C000203932

BOOKS BY S.E. LYNES

THE
WOMEN

S. E. LYNES

Bookouture

Published by Bookouture in 2019

An imprint of StoryFire Ltd.

Carmelite House
50 Victoria Embankment
London EC4Y 0DZ

www.bookouture.com

ISBN: 978-1-78681-906-2
eBook ISBN: 978-1-78681-905-5

This book is a work of fiction. Names, characters, businesses,
organizations, places and events other than those clearly in the
public domain, are either the product of the author's imagination
or are used fictitiously. Any resemblance to actual persons, living or
dead, events or locales is entirely coincidental.

For my sister, Jackie Ball, who fights not only for women but for human beings all around the world.

As long as I live I will have control over my being.

Artemisia Gentileschi

CHAPTER 1

ROME, ITALY, APRIL 2018

The light in Rome is like no other. Like yellow dust it falls over the restless queues that coil around the Colosseum, over the flaking ruins of the Forum, over the traffic cop who stands signalling in the middle of Piazza Venezia. It falls over the hordes on the Via del Corso, the tourists gasping at designer windows in the Via Condotti, over the *pietoni* on the Piazza di Spagna, the hand-laid cobbles hidden now beneath a thousand feet; other feet, bare, cool themselves in the fountains at the Piazza del Popolo.

Only April, but my God, how hot it is today.

There are ghosts too, ghosts everywhere, retracing their steps through the three-pronged fork of the old artists' quarter: Via Margutta, Via Ripetta, Via del Babuino; the ghosts of Caravaggio, Michelangelo, Leonardo da Vinci, names that melt in the mouth like the ice cream at Bar San Crispino, served gravely by men in gloves to gastronomes who, sun on their faces, Trevi Fountain at their backs, knees sagging in ecstasy, giggle in disbelief at the taste-bud-defying gelato, licking creamy trickles from their cardboard cups, wiping with greedy fingers at their chins. *Try mine! Taste this! It's like you're eating actual strawberries …*

The yellow light falls. Lands on lesser sights, lesser ruins, on the Santa Maria in Cosmedin church, where newly-weds Peter and Samantha Bridges and their baby, Emily, have taken their place in the chaotic queue. It is cooler here in the shade of the vaulted arches, beneath the towering minaret, where a human mass edges forward, fidgeting and twitching like children on a school trip.

'So, the Mouth of Truth,' Samantha reads from Peter's tattered guidebook, once she's sure he's listening, 'La Bocca della Verità, as it's known locally, is a huge stone mask in the portico here, which is part of the Chiesa di Santa Maria in Cosmedin.' She looks up, checks her bearings. The multilingual din all around and the damp heat of the baby against her back make it hard to concentrate.

'The square we're standing in now,' she perseveres, as a group of twenty or so Chinese sightseers presses in behind, 'is the Piazza della Verità. It's the site of the ancient cattle market, the Forum Boarium.' Her arms are flattened against her sides, the guidebook almost in her face. She can smell traffic fumes and cigarette smoke, feel Rome's greasy black dust coating her nostrils. She glances at Peter to check that he's still paying attention and sees a bead of sweat trickle down the right side of his face. He is overheating. Poor man.

He nods briskly at her to continue. Coughs into his fist, wriggles the rucksack from his back and digs out the two-litre bottle of water.

'The massive marble mask,' she goes on, 'is said to depict the face of the sea god Oceanus. Let's see ... ah, you'll like this ... historians aren't sure what the original purpose was, but it was possibly used as a drain cover near the Temple of Hercules Victor, which had an oculus in the ceiling ... that's the round hole, isn't it, like in the ceiling of the Pantheon?'

Peter has the bottle pressed to his lips. The water chugs. His Adam's apple bobs. The plastic implodes with a loud crack. She should keep going, lay the historical information on thick. With Peter, it's all about the credentials.

'It's thought,' she reads, 'that cattle merchants used the mask as a drain cover for the blood of cattle sacrificed to the god Hercules.'

She imagines the blood. A bestial red flood, gallons of it, running thickly down into the mask's open mouth. The memory she has had so often since giving birth to Emily flashes: helping her father pull a calf for the very first time – the hooves in the amnion, the viscera clotting in the hay, steam rising in the pre-dawn chill of the barn. Her father had patted the cow's sweating flank, nodded at her as she licked her calf clean. *She'll take it from here*, he had said in his thick Yorkshire accent. *All the bull does is leave his seed. It's the mothers that do the rest.* She thinks of her own primitive shock as her baby writhed out of her, their shared animal state; the pain, the blood, the strange lowing sound she made.

Peter is still glugging water. He has drunk almost a litre.

'Save some for me,' she says, one hand at her breast. 'I need it for milk.'

'I'm parched.' Awkwardly he wedges the nearly empty bottle back in the rucksack. His forehead glistens. 'Go on.'

'That's it really. In the seventeenth century, the mask was moved here. You put your hand in the mouth and legend has it that if you're a truthful person, nothing happens. But if you're a liar ...' She takes his hand, rubs the new wedding ring with the tip of her finger and fixes his deep brown eyes with hers. 'If you're a liar, darling – are you listening? – the mouth closes and takes your hand clean off.'

The crowd surges, pushing them forward. Peter flushes an even deeper crimson. He coughs once again. Too much red at lunch. Too many home-made tortellini. And he shouldn't have had the tiramisu.

'Superstition,' he almost wheezes. 'Hocus-pocus.'

'Of course. But it's amazing how many people will make a pilgrimage on nothing more than that.' She gestures to the jostling bodies around them, their latest iPhones, their selfie sticks, to the stout Italian woman immediately in front whose son is poking his sister in the back. 'These people aren't here for the history, are they? They basically want to put their hand inside the mouth and see if it closes, even though they know it won't. Ninety-nine per cent of their mind knows it won't. But it's the one per cent that brings them here, isn't it? That tiny, illogical sliver of doubt.' She smiles up at him, but he doesn't meet her eye. 'Superstition's like suspicion, I suppose, in that sense. A feeling you can't put into words. A one per cent of something you don't quite know.'

The babbling rabble advances a pace, two. The tonal highs and lows of Mandarin quicken in the hot air. They are getting closer to the entrance, where two male officials stand sentry. Peter looks towards the square, where once cows were bought and sold and slaughtered. Blood gushing on the ground. Blood running thick into the stone mouth. Sacrifice.

'We could go back to the apartment,' he says, 'if you think it's nonsense.'

'I didn't say it was nonsense. I was talking about the power of superstition. Anyway, we're here now.'

He pulls at his collar, wrinkles his nose. 'It's just … it's just so touristy. A bit naff, isn't it?'

'We're tourists. Tourism *is* naff, essentially.'

'Yes, but if we go back now, we could … take a nap.' He raises an eyebrow but it doesn't look convinced. Like a dodgy cheque; she's not sure he can cash it.

'You'll be looking after Emily while I sleep, so I wouldn't get too excited if I were you.' She lifts her face to his, attempting with a peck on the lips to unravel her confusion: the urge to apologise still comes to her, but she knows she should not, that it is habit, nothing more. She and Peter are going to see this damn mouth if it's the last thing they do. In their entire honeymoon, it's the only sight she's requested.

'Giorgio!' Immediately in front of them, the stout Italian woman smacks her annoying little boy over the back of the head. The boy bursts into tears. *Mamma!* is all Samantha can make out from the self-pitying wailing that follows. The boy is spoilt, she thinks. That's why he behaves badly. Spoilt boys become selfish men.

The woman and her children go ahead. Peter pays one of the guides, his expression begrudging, harassed. They step out of the shade. Heat comes at them as if from an open oven door. A hard Roman sun shines on a large stone disc. This is it: the mask, the mouth of truth. It is smaller than she has imagined when she has pictured them both here. The bearded face is monstrous, the eyes wide and staring, a deep fissure scarring the right eye. The mouth itself is a grotesque silent scream into the void. For a moment, she falters. But steels herself.

Peter drains the water bottle, wipes his mouth with the back of his hand. He looks, more than anything, appalled, though his colour is still high. The gargoyle is disconcerting, she admits. But the urge to put her hand inside the mouth is almost overwhelming. At the same time, she imagines the mythical severance, the bloody stump of her own wrist, the horror on the faces of the crowd as she staggers, bleeding, onto the street.

'A gargantuan gargoyle,' says Peter, but his expression is preoccupied, possibly due to his thwarted amorous intentions. In darker moments such as this, their relationship feels to her like a constant effort to appease him: to keep him fed, watered, sexually satisfied, conversationally engaged. Soothed. Emily has slept for most of the day, which means that when they return to the flat, she will wake up. And Samantha, desperate for sleep, will be faced with two sets of demands. Peter and Emily. Two children, in a sense.

They wander over to the monstrosity.

'You first,' she says, nodding towards the waiting mouth.

'I don't think I'll bother.' He coughs again; his hand flies to his chest.

Samantha waits for him to recover. She wants him to watch her. He looks up finally, and, holding his beautiful brown gaze, she slowly, resolutely slides her hand into the cool marble hole. An involuntary shiver passes through her, a shiver born of the sudden chill of the stone, of ancient legend and something like triumph.

Peter takes a photograph with his phone – if it's possible to do this sarcastically, then that is how he does it.

'There,' she says, withdrawing her hand and wiggling her fingers at him. 'I'm obviously *incredibly* truthful. Now you, Mr Grumpy. No getting out of it.'

He glances towards the crowd, back to her. Frowns. Clears his throat.

'Let's go.' His voice is thin, his breathing a little laboured. 'I need some more water.'

'Peter. Just put your hand in and let me take a photograph. It'll take one second and it's not like it's really going to bite you, is it?'

'It's just not my cup of tea, all right? I don't like these overt tourist traps. They make me feel used and … a bit grubby.' He pushes the heel of his hand to his chest and wheezes, looks again towards the entrance. The only way out is through the church. He will have to force his way back through the queue.

'Get over yourself, will you?' Her patience is all but at an end. 'I hardly have any photos of you from our honeymoon.'

'You don't need photos of me,' he snaps, then opens his mouth wide, as if to loosen his jaw. He grips his shoulder, rotates his arm. His face is the colour of red wine. 'I'm old and ugly.'

'Don't be silly. Haven't you seen *Roman Holiday*? Come on! I just really wanted to do the Audrey Hepburn and Gregory Peck thing.' She takes out her iPhone. 'Please? Put your hand in.'

'No.'

The follicles of her hair lift. 'It's just a stupid drain cover, for God's sake. Put your hand in, Peter.'

'I didn't get involved in art history to become a dumb sheep.' He pushes his fingers through his thinning brown hair. Still he doesn't look at her.

'Peter.' Her bottom lip stiffens. From the hovering throng comes a shush of voyeuristic curiosity. 'Put your hand in. Put your hand in and I'll take a photo and then we'll go back to the flat. You're being … vain and … stuffy and, I have to say, a bit foolish.'

One of the guides calls something to them in Italian.

'*Momento*,' she calls back, holds up her hand.

'Look.' Peter takes a deep breath, continues in a stage whisper. 'I'd feel exactly the same way if you asked me to ride a roller coaster or … or hire a gondola in Venice. It's no better than putting your head through the slap-and-tickle comedy boards in seaside towns. I just don't like this stuff. I don't *do* this stuff. They fleece you for the privilege of lining up like a … like a chimp and doing what every single other human being has done before you. And meanwhile … meanwhile they're laughing all the way to the bank. It's humiliating. Come on, Sam. You're an intelligent—'

'Put your hand in the fucking mouth.' They're both stage-whispering now. They are both ridiculous. The people waiting will have heard her swear, but right now, she couldn't give a—

'You're making a scene,' he hisses. 'You can't bully me into it. Sam, this is beneath you. It's beneath both of us.'

'No one's bullying you, Peter. No one's bullied you in your entire life. I've trailed round after you our whole time here. I've listened to Caravaggio's entire life story and your theories about everything from his homosexuality to the availability of paint pigments in the sixteenth bloody century. This is the only thing I've asked you to do, and yes, it's because I saw it in *Roman Holiday*, and I know you don't think that's a valid reason, but it's *my* reason. I mean, do you think you'll actually lose your hand? Or is this because it was my suggestion, not yours?'

From the doorway comes a murmur laced with delight: the honeymooners, having a fight, here, in public.

'*Signora?*' The guard stares at Samantha.

Again, she holds up her hand. And then, glaring at her husband, 'Peter.'

Peter has taken a handkerchief out of his back pocket and is dabbing at his forehead. 'For Christ's sake, Sam, give it a rest. This really is beneath you. You're an educated woman.' An eruption of coughing. He holds the handkerchief to his mouth.

She is about to reply with something flippant, an allusion to the fact that much of her education – albeit outside the classroom – has come from him, so many years her senior, but he turns away from her and staggers. Drops forward, hands to his knees, and gives a loud, rasping inhalation. The back of his shirt is soaked.

'Peter?'

He straightens but almost immediately lurches forward once more.

'Peter?'

He raises a hand, coughs into the other. Tourists chatter on long necks; there is the click of a dozen iPhones. One of the guards raises his arm at them.

'*Calma*,' he says. '*Un po di calma.*'

Peter is lunging into the crowd, pushing through, his cough hacking, raw. Samantha runs after him. The guards stand back to let her pass; they shout and gesticulate at the tourists to make way, but still the people push in, bleating like dumb sheep.

'*Scusi*,' she hears Peter say. '*Scusi. Scusi.*'

The raspberry-coloured bald patch at the back of his head zigzags a short distance away. He staggers up the steps, through the wide arched door of the church.

'Peter,' she calls out, almost slipping on the shiny tiled floor. 'Peter!'

He stops dead, as if he has heard her. With a great sucking sound, he clutches his shoulder, reels back and falls to his knees. She runs to him and she too drops down. In the backpack, Emily jolts against her shoulders.

'Peter?'

He collapses, his hands against the tiles, his chest against the tiles, his cheek now against the tiles. His mouth is slack, his eyes glassy, his forehead spritzed with perspiration. Shouts echo. Strangers are running, running towards her – from the altar, from the doorway.

'*Aiuto!*' she cries to them. '*Ambulanza!* Someone call an ambulance!'

CHAPTER 2
LONDON, OCTOBER 2016

Samantha Frayn sees Professor Bridges before he sees her. At least, that is how she will recall it later, in the light of everything that happens. But for now, nothing has happened, and all she can see is him. He is drinking red wine from a plastic cup on the far side of the English department foyer. His hair is a deep chestnut brown. He is slim. He dresses well – how she imagines an American academic might dress: soft blues, fawns, tan brogues. Would risk a burgundy V-neck, possibly has tortoiseshell glasses in a case in his breast pocket, though Marcia would say this was Samantha's *whole Gregory Peck thing*. She knows Professor Bridges teaches art history, here at University College, London. She knows he drives an old midnight-blue Porsche. And she knows that most of the female student population would give their last tenner for one look from him. Right now, he is talking to a girl from the year below Samantha. The girl laughs, knees sinking, looking down at the floor, only to glance up again. And there, look: she's tucking a loose strand of honey-streaked hair behind her right ear, better to expose her perfectly flushed cheek.

The thumb of jealousy in Samantha's chest is a surprise. Ridiculous.

There are about seventy people here. It is the beginning of term; autumn's nip is in the air. She misses the Yorkshire countryside in all its colours, the wellington boots in the stone porch, the smell of damp soot in the chimney stack, though these things haven't been part of her life for a long time now. Around her, chatter amplifies against the hard surfaces, brings her back to herself. She should move, mingle. She should at least smile. If Marcia were here, she would have got them both a drink by now. But Marcia has a hangover and is watching *I'm a Celebrity …* back at the flat.

Samantha glances towards the door; beyond, to the lifts. She could go, actually. She could just leave. It's not like she's interested in any of these people. Well, if you don't count one, and he is miles out of her league. Yes, go – turn and wander away, back into anonymity, onto the Tube. She could be in Vauxhall by—

'I took a chance and brought red,' a man's voice behind her says.

She startles, turns, finds herself looking into fathomless brown eyes, crinkled at the edges: the eyes of Professor Bridges. Oh God.

'Ah,' is all she finds to say – more of a noise than a word – fighting the heat that is climbing up her neck. She did not see him cross the room.

'I'm Peter.' He presses a plastic beaker into her hand. His lips are dark pink, the bow almost pointed, defined even against his weathered skin. The wine is warm, like blood. 'You're not first year, are you?'

'Final,' she says. 'I'm Samantha.' She offers her hand, which he shakes.

'Pleased to meet you, Samantha.' His hand is warmer than the wine.

'You too.'

He takes a slug of his drink, grimaces as if offended. 'Christ, the wine at these things is awful, isn't it?'

'Oh my God, yes.' Samantha rolls her eyes. Not that she's tasted better. Or worse. She really has no idea about these things; she's just trying to somehow throw a ring fence around the two of them, make some sort of lightning intimate connection.

'I'm not supposed to be here,' he says, glancing about before returning his gaze to her, as if the others are of no interest. 'I'm an interloper, strictly speaking.'

'Careful,' she says. 'You might get caught.'

He raises one eyebrow, as if surprised, before throwing her a suggestive smirk.

'Let's hope so.'

The quip goes right through her; her belly folds over. She has fantasised about a moment like this, but now that it is here, she has to look away. It's actually a bit embarrassing. A bit stressful. In her fantasies, she is much more self-possessed.

She manages to get herself together enough to look up. He is nodding towards the crowd, to someone; she doesn't see who.

'I'm good mates with Sally,' he says. 'She got me on the guest list.'

Guest list is ironic, Samantha gets that. It's not like this is some trendy club. She wonders if Sally is the young girl he was talking to, before realising that, doh, of course he means Professor Bailey.

'Head of English,' he adds, as if reading her mind, his pink mouth turning up at one side.

'Yes, yes,' she says. 'I mean, yes, I know who you mean. You're … you're history of art, aren't you?' Her face burns. Shit. In her surprise, she has revealed her hand.

But it isn't, apparently, a disaster. At least, his smile tells her it isn't. His teeth are even, creamy, a neat lacing of gum. He takes another sip of the terrible wine, his mouth immediately puckering. Beside them, a group of students from her year let out an excited shriek. She winces with embarrassment on their behalf. I am not like them, she wants to say. But can't, of course; that would be lame.

But he must pick up on exactly what she's thinking because he widens his eyes, leans towards her and whispers in her ear, 'What an amazingly exciting conversation they must be having.'

Oh my God, the telepathy! She giggles, tries to choose a spot on the floor, fixes on her DM boots, wonders if he finds them childish, finds her childish. She doesn't want him to find her childish, not nerdy and shrieking like the others. She wants, she realises, to appear older. When she's seen Professor Bridges around, in the uni cafeteria sometimes, she's put him in his late thirties, maybe as old as forty, but she wonders now how old he actually is, how much older than her. How much more experienced. It is not a question she can ask, nor does she, because he is lifting her beaker from her hand.

'Listen, shall we go and get a better drink somewhere quieter?' In his eyes there is no doubt, none whatsoever. It is as if he is saving her from something, as if he is teasing a bottle of cheap cider from the grimy hands of a homeless person and offering to take them to a hostel for the night. He knows she is not like the others. He's identified this in her. That's why he came over. He wrinkles his nose and she knows exactly what he means. 'I'll put these back, shall I?'

No objection makes it even as far as her throat. Why would it? He has chosen her. He, Professor Bridges, has chosen her, Samantha Frayn, a nobody with knobbly knees and flyaway dandelion hair. Out of all these rosy girls who know how to tuck their thick, shiny hair just so behind their ear, how to laugh on sinking knees when he hits them with that laid-back irony, he has chosen her. With no real preamble, no small talk. He has seen that she's someone who can ignore the petty, wheedling internal voice of reason, who is not afraid to rise to life's impetuous moments and meet them square on. Someone who can understand someone like him with no real need for words. *Shall we go and get a better drink somewhere quieter?*

Er, yes.

She watches him return the wine. The crowd parts for him. Girls throw sideways glances, meet each other's eye with almost imperceptible smiles. His blazer is smart, too smart for an academic, his deep blue trousers the perfect length against his tan brogues. At the back of his head is the hint of a bald spot, no bigger than a ten-pence piece. He has combed his hair over it and she thinks about him doing that – the secret vanity, the vulnerability in the act – patting the hair down with his hand, maybe using a second mirror to check it's covered. She has no idea what she has said or done to make him choose her, knows only that he has, and that possibly he intends to seduce her – properly, calmly, like a man. The thought fills her with a precipitous sensation. She is unbalanced, falling, the cave of her chest flaring with anxiety.

He is standing in front of her. His smile almost makes her panic. 'Let's go,' he says.

His Porsche is parked on Gordon Square. He unlocks the passenger-side door, which he holds open.

'No central locking,' he says as she lowers herself onto the cream leather seat. 'Makes me appear much more chivalrous than I am.'

Chivalry is a sexist anachronism, she *so* doesn't say. What she says instead is, 'Don't Porsches usually have, like, a fin thing on the back?'

'*Like* a fin thing?' he teases before strolling around to his side and getting in. His cologne smells expensive, a little like wet grass. 'This is a 1985 Porsche Carrera Coupé M491. No spoiler. No *like a fin thing*. I've had her a long time.'

'Was she new when you bought her? It, I mean. I mean the car.'

He laughs. Her face heats yet again. If Marcia could see her right now, she would freak.

'Just how old do you think I am?' Still chuckling, he starts the ignition. The engine gives a throaty growl. 'She was second-hand when I bought her. Now she's *vintage*.' He glances at Samantha when he says this, and his brown eyes twinkle – oh my God, the cliché of it, the actual cliché. She imagines telling Marcia later – or tomorrow! *Marcia*, she will say, *I know this is a cringe, but his eyes actually twinkled.*

'And which are you?' she dares to ask. 'Old or vintage?'

He grins, his canine teeth a little raised against the others. 'I'd say I've had a few too many careful owners.'

Cheesy, she thinks, but laughs despite herself as he pulls out into the city traffic. The pinkish blue of dusk has darkened to soft navy. White headlights flash and fade; red tail lights lure them forward.

'Where are we going?' she asks.

'Anywhere you want. There's a little pub I know not too far away. It's in Soho. Used to be ... well, not a brothel exactly, but it's an old prostitutes' hang-out and it still has the original booths, which back then had curtains you could pull across when you were ... you know, busy.' He glances at her, returns his eyes to the busy street. 'London pubs have such great history and some of them are beautifully maintained.' With the palm of one hand he spins the steering wheel, heads left towards Tottenham Court Road. 'And most of them serve a passable red.'

A passable red. Lol. The urge to giggle itches at her throat. She would text Marcia right now, but he would see.

Soho is dense with bodies. The car gives a low thrum as it slows to walking pace. He appears not to notice, asks her which modules she's studying.

'Eighteenth century,' she tells him. 'The Romantics and an option on Icelandic literature.'

'So, Pope?' he says. 'Addison, Fielding et al.?'

She laughs. Like all academics, his breadth of learning is intimidating, as if he has an entire library index stored in his head.

'Sheridan, Goldsmith,' she says. 'Loads. There's loads of reading.'

'Loads.' He gives a brief chuckle, though she's not sure why. 'You'd expect that, wouldn't you? Reading English? Clue in the verb there.' That laid-back irony again, the gentle tease of it. They are circling now around the packed Soho streets. Sharp-suited men and chic city women dawdle across the road without looking, spill from the doors of bars and restaurants she can't imagine ever being able to afford.

'Chaucer?' he asks, turning right into Frith Street for the second time.

'That was last year. It's all Vikings this year. Eddas and sagas and all that.' She is downplaying her knowledge so as not to appear too up herself. She hopes this will make her seem more intelligent. A double bluff, that's what she's going for. That's the idea, anyway.

The car stops. In front is a pushbike rickshaw, a polite chaos of pedestrians.

'Human traffic.' She frowns wisely. This time, an attempt to appear worldly, like someone who knows about these things.

He too frowns, mirroring her. 'This is hopeless, isn't it? Thursday's the new Friday; I didn't think it would be so busy.' He adjusts his position, leans against the steering wheel; one arm stretches over the back of his seat. He is looking at her. He is looking right at her. 'Tell you what, seeing as you're such a fan of all things vintage, why don't we blow the dust off one of my bottles of red, pour it into some decent glassware and talk where it's quiet and calm? If you don't object, that is.'

Oh my God. This is it. And so much better than *Hey, I've got some cans in my room if you want.*

'I don't object,' she says, attempting a small shrug.

'Fantastic.' He settles back into the driving seat, pushes his index finger to the stereo. Soft music fills the car. She thinks about her flat in Vauxhall. Marcia is literally going to die when she hears about this. She reaches into the footwell for her bag, but then remembers that Peter threw it onto the back seat. She should definitely text Marcy, let her know she won't be back, possibly not until tomorrow – *eek*. She'll do it when she gets to his place. Definitely. Oh my God, she doesn't know what the hell she's doing, why she's in this car. And yet she does know; she totally, completely knows.

From the stereo Marvin Gaye asks, 'What's going on?'

Too right, she thinks. What is going on?

He lives in Richmond, it turns out. For some reason, she'd assumed that he lived in the centre. But no, they drive for around an hour and she feels the city recede behind them, give way to lower buildings, darker, lonelier streets.

His house is a Georgian mid-terrace. She doesn't phrase it like this to herself, doesn't know that this is what it is; it is he who tells her as he unlocks the door, who told her a moment ago that they were in Richmond Hill, pointing out the kink in the Thames, the dark cloud of trees in Marble Hill.

'My father left the house to me when I was in my late twenties,' he says as they step inside. 'Along with a bit of money, which I used to fund a move from secondary-school teaching to university. I bought time, essentially.' He gestures for her to go ahead, into the hall. 'Time is expensive.'

'Your mother?' she asks, placing her coat into his waiting hands.

'She died when I was twelve. The big C, I'm afraid. You're not a smoker, are you?'

She shakes her head, as if shocked by the very idea. No need to mention binge-smoking Marcia's roll-ups on drunken nights out, the odd packet of menthols.

'Good.' He indicates a door further up, on the left. 'Go through to the living room.'

The hallway is wide. Her Docs squeak on the black and white diagonal squares. Her shoes are clean, at least, though she wonders if she should have taken them off at the door. Too late. She passes beneath an arch. Two plaster faces stare down at her: one angel, smiling; one devil, leering. Then a door on the right beneath the staircase. A moment later, she senses him behind her, turns in time to see him disappear into the dimness beyond. A wine cellar, must be. Oh my God, he wasn't even joking. He has an actual wine cellar. She edges towards where he has disappeared, hovers there. The steps lead down into semi-darkness. There is a bulb on a wire. She can hear him whistling below. Classical music, she is sure, though she doesn't – wouldn't – recognise the piece, the composer, anything about it really.

She steps back into the hall. Peter Bridges is a man with a wine cellar, she thinks. He is a man who whistles classical music, who drives a vintage sports car and lives in a beautiful house on a hill. It's literally the cheesiest thing ever, like a fairy tale or a dodgy romance. But still, if she's honest, *this* is the kind of guy she's half fantasised she might meet since she escaped the village, the grubby scandal of her father, the pathetic jokes of boys at the bus stop, off their bonces on weed. Until now, her degree has shown her only other boys. Boys with better vocabulary, better jokes, perhaps, but whose idea of a good time is still to get stoned, lit, or wasted on cheap lager in the union, enough to make groping, wet-lipped passes.

She shudders.

The whistling stops. The slap of leather sole on stone.

She shrinks back into the living room, warmed by the amber glow from a lamp in the corner. It must have been on a timer, she thinks. A precaution against intruders.

'Amarone.' He is at the door, holding up a bottle, dusty as promised. He places it on the smoked-glass coffee table, and when he releases his grip there is a burgundy handprint against the patina of pale grey. 'Glasses,' he adds and disappears once again.

He has a real fireplace. Smaller than the one at the farm, this one is surrounded by a tiled hearth, a blackened iron mantel. There are steel fire irons and a wicker basket of chopped logs. In the grate, a wigwam of kindling stands around screwed-up balls of newspaper. It is all waiting to go, prepared in advance, as if he knew she was coming.

A clink of glass comes from the kitchen. The running of a tap. She peruses the built-in bookshelves, the books in alphabetical order. One side is stocked with reference books – contemporary art, Caravaggio, masters of the Renaissance – the other side holds novels, contemporary and classic, and an eclectic selection of poetry: Tony Harrison, Dylan Thomas, William Wordsworth. There is no television. On the unit beneath the shelves sits a record player with a black Perspex lid. She tiptoes across the polished floorboards, the old – vintage? antique? – patterned rug and silently lowers herself onto the studded leather couch. She has never been in a house as elegant as this. Never seen such confident taste. And the proportions! White skirtings thirty centimetres deep, the ceiling miles away. The pictures on the walls are not even prints, she suspects. They are actual art. She studies an ink drawing of a man playing a trumpet, leans forward, squinting to read the signat—

'Here we are.' Here he is. He has taken off his jacket. His loose shirt is a fluid, soft denim and she wonders if he has undone a button since they were at the faculty; she can't remember noticing his chest hair earlier. The dust vanishes from the bottle stripe by stripe as he cleans it with a damp piece of kitchen roll, which he throws into the fireplace with one perfect shot. She is aware of how silent she is, they are. Her hands are clenched into fists, she realises, her knees pushed so close together they have started to ache. Where is her bag? It must be in the hall with her coat. She'll ask for it. In a minute. She really should text Marcia.

The bottleneck chatters on the edge of the glass goblets. He pours a shallow measure in each, offers one to her. She thinks of her friends: the tumblers – mugs, even – of cheap Cabernet Sauvignon, the pillow-sized bags of tortilla chips guzzled in minutes, the cigarettes extinguished in empty beer cans.

'To you.' He meets her eye and chinks his glass lightly against hers.

To you – who even says that? No one her age, that's for sure. Her stomach heats. She suppresses a giggle. At the hit of the wine on her tongue, she closes her eyes. She doesn't usually drink wine, or much at all really, but this is no cheap plonk.

'It's delicious,' she says, licking her lips.

'Yes, it's not bad. I've been waiting to open this one for a long time.'

They leave that there.

He pulls a small plastic bag from his trouser pocket. In it are sweets – or pills, coloured pills. Oh my God, they *are* pills. He places the bag on the coffee table but says nothing. A year from now, when she thinks back to this evening, she will remember how nonchalantly he did this, as if it were perfectly normal to bring out a stash minutes after meeting someone. As it is, in the moment, she presses her lips tight and pulls her eyes away, back to his.

'I can't explain why,' he is saying, throwing out his hands as he talks. 'Call it superstition if you like, but you … this … us coming here like this … What I mean is, the way we just … took off like that.' He laughs, shakes his head. 'Look at me, I'm a wreck.'

She frowns, as if to give this her serious consideration when in reality she can't think of a single thing to reply. He is not a superstitious man, she thinks. And he is definitely not a wreck. But isn't this what she has wanted, to find a man who knows what he's doing? And deeper still, there is the hope that this is more than sophistication, that he really has identified in her something special, something unique. She was worried that she'd let herself be led away too soon. Now she thinks it was the right move, that he finds her interesting as a result: daring, as free-spirited as a heroine in a black-and-white French film – Jeanne Moreau or Catherine Deneuve.

He runs his fingers through his hair. She makes herself hold his gaze, ignores the heat it triggers on her neck. He has crinkles at the edges of his eyes yet not one hint of grey. There's no getting around it: he's gorgeous.

'I know you're here in my house,' he says. 'I can see you. You're right in front of me and you are … you are … I'm not objectifying you in any way but you're really beautiful, and maybe that's why I can't believe you've come. I knew you would, from the moment you let me take that bloody awful wine from you, but at the same time I don't know why and maybe that's why I can't believe it. Knowledge and disbelief, all bound up together. It's … it's … well, it's worth celebrating.'

Her scalp tingles. Being permitted over the threshold of his private realm – and God knows, this house is like a kingdom – feels like a privilege reserved only for those whose behaviour is exemplary, like the time she was invited to the head teacher's office to be congratulated on a Shakespeare essay she wrote in sixth form.

'I feel the same.' It seems like the right thing to say.

'You do?' He appears to sigh with relief. 'Well, that's … that's everything, isn't it?'

She wants him to take her face in his hands. She wants him to bring her lips to his right now, but at the same time she wants to delay the moment. Her chest hurts.

But Peter doesn't kiss her. Instead, he stands up and heads towards the record player. A moment later and he's put a match to the kindling, slid a disc whispering from its sleeve and, with the precision of a surgeon, lowered the needle to the black vinyl. And now they are listening to what sounds like old jazz.

'Miles Davis,' he says in answer to her unspoken question, crouching by the fire and reaching for the tongs. He checks his watch and, carefully, places a log on the burning pile.

'We had an open fire when I was little,' she says.

'And where was that?'

'Yorkshire. I grew up on a farm. There was no mantelpiece; it was just, like, a square cut out of the wall.'

'Yorkshire,' he says. 'I thought I detected a slight accent.'

She giggles. 'That's nowt. Should 'ear us when I go 'ome.'

'Very good.' He laughs and places another log in the fire. An orange glow is establishing itself at the base. Another log and he stands and chafes his hands together before returning to join her on the sofa.

'Your house is so lovely,' she says. Lovely? That was lame.

'It's too big, really, for one.' He drains his glass, tops it up, offers her more. She lets him pour another splash; he stops when she raises her hand, which she finds respectful.

He reaches for the bag of pills and takes one out. 'Shall we indulge, as it's a special occasion?'

Indulge. It's the first time he's sounded old. But he's probably being ironic. Yes, ironic, definitely.

'Are they …' she says. 'Are they drugs?'

He grins and shakes his head, affectionately, as a parent might. 'Come on, you're what? Twenty?'

'Twenty-one.' Now *she* sounds older than she is.

'And you're telling me you don't do a little dab from time to time?'

She shakes her head.

'Not even at festivals?'

'I don't go to festivals. They're too expensive.'

'Clubbing, then?'

'I don't like clubs. I get claustrophobic.'

He raises his eyebrows in genuine surprise. 'So you don't do drugs at all?'

Again she shakes her head. 'I don't really drink much either, to be honest. Sorry.'

'I thought everyone your age did MDMA. I was with this girl, about ten years ago now, and she loved festivals and everything that went with that. I was like you, I never indulged, but trust me, this stuff is the secret the government don't want you to know about. All the feel-good, none of the hangover.'

She shrugs, tries to create the impression of an ambivalence she doesn't feel. She has always felt at odds with people her own age, for as long as she can remember. Only in her studies and her close friendships has she ever felt truly comfortable. Now, here she is, on the periphery once again. She expected to feel many things with Peter, but peer pressure was not one of them.

'I didn't go to a very good school,' she says, with no idea why. 'What I mean is, I had to work, like, pretty hard to get away. I mean, get my A levels. Only three of us went to uni.' She sounds defensive, worries he'll think she's chippy. His own background is clearly so much wealthier than hers. 'Some of my friends do Ecstasy,' she says. 'E. That's what it is, right?'

He nods.

'I know it's supposed to make you feel euphoric,' she adds, not wanting to appear naïve. 'And loved up, et cetera, but when my friends do it, they're actually quite boring. And then they, like, talk about having done it and when they're going to do it again, and that's even more boring. And a bit like clubbing, I never really saw the point. Plus, I've always been afraid of … I mean, I like to feel safe. And I guess they're not legal, are they, and so they're not, you know, regulated. And people have died. You hear about people dying. I mean, what if you get a bad batch, or whatever?'

He breaks one in half. 'You sound like a worried mummy, Samantha. Can I call you Sam?'

She shrugs. 'Pete?' She wrinkles her nose. 'No, that sounds wrong. You're not a Pete.'

He appears not to have heard. He is holding up a pill. 'Aren't you curious? You strike me as someone with an enquiring mind.'

She hears herself inhale sharply.

'Trust me, you're completely safe. How about we take half each? You'll like it, I promise. There's no way you can overdose on a half.' He places the tiny orange crescent in her hand. 'Neither of us knew this would happen tonight, did we? We're riding the wave. We're going with the flow. And something made you get into my car, even though you would never usually do that kind of thing, am I correct?'

She nods.

'What you need is a safe risk. A risk-assessed risk. That's what this is, trust me.'

A short laugh escapes her. 'I wouldn't exactly call it a risk. I don't feel like I'm in, like, danger or anything. You're a lecturer, aren't you? You're part of the university, you know, the establishment or whatever. You wouldn't throw away your career by molesting a student, would you? Not in this day and age. Anyway, you're not like that; I can tell. I'd know by now if you were a monster. I'd sense it.'

'Of course you would. I'm no monster, I assure you.'

Of course he's not a monster. He's too beautiful. But actually, she wonders then if she *would* sense it. She thinks she would. She's pretty sure. But he's right that she's acted outside of herself, and now here she is, with a man she has only observed from a distance. Admired. But he is vouched for. And he did open the wine in front of her.

'Ready?' he says.

Not really, she thinks. But he has built up such a fascinating idea of her, and she doesn't want to disappoint him. She'll pretend, tuck the pill up by her gum, take it out when he looks away and shove it in her pocket or something.

She takes a deep breath. 'All right.'

CHAPTER 3

Eyes locked, they press their hands to their mouths. She takes a sip of wine and throws back her head, pretends to swallow. But the half pill dissolves so quickly and a bitter taste spreads over her tongue. Oh, it's so disgusting. It's rank. There's no way she can keep it in her mouth, no way she can dig it out without making a fool of herself. She takes another slug of wine, washes it down, away, but a horrible hairspray taste persists. He only sighs and drinks a little more too. He doesn't comment on what they've just done, as if it's irrelevant, no biggie. She tries not to worry about the pill and focuses on him. He is talking to her, quite naturally, about his doctorate on Caravaggio – he tells her the title but it is full of academic jargon and she cannot hold it in her head.

'That's why my book is called simply *Caravaggio*.' He smiles and she wonders if he can tell that her mind is blown, despite her efforts to appear admiring, impressed but no more – not amazed to near breathlessness. He has written an actual book. That book on the shelf is by him. Oh my God, he is so accomplished; it's too much. What is she? Nothing, that's what, nothing at all in comparison. The best she can hope for right now is not to appear like a child.

'Do you have any, like, old paintings in the house?' She winces at the use of 'like', how stupid it sounds now, here, with him. And 'old paintings'? He'll think she's an idiot. And he'd be right. She sips her wine. Actually, she's pretty thirsty. She should ask for some water. She will. In a minute. And her phone.

'There's some less contemporary stuff upstairs,' he's saying. 'Downstairs, I prefer more modern work.' He nods at the ink drawing of the trumpet player. 'I dabble a bit. The odd sketch.'

'You did that?'

Bloody *hell*. He's so talented, as well as beautiful. Wait till she tells Marcia.

'It's really good,' she says. That's right, Samantha, hit him with that impressive vocabulary of yours.

But he's pointing at his drawing, his eyes half closed as if he's trying to remember something. It's possible he didn't hear her pithy appraisal of his work.

'I sketched that dude at Ronnie Scott's,' he says. 'It's a famous jazz bar in Soho. We went past it earlier. Do you know it?'

As if. She shakes her head, though she's secretly cringing at the word *dude*, grateful for it – no one gets everything right, not even him, and for the first time, she feels a small advantage in being younger.

'I'll take you there,' he adds.

The words hang. She is glad of the low lamplight, knows from the heat in her face that she is blushing. *I'll take you there.* Because he can. Because it is nothing to him. Because he is effortless. Even the way he sits on the sofa is easy, one knee tucked into the crook of his arm, the way he seems to command his glass into his hand like a lightsaber, the delicate but firm way he sets it down again. She has met people like him, other lecturers, but she has never been this close to someone of his … learnedness, or calibre, or whatever it is. Until this moment, she's only spoken one to one with lecturers in their book-lined offices, observed from a distance the specific weight of seriousness they all seem to carry so lightly within themselves. They have been other to her, these people, a separate breed. Peter is a part of that world, one she cannot imagine herself ever belonging to. Yet she doesn't really belong in the sweat-drizzled walls of student social life either.

And she no longer belongs back home – not now.

They talk about travel – he has travelled extensively in Europe and the Far East. Of course he has.

'What about you?' he asks.

'Erm, well, we went on a family holiday to a campsite in Brittany once. It was a year before my dad left.' She did not intend to say it, but out it has come.

Wordlessly, Peter gets up to tend to the fire, to change the record, which has reached the end with a *thm*, *thm*, *thm*. He turns the disc over in his clean, deft hands before pushing it snugly over the spindle and lowering the needle to a click of static.

'Your father left?'

'He … he …'

'You don't have to talk about it.' He is beside her on the sofa, topping up her glass.

She drinks; the wine is so rich, almost too rich for her. He pours some more for himself. He is facing her, intent, earnest, fascinated.

'So you live with your mother?'

'Yes. Well, no. I live in London, but when I'm home, I go to my mum's flat.' The fire is warm, the music quiet. It is so lovely to be listened to, to be looked at like that.

'My dad had an affair with an eighteen-year-old girl,' she says into the soft cradle of his attention. 'She was five years older than me at the time. She was at my school. There was only one school in the village. We found out that he'd gone bankrupt. It was kind of his reaction to that. My mum thinks, anyway. We had to sell our house. The farm.' She sounds like an automaton, she thinks, spouting out data.

He leans forward, and before she realises what he's doing, he has laid the flat of his hand on her cheek with such tenderness she feels her eyes prickle. His first touch. A moment and he takes his hand away.

'I'm so sorry,' he says.

'It is what it is.' She turns her gaze towards the fire. In the grate, flames lick the wood, curl up the chimney. She doesn't tell him the rest: that a couple of years later, she lost her virginity one dark night behind the school building to a boy she didn't even like, both of them off their faces on cheap vodka; that she slept with several more boys after that when she was barely of legal age, thinking herself a feminist, in charge of her body and her desires; that only later did she realise that this was her acting out after the heartbreak and humiliation caused by her father, that ultimately it was a punishment against herself, a form of self-harm. She never went in for the whole arm-cutting thing like some of the other girls.

'I'm sorry,' she says, after a moment. 'Not very cheery.'

He shakes his head, but fondly. He looks proud of her, or something. 'So where do you want to go on your travels?'

'I'm going to go around Europe with my flatmate,' she tells him, 'once we graduate.'

'Well, you have to go to Italy. I'll give you a list of places you must not miss.'

He asks her if she likes London, and she tells him the city is too loud and dense with people for her, even now. But that she couldn't go back to the farm, even if they still had it, or to the village. It strikes her that Richmond is the perfect place, though she doesn't say this out loud. There is plenty of green here, yet it is not the country; plenty of shops, yet not the town. She could live here.

'So, what will you do after uni?' he asks.

She shrugs. 'I'd like to teach, maybe use writing in some sort of therapeutic capacity, you know, to help people? I write poetry, so maybe one day I'll get a collection published. That's a ridiculous fantasy, obviously.'

'I bet your poetry's brilliant,' he says. 'And we all need fantasies, don't we? I went through a phase of socialist song-writing, angry young man stuff, back in the day. And I know what you mean about cities. They're noisy, dirty places. People are rude. But one day

I'll show you Rome.' He takes her hand in his. His second touch. It doesn't feel like a move. If anything, it's affectionate, nothing more, and the loosest knot of disappointment lodges in her belly.

'Ah, Sam,' he almost whispers. 'I can show you so much.'

Her eyelids are heavy. He fills his own glass but not hers. The bottle empties.

'It's weird,' he says from somewhere far away. 'I feel like I know you. Or knew you once.'

She doesn't have a clue what time it is, but she's drifting. He is talking, then not. He plays a record by Massive Attack, another jazz one she misses the name of. He is so nice. Gentle. Kind.

The music plays: classical now, has been for a while. The fire is an orange glow in her peripheral vision, a caress of warmth on her left side. They are listening to Bach now, or was that the last one? She knows no one who listens to Bach. She knows no one who lives in a house like this, with a wine cellar with dust on the bottles. No one who would say that her poetry was wonderful. Her whole life seems trivial; it has fluttered up in smoke. She strains to keep her eyes open, but the sofa is pulling her down. He said half a pill was safe, so it can't be that, although she's not used to it. And it's not the wine; she's drunk no more than two glasses, although those bowl goblets can be deceptive. So maybe the wine, actually, a bit, and maybe the drugs, a bit.

And something else, something deeper. He is kinder than she thought he'd be. Empathic. Safe. Or perhaps she is drugged on the effect she can see she has on him, the way his eyes slope at the edges when he looks at her. She never called Marcy, but it's OK, it's all right. He is safe. He is lying top-to-tail with her, his bare feet tucked against her side. She has no memory of him taking off his socks, herself taking off her boots, nor snuggling up together in this childlike way. Her eyelids close against the last image of him draining his glass. He said he wanted to find out about her, and that's literally all he's done. There will be no inexpert lunging, no wet mouth, no limbs trapped at awkward angles against the sofa cushions. She will not have to blurt her excuses and scuttle out of a bedroom that smells of trainers and socks and worse. Peter's house smells clean – scented, even. Peter is a man of culture. Peter is a man of the world.

She should go and see her father, she thinks. It has been a long time.

'Hey.'

Samantha opens her eyes. She is lying down. Peter is sitting beside her, looking – actually, no, not looking, *gazing*. Peter is gazing at her. In the daylight, the brown of his eyes is more complex, flecked with rich autumnal shades. She shifts, hears the creak of leather. Art on the walls. This is not her home. This is—

'I've brought you some tea,' he says. 'It's Darjeeling. I hope that's all right.'

She raises herself onto her elbows. A soft grey blanket falls from her shoulders. She is fully dressed, which is a relief, though she can't say why.

'Did I fall asleep?' She pulls herself up to a sitting position.

'I woke up when the record finished, so I grabbed you a blanket.'

'I'm so sorry.'

'What for?' He hands her the tea in a white china mug. 'It's lovely that you're still here.'

'I should text my friend; she'll be worried.'

'Is that Marcia?'

She stares at him, alarmed, but he laughs.

'Your phone was ringing. I didn't want to answer it, but it kept going, so eventually I took it out of your bag. That was probably the wrong thing to do, but I was a bit out of it and I didn't want to wake you.'

'You spoke to her?' It is then that she notices her phone on the coffee table.

'Don't panic. I told her exactly who I was and that we'd got talking and you'd fallen asleep on the sofa and it was too late and too far to send you home. I gave her my address. She seemed to know about the department drinks and she knew my name. Even so, I think you should give her a call, tell her I didn't take advantage of you. Yet.' He gives a wicked grin, hands her phone to her. 'I'm making waffles. Do you want some?'

Her stomach answers before she does – a loud, drain-like gurgle. She giggles. 'Yes please. Thanks.'

He kisses her on the forehead. 'And then I have to go. I'm lecturing later. Come with me if you like. It's a juicy one. "Caravaggio: sex and death, life and art".'

He leaves her. She listens a moment, hears cupboards opening and closing, the clank of pans. It is still odd to her to think of a man cooking. She never once saw her father so much as boil an egg.

She calls Marcia.

'Oh, thank God,' her friend says without saying hello. 'Honestly, I leave you on your own for one night … I wouldn't mind, but I've gone from thinking you were celibate or something to thinking you were dead in a railway siding.'

Samantha giggles; Marcia always makes her giggle her head off.

'Nothing happened,' she says.

'What? Liar. Not even a snog?'

'Stop it, you'll make me pee. Honestly. We talked. That's all.' She lowers her voice to a whisper. 'Marcy, he offered me an E! I think he was trying to be, like, cool or something. Down with the kids, you know?'

'Fuck! That's mental! Did you take it?'

'I took a bit, yeah. I thought with him being more experienced it would be, like, OK.'

'But he's a professor for fu— Oh my God!'

'I know, I know.' Samantha crosses her legs. She really does need to pee now. 'But he's not … he's not stuffy. I know he's, like, forty or something, but he doesn't seem it, you know? Except for in all the good ways. Like he's got an old record player and he listens to jazz and classical music and stuff from the nineties, he's got a wine cellar actually in the actual cellar and he's … he's making waffles. For breakfast.'

'Bloody hell, that's proper grown-up. Jacob buys me a Starbucks if I'm lucky.'

'I know! And he's taking me to see him lecture. In the car. You know, *the* car.'

'Oh my God, you got a ride in the Studmobile?'

Samantha laughs. 'Don't call it that.' She gasps, lowers her voice again to a whisper, covers her mouth with her hand. 'It's not like that. He didn't even try and kiss me. He didn't try anything. I know we thought he was a bit of a player, but he's the opposite of a predator, the absolute opposite.'

Peter appears at the door. He raises his eyebrows and points in the direction of the kitchen.

'I've got to go,' she says hurriedly into the phone. 'I'll text you later.'

At eleven, Peter drives them to UCL. As they weave through the London traffic, Samantha texts Marcia:

Breakfast = home-made waffles, home-made granola, Greek yoghurt and honey. Freshly ground coffee from a place in Covent Garden!!!!!

Marcia replies:

Stobbit! A GIF follows: a woman waxing orgasmic over a strawberry sundae. Samantha laughs.

'You don't mind me being here,' Peter says, 'while you're on your phone, do you?'

His tone is light enough, but Samantha apologises and slides the phone back into her bag.

He parks on Gordon Square, ushers her to the lecture hall; she feels his hand at the small of her back as they step through the door. Once inside, they part like lovers: he to the lectern; she to the front row, smiling occasionally at him as his students file in. From his bag, he produces a pair of black glasses, which he puts on. They suit him; he almost looks better in them, and the way he gazes at her is so direct, so intimate, it almost feels like they are doing something they shouldn't. For those few seconds, she feels the room recede, leaving her in a kind of void. Then the contact breaks, and her surroundings return in all their chattering aromas: charity-shop clothes and coffee, last night's gig, roll-up cigarettes and stale alcohol. Two girls pass in front of her. They nudge each other, glance sideways at Peter before exchanging a smirk. As they take their seats beside her, Samantha wonders if their excitement is real or whether she's projecting; whether she's falling prey to the mythology, the aura, the cult of Professor Bridges.

Peter, she thinks, her insides folding over. Peter, now.

At midday on the dot, he looks up from his notes. The room falls into an immediate silence.

'Amazing how the numbers swell when you put sex in the title of a lecture,' he says.

An easy laugh.

'Caravaggio was a cad and a bounder,' he announces from his pulpit with an ironic widening of eyes. 'A death-dodger, a cheap slut, a brawler, a murderer and a drunk. He was a genius, a fugitive, a master of chiaroscuro, an innovator and an enduring influence on the Baroque, on world-famous painters such as Rembrandt, Benini and Rubens.

'This morning I want to look at the psychological realism often praised in his work, and how his dissolute life might have given him the edge over ...'

Peter, who less than twenty-four hours earlier was merely Professor Bridges, no substance beyond his youthful appearance, his clean-cut style and his iconic car, continues for an hour: pacing, pointing, raising his voice, lowering it, polished as a stand-up comedian. And like a stand-up, he makes it look as if he's making it all up there and then, as if these informed observations have come to him only now. Watching him, Samantha thinks about the night they spent together, how differently it played out from how she'd imagined. This private side of him, known only to her, thrills her like a secret, especially here in the packed, public lecture hall.

He talks without notes, his thumb deft on the remote. Behind him, paintings bloom on the screen. Under his analytical commentary, the sacred historic scenes come to life: blood oozes from Holofernes' throat as Judith slits it, holding her poor victim at arm's length while her maid cowers behind her; when he introduces a painting called *Saint Francis of Assisi in Ecstasy*, she thinks of that bag of pills and allows herself a childish smile; and then, into the rapt silence, comes the disembodied head of the Medusa.

'Caravaggio used his own face, as you can see.' Peter gestures loosely at the screen. 'Which creates a kind of hermaphrodite, grotesque grimace, framed by the famous writhing snakes of hair. This is the gorgon caught in the terrible instant of self-recognition. Look at that horror. It is the moment the monster realises who he – or she – actually is.'

Samantha feels a chill pass through her. She looks about her to see if any of the others feel it too, but Peter is off again, leading her through Roman streets with nothing but words: pungent ale sloshing in the taverns of the Via Margutta; the raucous hullabaloo of the brothels; violent brawls on the slimy cobbles. He transports her, transports all of them, to the Eternal City at the turn of the seventeenth century, a time of murder, rape and danger.

'If you ever get the chance to visit,' he says at thirty seconds to one, 'make bloody sure you do.'

The lecture is over. After a brief moment of silence, a roar of applause. Samantha has never seen a lecturer applauded before. Afterwards, the students pack up their notebooks, throw their bags over their shoulders and leave talking nineteen to the dozen.

Samantha sits perfectly still, last night a foggy dream to her now. On his leather sofa in the firelight, Peter promised he would take her to Rome. This morning, he has. Now they will return to his beautiful house on the hill together. There is no doubt in her mind that this will happen. She watches him fend off the gaggle of female students who flock around the lectern like geese around a bucket of cornmeal. Peter will drive her to his house and he will press his hand to the small of her back as they step inside. The door will close and she will turn to him, and finally—

'Ready?' Bloody hell, he moves quickly.

'Yes,' she says.

He leads her to the car. Brushes his fingers across her thigh and starts the ignition. Her throat is dry.

'Let's go home,' he says.

CHAPTER 4

'Move in with me,' Peter says.

They are propped up on pillows against the headboard of Peter's white king-size bed. They are drinking freshly ground coffee as stripes of weak sunlight filter through the Venetian blinds, and Samantha has no idea how to reply. Yesterday is like a dream. She can't believe she's even had that thought, framed it with that word. But it really was like a dream, that's the problem.

On the way back to Peter's house, she found yesterday's knickers balled up at the bottom of her coat pocket. All she wanted was to grab a fresh pair of pants, her razor and a few toiletries, maybe a change of top.

'Is it too out of your way to call at my flat?' she asked.

He'd put on an album by that old band that was still quite cool, The Chemical Brothers, was it? Cousins? Whatever, he'd raved about them anyway, asked her if she'd seen the film *Trainspotting*, which she hadn't, and again she felt the keen stab of her own ignorance.

'Why do you want to go to your place?' he asked, turning the volume down.

'I need a change of clothes, that's all. You know, if we're going back to yours.' A hot flare of near panic; she'd assumed too much.

He gave a slow nod of understanding. 'Sorry, I should have thought.'

But he didn't take her home. Instead, he drove into Richmond and took her to House of Fraser, the big department store on George Street. In the women's department, he told her to choose an outfit and some underwear and stood at a distance looking into his phone. She flicked through the rails, barely seeing anything but the tags. Everything was too expensive. She didn't know what he meant by an outfit. Not wanting to keep him waiting, she chose a dress she thought he'd like: short, black, strappy. She didn't try it on.

'Is this OK?' she asked.

He looked up from his phone, took the dress from her and, hooking the hanger on one finger, held it out in front of him. 'You're not going to want to wear that tomorrow, are you? Buy something practical. Jeans, a sweater, whatever. It's cold out.'

He chose some designer indigo jeans, three tops by a brand she'd only ever looked at online and a merino wool sweater with a label she'd never even heard of, and waited while she tried them on. With a loose wrist, he flipped his bank card at the shop assistant, keyed his number into the terminal as if bored. When she looked in the bag, she saw he'd included the strappy black dress she'd originally chosen. It was all a bit weird. But the feeling was not unpleasant. And it'd been years since she'd bought clothes from anywhere other than charity shops and the cheapest high-street chains.

In the underwear department, again he stood at a distance, looking elsewhere. She sidled up to the racks of bras, traced the lace contours with the tips of her fingers. The colours conjured up saloon bars, the Moulin Rouge, busty, confident women laughing in red lipstick. But what was the right thing to pick? They both knew why they were going back to his place. She didn't want to seem naïve. But she didn't want to seem like a slut either. He was being so nice, but it felt like a trap. She would never have worried about any of this with boys of her own age. She'd never have found herself in this situation, full stop. She was a feminist, she was, but … It was like that podcast she listened to: she was a feminist, *but* she wanted to look hot when she took off her clothes. There. A rubbish feminist. Tentatively she lifted a turquoise and acid-pink set from the rail and walked over to where Peter was waiting.

'Are these OK?'

He frowned. 'If you like them, we'll buy them. But don't buy them for me. I would never objectify you, Samantha, you must know that.' He looked away, then back at her, his intense brown eyes on hers.

'I … Sorry,' she stammered. 'I've got it wrong. I don't know how to be.'

He gripped her wrist and put his lips to her ear, as if to threaten her. 'Yourself,' he said softly. 'That's all you need to be. That's all you ever need to be. If you're not sure, I'll help you.'

Together they walked over to the more practical underwear: packs of five, sensible schoolgirl neutrals. He waved his hand over the selection.

'Choose something comfortable. Choose for yourself. You're the one that's going to wear it, not me.'

Again he paid, with the same unceremonious wave of his card, as if money were an unlimited commodity to be exchanged for … well, for whatever he happened to want. And later, much later, when she looked back with the wisdom that only comes from experience, she realised that what he wanted that day was her. But this was not later, there was no hindsight; her thoughts had not refined themselves quite yet. Dreams are blurry realities – time slips, shrinks and warps; opinions are but embryos.

'For you,' he said, handing her the bag. 'If you like the fancy stuff, wear it. But wear it for yourself.'

Later, at the house, before the door had fully closed, she pushed him against the coats and kissed him hard on the mouth.

'Sorry,' she said. 'I couldn't wait another second.'

They staggered as far as the living room. Once he discovered her lack of underwear, the whole thing lasted seconds, but they laughed at themselves, still half clothed and breathless on the antique rug. Afterwards, he opened a bottle of red.

'To us,' he said.

She was getting better at stifling the giggles and replied simply, 'To us.'

Leaving him to cook a sauce for spaghetti he boasted would change her life, she left her second glass of wine in the kitchen and went upstairs. She showered and shaved her legs with his razor, which she rinsed carefully, dried on the towel and replaced. She put on the new, fancy lingerie – why not? She considered the new black dress but at the sight of his soft denim shirt on the back of the chair, she threw that on instead. Cheesy, but she was caring less and less.

At the sight of her, he turned off the gas and held out his hand.

'Come on,' he said. 'Let's do this properly, shall we?'

Later still, after dinner, he made love to her again, and in the night she woke to his kisses down her spine, his hands sliding around her. Afterwards, when he told her he was crazy with love for her, she kissed his chest and told him she felt the same, the urge to giggle almost gone.

And now here they are, in his white king-size bed with sun filtering through the blinds. A dream. A blurry reality that has left her absolutely exhausted.

'I know it sounds sudden,' he is saying, taking her hand in his. He has little tufts of dark hair on the backs of his fingers; his nails are manicured perfection. 'But trust me, when you get a little older, you realise that this' – he waggles his finger between the two of them – 'doesn't happen very often. If at all. It's never happened to me, at least.'

A current of what feels like electricity passes through her. 'But what about Marcia?' The question is practical enough, but in reality, she can't take it in, can't take any of it in. A dream. Shut up, Samantha.

His brow knits. 'What do you mean, what about her?'

'It's just … I live with her. I'd be letting her down. There's no way she can pay the rent without me.'

'Oh, don't worry about that. I'll pay your share until the end of the year. And she has a boyfriend, didn't you say? Jake?'

'Jacob. Yes, she does.'

'So you're not leaving her alone. And she can visit.'

Visit. He makes his house sound like prison. He lifts her empty cup from her hands, places it on the bedside table. Another second and his lips are on her belly, his hands under her buttocks. 'So, Marcia will be fine, yes? What else?' His breath is hot on her navel. He is smoothing his hands over the tops of her legs, now over her hips, her waist. He makes a soft hum of appreciation, plants baby kisses on her abdomen.

I could live here, she thinks. In his house on the hill. This would be my home, my life. She imagines it, this life, unfurling before her. In her mind, it takes the form of the last twenty-four hours: intimate conversation and fine wine, listening to him talk, passionate sex the moment they walk through the front door, clothes strewn in the hall. A little reading, an afternoon glass of wine, a ragout simmering on the range, Massive Attack through the ceiling speakers in the bedroom, more wine, more sex, her body attended to with sure hands, an expert mouth. And on … Conversation. Theatre trips. Travel. A home to return to. Not the village, not the city. Here.

'All right,' she says. 'I will.'

CHAPTER 5

LOTTIE, LANCASHIRE

The Stevensons arrive on the dot of ten. At the end of the long tarmac drive, iPad clutched against her chest, Lottie watches them park their bronze Audi at the kerbside of the cul-de-sac. She smooths out her pencil skirt, checks her name tag is straight and, seeing a spot of muck on her court shoe, gives her foot a quick rub against the back of her shin. Never explain, never complain and always look your best, her nan used to say. Wise words – not that Lottie's got anything to complain about. It's a lovely day.

The Stevensons are smartly dressed. Clean-looking. Lottie shakes their hands with a firm-but-not-too-firm grip and wishes them a good morning.

'I'm Lottie,' she says, her best professional smile in place. 'We spoke on the phone. Keith? And you must be Bev, is that right?'

They return her greeting and together they wander up towards the detached four-bed new-build.

'It's a corner plot, as you know,' Lottie says, really for conversation. They have the schedules in their hot little hands, but it doesn't hurt to emphasise the unique selling points. 'There's roughly thirty per cent more garden, so that'll come in handy if you have a family – extra playing space, washing line and what have you. There's a patio to the rear, ample flower beds for planting if either of you have green fingers and the rest is laid to lawn.'

She unlocks the front door. It's one of her favourite bits, this: the sound of the key sliding into the lock, the click of the turn, and Open Sesame! In these moments, it's as if the house is hers, as if she's coming home after her day at work, and she has to stop herself from calling out: *Cooee, Joanne! Mum's back!*

She doesn't do that, obviously; that would be nuts. Instead, she shows the Stevensons through to the fitted kitchen, the double reception room, the under-stairs loo and hand basin.

'The garage you can access from the drive via the door, obviously,' she says. 'Which incidentally has its own remote. But there's also an internal door here, to the immediate right of the front door, which is very practical.' She throws open the door and stands back to let them have a nosy. 'The back of the garage has enough space if you wanted to set up some kind of utility arrangement, washing machine, dryer and what have you, give you more storage then in the kitchen, if you needed it.'

'That is spacious,' the woman, Bev, says, nodding at the empty garage. 'Plenty of room for shelves, isn't there, Keith?'

If Keith reacts, Lottie misses it.

'Shall we look upstairs?'

She bends to slip off her court shoes. The stair and landing carpets are cream, some developer's bright idea. She's not about to point out how impractical that is, obviously, just hopes that when they see her … Ah, bingo, they're following her example, taking off their winter boots and dropping them onto the more durable laminate floor of the hall.

'It's a four-bed, is that right?' Bev is obviously the chattiest, bless her. The women usually are.

'That's right.' Lottie goes up ahead, sliding her hand lightly up the pine banister. 'I don't know if that suits your situation, but it's always good to have spare rooms. Depends what you need, I suppose. I'm in a two-bed flat myself, but there's plenty of room for me and my daughter so it suits us perfectly.'

'How old is your daughter?'

'She's coming up for nineteen. She's at uni, actually.'

They've reached the top of the stairs. Bev gives her a warm woman-to-woman smile and says, 'Nineteen! You don't look old enough!'

Lottie bats off the compliment, even though it's true. It's just something people say, isn't it? Like, if you said *guess my age* to someone, they'd lop off at least ten years, wouldn't they? So it's not as if Bev was going to say, bloody hell, I thought you'd have grandkids by now, you old bag. Nah. No way. People are much more polite than that, especially in professional transactions. Along with the moment of the key going into the lock, it's another one of her favourite aspects of the job: the politeness. There's never any need to be rude – another of her nan's old sayings – and the more professional you are, the less chance there is. If there's one thing Lottie can't stand, it's rudeness.

It's probably why she's won Nash and Watson Regional Agent of the Year from 2010 through to – and including, she hopes – 2016, which will be announced soon, what with it coming up for December. She's smart, she's clean, she's literally never late and she knows the houses like the back of her hand. When a client comes into the office, all they have to do is describe what they're looking for and she doesn't even need to get the files up. It's like they're all stored in her head. She knows how to make conversation with the clients without getting too familiar, so to speak, and she knows how to share a little about herself without bombarding them with personal information. It's funny, because if you met her outside work, you'd say she was quite shy. Not snotty or anything, just keeps herself to herself. She doesn't go out, only stays half an hour at the work Christmas drinks. She's happier at home with a book and a hot chocolate, or a Baileys if it's Friday. But once the work shoes go on, the uniform and her badge, she's a different person. She's a professional, that's what she is, from her head down to her toes.

Professional.

CHAPTER 6

Marcia is gaping at her like a goldfish. They are in the shabby kitchen of their Vauxhall flat. If you stand on a chair, you can see the MI6 building. Well, a corner of it.

'But you've only just met him,' she offers.

'I know. I know that. But it feels right. I can't explain it. And he's so sure too. He says he's never felt like this before.'

'Does he now? Do you love him?'

'I love the way he makes me feel. I love the way I can see I make him feel. Does that make sense? So yes, I love him.'

Marcia is still unsure when she helps Samantha move in a week later. Greets Peter at the door with a wary eye.

'I told you I'd come for your bags,' Peter says as Samantha stumbles down the chequerboard hallway, beckoning Marcia to follow.

'I only had two,' she says. 'And Marcia wanted to see the house.' She giggles. 'That sounds wrong. Marcia wanted to meet you, didn't you, Marcy?'

When she looks back over her shoulder, Peter is shaking Marcia's hand, telling her he's heard a lot about her, which Samantha doesn't think he has, not really. Marcia is still on the step.

'Come in,' Samantha says. 'Stay and have a cuppa.'

Marcia thrusts her hands into her pockets. 'Actually, I have to get going. I'll see you soon, yeah?'

Samantha follows her down to the front gate, onto the street. 'Are you OK?'

Marcia is staring at her trainers. 'I'm fine.' She glances up, one eye closed, a freeze frame of a wink. 'He's quite a bit older, isn't he?'

Samantha shakes her head, defensiveness flowering in her chest. There is something in the air that she can't name, something final.

'He's not even forty yet, but yes, he's a … a grown-up,' she stutters, strengthens. 'And that might not be what you want but it's what I want, OK?'

'I just wish you could have waited a bit longer, made sure of your feelings, yeah?'

'I am sure.'

Marcia shrugs, yields grudgingly to a hug, hands still in her pockets. Samantha watches her go, all the way to the end of the street, watches her become a silhouette, then disappear around the corner, back towards the town.

Out on Richmond Hill, the light is falling. It is the end of October, barely five o'clock. This time next month, it will be dark at this hour, and when Samantha looks back on this moment, she will wonder whether it was now that the subterfuge started. As it is, she feels only the setting of her bottom lip, the burgeoning resentment at her friend passing comment, passing judgement. Her relationship with Peter has nothing to do with anyone – not her mother, not Marcia, not anyone. In future, she will keep it to herself. She turns away from the empty brow of the hill, heads back and moves in with Professor Bridges.

And yes, it is darker in November, darker still in December. The air turns chilly. At the end of term, she takes the train to Yorkshire, drinks strong tea in the kitchen of her mother's aggressively clean two-bedroom flat.

'So I've moved in with Peter,' she says. 'You know, that guy I've been seeing?'

'Moved in? Haven't you just met him?'

She gives a little laugh. 'Not at all. We've been seeing each other on and off for a while. I just didn't think it was worth mentioning until it was something, you know?' She cannot look at her mother, cannot look anywhere near her.

'Well, you're a grown woman now,' her mother says. 'I can't tell you what to do anymore.'

Later, much later, when she thinks back to this visit, the same feeling she had watching Marcia fade to black the night she moved in with Peter will come to her – that growing sense of going underground, as if she is hiding something from herself as well as them. She will be haunted by the expression on her mother's face when she said goodbye. She will remember how ninety-nine per cent of her felt so happy, so exhilarated, so in love. She will remember a much smaller feeling, a tiny one per cent in her gut. And she will remember pushing that feeling aside.

But it is not much later. She has not yet lived through all the things that will make her look back on this moment and see it differently. And when her mother asks, 'So you're sure about this fella, then?' she answers, 'Yes, I am. Completely.' Adds, 'Why don't you come to us for Christmas?' Without her mother knowing that she's trying to change the subject. Because, actually, Samantha already knows that her mother is going to her sister's, since it is where she was supposed to be going too. So she stays another couple of days, to try to even things out, and doesn't return to Peter until Christmas Eve.

At the station, her mother pushes a twenty-pound note into her hand and gives her a kiss on the cheek.

'Bye, love,' she says, and Samantha feels her heart split in two.

'You're back,' Peter says when she gets home and leaves her in the hallway. A moment later, the door of his study shuts and doesn't open again until evening, when it is time for their glass of wine, by which time he appears to have forgiven her.

*

'So many presents!' The next morning, Christmas Day, Samantha surveys the exquisitely wrapped pile of gifts under the Nordic pine that Peter bought from a garden centre out near Feltham because they sell the best trees and he doesn't want needles dropping all over the house.

'Our first Christmas together,' he says, taking from her the one thing she has bought for him, a Swatch that cost her the rest of her loan.

It is eleven o'clock, later than she's ever waited to unwrap her gifts. Peter doesn't like to rush, says it isn't civilised. And so he brought coffee up to bed, they made love then took a long shower together, followed by a breakfast of smoked salmon and scrambled eggs. After that, he relaid the fire and lit it, and now here they are.

He has wrapped her gifts in thick single-sheet paper, tied them with red ribbon. She opens them one by one: a book, a red cashmere hat, scarf and gloves. A black parka coat, by a brand he tells her makes the finest arctic gear. The weather in the south of England doesn't strike her as anything like arctic; it is much warmer here than in Yorkshire, but she doesn't say this to Peter.

'Oh my God, thank you,' is what she says and sips her Bellini. It is over an hour later, when they are out walking hand in hand to build up an appetite, that he suggests, kindly and politely, that she refrain from punctuating her speech with *oh my God* all the time.

'It's not that I object on religious grounds,' he tells her. 'But it makes you sound stupid. And you're not stupid.'

He has already taken off the watch. It is cumbersome for cooking, he says, in a way that his leather-strapped Breitling is not. And he has the bird to prepare. By bird, he means the goose, which he bought from a specialist butcher in Strawberry Hill.

'Can I help you cook?' she offers, but he tells her he prefers to do it himself.

She sets the table, for something to do, but later finds him realigning the cutlery, adjusting the glasses, and pretends she hasn't seen. She returns to the living room, picks up the book he has bought her: *What a Carve Up!* by Jonathan Coe. It is very funny, he tells her. He can't believe she hasn't read it.

She reads forty pages but doesn't laugh once. She can see what he means, how someone of his age might find it funny. The book lolls in her hand and she thinks about the months she has lived in this house. It is nothing she can tell Marcia, and certainly not her mother, but living with Peter is taking a little more getting used to than she anticipated. There's still plenty of wine and good food and a surprising amount of sex, given his age. In fact, these things form the basis of a comprehensive evening routine, in that strict order. Not one of the three, it seems, can be missed, unless the circumstances are extenuating. There are other things that must be adhered to as well. There is the matter of the shower screen. She keeps forgetting to go over it with the squeegee, which is kept in the cupboard under the bathroom sink. When she does remember, she leaves the squeegee in the shower tray, which also annoys Peter.

'Everything in its place,' he tells her, not unkindly, 'and a place for everything.'

He has lived alone all his life, she thinks. He is not accustomed to sharing his space with another human being. They both have a lot to get used to. So she does her best. Keeps her laptop and books tidy, always hangs up her clothes, never leaves her knickers on the bedroom floor. Even if it is he who has taken them off during the night and thrown them there, she creeps out of bed in the dark and hides them in the laundry basket before morning.

Mornings, she learns, he likes his first cup of coffee in bed, his second in the kitchen with his hot buttered soda-bread toast. The first few times, he brings coffee upstairs to them on a small tray, a precursor to their morning lovemaking, since that was what happened the first time they woke up together. It will be over a year later that she'll realise how quickly this coffee–sex routine turned from spontaneity to simple expectation. How one morning, about a week after she moved in, when he kissed her shoulder and whispered, 'Hey, don't suppose you fancy making the coffee for a change?' she was only too happy to oblige.

'Of course,' she said, almost leaping out of bed and pulling on his Japanese silk dressing gown.

She had no idea, none whatsoever, while she was waiting for the coffee to bubble through the pot, that Peter had just effected a permanent change. From that day on, it would be her who brought their morning coffee to bed, who would ask if it tasted OK, who would close her eyes when he slid the silk robe from her and pushed her back into the soft white pillows.

She doesn't complain. About anything. It is his house and she still feels like a guest, keen to be sensitive to her host, to make herself welcome. Once the morning coffee–sex routine is established, he begins to go running immediately afterwards, explaining to her that he has let this habit lapse because of her but that he must now pick up his training. He puts on his kit, talks her through the special breathable fabric of the T-shirt, the trainers that he had professionally fitted at the specialist running shop in Teddington. She can't understand why he thinks she would find this interesting, but she smiles and tells him it sounds amazing. He seems pleased and leaves her to read in their large white bed.

The moment he has gone, she feels the emptiness of the huge house surround her. Restless, she runs downstairs and grabs her phone, taking the opportunity to cruise through Facebook while he's not there to pass comment. When she hears the front door slam, she hides her phone beneath the covers and, not wanting him to think she's lazing around like a sloth, quickly jumps into the shower before he reaches the bedroom. A mistake, as it turns out.

'Did you wait until I'd got back to have a shower?' he asks when she returns to the bedroom wrapped in a towel.

'What?'

His feet are bare. She can smell them, sour in the humid room. He pulls his special breathable T-shirt over his head, releasing a strong, weird whiff of sweat and something like nylon. 'I was wondering if you'd waited till the exact moment you knew *I'd* need a shower just to piss me off, or if it was simply sheer thoughtlessness?'

She scrutinises his face, sees that he's serious.

'I'm so sorry,' she says, feeling the burning heat of shame creep up her cheeks. 'I ... I thought you'd need to cool down first.' This is a lie; he is right, she didn't think, but she doesn't want him to know this. 'I was only in there for a few minutes.' That at least is true. She's already in the habit of timing herself after he remarked that she was taking too long, wasting the planet's resources. She's got it down to three minutes, including hair wash and express leg shave, no mean feat. 'Sorry,' she says again.

Wordlessly, he leaves her to get dressed. A moment later, the luxurious rush of the German Raindance shower head reaches her from the en suite. Miserably she resolves to be reading, or at least pretending to read, when he gets back from now on, or better still, to grab her shower the moment he leaves so that she can prepare breakfast once he returns.

After breakfast that morning, he gives her a peremptory nod and asks if she's ready, and thinking that he's still cross with her, she replies quietly that yes, she is. And as with the coffee–sex routine, only much later will it occur to her that another routine was substituted that morning: the soft kiss on the back of her neck, the casual remark on the colour of the sky or the wonderful surprise of birdsong was in that moment replaced forever by the irritable twitch of his head, the dull, unsmiling way of speaking to her. She will not be able to remember when exactly these things became part of the fabric of their life, nor when the chatty drives into London or to Richmond station became silent, the CDs he longed for her to check out replaced by Radio 4 news, which, if she tries to talk over, is met with a brusque, frowning *shh*.

When Marcia asks her how it's going, Samantha tells her that Peter is a bit of a stickler. Grumpy, she would say, though not out loud, and definitely not to Marcia. 'Cold' is the word that nestles lower, much lower down. But this is part of what it means to live with someone romantically, which of course she has never done before. And the thing is, he is right about so many things. It is important to listen to the news, rude to talk over the top when someone is listening, inconsiderate in the extreme to take a shower when you know your partner needs one. If she wants to be worthy of him, she has to grow up; she knows that. And in the evenings, particularly after their seven o'clock pre-dinner glass of red, he softens, he really does.

'Come here,' he says, beckoning her to join him on the couch, pushing back her hair and kissing her neck. 'God, you're gorgeous.'

It is the stress of his day diluting, she thinks. And hers too. In fact, she feels herself de-stress along with him, closes her eyes to the feel of his hand as it traces its way to her waist. Yes, her evenings are never lonely. And Peter has helped her to become so much more organised. Where before she studied whenever the hell she liked, sometimes until two in the morning, a turret of Hobnobs diminishing rapidly on her desk – chaos! – now she drinks camomile tea, eats proper food at the proper time, has a regular bedtime of ten thirty.

Daytimes, if Peter's at home, she writes her essays at the dining-room table while he works in the study. If he's going into the uni, he likes her to study in the library until he's finished lecturing, so that they can travel home together. Evenings are for reading, nothing heavier. Her iPhone is not allowed after eight o'clock. Together they lie top to tail on the sofa, wine on the coffee table, fire in the hearth. In these moments, she feels a little more at peace, and it is this peace she focuses on, hoping that it will permeate the rest of her days, gradually overtaking and obliterating that small seed of unease.

The new year dawns: 2017 is ushered in by firelight and an incredible bottle of vintage Veuve Clicquot. Just the two of them, together in their love nest.

And then one Saturday in February, just after Peter's thirty-ninth birthday – which he celebrates at home with a 1968 Saint-Émilion Grand Cru Château Cheval Blanc – she realises that her period is late. She missed one in January too, and she thinks back to that drunken time with Peter over Christmas. While he's out running, she stares at the calendar, racks her brains, but she can't think, can't think, can't remember exactly. All she knows is that the possibility alone is making her nauseous. God only knows what confirmation will do. If she even is, which she can't be. She isn't. Oh please God, make her not not not be pregnant.

She calls Marcia. 'Hey, can I come over? Like, now?'

'Sure,' Marcia says, and even in this one word, Samantha can hear the surprise of former closeness now lost.

But perhaps not forever. She tells Peter she is meeting Marcia for coffee. She's so sorry, she forgot to mention it and now she's late. She waits until he is in the shower to tell him, shouts it to him through the steam.

'What?' he protests, but for once, her stress levels trump anything he might have to say, even as he complains that he's bought some Guatemalan Finca Capetillo for them from Monmouth Coffee, that he'd thought they'd drink it together this morning with the papers, that he wishes she'd mentioned it earlier.

'I'll have some later,' she says, running down the stairs before it becomes an argument. 'I won't be long,' she calls up, knowing he can't hear her. She feels like she's abandoning him, guilty that he is now upset because of her, but panic wins over guilt and she legs it all the way to the station, stopping only at the chemist on George Street.

Marcia makes tea in the flat they used to share while Samantha goes into the loo and pees on the white stick. They sit on the sofa and Samantha tries not to think of giggling fits and boozy, smoky nights in front of crap telly. Marcia takes her hand and holds it, grips tight when two blue lines appear like magic in the tiny window.

'Oh my God,' Samantha whimpers, a gut-churning memory she has pushed aside over and over emerging now from the fog in a hot, anxious wave. These multiplying cells – she cannot say 'baby' even in her mind – are the result of that—

'But you were being careful,' Marcia says. 'Weren't you?'

'Yes,' Samantha replies, thinking of that night. 'But …'

They had been out for dinner at Luigi's, Peter's favourite Italian restaurant, over the bridge. As had become their habit, they had drunk an early-evening glass of expensive wine – a Chianti that night, she thinks she remembers – from Taylor's, the wine merchants Peter always uses. Later, in bed, when Peter discovered that the box of condoms in the bedside cabinet was empty, he said he was too lazy and too drunk to fetch the spare packet from the bathroom. It had made her laugh, in the moment. *It's OK*, he said. *I'll be careful. Trust me.*

'So you let him do it without?' Marcia is incredulous; she just doesn't get it.

'I was … we were … you know? Quite far along. I didn't want to ruin the moment.'

Marcia sighs. 'But you know how babies are made, right?'

'Of course I do. Stop being so judgemental. I … I suppose I trusted in his experience, you know? I trusted him in a way maybe I wouldn't have trusted someone my own age.'

Trust misplaced, as it turns out. *Oops,* he had said, forehead crashing on her chest. *Don't worry about it; it's only once.* She put it to the back of her mind, told herself it would be OK, she'd have to be so unlucky for …

Marcia says nothing, rubs her back. Samantha is more grateful than she can put into words.

'It's one of his favourite albums,' she says after a moment, the test limp in her hand.

'What is?'

Samantha nods to the white stick. '*Blue Lines*. It's by Massive Attack. They were big in the nineties.'

They laugh, because in that precise moment there's nothing else they can do, until Samantha lets her face fall into her hands.

'What the hell am I going to do?' she wails. 'Peter will be nearly forty by the time it's born. I'll only be twenty-two. I can't have this baby. I just can't.'

She takes the train back to Richmond, stares out of the window and wonders how the hell she will tell him. He will not want to be tied down. By anyone. He is the dishy professor, the driver of the vintage Porsche, a few too many careful owners. He asked her to move in, yes; he has told her he loves her, yes; he has asked her to marry him twice already. Yes, yes, yes. But he has not expressed a wish for a child. He has told her he's never before asked a woman to live with him, and while she does believe him, of course she does, it's just that she doesn't know absolutely that this is the truth or whether it's the absolute truth. What is the absolute truth anyway? Most truths have something beneath: unspoken or unacknowledged or incomprehensible. Sometimes that tiny, hidden lie is only apparent or understood much later, even by the mouth that uttered it.

The truth right now is that she feels sick – not at the hormones but at the fear of what Peter will say. Maybe she should take matters into her own hands. Marcia would help her. But no, that would involve outright lying. She thinks of the pervasive, insidious dishonesty that her father inflicted on her mother. She knows first-hand how devastating that is. God knows, her mother is dealing with the toxic fallout even now.

She manages to wait until the next morning, a Sunday. She didn't want to ruin their Saturday-night film – there is a television, as it turns out; it is in the snug, a separate small sitting room at the back of the house that they use on Saturday evenings. She decides to tell him not while they are alone in the house, but outside, where there are other people around. Why she does this hovers in some foggy, soupy place she cannot reach, or does not want to.

She waits until they're at a table outside the veggie café under the arches of Richmond Bridge, the one that serves the best spanakopita in Surrey, according to Peter. Boats sail by, geese drift in arrowheads on the murky water, weekenders amble along the riverside. It is freezing, but she has on her new arctic explorer coat, her cashmere hat. And there are outdoor heaters.

'Peter,' she says. 'I need to tell you something.'

And she tells him, wincing a little, her shoulders hunched.

The silence lasts a second, two, three, oh God. She makes herself look at his face. But instead of a grimace, there is a grin of what looks to her like pure joy. Confusion fills her. He half laughs, picks her up in his arms and sinks his face into her neck.

'Marry me, Sam.' The delicious scratch of stubble against her exposed skin. 'Marry me immediately.'

A giggle escapes her. It is so nice to be wanted *this much*.

He sets her down and she takes her seat, still giggling a little, her face hot.

'You're not furious?' she asks.

But he has knelt in front of her, and her face grows hotter still.

'Samantha Frayn, will you marry me?'

'Stop it,' she says, panicking. 'Get up.'

He does, thank God, though not before people have turned and thrown indulgent smiles their way. He sits on his chair, apparently quite unable to wipe the grin off his face. 'Well then? Will you?'

'I don't believe in marriage. As you *know*.' She is trying to keep this light, but she's told him countless times. He's said he understands. But here he is, putting her on the spot yet again.

'I'm not your father,' he says.

'I know. But I'm only twenty-one. I'm just … I mean, I … I haven't travelled, I haven't seen anything, I haven't even graduated.'

He reaches for her hands. 'Listen. I'll look after you, dummy. We'll have this baby, and after that I'll take you all around the world. I'll make sure you don't miss out on one single thing, trust me.' He pushes her hands to his lips and kisses her knuckles. There are actual tears in his beautiful brown eyes. 'I'm so happy, Sam. You've made me so happy. And we don't have to get married immediately if you don't want to. We have plenty of time.'

It is days later that she reflects on how he never once asked how *she* felt about it, if she was happy, whether it was right for her. It is her life, after all, not his, that will be turned upside down, though on that perfect wintry morning by the river, she has no idea just how much.

CHAPTER 7

It is her mother who is the most difficult.

'But … but you've only known him five minutes.' Her voice is sharp down the phone. 'You were only moving in with him the other month; now you're having his baby? Why do you have to be in such a rush, love?'

'I'm not. It just happened. And Peter's delighted.'

'Peter.'

Samantha waits, but her mother says nothing more.

'Mum,' she says. 'I know you're worried, but if you met him, you'd like him, honestly. He's very … well respected.'

Unlike my father, she doesn't say. Doesn't have to.

Her mother gives a great exhalation, a trailing cloud of hot steam from a train travelling all the way from God's own county to here, the mistrusted south of England. *The south*: syllables spat from downturned mouths by everyone she still knows in the village.

But Samantha knows it's only love that makes her like this. Quite simply, her mother cannot bear for Samantha to suffer as she has. It would kill her.

'It's all right, Mum,' she says before she rings off. 'Everything will work out, I promise.'

Everything does work out. With military precision. Peter makes sure she finishes her degree, gives her regular lifts into town and to her medical appointments. And on a hot day in June, when she logs on to her student portal to find out her results and discovers she has gained a 2:1, she shrieks and runs into Peter's study to tell him the amazing news.

'Er, knock?'

'Sorry!' She waits for him to turn. He swivels around on his chair and pulls his black glasses from his nose. He is smiling at her before she even has time to say it.

'You've heard?' he says.

'I got a 2:1!'

His smile realigns itself; his eyebrows lower a fraction, then worse, shoot further up than they were at the start.

'Well, I think that's brilliant,' he says. 'Under the circumstances.'

Her delight shifts shape as an animal cowers under a whip, still recognisable but so much smaller.

'Under the circumstances?' she asks.

His eyebrows are still high, his hands clasped in his lap. He is nodding encouragement, but encouraged is not what she feels.

'It's really great.' He reaches then for her hands and holds them in his as he often does when explaining a point. 'I just meant with the pregnancy and everything. I meant that it's a marvellous achievement and I have no doubt whatsoever that you would have gained a first if you hadn't had all that to deal with. You clever, clever thing.' He pulls her towards him to kiss her. It is awkward, with the bump.

'Thanks,' she says quietly. 'I'm actually really pleased.'

She leaves him, telling him she'll let him work, and, without a clue as to why, goes and stands by the front door and cries. It is cool here, cooler than anywhere else in the house. She pushes her face into the coats and breathes in and out. He meant it kindly. His faith in her is rock solid and she is grateful for it. But he has no idea how he has crushed her. He didn't mean it like that. He doesn't, cannot possibly know or understand that for her, getting into UCL was a pipe dream, to have come out with a 2:1 beyond anything she imagined. For a few moments, her delight was tall and whole. Until he brought down the whip.

After a brief holiday in Dorset – he doesn't want to risk flying – Peter books her on to a twelve-week adult education course. A teaching qualification will be a string to her bow, he tells her. It's good to have a flexible profession to fall back on. By the time she finishes the course, it is late summer and she is as round as a hot-air balloon, breathless, astonished at how her ankles have swollen. This is a sick joke, she thinks. Nature is a mad sadist. How does any woman have more than one child? She doesn't care how much childbirth hurts, she just wants the baby *out*.

Peter pays for a private clinic in Cobham, a private room, a private delivery.

And it is perhaps only at that point, when they enter the delivery room, that Peter's confident order is obliterated by a force stronger than both of them: nature, in all its bloody and painful reality. Samantha lows like a cow, panting, sweating, swearing, pushing out with all her animal might this purple, sticky and raging baby girl, who for now at least is not taking any shit from anybody. Right now, this child will not be told what to do or how to do it or how to be. No, she comes out fast, fists tight, yelling like a barbarian.

'Is she all right?' Samantha asks, her own pain forgotten instantly.

'Oh yes,' the midwife says, placing the tiny naked warmth on Samantha's chest as Samantha bursts into tears of relief and joy. 'Don't you worry about her. She's a feisty one.'

'Special delivery,' Samantha quips later, when her baby girl is returned to her, clean and wrapped in a soft cotton blanket. She holds her swaddled daughter in her arms, nuzzles her nose against the soft, warm, angry little mite, kisses the world's tiniest fists.

The love is instant, like a light beam or an injection or something, designed to obliterate the hell of the last weeks and hours.

'We should call her Emily.' Peter stands over them, his face lit with pride. 'It's a good writer's name.'

It's also his mother's name. Samantha thought maybe Laura, after her own mother, but she hasn't voiced it, and now Peter is looking at her all joyful and sure. Unable to be marked by childbirth, he's going to stamp his family name on the baby like the farmer brands the cow. Samantha says nothing. Peter's health insurance has earned him the right to pick whatever name he wants, she supposes. She doesn't want to seem ungrateful.

Her mother can't believe what she's seeing when she comes to visit.

'Looks like you've landed on your feet,' she says, with almost no trace of bitterness in her voice.

Samantha shows her up the wide staircase with its dark brass runners and white eggshelled edges. The spare room and the third bathroom, which her mother will have sole use of while she stays, have been freshly painted by a guy who Peter said *takes care of things around the place for me*. Her mother sits on the soft double bed, runs her hands over the crisp new White Company bed linen; the gesture is not casual, it is appreciative. She gathers the new snowy bath towel in her arms and presses it to her face.

'Money isn't everything,' Samantha says, with no idea why, or what she means by this. Sorry, perhaps. She wants to say more, but at that moment Peter appears on the landing.

'Ah, there you are,' he says. 'Who'd like to join me in the sitting room for a glass of wine before dinner?'

It is a Sunday evening in October, almost a year to the day since they met.

'So I've hopefully lined up a job for you at Richmond College,' Peter announces over dinner, an organic rabbit casserole he has prepared with the rest of the second bottle of Barolo he opened last night. 'It's only two hours a week, but it'll be good for you to get out of the house and exercise the old grey matter.'

Immediately, her eyes prickle. She hasn't had much sleep. Emily is only a month old and Samantha still feels like a leaking bag, like a cow, like a shapeless mess of flesh she no longer understands. But he has only moments ago told her how wonderful she is, how amazing.

'What's the job?'

'Creative writing course. Beginners. Piece of cake for someone like you.'

She flounders. 'But my degree is English lit. I don't really—'

'Of course you do.' He reaches out and takes her hands. He is so very tender – he is the man who pressed his palm to her cheek that first night, who wanted nothing more than for her to be brilliant, listened to, understood. 'You write poetry, don't you? You only need to be half a page ahead, trust me. It's all about confidence.'

She pushes the stew around her plate. It is delicious, like everything he cooks, but her head is mince. 'I'm not sure my confidence is at an all-time high just at the moment.'

'Nonsense.' Softly he strokes the back of her hand. 'Trust me, you'll ace it. It's only ten weeks' maternity cover. And it doesn't start until January. Perfect foot in the door, nothing too strenuous, and I'll help you.'

'But I want to teach English as a foreign language. Or teach people to read. I want to help people.'

'Exactly.' He smiles. 'That's what I told Harry. It's a stepping stone, but you need to keep your hand in, not let the grass grow, et cetera. A woman of your intelligence and capabilities can't be stuck at home. It'll look bad on your CV.'

'But what about Emily? And who's Harry? And how do I get from there to helping people?'

He chuckles. 'Slow down. Harry's head of humanities at the college. I went to school with him; he's a good bloke. And I'll arrange my schedule so that I can look after Emily. You'll only be out of the house for three hours, three and a half at most, and she'll be, what, nearly four months old by then? Trust me, darling, this will be brilliant for you. And it'll help if you ever want to get your collection published. Editors would take you more seriously.'

She can't believe this is true. She would need to be a university lecturer, surely. An academic. But still, Peter looks so pleased with himself, and she is so tired, too tired to argue, and it's not until after Christmas. She doesn't have to think about it now.

'I'll help you,' he says in his soft, low voice. 'Don't worry – you'll be fine. You can do it for a while and then take a break to do your MA, maybe when we have another child. The contracts will arrive a week or two before.'

It really is all sorted, she thinks. A little like her pregnancy: no sooner announced than taken over, supervised, organised. Peter is looking after her is what she tells herself. He has everything under control. So why does she feel as if control is the exact thing she has given up?

CHAPTER 8

LOTTIE

Lottie watches the Murphy family through the windscreen of her car. They can't see her, there in the road, wouldn't notice her if they did, not from this distance. They're leaving fifteen minutes after they said they would, which is irritating. Their Ford Galaxy follows the A-2-B removal van out of the close and then, after a moment, she pulls forward, turns into their drive and parks her car. The Smiths won't be here until this evening. They're driving up from Exeter and it takes at least four hours to get to Lancashire from there, more if the M6 is jammed, unless they pay the rip-off toll, of course. That's why she always goes early: no traffic, no toll.

She slides the key in and out – once, slowly. That's the way with a newly cut key – a bit like heating oil in a new frying pan, then wiping that oil off and starting again with new oil so that the omelette doesn't stick. She loves omelettes, makes them all the time … but anyway, with new keys you have to be careful or they jam up on you. She slides the key in again, closing her eyes at that lovely scratchy sliding sound … pulling the door hard towards her, the click when the key turns. That's the knack with this particular door. She opens her eyes to it swinging away into the ample hallway. Open Sesame.

Inside, the house feels empty already. Weird how quickly that happens. When she showed the Smiths round, you could hear the kids' music upstairs. You could just feel that there were people in. But now that they've gone, the house has that echo to it when she shouts, 'Hello? Is anybody home?'

The word *home* bounces off the polished floor tiles – *home*, *home*, *home*, like that. There are pale rectangles on the staircase walls. A wedding photo; a boy of about ten with his arms around his younger sister, both in school uniform; a grinning man holding a salmon. These photos are not there now; the empty rectangles are their ghosts. The actual pictures have been packed into boxes along with the rest of the family's things, on the way to the coast to be hung in another happy family home.

In the kitchen, the white goods have been left as agreed. The curtains and blinds are all here, which she always likes. In the dining room, the carpet's got those funny flat patches where the table and chairs and the sideboard were, and when she presses her hand to the dining-room radiator it's still warm. The boiler is in the downstairs utility, so it's easy enough to pop the heating back on. Back in the kitchen, she pulls her dirty linen from her holdall and puts it in the washing machine. They haven't left any detergent, but that's all right; she always brings her own. She measures out 35 ml because it's a small load, and selects the mixed wash quick option. Hopefully she'll have time to take advantage of the dryer too while she's here. She has another viewing at one, so she'll have to get a move on obviously.

The slosh of the washing in the drum is a cosy, homely noise. Already the place feels like it's got a family in it again, which is what a house should have. Her little portable radio adds some music to the mix. She's extra lucky today because the Murphys' leather three-piece suite and their beautiful pine super-king-size bed are too big for the cottage they're moving into, and the Smiths are coming from a smaller place, so they did a deal on the suite and the bed and the matching units. She doesn't know how much the Smiths paid, but she bets they got a right bargain. She doesn't have any super-king bedding, which is a shame, and it wouldn't have been her place to suggest the Murphys leave theirs. She's way too professional for that, and some people are weird about that kind of stuff. Some people are weird full stop. You see all kinds if you work for an estate agent. Beggars belief, some of it.

It's getting on for eleven, so she puts the kettle on. From her handbag she pulls coffee, powdered milk and a couple of mugs, both with *Coffee Time* on the front in a red handwriting-style font. A nice cup of coffee each, that's what they need. It's instant, but it gives that barista taste. It doesn't, actually; it just tastes like any old coffee, but that's what it says on the tin. To be honest, it's nowhere near as good as Costa. Costa's her favourite, but only for a Friday treat. Too expensive to have it every day like some do. She always nicks a few sugar sachets while she's in there, keeps some in her bag in case Joanne fancies some. She likes hers sweet, especially if there's no biccies on the go.

The Murphys' sofa is as soft as it looked when Lottie was showing the house. She didn't sit on it then, obviously – that would be totally unprofessional – but she sits on it now all right. It's so soft she sinks right down into the cushion and the coffee almost spills into her lap. She has to put the mugs on the floor while she rights herself because there's no coffee table. It's OK because there's no rug either, so there's no danger of spoiling anything, although she'd move pretty quick if she knocked a cup over, obviously, because liquids stain wooden floors if you leave them to soak in. Cripes, that would give the game away, wouldn't it? Talk about red-handed – it'd be someone else's name engraved on the Nash and Watson shield this year before you could say *show home*. Not that she's doing anything wrong as such. Not really. It's unprofessional, obviously, but what the eye don't see …

The coffee is too hot to drink but it'll soon cool down, so she wanders to the foot of the staircase.

'Joanne!' she shouts up. 'Your coffee's ready, love. Don't let it get cold.'

She knows what she's doing isn't, strictly speaking, on the level, but this house is going to be lying empty for the next few hours, and she's not hurting anybody or damaging anything, so as far as she's concerned there's no harm in it. There's plenty of people doing much worse than her in this world – blowing up buildings and sending bugs through the post. She'd never do anything like that. All she wants is an hour with her best girl.

CHAPTER 9

Standing on the front step, Samantha nuzzles Emily on the head before stretching up to kiss Peter goodbye.

'Sure you'll be OK?' She pushes her folder of teaching notes into the new Hermès leather satchel that Peter bought her for her first day.

'Don't you worry about us,' he replies, Emily in his arms, the burp cloth that Samantha handed to him moments ago draped over his left shoulder. He looks a little like he does when he cooks dinner – the tea towel replaced by a milk-infused piece of muslin.

'I should be back by half two, three at the latest.'

'As long as you're back by four. Go on, off you go. You'll be brilliant. They'll love you almost as much as I do.'

She walks. It's strange, walking without first having to load the car seat into the pram chassis, make sure she has her rucksack with nappies, nappy bags, wipes. All she has is the lesson plan, the handouts and her purse, packed into an elegant burgundy leather satchel, as if her professional self is a change of identity made possible by a change of bag. Her limbs bounce, almost, as she strides down the hill, their lightness astonishing, new. By the time she reaches the roundabout – Bill's Restaurant on the corner, the Odeon standing guard over the bridge – she has got used to her single status. But still when she passes herself in a shop window, she looks to see who she is. The woman who stares back at her is different from the one she was a year ago, but not noticeably a mother, not without Emily. She looks tired, a little puffy. More than anything, she looks young, too young for what she is, as if her life is a garment that doesn't really suit her and doesn't yet fit.

She arrives at the college fifteen minutes early. Taking advantage of the silent solitude of the empty classroom, she keys the password she's been given into the computer and is relieved when it lets her in. She brings up the register and skims down the list of names, amused to see that one of the students is called C. S. Lewis. There is a Daphne, who makes her think of du Maurier, a Reggie, who makes her think of an East End gangster, a Jenny, a Thomas, a Svetlana, an Aisha and a Sean. Eight students in total.

A flash of nerves. Ten minutes to go. She has planned her lesson, her first ever lesson, sounded it out with Peter last night. She showed him her notes, told him she was planning to do limericks to warm the students up, have a few laughs and build their confidence, but taking the notes from her, he frowned.

'Limericks? No, hon. Too basic, even for beginners. Anyone can write a limerick. If you want to break the ice, use the clerihew.'

'What's that?'

'Exactly.'

Peter explained what a clerihew was and why it was better. He helped her to change her notes – so generous; he was working on her handout until eleven last night. Once he was happy with it, he hugged her and told her she would be brilliant, that he couldn't wait to hear how she got on.

Samantha yawns, wonders how he's coping on his own with the baby – he's not very hands-on, which she's put down to the fact that he does all the cooking while she feeds Emily. At that thought, her breasts tingle and harden. Keeping one eye on the door, she checks her breast pads are in place. Teaching elementary poem forms with rivulets of milk staining your blouse is not a good look. A flutter of butterflies. They will be here soon, expecting an expert. She is not an expert. They will be expecting someone mature. She looks like a girl, a haggard girl but still a girl. She feels like a girl. They'll see straight off that she's a fraud. She *is* a fraud … oh God, for a penny, for nothing at all, in fact, she would run out of this room and take the first bus—

The door opens and an elderly woman with spiky fuchsia hair enters. She is wearing a loose pale pink smock dress, black leggings and black Doc Marten boots tied with bright stripy ribbons, and she is smiling. Samantha loves her instantly.

'Is this creative writing?' she asks.

'Yes.' Samantha smiles back in what she hopes is a confident way. 'Please take a seat.' Unsure of what to say next, she sits at her desk and shuffles through her notes, pretends to read something, picks up her pen, puts it down again.

The woman sits. Out of the corner of her eye, Samantha watches her. Outside, the sky is a pinky yellow over the office buildings next door. On the opposite side of the classroom, internal windows give on to the corridor, where another classroom spews noisy students out of the door. Pink-hair woman pulls out a notepad and pencil case from a canvas bag decorated with a modern art design. Samantha sorts the handouts into piles, fighting off those annoying butterflies. She should chat to this woman, she knows, but she can't think of anything to say.

A man of no more than twenty enters: black curly hair and dark shadows under his eyes. He nods at her, sits in the chair nearest the door. Two women who clearly know one another follow, chatting comfortably. Friends. Mums, she guesses, here to catch a class that will allow them to get back to the school gates in time. They both smile and say hi. Another woman strides in, her hair undercut on one side, several ear piercings and the hint of a tattoo on her neck; an old man – woolly hat, blinking behind thick spectacles; a middle-aged woman – thin, almost birdlike at the top, voluptuous at the bottom, as if her body belongs to two different people.

Samantha waits, keeping her face in a neutral but, she hopes, pleasant smile, a smile that says *welcome*, that says *I know what I'm doing*, that also says *please be kind*. The door closes. Rustles and murmurs, takeaway cups planted on the corners of desks. Notebooks, laptops, pens, tissues, a half-eaten flapjack, a packet of liquorice allsorts – people are funny. She waits for the shuffling to subside.

'Hello, everyone,' she begins when silence comes, cursing the giveaway tremor in her voice, the heat now creeping up her neck. 'I'd like to start by—'

The door opens. A man of about thirty-five pokes his head into the classroom. 'Creative writing?'

'Yes. Come in. We're just starting.'

He nods. 'Sorry I'm late. Roadworks on the A316 and I got caught in the traffic jam. It was a bad idea to drive. I'll check before I leave next week and probably take public transport. I can get a bus and a train. I'm Sean Worth.'

'Hi, Sean.' Samantha seizes the moment to interrupt. 'Take a seat. We were about to introduce ourselves, so you've got the ball rolling nicely there, thank you.'

The other students shunt their chairs as far as they can under the desks. Sean sidles around, apologising as he goes. His hair is greasy. His anorak is stained and zipped up to the top.

'Hello, everyone,' she says again and introduces herself before running through her background. She tells them that she writes poetry, that she's hoping to publish a collection next year. This was Peter's idea, another correction from last night. She'd argued, said it sounded pompous and that it was untrue.

'Not at all,' he said. 'It is the truth, if you think about it.'

'But it implies there's something in the pipeline, like it's only the timings that are yet to be finalised.'

He waved his hand, frowned. 'That's for them to interpret. All you're saying is that you hope to be published next year, and you do, so that's not a lie at all. It's not about what you've done or what you do, it's about what you can get away with. Everyone does it. If you want to be successful, you have to be realistic.'

And so she's said it, feels horrible, but breezes onwards now to her recent graduation in English literature and her teaching qualification. She does not tell them that her partner pulled some strings to get her this maternity cover but instead suggests they go around the room, taking turns to introduce themselves. The young man with the black curly hair is on her left, by the door. She nods to him to go first.

He cocks his head to one side, which makes him look coy, though his eyes are bloodshot. He takes his pen and holds it horizontally between the tips of both forefingers.

'Yeah,' he says. 'So, I'm Tommy. I'm a musician? Keyboards mainly. Recovering addict. Done a lot of rehab, but I'm getting back on track now.' He pauses, glances up at her. 'I signed up to get some tips on songwriting. I write songs.'

'Lovely. Thanks, Tommy.' On a sheet of paper Samantha writes: *Tommy. Drugs. Musician.* She looks up, catches the eye of the woman sitting next to him, the one with the undercut and the neck tattoo.

The woman glances about her, as if to meet the gaze of every other student individually. 'My name is Lana.' Her accent is Eastern European. 'I'm from Poland. I'm living in UK for five years. I have bad experience with boyfriend so I want to write about that.'

Samantha nods, scribbles on her aide-memoire: *Lana. Polish. Bad boyfriend.*

'I'm Aisha,' says the woman next to Lana, one of the mum friends. 'Like you, Samantha, I'm an English literature graduate. UCL, a few years ago now. I've come with my friend Jenny. I'm here because I've loved literature all my life and I'd like to create some, if I can.'

Samantha smiles while she writes, refrains from adding that she graduated from the same university – it's not the right moment to get into a conversation. Aisha's friend with the red hair goes next.

'Yes, I'm Jenny, like Aisha said. Also a UCL English grad, a few years after Aisha. We met at uni, well, in the pub near the uni.' She gives a brief laugh. 'We share a flat and she suggested I come along. I'm looking for work at the moment so I'm pretty much here to enjoy myself and try something new. Er, yeah, that's it really.'

Not school mums then, as she had first thought. Samantha scribbles, nods, looks up to encourage the elderly man with the thick glasses, who has taken a seat in the corner.

'Hello, my name's Reginald Spark. Reggie.' He speaks in a broad London accent. 'Used to be a session musician and I've worked with some pretty interesting people over the years ... Elton John, the Stones in the early days, even did a gig with David Bowie once, so I'm hoping to maybe write a memoir or something in that vein.'

There is a collective murmur of approval. Reggie has taken off his woolly hat to reveal a bald head, shaved close at the sides, and his navy cardigan opens on a grey T-shirt with a rainbow passing through a prism, a design Samantha thinks might be an album cover, though she doesn't know which one.

'My name's Suzanne,' says the middle-aged woman, looking thin now that she has sat down and only her narrow shoulders are visible. 'I left school at sixteen and I've always regretted it, so I just wanted to see if I could come up with something. Thought it might give me a bit of confidence.'

'I'm sure it will. Thanks, Suzanne.' *Suzanne. Left school 16. Confidence.*

'Sean?'

'Yes, hello. Like I said, I'm Sean Worth. I'm writing a futuristic fantasy novel where this guy is basically the last man left on earth, or he thinks he is, but then he goes around the world and one day he discovers this tribe living in the jungle and they're all women and the only way to save the world is if he gets them all pregnant, so he—'

'Thanks, Sean.' A giggle bubbles up in her chest. She bows her head and writes, pushing her teeth hard into her bottom lip. The air has thickened. But everyone has to be made to feel safe and she cannot – must not – laugh. *Sean*, she writes. *Sci-fi. Last man on earth.* Wait till she tells Peter.

She looks up, careful not to catch the eye of any of the women in case one of them so much as twitches in amusement. If that happens, she will collapse into hysterics. Not good.

Pink-haired Daphne saves them all, however, announcing with a cheeky chuckle that she hopes to write erotica to supplement her pension.

'Something saucy to keep the heart beating,' she adds and giggles, which allows the others to release the laughter that they've undoubtedly been stifling for the last few minutes. Thankfully, the tension bleeds out of the room.

Samantha feels herself lift. People are incredible. They are wonderful, she thinks. Peter was right. He said she would enjoy this, and she thinks, once the nerves die down, she will.

After the break, Samantha tells them they are going to write some simple poems. A collective groan ensues, which she bats away with a smile.

'We're going to pull poetry apart like a wind-up radio,' she says. 'To see how it works, how it's put together and how you might build one yourselves.'

'Is that a metaphor, Miss?' Tommy's smile looks more like a sneer.

'It is, Tommy. Well spotted.' She smiles again and presses on. 'Today we're going to learn how to write a clerihew,' she tells them. 'Does anyone know what a clerihew is?'

Blank looks all round.

'OK, well, the clerihew is a simple four-line satirical verse. It was invented by Edmund Clerihew Bentley in the early twentieth century.' She reminds herself to stand up straight and to keep her speech slow, loud and clear. 'If you look at your sheets, we can read his famous example.' She clears her throat, takes a sip of water and reads the poem aloud:

> 'Sir Christopher Wren
> Said, 'I am going to dine with some men.
> If anyone calls
> Say I am designing St Paul's.'

The group gives a low harrumph of amusement. Samantha feels her nerves abate a little. The ice is breaking, hopefully.

'If you look at the first line,' she says, 'you'll see it's simply the person's name. The second line is something whimsical about the person that rhymes with that name, and the last two lines rhyme with each other.' She looks up, scans their faces. So hard to tell if they are listening or bored rigid. 'Can anyone name a celebrity?'

Eight blank looks.

'Mick Jagger,' Reggie says, a split second before the silence becomes painful. She wants to kiss his bald pate and say *cheers mate*.

'Very good, Reggie.' She writes *Mick Jagger* on the whiteboard. 'So, can anyone think of a line that rhymes with Jagger?'

'Walked with a swagger?' Reggie suggests.

'Brilliant, Reggie.' Her heart fills. Of course. Reggie is a musician. He will have a good ear. She writes it up, hoping the others will have the confidence to join in now. 'So, the third line can be any length at all and it doesn't have to rhyme with the first two. Anyone?'

Nothing. Her heart shrivels.

'How about,' she says, '"But sometimes when he did a dance."' Without waiting, she writes it on the board and turns again to face the class. Some of them are almost smiling, though it could, as her mother would say, be wind. 'Can anyone think of a last line to rhyme with dance?'

'"A million girls were in the mood for romance"?' It is Aisha, her face eager. She is very pretty, Samantha notices. Huge brown eyes like a doll's.

'Aisha, thank you, that's perfect.' She completes the poem on the whiteboard and reads it aloud:

> 'Mick Jagger
> Walked with a swagger.
> But sometimes when he did a dance,
> A million girls were in the mood for romance.'

'That's great! And did you see how easy it was?' She wonders if the class can hear her heart beating. 'Once you've it written down, of course, you can play with it. You can change one of the words, or a whole sentence … You can say "All the girls in the world", or "a sexy dance", whatever, because there's no limit on line length or the number or syllables like there is in other forms. If you stick to those simple rules, you will nail it, trust me.'

The students bend their heads and write.

Samantha's shoulders straighten. Her chest swells. Even the muscles in her jaw relax. After that, the class passes quickly. She talks to them about rhyme schemes, about comic timing. They attempt a clerihew and seem lost in concentration.

'Thank you so much for a lovely first class,' she says as the lesson draws to a close, realising that she's completely forgotten about Emily, about Peter. She's even forgotten to be nervous. 'If you can pass your poems along to this end, I'll take them home and mark them. For homework, I'd like you to have a go at writing something you'll all know from school: a limerick. Don't worry if you find it difficult, but have a go, for fun, as we'll be pulling them apart next week in class. See you then.'

They file out. All except Lana, who hands her the stack of collected poems with a solemn expression.

'What is limerick?' she asks.

Bugger. Her first week and already she's infringed the guidelines of equality and diversity.

'I'm sorry, Lana, I should have explained that better. Tell you what, just look it up on Google and have a go, but don't worry about it if you can't.' She scribbles her email address on a scrap of paper. 'If you're really stuck, drop me an email,' she says, handing it to Lana – she shouldn't really, but she can't see the harm.

Lana gives a grave nod and makes her way out.

Samantha leaves the college buoyed up with pride. She has lost so much confidence since the pregnancy, so much energy too. But today, she's managed a class on her own! No one has corrected her, no one has run screaming from the room and no one has pointed at her and yelled, 'Fraud!'

It is only when she is on the bus that she takes out her folder to read through the clerihews.

There were eight students.

There are nine poems.

CHAPTER 10

Samantha can hear Emily crying before she puts her key in the lock, a sound that amplifies as she pushes the door open. The hallway is dark, even though it's only quarter to three in the afternoon. The soft tinkle of classical music drifts under the closed door of the living room.

Peter is on the sofa, listening to Debussy, one hand across his eyes.

'Peter?' she says. 'Can't you hear the baby?'

'I can.'

She hesitates. 'But … she's crying. She's crying, Peter.'

'I tried everything. I tried the milk; she wouldn't take it. I tried changing her, I tried burping her.' He takes his hand from his eyes and peers at her. His hair is too brown, she thinks; it looks like a wig.

She stomps up the stairs without taking off her shoes. Sod him. Emily is wailing like a professional mourner: deep sorrow, oceans of pain. From the wall of the staircase, Peter's parents stare out from a photo taken here, in this house; her own parents squint against the sun, stiff as convicts outside the farm, a picture taken before the divorce. There is one of her, aged ten, with a home-cut fringe, a real knife and fork job; and herself and Peter with Emily when she was first born, the one she posted on Facebook to announce her baby's arrival into the world. It is Samantha who has framed and hung these pictures, to give the house a bit of soul.

Emily is crying hard now: great howls, trembling aftermaths, shocked silences as she sucks in another lungful of air. She is in her cot, her face crimson, almost purple. Samantha picks her up, holds her fraught and furious body close. Almost instantly, she calms. Sh-sh-shushing, Samantha sits on the armchair in the corner of the nursery and unbuttons her blouse. Her left breast is the fullest, firm as a rubber ball, and when Emily closes her mouth around it, she almost yelps with that still strange yet familiar blend of pain and near ecstasy as the baby draws the milk down.

Hush descends. The soft smacking sound, Emily's eyelashes, her tiny soft head. Samantha tries to contain her fury at Peter. Illogically, she fears it might transfer, might sour the milk.

Peter appears at the nursery door.

'That's what she needed,' he says, smiling.

She glances at him, but only briefly, before looking away. She cannot look at him, not right now.

'I left a bottle,' she says.

'I tried, but she wasn't interested.'

She glances at him. He is not upset. He is not mortified. He is not ashamed to have been caught lying on the sofa while their baby—

'I've been out of the house for a few hours,' she says. 'A few hours. This is the first time I've been out on my own. You could have comforted her, Peter. She's a baby. They need comfort. And instead you comforted yourself with a little lie-down and some nice music.'

'I couldn't do anything for her, Sam. I thought the best thing to do was leave her to cry it out. There's no point me draining my battery, is there? I have a lecture at five.'

She closes her eyes to the rage that boils within her. 'I won't leave her with you if you're not going to look after her. I'm not going to go and teach if you can't even—'

'She was perfectly safe. She hadn't been crying that long. I just needed a break.'

'You just needed?' She has raised her voice, damn him. He doesn't like it when she raises her voice. Well, tough. 'What about *her* needs, Peter? You're missing something, some vital piece. It's about her needs now, not yours. Don't you see that?'

'I'm not going to talk to you if you're going to shout.'

'I'm not shouting. But you can't have tried very hard. I would have tried for the whole time. I would have sat there for hours and got her to take her bottle if it killed me. It's bound to be difficult, but you have to persevere, otherwise, I can't go out to work.' She looks up. The doorway is empty. From downstairs music amplifies, dies away.

'Twat,' she mutters, relishing the illicit swear word. 'Bastard. Stupid wiggy twat bastard fuckface.'

She has made herself laugh at least. But it is not the first time he's left her muttering and swearing like a madwoman. And as often happens since she had Emily, in these moments, when she finds herself so utterly alone, the memory of giving birth comes to her, followed always by the first time she pulled a calf with her father, over and over, like a dream: the hay and the heat, the smell of iron and dung, the mother licking the calf with her pink speckled tongue. Herself, no more than ten, crouched by her father's side, listening to his soft whispered words ... *She'll take it from here.* The day she gave birth to Emily, Samantha put her trust in the midwives as the cows put their trust in her father. Maybe that's why the memory comes to her when she's cross and confused. Maybe it's to do with her father, her father who, in the end, couldn't be trusted.

'Hey, my little baby calf,' she whispers, lips pressed to her daughter's soft head.

But now she's made herself cry when what she wants is to be furious. As furious as her beloved baby girl when she came slithering out, livid as a bruise, outraged. This part of her own body, this hot blood shared. How could Peter leave their child to cry when she is part of his flesh too? His emotionless response is so at odds with the way he can be at other times: so affectionate, so understanding, so beautifully civilised. Day and night. It is as if he is two people.

She hears the oiled click of the latch, the profound roar of the Porsche pulling out onto the street. She carries Emily to the front window and watches Peter drive away. Her anger is already beginning to confuse her now, after the event, as it so often does. Peter has a way of making her out to be the unreasonable one. He does it so eloquently, so rationally, that she is left no longer sure if she is entitled to feel what she undeniably does feel, whether she is being too demanding, too sensitive, too … whatever. And she always ends up being the one to say sorry. Peter doesn't say sorry. Ever.

'Never argue with a professor,' she said to Marcia last time they met for coffee, before Emily was born. 'Even when they're wrong, they're right.'

Seven o'clock. Emily is in bed and Samantha is starving. Peter should be home by eight, but she is too hungry and, frankly, not in the mood to wait for him. In the living room, she finds a low bank of glowing coals in the grate and tops them up from the bucket. The house is cosy, at least.

In the larder there's some dried pasta and half a carton of fresh pesto in the fridge. While the pasta boils, she calls her mother, whose village gossip always straightens her out.

Sure enough, her mother regales her with the story of the stranger who, on Tuesday evening, sat in Charlie West's chair in the Dancing Drake, the pub where her mother works, the silent scandal that followed; Fiona Kelly, who organised the maypole dance for the last spring fete, is in hospital again with her nerves; Tara Munday's lad broke his wrist coming off his quad bike and had to be taken to York to have it reset.

Last of the stoics, her mother never once mentions the farm, the life that was sold from under her.

Samantha eats two rounds of toast while she listens, several slices of Cheshire cheese, a lone leftover falafel and a handful of walnut halves. Peter has never, in all the time she's lived with him, stocked crappy foods. Which is a shame. Right now, as she tells her mother about her first ever class, she longs for a treat from the packed lunches Mum used to make: prawn cocktail crisps or cheese strings or a greasy, salt-saturated Peperami.

'How's Dad?' The inevitable question, always asked at the end. She drains the pasta, phone in the crook of her neck.

'All right,' her mother replies. The tiniest inhalation.

'What?'

'Rhianna is pregnant.'

'Oh for fuck's sake.'

'Hey! Swearing.'

'No but really.'

'I know,' her mum sighs. 'He's a fucking arse.'

They both laugh. Samantha eats the pasta standing at the kitchen counter while her mother fills her in on her father's embryonic new family. Rhianna, Dad's new girlfriend, is five years older than Samantha. Her pregnancy means that Samantha's new half-sibling will be a year younger than her own daughter. But then, at forty-one, her father is only two years older than Peter.

'Let's hope that by the time the silly bitch hits forty, he'll be too old to muck about where he shouldn't,' her mother says, by way of a wrap-up. 'For the baby's sake.' She gives a dark laugh. 'You should go and see him, you know. You have to forgive him sooner or later.'

It is only once Samantha puts the phone down that she remembers the extra poem. The argument with Peter, the baby's constant demands and the rather depressing talk with her mother have conspired to flush it from her mind. She read Tommy's, Lana's and Jenny's clerihews on the bus before she reached her stop, but now she settles with her folder and a cup of decaf coffee on the sofa. She is calmer than she was; she has rationalised it. Quite simply, in a fit of enthusiasm, one of them has written two poems and wants her to look at both. No big deal.

Lovely Daphne's is top of the pile:

> Michael Jones
> Had good bones.
> His smile she trusted.
> After his Greek-god bod she lusted.

'Brilliant,' she says aloud, laughing softly, and flicks to the next one:

> Sean Worth,
> Last man on earth.
> Everyone's disappeared without a trace
> So now it's down to him to save the whole human race.

'Bravo, Sean!' She jots some encouragement before leafing through the rest. Aisha's is a political verse about Boris Johnson, which ends on a clever rhyme concerning VAT and Macavity the cat. Trust an English graduate to throw in a reference to T. S. Eliot. Suzanne has written about Kylie Jenner, who borrowed a tenner – she spent it on an exotic pet, apparently, and is now in debt, ha!

Reggie has written an accompaniment to the Mick Jagger poem from this afternoon. 'Bill Wyman,' Samantha reads under her breath, 'broke many a hymen.' This makes her laugh out loud. Good old Reggie, giving her a giggle after the tension of the evening, her father's continuing and barely believable crassness, her poor mother.

Still chuckling to herself, she slides Reggie's work to the bottom to find the last clerihew – the ninth poem. Anticipation catches in her chest. There is no name at the top or bottom of the page.

The sheet is unlined. The poem has the correct number of lines: four. But when she sees her own name at the top, her laughter dies on her lips.

> Little Miss Frayn
> Will be driven insane.
> She thinks she's the only one
> But her happiness will soon be done.

CHAPTER 11

Samantha drops the poem, watches it skitter to the floor. She jumps up, tears a strip off her thumbnail with her teeth. The shutters are closed. She strides over to them and pushes them open, just a little. Outside, the black sky is hazed in orange from the street lamps. She paces out of the living room, across the hallway to the kitchen. Checks the back door. It's locked. She lowers the blinds on the back windows, pulls the heavy curtains across the patio doors. Opens the curtains a centimetre and, hand visor-like to her brow, nose touching the cold glass, peers out.

The garden is in darkness, the shrubs and trees gothic shadows under the starless sky, the white sliver of moon. She strains her eyes, scrutinises the scene for movement, but there is nothing. No one.

She closes the curtain, tells herself she is being stupid. Pathetic even. Her heart is racing over what? A poem. A stupid poem that could be, probably is, actually, a silly prank. Yes, a joke. A student with misjudged ideas about what's funny, with what Marcia would call 'a shit sense of humour'.

She was not looking forward to Peter's return, but now she wills him to come home. She calls him but he doesn't answer. A good sign; it means he's on his way. Hopefully. She paces, looks out of the window, tells herself that pacing is a cliché, to stop, stop it, stop it. She sits, finally, tries and fails to read the new Kate Atkinson, checks Facebook, feels a pang at the picture of Marcia and Jacob outside the Barbican, about to go to a gig.

She scrolls through her own page, the photos of her and Peter, of her, Peter and Emily when Emily was first born, when she was a few weeks old; her announcement that she would be teaching at the local adult community college in the new year, the link to the course her feeble attempt at advertising. It's all so recent, yet it feels like so long ago. She puts this down to the dramatic changes in the last year or so. It's been intense, a life concentrated to a pulp.

She uploads a picture of Emily sleeping, tags Peter, and adds the caption: *Zonked out after a super-busy day!* She throws down her phone, paces some more, looks out of the window. Listens.

She is checking her non-existent notifications for the tenth time – only Marcia has liked the photo – when she hears the roar of the Porsche on the drive. She leaps up from the sofa, half runs to the front door. The freezing January night rushes in, making her shiver. In the porch light, Peter's face is tired and stern, his neck a little forward, as if he has something heavy on his shoulders. He doesn't know she is watching him, has not seen her. She wonders whether this is how he moves when he thinks she isn't looking, how he *really* moves. It is nine o'clock. He is over an hour late, but that's the least of her concerns.

He looks up, seems to straighten his shoulders, lighten his step as he walks towards her.

'Hi,' she says. 'Sorry about earlier.'

'That's all right.' He leans in to kiss her on the cheek. He smells of cigarettes.

'Have you been to the pub?'

'Supervision meeting with a PhD student,' he says, hanging up his coat. 'We were both starving, so we went to the Marlborough Arms. You haven't made dinner, have you? I grabbed steak frites.' He heads through to the kitchen. She stands in the doorway while he pours a glass of red, takes a large slug – about half the glass – and tops it up. He sighs, rests his hand on the counter, looks at her, finally. 'Emily go to bed all right?'

Samantha nods. 'She's asleep.'

'Good, I—'

'Peter?'

'What?'

'I need to talk to you about something.'

She gestures towards the living room and goes in. Sits down.

'Peter?' she calls after a moment.

'One second.' A minute or two later, Peter appears at the door, chewing a breadstick and carrying two glasses of wine. 'You look like you need one,' he says, handing her a glass and sitting beside her on the sofa. He glances about him. 'This is all a bit ominous.'

'It's not about us, don't worry.' She does, she realises, fancy a glass of wine. Tonight, with Peter not here to pour it, and her so preoccupied, she has forgotten to have one, but it is her habit now as much as his. She takes a long draught, another, enjoys the alcohol hit. Her head swims a little, pleasantly, and she feels a bit calmer.

'At the end of the class today I took in their clerihews,' she begins. 'Anyway, there are eight students, right? But when I looked in the folder, there were nine poems. I thought nothing of it. And then I got home and had to tend to Emily and all that so I didn't get round to checking them until after dinner. But anyway, one of the poems didn't have a name on it, the handwriting doesn't match any of the others and it's … it's a bit … I don't know, have a look.' She hands the sheet to him and studies his face while he reads. 'I guess it's just given me the creeps a little bit.'

His frown deepens. He runs his fingers through his hair, takes another slug of wine. 'Did you see anyone hand this in?'

The dull pain in her sternum tells her that she was longing for him to dismiss it instantly as nonsense. But he has not.

'No,' she says. 'They collected them in a pile and one of them, Lana, she gave the stack to me, I think … Yes, she did because she asked me about limericks.'

He presses his lips together in thought before shaking his head. 'It's probably meant to be funny. They might even have handed it in by mistake, you know. What about the paper? Does it match any of the others?'

She flicks through. 'No. No, that one's plain white. The rest of them are on lined sheets. It could have been stolen from the photocopier or something, so that suggests something a bit more purposeful.' She meets his eye, their grumpy exchange from earlier forgotten. 'What should I do?'

'Nothing,' he says. 'Do nothing at all. Just hand out the named sheets and throw this one away. Whoever it is either gave it in without meaning to or is trying to provoke some sort of reaction. It's classic attention-seeking – I get it sometimes. Is there anyone who appears odd or needy in any way?'

'Not really. Well, a bit. There's a guy called Sean who's slightly geeky, nerdy, you know? Stained anorak, writes speculative fiction in which he features as a priapic love god.' She feels a wry smile spread across her mouth. 'There's a recovering drug addict, Tommy, a Polish girl who's more serious than anyone I have ever met and a punk septuagenarian writing soft porn, but apart from that …'

Peter laughs. 'The joys of adult ed.'

She can't quite laugh with him. 'So I just do nothing?'

He nods. 'Just ignore it and they'll give up eventually when they see you're not reacting.'

'Thank you.' She leans in for a kiss, recoils a little. 'Have you actually been smoking?'

'Young people,' he quips, draining his glass. 'Such a corrupting influence. Why don't we head upstairs? I'll clean my teeth twice, I promise.'

Samantha follows him up. Despite his advice, she knows she will not be able to stop herself from asking next week who wrote that poem. She can dismiss it, laugh it off, as long as someone claims it. As Peter said, it's probably a wind-up. Someone has got the tone wrong, so that could mean Lana. Perhaps her grasp of nuance in a language that isn't her mother tongue isn't quite on point. And that's the thing about writing, it can be hard to get the tone right. Hasn't she found this in her own poetry? Getting the exact thought, emotion, feeling, crystallising that with words – that's difficult, that's what she's trying to teach them, after all.

But as she waits for Peter to shower and clean his teeth, the poem turns over in her mind, memorised now to perfection.

> Little Miss Frayn
> Will be driven insane.
> She thinks she's the only one
> But her happiness will soon be done.

She tries to remember Lana's clerihew, can recall only the first two lines:

> Stan
> Was very bad man.

Lana misses the definite article even when she speaks. She wouldn't, probably couldn't, have written the offending clerihew. She would have written *She thinks she's only one*, not *She thinks she the only one*. So no, probably not Lana, gruff as she is. The others drift into her mind's eye: Sean, Aisha, Jenny … Reggie, Suzanne … Tommy, Daphne … Who is a bit odd? All of them. None of them. We are all a bit odd. All of us prey to all sorts of issues and neuroses, jealousies and rage.

It's just that some of us hide it better than others.

She of all people knows that.

CHAPTER 12

Samantha gets to the college fifteen minutes early to prepare the classroom. The week, with its routines, daily walks and baby groups, has helped her to settle, to reassure herself that Peter will do better in her absence this time and to process the nasty clerihew, which she now thinks is nothing more than some ill-conceived mischief. She has been busy preparing her classes too, which has helped. Peter sent her three books on writing prose fiction from his Amazon Prime account. She has spent hours poring over them, taking notes and devising the most interesting classes she can. She has even started to write a little herself, while Emily sleeps, and has started work on a short story.

'Hello there.' It's Daphne, first again. 'My bus gets here early; I hope you don't mind my coming in.'

'Not at all,' Samantha replies. 'No point waiting in the cold, is there?'

Daphne sits heavily and sighs. Her colour, now that Samantha looks more closely, is a little grey.

'Daphne, are you all right?'

She nods, but her smile is watery. 'It's really rather chilly out.'

Samantha crosses the room and without thinking reaches for the older woman's hands. They are like ice, a bluish purple. 'Daphne, you're freezing.'

'I got to the stop too early. I'm too early for everything. I do so hate to be late.'

Samantha leans forward and brings Daphne's hands to her lips. Softly she blows hot air on them before chafing them together in her own hands. 'Wait there and I'll run and get you a cup of tea.'

'Don't be silly, dear, I'm fine.' Daphne's pale grey eyes are filmed with tears.

'Tea or coffee? If you don't tell me which, it'll be tea whether you like it or not.'

Daphne's smile widens. 'Tea would be lovely. That's kind of you, thank you.'

Samantha runs across the courtyard to the cafeteria. With an apology, she joins the front of the queue. A minute later, she's back in the classroom, armed with takeaway tea, two cartons of milk and two sugar sachets. 'Here,' she says. 'Put your hands around the cup for now. I think I should add some sugar – shall I do that?'

Daphne stuffs her tissue into her sleeve and does as she's told. Her elegant fingers are bedecked with rings. 'Thank you, dear. How much do I owe you?'

'Don't be silly.' Samantha adds the milk and sugar and stirs the tea.

'Hello.'

She turns to see Sean shambling in, talking all the while. He is on time, he tells her, in case she didn't know, and goes on to explain in some considerable detail that he came on public transport today as the roadworks were ongoing. Daphne sips her tea, her colour returning. She glances up and gives Samantha a beautiful smile.

The others file in. By midday, seven students are sitting ready for the class to begin, but Reggie is still missing. Perhaps he didn't enjoy last week's class and has decided not to come back. Maybe he is the author of the horrid poem – a parting shot after a disappointing first lesson. No. No, it can't be.

Samantha pulls back her shoulders, faces them. She will not be intimidated by four lines of silly poetry.

'Hello, everyone. Looks like Reggie might not be joining us today, so I'll crack on. I read your poems and they were all very good. Very amusing, well done.' She hands out their work, making sure to give a little word of encouragement to each student in turn. It was such a small task, but these early attempts are important, she feels, for building the necessary confidence to tackle harder, perhaps more exposing work. Whilst they're in this room, it is her job to make them feel safe.

Even if she herself doesn't.

Once everyone has their poem in front of them, she rests her bottom against her desk, crosses her feet and takes out the remaining sheet of paper.

'So, there was one extra piece.' She waves the sheet as casually as she can manage. 'Anyone?' She tries to decipher all their faces at once. She doesn't want to read out the poem; it is too unpleasant, has affected her too much and she doesn't think she can give it the flippancy it requires. Sean sips his coffee. Jenny tears the end off a croissant and shakes her head.

'It's on a plain sheet, no lines,' she adds. 'No? Anyone remember writing two poems, perhaps one with my name in it for a joke? It's OK, I'm not angry or anything, and it's a perfectly good clerihew. I was just curious who wrote it, that's all. Perhaps handed it in by mistake? No?'

No one looks away. No one coughs or fidgets. Nothing. Which leaves Reggie. But not for one second can she imagine that lovely Reggie is capable of anything mean-spirited. Besides, it doesn't really seem like his sense of humour, which is warm and harmless and, frankly, funnier. But then, she doesn't know Reggie. She doesn't know any of them, not really. She doesn't even know if this poem *is* mean.

But no one owning up is worse than someone admitting to it.

'All right,' she says, hearing herself falter. 'Let's … let's have a look at your limericks.' A faint fog of stress clouds her brain a little; she has to steel herself to persist, to force the confidence back into her voice. 'How did you all get on?'

Like kids, they mumble and fidget and glance at each other.

'I enjoyed it enormously,' Daphne says, the colour returned to her cheeks. 'I haven't written a limerick since primary school. And I never owned up to that one.'

The others laugh.

'I find difficult,' Lana says.

'That's OK.' Samantha notices, can't help but notice, the speech patterns in Lana's second language. 'We'll try again once we understand what we're aiming for, how does that sound?'

Lana nods. It has to be said, her intense seriousness is really quite unsettling.

For the next hour, Samantha uses *There was an old man from Peru* and other popular limericks to teach them about rhyme and meter. She gets them to tap the beats on the desks. The familiarity will, she hopes, take the fear of poetry away. Peter was working last night, so she didn't run the class through with him, and she is pleased now to see her own ideas being enjoyed. Together they reverse line lengths, try lines with too many syllables, make limericks that don't rhyme. Together they discover what happens when the rules are broken.

'So if the line length is wrong or the rhyme is off, you lose the comic effect, see? Like a mistimed joke.' She returns their smiles, feeling that she has communicated something. 'For those of you wanting to write comic dialogue, that's something to think about later perhaps – rhythm, timing.'

Still Lana looks unsure. Samantha makes a concerted effort to keep meeting her eye. Together the class corrects a 'broken' limerick by rearranging the lines into the correct shape.

'The trick is to keep playing,' she says. 'If you just keep playing until you get everything spot on, you're basically manipulating language. You're bending sentences into different shapes, for different effects. You're putting yourself in control. Once you put yourself in control of things like word order, punctuation and all the things that make up writing, once you understand how those things create particular effects, you step from the world of writing for your own daily needs into the world of writing as an art form, which is basically telling lies. If you tell longer and longer lies, you become a writer. You gain all the power and arrive at your own truth.'

It is a satisfying note on which to end the class. The students give a hum of appreciation, which lifts Samantha's spirits, almost makes her forget her sliver of unease.

'If any of you have limericks to hand in,' she says, 'just leave them on my desk.'

A scrape of chairs, the indeterminate rustle of notes and coats, of stuff going back into bags, chatter.

Samantha gathers her things, pretends to be glancing up only to smile, say goodbye and acknowledge each sheet of paper as it lands, when in reality she is watching for another anonymous sheet, the hand that delivers it. Tommy looks a little red around the eyes, Daphne squeezes her arm and waves goodbye. Lana gives a perfunctory nod.

'Thanks,' Samantha says, and, 'Cheers,' and, 'That's great.'

Aisha and Jenny stop a moment.

'See you next week then,' Aisha says.

They are both smiling at her; both appear to be lingering a little.

'Did you want to ask me something?' she says.

'There's mine,' Sean interrupts. 'I wrote three.'

Perhaps seeing Samantha can't talk, Aisha raises a hand and she and Jenny slope away.

But Sean has not moved. His anorak is still zipped up to the top as it has been all class.

'I've got to go into Kingston now,' he tells her. 'Do you know the Games Workshop?'

'Can't say I do, Sean,' she says, walking towards the classroom door and holding it open for him.

'It's behind the Bentall Centre and Marks & Spencer, next to the art shop. I need a new crystal fortress for my blood angels.'

'Well, I hope you find one.' Looking at him, she wonders if he's lonely. She fights the urge to ask if he'd like a cup of coffee, some company just for half an hour – wouldn't hurt her to give him that, would it? But she has to get back for the baby. Instead, she gives him a warm smile, walks with him down the length of the corridor to the outer door and waves him off. 'See you next week! Hope you find your blood angels!'

'I've got the blood angels,' he replies. 'It's the fortress I'm going for.'

'Of course. Well, I hope you find your fortress.'

He gives a shy grin, the merest hint of a raised hand, and turns to go.

She watches him a moment. The hems of his jeans trail on the floor. They are frayed and darker at the bottom where they have absorbed rainwater from the pavement. He is a fragile soul, she thinks, not quite tethered to the earth. She hopes that the world has some kindness to offer him as he goes along his way. With a pinch in her heart, she returns to her desk.

At the sight of the small pile of paper, her heart beats faster, harder than it should. Ridiculous. She is ridiculous. Last week, someone pulled a silly prank that this week they didn't want to own up to. They will have been too embarrassed. It is ridiculous to let it bother her so much.

But still.

She picks up the pile, torn between the desire to count the poems and the urge to drop the whole lot in the bin unread; to read them all here, now, or to save them until she gets home to safety. She stands by her desk and looks at the top one – Sean's.

The last man on earth was called Sean.
Into a brave new world he was born.

There are two more limericks on the sheet, which look like variations on Sean's favourite theme. She exhales, lifts the page. The second one is Daphne's. So that would mean Sean has left only one sheet. Or would it? He may have slid a second, anonymous one underneath while she was talking to Aisha and Jenny. God, this is horrible, thinking badly of Sean, poor man. She reads Daphne's offering.

> There was a young girl name of Sue
> Who needed help tying her shoe.
> She called a kind man
> Who could dance the cancan
> And whose high-kicks made her go woo-woo.

Despite herself, she smiles. Emboldened, she peels the corners of the sheets one by one, like banknotes. One, two, three …

There are eight.

'Fuck,' she whispers into the silent room. 'Fuck.'

She should not have walked Sean to the outer door. She left the classroom open, the pile of homework on the desk, not to mention her bag, her phone. Idiot. Anyone could have slipped an extra sheet in; it would have taken seconds. Idiot, idiot, idiot. She checks the names. Most have been typed up; some sheets have one verse, some have a few attempts. The typed verses are printed on blank paper. The two handwritten ones, from Daphne and Tommy, are on lined paper pulled from a jotter.

One, typed on a blank sheet, is anonymous.

> There was a young girl, easy led,
> Whose husband took many to bed.
> But she was the one
> Who stopped all his fun
> And now she'd be better off dead.

CHAPTER 13

LOTTIE

The Wolffs' house isn't as grand as the Murphys', but it's cosier in many ways. A well-appointed three-bed end of terrace within easy reach of local amenities, with a good-sized patio to the rear. Lottie pops her washing on and makes coffee for Joanne and herself. There's no one to watch her. It's no one's business what she does, who she does and doesn't make coffee for. She's got an hour and a half before she has to be over in Edge Hill to show a two-bed and box semi to a young couple hoping to buy their first home. Was a time she hated anyone with a baby, but she doesn't hold it against them, not anymore. Not fair, is it? Not their fault. Was a time she hated so many people, with their baby showers and their strollers and their Facebook posts about their perfect family life. Now there's only one person she hates.

Well, two.

She leaves Joanne's coffee on the side and takes her own upstairs. Feeling a bit antsy today. There's no furniture upstairs, so the bedroom floor will have to do. It's hard on her shoulders, and the small of her back hurts, so she has to bring her knees up before she closes her eyes. That's better, flattens her spine out nicely. She's forgotten the bloody radio; the house roars with quiet. That's because of what she's found out; it's got her all over the place, and with the new year coming in and that. That always makes things a bit raw, doesn't it?

She starts singing to calm herself: a bit of Adele – really belts it out – and that lovely song by Corinne Bailey Rae from ages ago. She's good at remembering lyrics, knows all her favourite songs off by heart: 'I Believe I Can Fly', '… Baby One More Time', 'Wonderwall'. She loves the nineties ones. Sometimes she even writes her own songs, when the mood takes her. She always was quite good at English, though she worked hardest in history. Because of him.

It was a mistake, looking on the internet. Obviously. She told herself she wouldn't search. She'd lost track of him years before, but there's always been that shadow hovering at the back of her mind. Then Facebook came along. She looked, but nothing, and she thought maybe he'd changed his name. But these last few years, well, you can find anyone now. You're no one if you don't have a profile of some sort – a digital footprint. Even her, a loser who spends her free time pretending to live a life she could have had but didn't in houses she doesn't own – yes, even she has a digital footprint, and like everyone else's hers is made with her best shoes and not the smelly old trainers she keeps in the shed. She made sure she posted her award at the end of last month. Nash and Watson Regional Agent of the Year. Oh yes, up that went, all smiles. But she's not posting this, is she? Not posting herself lying on someone else's floor crying her eyes out, heart breaking all over again.

Best foot forward. Her nan used to say that. Never complain, never explain and always look your best. Her nan used to say that as well. Her mantra, that was. Times don't change, not really. At the end of the day, Facebook, Instagram and all that crap is just your Sunday best, isn't it? It's your best foot forward, in its best shoes, making its digital print.

Obviously, he was always going to turn up online eventually. And like everything else, just when she'd stopped looking. Doing very well for himself, thank you very much. Still a handsome bastard. Still has that house on the hill. Now that was a house! If pushed, she'd say that was probably where her whole interest in the property market sparked. It was definitely the first time she felt the rush of a cold set of keys in her hand as she slid them into her pocket. She bloody loves keys. People collect all sorts. You see that, working in this game. She's seen everything from stuffed owl collections through tin soldiers to all that train set stuff a certain type of man has in the attic. With her, it's keys. House keys particularly. They're easy as pie to copy; you just take them to the cobbler's, and if you have the key to someone's house, their front door might as well be wide open. If you have their digital footprint as well, you have their habits, their haunts, their place of work, their friends. You have the key to their whole life then, don't you?

And you may as well step inside.

And if that someone ruined your life, ruined you, in fact, then it's only fair that you should ruin theirs right back. There she is again, her nan, God rest her soul, coming in with another of her old sayings: *Revenge, Lottie. Revenge is a dish best served cold.*

CHAPTER 14

Samantha almost falls into the house when Peter opens the door.

'I hate it when you don't use your key,' he says. 'It's so lazy.'

'Sorry,' she says. 'I was rushing and I got flustered. I've had another poem and it's not a joke, it's definitely not a joke this time.'

She pushes past him and into the living room. On the coffee table is an empty wine glass, the smallest bud of burgundy at the bottom. It stops her in her tracks.

'Have you been drinking?'

'I had the leftover lasagne,' he says. 'There was literally a dribble of the Pinot Noir left.'

Momentarily derailed, she sits on the sofa. After a moment, she digs her folder out of her bag. 'Is Emily asleep?'

He nods, yes, and sits beside her. 'So, let's see the offending article.' His tone is light, almost amused.

'What's that supposed to mean?'

He stares at her as if perplexed. 'Nothing. Sorry. I just meant let's see the … what is it, another clerihew?'

Warily, she hands it to him. 'A limerick. I'm trying to build their confidence by getting them to play around with words. Lose their fear, you know?'

He reads, his frown line deepening at the centre of his forehead. She reads it herself, yet again, upside down.

There was a young girl, easy led,
Whose husband took many to bed.

But she was the one
Who stopped all his fun
And now she'd be better off dead.

'Just how promiscuous were you?' The question is out before she is able to stop herself, and as she could have anticipated if she'd had the presence of mind to keep quiet, Peter looks at her aghast.

'What? Where did that come from?'

'I'm sorry. Sorry. I'm just … It was nerves. I'm just, like, really creeped out, that's all.'

He winces. She has said 'like' – his pet hate – and he won't like the term 'creeped out' either.

'Samantha.' He has used her full name, never a good sign. 'I told you the first time we met that I've been with other women. I know we don't think about our age difference much, but it really is an inevitable aspect of me being a little older, you know that. We talked about this.'

'Sorry.' She nods, a little ashamed. They did talk about it, back when he asked her to move in. She'd been concerned about this very thing. He told her how unhappy he'd been, how he'd searched and not found for years. Until her.

'I've never asked anyone to move in with me,' he said. 'And I've certainly never asked a woman to marry me. Only you. Only you, Sam. You are my one, you know that.'

She promised him it was enough, that she would never use his past against him. Which is what she's just done.

She apologises again.

'The point here,' he says, 'is that this isn't about me. And it's not about you either. You're reading it through your own subjective lens.'

She takes the poem from him and reads it again. There are no names. And she's not easily led. And Peter has a past, yes, but he's hardly a gigolo.

'The thing is,' Peter says, 'it's actually pretty generic, isn't it? There are no names, it's a standard set-up and pay-off, just that the pay-off is a bit ... misjudged.'

'Misjudged? Is that, like, code for sinister?'

'Don't say like.'

'Soz – sorry.' She bites her lip. She's almost eradicated any trace of youth-speak along with *oh my God*, but in her stress, it has popped out.

He scratches his head, blows air through pursed lips. 'Let me think about it. I don't think it's anything to get hugely panicked about. It's not malevolent. Just someone with a terrible sense of humour or maybe lacking in social skills. It could still be innocent, someone trying to be cheeky but getting the tone wrong. As I said, we're not named.'

'I suppose.' She leans into him, presses her face to his chest.

He puts his arm around her and kisses her on the head. 'Above all, don't worry. Nothing bad can happen to you while you're with me, OK? I'll keep you safe.'

'Thank you,' she says, sliding her arms around his waist. 'I wish you didn't have to go to work.'

'I'll be back before you know it.' He loosens her arms and stands up.

Panic fizzes in her guts. She really doesn't want him to leave her here alone. But there's nothing she can say. A student with a taste for sinister humour is not enough to make him miss his lecture. And he's right, it's not about them.

He pulls her up, into his arms, and kisses her on the mouth. 'Don't worry about it.' His eyes are so deep and so brown.

'You don't think he or she knows where we live,' she says, 'do you?'

He frowns. 'Don't be ridiculous. It's just a stupid verse written by a stupid human being. Let's not blow things out of proportion.'

*

She watches him pull out of the drive. Once he has gone, silence hisses through the house like gas. She stares out of the front window, over the hedge to the street. There is no one outside, no one watching the house – of course there isn't, for God's sake. And Peter won't be gone that long. It isn't even four o'clock, and he'll be back around eight; it's nothing, no time at all. To resent him going to work is beyond pathetic.

She goes upstairs to check on Emily, who is fast asleep, fists raised. This isn't good; she should be awake now. Yet again, Peter has managed to disrupt the routine it has taken Samantha months to establish. In all likelihood, he has done it to please himself, and this annoys her even against the worry of the potentially malevolent poet. She shouldn't complain, even in her mind. Her dad never lifted a finger inside the home; his domain was outdoors and that was that. Outdoors – pretty far out of doors, as it turned out. *Stop it, Samantha. Stop.*

With her and Peter, the boundaries are less defined, less easy *to* define. The demands on his time are more ad hoc, and of course he has lived most of his life on his own and she gets that, she really does. Plus, he is around much more than other husbands, from what she can glean from the mums in the two baby groups she has joined. So what if he's often home late and has to hide away in his study at weekends? The other women seem to spend a lot more time alone, long evenings waiting for their partners to return and hold the baby while they grab a shower or prepare a hasty meal. They see her as a girl, these women, she knows that. Last week, one of them asked in super-slow English if she was the au pair.

Downstairs, she makes herself a cup of tea and sits on the sofa. If Emily is going to sleep, she can at least put her feet up for five minutes.

There was a young girl, easy led,
Whose husband took many to bed.

She stands up, walks over to the record player. Tom Waits is on the turntable. She's not in the mood for that maudlin growl but can't be bothered to flip through the other discs.

And now she'd be better off dead.

Stop it. If only there were some biscuits in the house, but Peter doesn't like her to eat too much sugar. And he's trying to persuade her to take up running. He says it's good for low mood and excellent for aerobic fitness, though she suspects he is keen for her to lose the half stone she gained during pregnancy. Just the thought of running makes her feel tired. Besides, the Fitbit he bought her tells her she walks almost ten kilometres with the pram every day. How much air does one pair of lungs need?

… better off dead.

Stop. It. She could make some toast. Or call her mum. Or take a nap.

No chance.

Peter's wine glass is still on the table. She puts her mug next to it and lies down. The cushions shift; she can't get comfy. Her eyes sting. She opens them, props herself up on her elbow. The cushion slants. The corner of what looks like one of the plastic bags she uses to store her breast milk pokes out from behind the cushion. She pulls at it. A moment of resistance and it comes free. In it are coloured pills.

'Oh my God,' she says aloud. 'You are joking me.'

She puts the bag to her nose and sniffs inside. It smells of nothing; she has no idea why she even did that.

'What the hell?' she asks no one at all, the habit of talking to herself one she has acquired since Emily. Is this what Peter does when she's out teaching – gets Emily to sleep and then takes drugs? In their home? Her head throbs.

The pills could have been there for ages. He offered her Ecstasy many times in the early days, though never calling it by that name and never in pill form since that first night. *Fancy a cheeky bit of Mandy?* he would say, or *Few sprinkles in your wine?* She always refused, telling him to go ahead, which he did the first few times, then didn't. And he has not offered her anything since she was pregnant, before that even. She assumed he'd forgotten all about it, had moved on now that they were a family.

But they have never openly talked about it. A mistake.

She wonders if and how she can broach the subject. It isn't as if Peter was out of it just now. Which points to him having forgotten about them. In fact, it's possible they got lodged behind the sofa cushions the first night she spent here. It's not like they're at risk of friends discovering them. Apart from her mother coming to stay that one time, they've never, in all the time she's lived here, invited anyone over.

She pushes the bag back where she found it. She will pretend she hasn't seen it, check in a few days and see if it's still there. If it is, she can make light of it, or maybe pretend to discover it by accident when he's here with her.

'Peter,' she could say, the trace of laughter in her voice. 'Look what I just found. Shall I throw them away now that we've got Em?'

Yes, something like that. They're a family now. Peter is nearly forty. He can't expect to hold on to his youth for ever.

CHAPTER 15

The week goes pleasantly enough. Samantha takes her cue from Peter, who doesn't mention the poem again, though that doesn't stop her students flying about her mind like spirits. She reminds herself over and over that the poem didn't mention any names, that there's no point dwelling on it, that to talk about it is to give it oxygen.

And she doesn't mention the pills.

How easily and how soon she has slipped into secrecy, she thinks sometimes. She remembers her mother's one daily cigarette, smoked at the back of the farmhouse. *Don't tell your dad* was all she said when Samantha caught her. And despite being barely twelve, Samantha understood that this was a confidence never to be broken, that it had to do with the unique and subterranean solidarity of her sex, the secret armoury of survival in a world made by and for men. Her father's secrets were a different kind. They were weapons of destruction.

And so, in secret, she checks the sofa every day and finds the pouch of pills still there. On the second day, she has the presence of mind to count them – there are twelve – and at the end of the week there are still twelve.

'It's obvious,' she says to Marcia over the phone. 'They've been there for ages. He must have forgotten all about them.'

'So throw them out,' her friend says. Of late, her tone has been impatient. She is doing a PG Cert and it is tiring her out, although it's always possible she's curt because she finds

Samantha's situation ridiculous. Even more possible is that she still harbours resentment for Samantha's sudden abandonment of her and the flat they shared. Peter did pay the remainder of the rent, but now that Samantha is out of the heady reel of the first year of romance, now that she has faced childbirth and its aftermath, she can see that, at least for Marcia, rent wasn't the point. Friendship was the point, and at that thought Samantha's cheeks blaze with regret.

'I can't throw them out,' she says. 'If he remembers them, he'll know I've found them and chucked them away.'

'So? Tell him you don't want to bring your daughter up around drugs. Fair enough, isn't it?'

'It's hardly bringing her up around drugs, Marcy.'

'Well, leave them where they are then. Listen, I have to go, I have a load of Hamlet essays to mark.'

I don't have time for this is the phrase that lies beneath. Samantha's just made notes on subtext for a class on dialogue later in the term. *I don't have time for you* is another possible meaning. Marcia doesn't exactly hang up on her, but where they usually sign off with *love you*, all she says is *see you later*, which stings.

They won't see each other later. Later, Marcia will go out with the friends they used to have in common, or with her boyfriend. They will see a band or go for drinks or a pizza or … do whatever people of her age are supposed to do. Whatever it is, Samantha will not join them. After Emily was born, Marcia asked her to come out once, twice, even three times. But she was too exhausted; she couldn't get out between feeds; Peter was late back from uni.

She has not been asked since.

The class comes around once again. Samantha resolves not to ask about the limerick. Peter is right, she should not. But this is not why she stops herself from asking. Honestly? It's because she cannot stand the thought of no one admitting to it once again, what that will do to her ability to lead the class.

No one can function properly in fear.

Reggie returns, wearing a white T-shirt with a brick design and on it the words *Pink Floyd The Wall* scribbled in red. Samantha has heard of Pink Floyd, though she can't remember from where or whom … her grandparents, possibly, when she was a kid.

'Apologies for my absence,' Reggie says, sliding a piece of paper onto her desk. 'I had a hospital appointment. That's my limerick from last week.'

'Thank you.' She glances down, reads enough to reassure herself.

> There was a young man called Syd B
> Who dreamt he was but four foot three.

Daphne arrives just as the class are settling down.

'I took a later bus,' she says, winking at Samantha.

Aisha and Jenny carry in takeaway coffees in bright blue cups. Neither of them looks like the kind of woman who would send a poison poem to another woman, but then what does that kind of woman look like? *Bitch* is a word Samantha hates, never uses, but it is the word that comes to her now: how do you spot a bitch?

Lana strides in in her own serious way. She has re-shaved the side of her head and Samantha thinks she may have a new piercing, a bolt at the top of her ear. She glances at Samantha, and while her smile is peremptory, there is no overt malice in it. Over sixty per cent of communication is non-verbal, isn't it? Surely Samantha would pick up on any animosity? Two weeks ago, she would have said yes, absolutely. Now, her world is as solid as cloud.

Sean follows, still with his anorak zipped tight to his neck. He is carrying a motorcycle helmet

'The roadworks on the A316 are still causing traffic delays. They're re-laying the gas main. I took the thirty-three from Hammersmith, but then I got off and went back for my motorbike. It's only a scooter, it's only a hundred and twe—'

'Great, Sean,' she says. 'Take a seat.'

There are seven students. Who is missing? Tommy. No, Tommy is here, his eyes red and sore-looking. He was sarcastic in that first lesson, but, frankly, he doesn't seem compos mentis enough to write something purposefully nasty. Besides, with his self-conscious louche irony, he seems to enjoy his former drug addict status, its power to shock, and Samantha suspects he is too self-obsessed to contemplate targeting someone he's never even met before.

Suzanne. Suzanne is missing. A flare of doubt courses through her. Perhaps she didn't like the last class. She was very quiet. Could it be her? Samantha doesn't think so. Her clerihew suggested a liking for daytime television and celebrity gossip magazines, and if the first poem hinted at some sort of connection with Peter, then that is highly unlikely.

'All right,' she says, forcing herself to focus. 'I thought today we'd try some flash fiction …

She explains the super-short form. It is a slice of life, an odd story that captures a moment or a mood. It can leave the reader on a troubling precipice or with a lasting image. And it is prose, a break from poetry.

Together they make a word map on the whiteboard.

'A word map is all about freedom,' she tells them. 'Just shout out any old random thing. There are no wrong words, no wrong ideas. The fear of getting it wrong kills creativity.'

They shout out words. They are more confident than in week one, she thinks, and this delights her. In no time, twenty words have gone up on the whiteboard: fire, sun, red … now thirty, now forty … desert, blaze, madness; boots, fight, hell.

'This is wonderful,' she says, her wrist beginning to ache from all the scribbling. 'Is anyone getting a sense of a narrative at all? Anyone got a character coming out of the fog?'

'I have an old cowboy,' Daphne says.

'That's good.' Samantha gives her a smile. 'And do we know where he is and what he's doing?'

A story emerges from some mysterious collective. The energy in the room is palpable.

'An old cowboy has to bury his horse out in the desert,' Reggie says, and Samantha sees an affectionate glance pass between him and Daphne.

'Yes,' she says, clearing a patch of board and scribbling sentences now.

'It's hot, damn hot,' Reggie drawls, making his classmates giggle. 'The work is tough but he owes his hoss a proper burial.'

'Why?' Samantha asks. 'Why is it so important?'

'The horse is the last living thing he knows,' Jenny chips in. 'His only remaining friend.'

'Yes!' Samantha is breathing fast, trying to keep up. 'And the why of that is potentially our real story.'

They carry on. They seem fired up. All thoughts of the malicious poems drain from Samantha's mind, and when her watch alarm beeps to signal half-time, she startles, is genuinely shocked to see that an hour has passed.

The students file out for their fifteen-minute break. Aisha hovers with Jenny at Samantha's desk, asks if she would like anything from the canteen. God, these women are keen. They're like a couple of Peter's acolytes.

'That's kind,' Samantha says politely. 'I'm fine with my water, thanks.'

They seem to be waiting for her to say something else. Looking at them both, she cannot help but wonder again if one of them might be capable of writing something with malicious intent. She doesn't think so, but again, who is she to say? Just because someone is pleasant-looking on the outside doesn't mean they're equally pleasant inside. It's a perfectly bog-standard reflection, something everyone knows. Why then does the world respond otherwise? Why does the world place so much value on external beauty?

'Did you want something else?' she asks. 'Can I help you with something?'

'Actually, it was just … We're going to grab a quick coffee after class,' Aisha says. 'Would you like to join us?' Her manner is shy. She glances to Jenny, as if for reassurance.

Jenny's grin is guileless. 'Just a quickie,' she adds. 'If you can stand the thought, obviously.'

Samantha hesitates. She has left milk for Emily. And Peter tends to leave almost an hour after she gets in. Things are a little cool with Marcia, she doesn't see the rest of her friends from uni and the mothers at the baby group are so much older, so much more at ease with motherhood and all that goes with it. It would be nice to talk to some intelligent women. After all, it's possible their good looks match perfectly lovely personalities. The two things aren't mutually exclusive. And frankly, friend-wise, Samantha isn't exactly fighting them off with a shitty stick, is she?

'I can only stay for half an hour,' she says. 'But that would be lovely, thank you.'

At the end of the class, she tells them to leave their flash fiction pieces on her desk.

'I'll have a quick read through,' she says as they begin to pack away their things, 'and feed back to you next week.'

She tries to say goodbye as politely as she can, to wish them all a good week, while keeping her eyes trained like lasers on the papers as they land. One by one they place their sheets on the pile. But none of them leaves more than one, she is convinced. She puts the papers in the folder. She has not left the room. No one, no one could have tampered with her stuff.

Aisha and Jenny are waiting for her outside the classroom. There is a moment of shyness, of awkwardness, as if all three of them sense some kind of boundary about to be crossed. But it is only a moment before they wander together across the courtyard to the canteen, where, in the corner, some music students are setting up for a recital. No sooner there, however, when Samantha realises she needs to pee.

'I'll grab the coffees,' Aisha says. 'What would you like?'

'A peppermint tea, please, if you don't mind,' Samantha replies.

It is only when she gets to the loo that she realises she has left her folder on the canteen table. Bugger. After she's been so careful! Jenny was sitting at the table watching the bags while Aisha got the drinks. But it is too late for Samantha to dash back. Even if she pleads forgetting something, Jenny will have had time to add to the contents by now. No one would notice a slip of paper going into a folder. No one would even know it's not Jenny's folder. But then, she would have to risk Aisha seeing her. Aisha would know she was rummaging in Samantha's folder and ask what she was doing.

Unless they're in it together? God, this is horrible.

Samantha washes her hands, chest tightening. In the mirror, her face is drawn, strained. There are black shadows under her eyes; her cheekbones look more defined. She looks older than twenty-two. God, she looks almost thirty! Suspicion is exhausting, ageing. And here she is, about to have coffee with two women she doesn't even trust.

'We got you a muffin,' Aisha announces when Samantha returns. 'You look like you've lost weight since the start of term; we need to feed you up!'

'Oh,' Samantha says, wondering what on earth her weight has to do with Aisha while at the same time wondering if it's true and whether what Aisha really means is what she herself has just noticed: exhaustion, strain.

'Peter calls these cupcakes on steroids,' she says, to keep things light. 'He says they're artificially inflated with all kinds of rubbish.'

Oh God, that was tactless. She tears at her fingernail with her teeth. What the hell has happened to her?

'Sorry,' she says. 'I didn't mean … Thanks, though, it looks amazing.'

'It's blueberry.'

'Blueberry? Yum.'

She sits down, lays a proprietorial hand on the folder, tries to act normal. What is normal again? How does it go? She can't eat that cake. It isn't Peter's objections, it's Aisha and Jenny. They have been so friendly … too friendly? Obviously they haven't poisoned the muffin. Ninety-nine per cent of her knows they haven't, that it's outrageous, the stuff of fiction. But the one per cent …

She takes the knife and cuts the muffin into three. 'Here,' she says. 'Let's share it.'

Ridiculously, she waits until the other two have taken a bite, but by now her stomach has closed with stress. Her throat too feels swollen; she can barely swallow her drink.

'So you both went to UCL?' she manages to ask, sliding her folder into her satchel.

Jenny looks at Aisha, something indiscernible in her expression. 'We met in the pub, didn't we, Aish?'

Aisha brushes her mouth with her fingers. 'The Marlborough Arms.'

Samantha feels her neck heat. That's Peter's after-work local. But then it used to be hers too. It's the local for loads of UCL students. It's where she first noticed Peter, asked Marcia who he was.

So. Hardly a clanging coincidence.

'I thought you were in different years though?' she says, nibbling a crumb from the cupcake.

'We were.' Again it's Jenny. 'Aisha is much, much older than me.'

Aisha laughs. 'Cheeky bitch. I'm a couple of years older.'

'Five,' Jenny coughs into her hand; both of them laugh. They are clearly close; they clearly enjoy one another's company very much. Samantha feels a pang. She and Marcia had this. In fact, lots of her friends made her laugh easily. She has stopped laughing. She can't remember when she last got a fit of the giggles.

'I was back at UCL for my masters,' Aisha is saying. 'I was working for this frozen food company – so random – and hating it, so I went back thinking I might go into academia. My boyfriend at the time encouraged me to do it.' She looks at Jenny. Again, something passes between the friends but Samantha has no idea what. 'Anyway, Jenny was in her final year, weren't you?'

'I was,' Jenny says once she's swallowed the last of her blueberry sponge. 'And now I'm working at Starbucks *and* the Prince's Head – you know, the pub on the green?'

'Mm-hm.'

'That's the kind of career highlight a good honours degree from a top uni will get you. Next time you fancy a drink, go there and I'll give you a free pint.'

'Because of course it's your pub, isn't it, Jenny?' Aisha teases and they both snigger.

Samantha giggles too. Her anxiety about the two of them fades a little. Not enough to eat or to want desperately to check the folder, but enough to release the lock in her jaw.

'I actually went to UCL too.' It feels like a confession.

Aisha glances at Jenny. Yet again, something is exchanged in the way they look at one another, and Samantha's unease returns. But it is impossible to remark on it. What the hell could she say without appearing paranoid?

'Small world or what?' Aisha says.

'I'm … I'm actually living with someone who works there …' Samantha trails off, realising that she doesn't want to say who. Peter isn't an English lecturer, there is no reason why they would know him, but he is good friends with the head of the English department, and of course, there are the unsettling poems to consider. Poems that could have been written by either of these women, or both. 'Speaking of which, I'm going to have to run. My partner's waiting for me to get home so I can take over with the baby.'

'Aw, little Emily,' Jenny says. 'How old is she now?'

Samantha smiles at them both, a shy heat climbing up her neck. 'She's nearly five months.'

'Five months? How cute,' Aisha coos. 'Well, hopefully you can have coffee again next week. We always have a quick one after class, so you can join us any time. We promise we won't lead you astray.'

'Unless you want us to.' Jenny laughs at her own joke; Aisha is not far behind.

'Listen,' Aisha says, taking out her phone. 'Let's swap numbers then you can always text if you've had to dash off or whatever.'

Samantha recites her number, really out of nothing more than politeness because, despite everything, she has been raised not to be rude. Biting her bottom lip with irritating cuteness, Aisha taps the digits into her phone.

'Great,' she says. 'I'll text you now. There you go. Now you've got mine.'

Samantha's phone buzzes in her pocket. Anxious now, she thanks them for the tea, promises to pay next time, and leaves the two of them chatting in the effortless, good-humoured way that gives her a pain in her heart. She walks quickly, texting Peter as she goes.

Running late be home soon going as fast as I can.

She hasn't punctuated but he'll have to lump it. And she won't even tell him she's had a third of a muffin. Despite her nerves being all over the place, it felt good to spend time with women who are nearer her own age and with whom she thinks she might have things in common. Aisha is around thirty, she thinks, Jenny a little younger. Neither of them has a decent job, despite being graduates. Samantha is lucky that Peter was able to swing her this teaching gig. Even if it feels too soon after Emily and is only two hours a week, it's something from which she can build.

Yes, she is lucky, she is, only …

She speed-walks up the hill, stops for literally two seconds at the brow. She is so lucky, she thinks, taking in the green sweep of the bank that runs down to Petersham Nurseries, to the flash of winter sun that splashes like cream on the kink in the river. She is so lucky. She feels it acutely now, in almost every part of her. Almost. She runs then, down Rosebush Road, the tiniest something that has been niggling her since she left Aisha and Jenny pushing darkly at the edges of her mind. Some peace-wrecker, some latent gremlin. The private looks exchanged between them, herself on the outside of their friendship, looking in – perhaps it is only that.

But as she pushes open the gate, the gremlin steps out into the light and she sees it so clearly that she wonders why she didn't before. When she mentioned the baby, Jenny said: *Aw, little Emily. How old is she now?*

Samantha has not mentioned her daughter to the class. She knows this because she decided before the course started to keep her worlds separate. In the months that Emily has been alive, everyone she has told about her, or introduced her to, has reacted with an infinitesimal delay, a kind of benign surprise, and she knows this is because she is so very young to be a mother.

But Jenny didn't do that. There was no such moment.

And she knew Emily's name.

CHAPTER 16

Before Samantha gets halfway up the path, Peter opens the door.

'Where the hell have you been?' he says. 'I've been waiting to go.'

'Sorry,' she says. 'It's not yet half past three though, is it? And you don't go till nearer four.'

'That's not the point, Sam.'

From inside the house, Emily cries.

'I'm sorry.' Without pausing to wait for a kiss that will clearly not be forthcoming, she steps into the house and heads for the living room. 'I went for a very quick coffee with a couple of students. I sent you a text. Anyway, I'm back now.'

Emily is in her car seat in the living room, her face a raging raspberry. Samantha picks her up, shushes her. The baby's little head is hot against her shoulder.

'I'm off then.' Peter is at the door, his expression still stern.

'I'm so sorry,' she says. 'I just wanted to chat to someone.'

No reaction. As if she hasn't spoken.

'I'll be back late myself,' he says. 'Don't wait for me to eat. I'm trying to fit some of my PhD consultations into the evenings to give me more time at home.'

'Thanks.' She is wriggling Emily's arms out of her fleecy jacket. The poor child is boiling. 'See you when you get home. I really am sor—'

The front door clicks shut. A moment later comes the lupine growl of his car, the vintage Porsche that so impressed her a little over a year ago now. Only after the roar has died away does she reflect on his parting shot. Whether or not he meant to be passive-aggressive, it is hard to say, which she supposes is the whole point of passive aggression. And at that last she laughs to herself.

Sod him, grumpy old bugger.

As for Emily, Samantha has no idea what time she was last fed, since Peter was too busy making a petty point to have time for a handover. What is apparent is that she has not been changed all afternoon; her nappy is as heavy as a bag of potatoes. It is as if Peter will deign to look after their baby for a short time but that he regards this as a favour he is doing for her, one for which she is expected to pay by clearing up the mess he chooses to leave her. He is so much older than her, she thinks. And yet sometimes he behaves like the child.

Too unsettled to stay indoors, despite the threat of an imminently darkening sky, once she has changed Emily, Samantha clips the car seat into the chassis of the buggy and heads out. Yes, the sky is bruising already, but the air is crisp and cool. She walks around the block, calls at the shop for some milk and a loaf of bread. On the way back, she goes to the top of the hill again and stands opposite the Roebuck pub, looking out. The river is almost in darkness now. The view reminds her of the first night she came here, when, half sick with awe, she let him drive her to his home within minutes, no, within *seconds* of their meeting. It seemed to her then to be a dream. Now it's more like madness, a kind of fugue state. She can't put herself there, can't imagine herself behaving in that way anymore. She felt like a schoolgirl. It's possible she behaved like one.

She heads back. It is really quite dark now – a thunderous blue-black. Emily will need feeding the moment they get in. She'll need a bath, a story, a top-up feed before bed. Samantha reaches the end of Rosebush Road. On the pavement near her house, a figure loiters in the gloom, begins to walk. Something about the way his head moves side to side is familiar. He is carrying something round. The dusk makes it hard to see his features, but it looks like Sean, and as he draws nearer, she sees that yes, it is him. It is Sean, his motorcycle helmet in his hand.

'Sean?' she says when there is no more than half a metre between them.

His smile is uneasy. He is wearing headphones.

'Hello, Miss.' He raises a hand before returning his gaze to the pavement.

She dismisses the absurdity of him, possibly fifteen years her senior, calling her 'Miss'. He has on the same anorak as earlier today, but no woolly hat, no scarf or gloves, and even in the dull light she can see that the base of his nose is pink, his eyes glistening with cold. There is something heartbreakingly vulnerable about him, and she is filled with her mother's advice to *be kind, always*.

She stops, there on the pavement, expecting him to stop too. But he doesn't. Instead, he passes her by, shooting her a furtive glance. Perplexed, she turns, watches him head away, up the street.

'Sean?' she calls after him, wanting to ask him if he's all right, or at least to find out what he's doing here, so near her home. But he either doesn't hear her through his music or chooses to ignore her.

Perhaps he lives nearby. But as he rounds the corner and heads away towards the town, it occurs to her that no, he doesn't live around here. He was late for the first lesson because of roadworks. If he'd driven in from Richmond Hill, he would not have hit those roadworks, only the heavy traffic that chugs through the one-way system in the centre.

Why, then, is he wandering around near her house?

She calls out again, a ball of heat in her chest. 'Sean?'

But he is gone. She would have to run to catch him, but she has not moved. She is standing there with the buggy as if her feet are attached to the paving stones, staring and thinking that she did not check the folder before leaving college today, after her coffee with Aisha and Jenny. She did not check it when she got back just now. Sean was coming from the direction of her house. It's possible, she knows it, that in her haste to get some fresh air, she left the back door open. It's possible, then, that Sean was able to enter the house when no one was there.

'Shit.'

Her rubber soles fall quickly on the pavement. Another few seconds and she is shoving open the iron gate, pushing the buggy up the path, plunging the key into the front-door lock. From the living-room window, the lamp glows. Her stomach clenches before she remembers that it's programmed to come on at five.

The hallway is chilly and dark. Keeping her coat on, she leaves Emily in her pram, heads for the kitchen and flicks on the overhead light. The homework folder is on the kitchen table. She has no memory of getting it out of her bag, which she discovers on the floor next to a chair. She blows into the roll of her fingers and puts the heating on. Chafes her hands together. Maybe she threw her bag down after pulling out the folder to look at later.

'No,' she says, to no one. She didn't take the folder out.

Which leaves Peter. Or …

She tries the back door, feels her chest heave when the handle gives, a surge of nausea when the door opens.

A soft whine escapes her.

On the table, the folder stares at her in challenge. She cannot open it, not now. Her nerves are too frazzled. Pathetic, but there it is. She cannot open that—

She picks it up, grabs the pieces of flash fiction. The names of her students barely register as she throws the sheets one by one onto the table. They slide on the smooth surface; one skids over the edge, lands a moment later with a soft shush on the terracotta floor tiles. And there it is, the blank, anonymous sheet. Handwritten this time, a short paragraph. A paragraph she reads against a terrible heat that climbs from her chest, up her neck to her face, her ears, her scalp.

A very sociable man

    He was a very sociable man, everyone said so. And smart, liked to dress well. He made his girls laugh, made them think, made them want him. He offered them the world, his lovely house on the hill with all the pictures on the walls. He liked pretty things. Like girls. He liked girls almost as much as he liked clothes and red, red wine. Chose his girls like fruit: just as their colour changed, but still a bit green. Just like his daughter, all grown up now. And him, Peter Pan. His childhood never ends. Mine ended long ago.

    The paper shakes in her hand; her breath is hot against her palm. The piece has that same mix of vagueness and specificity, enough detail to send a chill through her veins, not enough to take it to the police. Planted secretly enough to be sinister while allowing the possibility that this was done in plain sight. Sean was right outside her house. He looked sheepish. He must have written this and put it in her folder while she was out. That means he must have been watching the house, waiting for her to leave. He could be watching it now, from a distance. God knows, he could be *in* it.

    She shivers, pulls her coat tight. Emily.

    In the hallway, Emily is still asleep, fists raised, lips pursed in a kiss. Samantha tears her hand away from her panting mouth, forces herself to think clearly.

    Lock the back door. Yes.

    She returns to the kitchen, turns the key, leaves it in. She doesn't want to lock anyone in. Her breath is ragged in her chest. She calls Peter, but his phone is off, as it always is when he is teaching. She thinks about calling the police, but what would she say? She is not in mortal danger. And yet she can taste danger like stale breath on her tongue, can feel the solid lump of it in her belly. Something is not right. Even Peter, by turns so loving and tender, then so cold and disapproving ... There is something, something ...

She runs upstairs. In her and Peter's room, she looks out of the front window on to the street. There is nothing, no one. In Emily's nursery, out of the back window, the dark shapes crouch like monsters: the shed, the neighbours' gardens, the pale squares of light in the other houses. There is no living shadow lurking, no rustling movement in the hedges.

She runs down the stairs. Emily sleeps on, oblivious. Samantha is pretty sure there is no one in the house. She would feel it if there were. She would sense it. Wouldn't she?

In the living room, she slides her hand behind the sofa cushions. The pills are gone.

With a cry, she pulls the cushions onto the floor, digs down into the base. The bag is not there.

She replaces the cushions, runs out of the living room, takes the stairs two at a time. In the bathroom, she rifles through his toiletries – hair wax, hair gel, hair fudge, shaving foam, Dior eau de toilette, liquid facial cleanser, a small wallet of grooming tools – scissors, tweezers, cuticle removers ... Good God, he has more of this stuff than she does.

In the bedroom, she throws herself to the floor, peers under the bed. Nothing. Peter doesn't approve of keeping things under the bed, says they attract dust.

At his bedside table, she hesitates. This is an infringement of privacy. And Peter has done nothing wrong. She has no right to—

She opens the drawer. At the top, a box of condoms. She thinks about the night they ran out, how, caught up in the moment, they carried on regardless. Would she change that now? Would she grab her stolen youth and run? She shakes the thought away. She would not be without Emily, that's all that matters. There is a pot of cufflinks, a book of Dylan Thomas poems. There is a red paper wallet of what look like photographs. Are photographs.

She sits on the bed and spreads the glossy pictures on her lap. It is weird to have them printed out like this, to physically touch and handle, not thumb through on a screen. There is a small picture of a teenager dressed in an elegant school uniform: black blazer with a gold insignia on the breast pocket, white shirt and black tie with diagonal gold stripes. He is standing by the Leaning Tower of Pisa. He is in the foreground, holding out his hand so that the tower balances in his palm. It is Peter; she recognises his eyes, his smile. He is no more than a child, but still it strikes her as ironic that he should be posing in exactly the kind of naff tourist stance he would openly deride now. Another photograph is of him at university by the looks of things – his hair is less long than big, almost fluffy, and this, his square clothes and the fact that he is quite obviously inebriated makes her smile despite everything.

Another photograph shows him aged twenty-five or so, with around twenty young girls, all in rather less elegant grey school uniforms and a mixed array of winter coats. He is standing in the middle, his arm around some of their shoulders. He is wearing a shirt, tie and V-neck sweater and he is grinning. The girls are laughing, a couple of them looking at Peter with the expression of goofy adoration she has seen him elicit so many times. The group stand in front of a cathedral she half recognises. On the back of the photograph, in a version of Peter's handwriting, she reads: *St Catherine's trip, York, October 1999.*

So he must have been around eighteen, nineteen. This must have been a training post or work experience. He looks older, probably because he is dressed in a shirt and tie, and surrounded by girls of around fourteen, fifteen. Perhaps he was a sixth-former and had volunteered to help on the outing.

She doesn't, she realises, know much about that period of his life.

At the next photograph, she catches her breath. Peter, older in this shot – perhaps thirty, thirty-five? – with his arm around a beautiful woman. They are clearly a couple, though Samantha cannot pinpoint exactly how she knows this – something about the way the woman leans into him, the angle of her head tipped towards his – but they are together and she … she is—

'Aisha,' she hears herself say into the silence. 'Aisha.'

Behind them are railings, a green city square. Gordon Square, she's pretty sure, opposite the history of art department. The photograph is uneven at the bottom, where it has been trimmed with scissors. On the back, a pale brown scar of old glue. It was clearly in a frame. Possibly hung on a wall in this house …

She pinches the bridge of her nose, battling, battling to keep her breathing under control, to sit still, to not throw the photographs across the room. She cannot pull her gaze from the picture, from Aisha, the amusement in her eyes, the way her head tilts both towards Peter and back a little, as if this narrowing of eyes, this white and wide smile, is about to blow up, the eyes about to close, the mouth about to open fully, Aisha's long, soft brown neck about to lengthen as her head falls back in helpless laughter.

Peter has always been open about having a past. Samantha has tried never to mention his ex-lovers, no matter how difficult she has found it sometimes. She has not wanted to appear younger than she is; his age, his knowledge, his status already make her feel all too often like a child. She has wanted to be an adult, like him. He has made it clear that to ask about his life before her is childish, beneath her, beneath both of them, though she cannot say how he has done this, cannot point to any actual words he has said. Somehow the topic has been off limits, almost a taboo. And he has never, ever mentioned an affair with a student.

Although Aisha was not a student, at least not one of his. She said she'd studied English literature, not art history. Samantha casts her mind back to the conversation with Aisha and Jenny over coffee. She thinks Aisha mentioned an ex-boyfriend, but she didn't say he was a lecturer. But she, Samantha, definitely told them that she was living with a UCL lecturer and that they had a child together. Then there was that look that passed between Aisha and Jenny. It would have been natural at that point for Aisha to chip in that she'd once been with a lecturer, or was that a leap too far? Perhaps she meant to get to it but Samantha had to rush off and the moment never came.

A sick feeling starts in Samantha's belly. It hardens, becomes a rock. She runs downstairs and retrieves the flash fiction from the folder, her eyes skimming across it.

… liked to dress well, she reads *… made his girls laugh, made them think, made them want him.*

Her hand flies to her forehead, runs through her hair. When she gets to *his lovely house on the hill with all the pictures on the walls*, she stops, presses the sheet to her chest. The house on the hill with all the pictures on the walls. It is too on the nose. Whoever wrote it knows Peter. Whoever wrote it has been in this house.

… red, red wine, she reads in a half whisper in the dim kitchen. She thinks of the dusty bottle of Amarone, the shiny stripes as he cleaned it with a cloth that very first night.

I've been waiting to open this one for a long time, he had said.

Chose his girls like fruit, she reads on, punishing herself now, *just as their colour changed, but still a bit green.* That's her; she can see that her colour has changed now, the green all but gone. Aisha would have been green still when they met.

His childhood never ends. Mine ended long ago.

It was Aisha who wrote this; Aisha, the friendliest of the students. Aisha who asked if Samantha wanted anything bringing from the canteen, if she wanted to come for coffee, Aisha who is always so keen to contribute in class, who lingers at the end as if she wants to chat or simply … connect. She knew Samantha was going to be the tutor and enrolled just so she could inflict some mental torture on her. She has been the sweetest but is in fact the deadliest, motivated by that particularly poisonous breed of jealousy: that of the jilted ex.

CHAPTER 17

Samantha returns the photographs to the drawer, an awareness dawning as she does so of something new within herself, and within her relationship with her lover and the father of her child. It seems to her, putting these photographs back, arranging the drawer with everything exactly where it was before, that this is the behaviour of deceit but that this is how she must behave now, at least for the moment. Though isn't this how she's been behaving for a while, perhaps since she found the pills behind the sofa cushions, or maybe even before?

And that is how a hole opens up in the life of a couple, she thinks. Small acts of subterfuge. Tactics. It isn't as if he has betrayed her. It isn't as if he's been having an affair, but something has been lost between them and she wonders if they will get it back.

Peter returns home late. Like last week, he smells of cigarettes and beer. She doesn't question it, barely notices it, other than to remember that he mentioned he was meeting a PhD student and presuming that is what he has done. Nor does she remember in that moment the pills now disappeared from the back of the sofa. On her mind and on her lap are only the three pieces of creative writing she knows now were written and delivered with malicious intent, most probably by Peter's ex-girlfriend, Samantha's student, Aisha.

'Peter,' she says when he appears at the door of the living room.

'One moment,' he replies, and she listens to the fall of his shoes on the floorboards, hears him go whistling through to the kitchen – Rachmaninov, she recognises, Piano Concerto No. 2. A clank of glassware and she knows he will appear in a few moments with their customary evening glass of red. He never asks if she wants one. She wonders now if he ever has.

'So,' he says, joining her on the sofa and handing her a glass.

'Peter, I've had another one of those pieces,' she says.

'What? Show me.' He takes a large slug as she hands over the latest sheet.

She watches him, drinks her wine. Unusually for her, she finishes half the glass in one go. Just the taste of it helps, the trickle of heat in her throat.

Peter's brow furrows. He stands up, wanders over to the record player, opens the lid. She is about to tell him not to put a record on, to focus on this, on her, when he appears to reconsider. He lowers the lid, returns to join her on the sofa. He drains his wine.

'I think you should go and see Harry,' he says.

Harry Boyd, the guy Peter persuaded to let Samantha cover the maternity leave. She ponders on it sometimes, this network of men pulling strings behind the scenes, as if the rest of them are puppets. But going to see Harry is not what she expected Peter to suggest. He has not reached the most obvious conclusion: that this must be an ex of his, bound for revenge. Or perhaps he has.

'But don't you think it sounds personal this time?' she pushes. 'The house on the hill with the pictures on the walls? Whoever it is has been here.'

He shrugs. 'I'll admit it's creepy. But a house on the hill is a dramatic staple, isn't it? What's that Fleetwood Mac song?'

She looks at him blankly, no idea what he means.

He shakes his head. '"Big Love?" Never mind. All I'm saying is that it's a well-worn phrase and lots of houses have pictures on the walls. Most, I expect. It's how we customise where we live; it's part of how we show who we are.'

'But what about that stuff about liking girls and clothes and red wine? And Peter Pan? Your name is Peter!'

He gives an amused exhalation through his nose. 'My name is not Peter Pan though, is it? I can see why you feel unsettled, I'm not minimising it, not at all. Which is why I think you should go and see Harry. But it's the quintessential predatory male, isn't it? Likes girls, well, that's bog standard; men like women, so what? And clothes, well, I wear clothes but I wouldn't say I'm particularly interested in them. I need them. They serve a purpose and I don't want to look like a Central Casting academic, which is fair enough. As for red wine, well, everyone likes red wine, don't they? And again, it's synonymous with sophistication, seduction, sensuality.' As if to illustrate the point, he pours himself another glass. 'Peter Pan is a household name, a byword for youthful men everywhere and, look, you're overlooking this bit here ... *his daughter, all grown up now*. I don't have another daughter, only Emily, and she's a baby. Honestly? I think whoever wrote this is a woman who has been jilted. Didn't you mention that your Polish student had had a bad boyfriend? Didn't she even say that was what she was going to write about?'

Lana. Yes, she did. She did say that. Samantha has thought this before, and now Peter's said it too. If Peter hasn't mentioned a former student lover, so what? It's none of her business and it looks like it was a few years ago, four or five, yes, that's years. She hasn't mentioned Aisha by name, so he has had no reason to feign ignorance. He *is* ignorant. He has no idea that his ex is in Samantha's class. And Aisha was probably about to tell her when she rushed off.

Suddenly it doesn't seem possible that Aisha wrote this. Or at least it seems possible that she didn't. It is too mad for Aisha, too bitter. And the writing itself is perhaps too basic for an English literature graduate who casually drops a T. S. Eliot reference into four lines of verse. But then it doesn't seem likely to be Lana either. The correct use of the definite article suggests it was written by someone with English as their mother tongue. Jenny? Jenny is pretty strident. Jenny was alone with the folder today. Jenny is close to Aisha; could she have some sort of crush on her, be in love with her even?

Could Jenny be writing on Aisha's behalf, perhaps even without Aisha knowing?

'Samantha?' Peter says. 'You're miles away.'

'Sorry.' She smiles, sips her wine. 'Do you think I should call the police?'

'Don't be silly, what would you say? A student with mental-health issues is writing dodgy poetry? I'd like to report a sinister piece of prose?' He laughs, reaches for the back of her neck, strokes it.

'But …' She flounders. He is right, of course. It's hardly a body or a burglary. 'But the other thing is that I went for a walk with Emily earlier, just after you'd gone, and I bumped into that guy I told you about, the one who's writing about the last man on earth.'

'What, here?'

She nods. 'Outside. Sean, his name is. I mean, I thought he was harmless, but he was coming up the road from the direction of our house. It was quite dark by then, although he did see me and say hello, but he looked … weird. Off, you know? He didn't stop. Usually he tells me a load of stuff I don't need to know, like where he's going or about roadworks or whatever. It's a sign of anxiety, that whole over-explaining thing, I think, but I've never felt threatened by him.' She doesn't mention the open back door. Peter would kill her. The lamp on a timer, the safe in the cellar, the alarm she secretly never uses, the double locks on the windows … He is very security conscious.

Peter is silent for a moment. Samantha finishes her wine. She feels better for having told him, for his poise, his logical reasoning, and for his hand on the back of her neck. His life before he met her belongs to him. For all she knows, Aisha was just a fling. Peter has the right to have had flings, girlfriends. To get worked up over a photograph is silly, paranoid. He's with her, Samantha, now, and Aisha turning up in a local writing class is not exactly the weirdest coincidence in the world. She obviously got to know the area while dating Peter. Samantha herself loved this area from the moment Peter introduced her to it; it's completely understandable that Aisha loves it too. And besides, even if Aisha did enrol with some dodgy agenda, that isn't Peter's fault, is it?

It might have seemed strange that the piece of writing didn't appear to freak Peter out even a little bit, but then again, if he has nothing to feel guilty about, he would be exactly as calm as he is now. All he has been is kind and calm. She loves his calmness. She loves him. She needs to stop being so suspicious.

'I think,' he says slowly as she curls up against him, 'you should take the three pieces of work to Harry next week and just chat it through. I think it's time to let the college know and put it on record. I can have a word with this Sean guy—'

'No, it's OK. I can do it.'

'OK. Well, you can ask him what he was doing in your road, and if he can't provide a decent answer, tell him gently and kindly that if you see him near your house again, you'll call the police.' He puts the flat of his warm, dry hand to her face, presses her head softly against his chest. 'But most of all, don't worry,' he says. 'I won't let anything bad happen to you. Some people are just a bit messed up, you know? Most cases of actual violence come from people we know. Trust me.'

'If it gets worse,' Peter says over breakfast the next day, 'I was thinking you can hand in your notice. The pay is peanuts anyway and you should do an MA come September. If your poetry collection is accepted, we'll get you something in a university, all right?'

She nods, although that's not what she wants. She hasn't given her poetry a single thought. It belongs to a past life, a past her, a youthful obsession, a phase. Her priorities have changed. She wants to help the illiterate and the dispossessed. She has seen foreign students in the college, heard them speak. She cannot imagine where they have come from, what they have come from, but she knows enough to understand that they are seeking better, safer lives.

'I'm sure it won't come to that.' She spreads butter on her toast. When she looks up, she sees that Peter is watching her. She passes the knife back over the butter, scrapes off the excess, wipes it on the side of her plate.

Peter grimaces, tears off a strip of kitchen roll and, with one swift swipe, removes the butter from Samantha's plate and puts it in the swing bin.

Wordlessly he returns to the table and spreads sugar-free strawberry jam on his own butter-less toast. He is still a little flushed from his early-morning run.

'Oh,' he says. 'I need to tell you I can't have Emily the week after next.' He bites his toast, smiles, as if this represents the most minor inconvenience. His matter-of-fact delivery, his whole demeanour in fact, is so different from the tender way he was last night, his willingness to take her worries seriously, and later, when they were in bed. Last night he was a warm and gentle breeze; this morning an icy blast.

She tries to meet his eye but he is looking at his phone. 'But it's only for a few hours. And you know I don't have anyone else.'

'I know, it's a pain. Could you ask your mum to come and stay?'

'She has to work, you know. She can't just take a holiday when she feels like it.' Most people have to work to eat, she doesn't add, much as she'd like to.

'What about the crèche at the college? Yes, that's it.' He is standing up, throwing his navy Harris Tweed jacket over his shoulders. 'Book Emily in next week as a practice run. She'll barely notice. But it'd be good to try her out while I'm here to come and get her if it doesn't work out. If it does, it might be better to have her there anyway going forward. I'm losing a lot of time on Tuesdays.'

He bends and kisses her on the cheek. Before she can respond, he has grabbed his keys from the raku bowl on the hall table and is opening the front door.

'Bye, girls,' he calls.

The door shuts.

CHAPTER 18

Samantha stares after him, seething, though she is not sure why. Perhaps because he cannot even commit to looking after his own sodding daughter for a few hours once a week. Yes, perhaps it's that. But if he has to work, he has to work. And the crèche might not be such a bad idea. It means she won't have to rush home, and she fully intends to meet up with Aisha and Jenny after class.

There are questions she needs to ask.

She calls the crèche and books Emily in. When she goes to write it on the wall calendar, she realises that next Monday is the fifth of February, Peter's birthday.

'Oh my God,' she whispers.

It's his fortieth. A landmark birthday. In all the turmoil, she's totally forgotten. She is a rubbish, rubbish girlfriend.

But when Peter returns and she asks him if he'd like her to invite some friends over at the weekend, or organise a meal out, maybe some drinks in the Marlborough Arms if she can find a babysitter, he replies with a good-natured wave of his hand.

'Good Lord, no. Always low-key if there's a zero on the end. Why on earth would anyone want to celebrate being a decade older?'

Relief washes over her. He's not angry. And she's not expected to do anything grand. 'Are you sure?'

'Of course I'm sure. Besides, it's too much with the baby and everything. And it's a Monday, for God's sake, no one wants to go out on a Monday. Let's go to that new pizza place near St

Margaret's. I'd rather open a decent bottle of wine and have a quiet dinner with you.'

'Fine,' she says. 'I'll book it. What's it called?'

'Pizza Romana. I'll send you the link.'

He seems genuinely happy, tells her to relax in the living room while he fixes them a drink. She goes through, sits on the sofa, kicks Emily's furry giraffe underneath just in time.

'You see, people have babies,' he says, coming through to join her with their drinks and a small plate on a tray, which he puts down on the coffee table. She stares at it.

'Thinly sliced raw fennel,' he explains. 'Good for digestion.'

'Right.' They're going to eat it, she supposes.

He hands her a glass. 'Bourgogne,' he says before returning to his theme. 'Yes, I was just thinking as I was pouring our drinks just now how important it is to have this ritual, don't you think? Our little aperitif. It's important to keep a handle on adult life, especially now that Emily is here. I've seen friends have babies and from one moment to the next they go from civilised human beings to blithering idiots, apparently no longer capable of decent thought or deed, their whole lives descended into a wash of breast milk, puke stains and shit.' He chinks his glass against hers, takes a long slug she suspects is not his first. 'I don't want that for us, do you?'

'No,' she replies, nibbling on the fennel, which tastes of liquorice.

'That's why our routine is just as important as Emily's. We have to stay civilised or we'll fall into the abyss.'

'Yes,' she replies, not wanting to tell him that sometimes, when she has slept little, the wine gives her a headache, that she often still has that headache in bed. 'I read that an early-evening glass of red wine can help with milk production.'

'Really?' he replies, and she tries not to notice the mild expression of distaste that crosses his face. 'Excuse me, I've left the gnocchi on.'

*

On Monday evening, Samantha gives Peter the card she has made and signed from her and Emily, together with *Egon Schiele: L'oeuvre complet, 1909–1918*, a book that cost over a hundred pounds but for which he sent her a link that took her to his Amazon Prime account.

'This wrapping paper is lovely,' he tells her as he plants a kiss of thanks on her forehead.

Later, he even sings to the baby while Samantha has a shower, takes five minutes to apply a quick lick of mascara and throws on the black strappy dress. It's too elegant, really, for a Monday night in a pizza restaurant, but it is Peter's birthday and so far she's only worn it for him inside the house.

She returns downstairs brushing at the smooth fabric, a little embarrassed suddenly.

'You look stunning.' His eyes are soft, sloping at the edges in the way she loves. He hands her a glass of red and clinks his larger glass against it. 'This is Pinot Nero, very light. Did I tell you this place uses polenta in the pizza bases? The guy is from Naples, apparently, and it's bring-your-own, so we can take the rest of the wine with us.'

He brings a chilled bottle of champagne too, so that they can toast, which he is about to do when she stops him.

'Let me,' she says, and he smiles his permission. 'Here's to—'

He throws up his hand. 'Just … don't mention the age, all right?'

She considers him for a moment. It isn't like him to be vulnerable. But she remembers her first sight of him, how she was moved by his carefully covered bald spot. The bald spot that is undoubtedly bigger this year.

She holds up her glass of fizz once again. 'Here's to your no-big-deal birthday, which means little to me apart from my gratitude that you were born in the first place. How's that?'

He chuckles. 'You're a wonder. Cheers.'

Over dinner, perhaps keen to move the conversation away from a birthday he is clearly not comfortable celebrating, he asks her with real interest more about her teaching, about the students. Emily is asleep in her stroller, zonked out by a good feed before they left the house. Samantha finds herself more animated than she has been in weeks.

'I sometimes feel like I'm winging it,' she confesses. 'And it's taking me hours to plan one lesson because I'm having to learn it myself first. It took me two days to write the class on subtext in dialogue. But I guess it'll get easier, won't it?'

'It will, it will. And then you'll be bored.'

'I don't think so. I love the people, that's the main part of it. I could be teaching anything, really. I'd ... I'd quite like to teach English as a foreign language though. Or teach people to read. You remember I said that?'

He frowns, presses the paper napkin to his mouth. 'I wouldn't. You're too intelligent.'

She pauses to see if he's joking, but he cuts another triangle of pizza and lowers the wilting point to his mouth.

'But surely,' she says, 'it's good to put intelligence to real use? Meaningful use? I think I could really help people, make a difference. Some of them look totally lost, and without English, what possible job opportunities can they have here?'

'Absolutely, absolutely. But someone of your ... calibre ... I just don't see you doing that.' He drains his champagne and, finding the bottle empty, signals to the waiter for another wine glass. When he returns his eyes to hers, he must read something there, because he adds, 'But if you want to, then go for it, obviously.'

For a moment, their two worlds hang in orbit. This is a whole conversation they cannot have, she realises, one that revolves around perceptions of success, meaning, life itself. In those first weeks and months of late nights and constant sex, she thought they'd talked about everything. She thought they were so aligned.

But perhaps she's overthinking. Peter tells her she does that sometimes. She remembers the photographs in his bedside drawer. Now would be a good time to change the subject.

'So, did you go to school around here then?' she asks.

'Hampton,' he replies. 'Hampton Boys. Nearby, yes, why?'

'Was that a private school?'

'Still is.'

The waiter arrives with a clean tumbler into which Peter pours a generous measure of red. Samantha has still not finished her first glass of champagne.

'Remember I told you my father left me the house and some money?' Peter says. 'Well, it was a lot of money. He was the CEO of a pharmaceuticals company. So yes, I went to private school. In fact, I don't really need to work.'

'You don't need to work?' She can barely stretch her brain around the concept. She knows people like that exist, but …

'Close your mouth,' he says.

'Sorry. I just can't believe I didn't know that.' She can, actually. Their relationship has been such a whirlwind, and now here they are with a baby, getting to know one another retrospectively.

Perhaps he feels it too, because he leans forward, grasps both her hands in his and kisses her knuckles. 'Which is why I keep asking you to marry me.'

She shakes her head. 'A wedding ring didn't protect my mother from anything, did it?'

'But that's because your father was bankrupt as well as a philanderer. I sowed my wild oats at the appropriate moment. And if I've told you about my situation now, tonight, well, consider it my declaration of trust in you. You're safe, Sam. As I keep telling you, I'm not your father.'

'I know.' She kisses the inside of his wrist. 'I know that. Maybe one day. Keep asking.'

His eyes shine, the pupils black and enlarged in the low light of the restaurant. He pushes his plate away. 'I think we should head home.'

'All right.' She glances at the table. She has left her champagne, due to the beginnings of a headache, but has eaten all of her pizza as well as a home-made panna cotta. Peter has left half his pizza, but both bottles are empty.

Peter suggests they walk home rather than taking the bus or a cab. For exercise, he says. It will do her good after eating so much. They stroll back over the bridge, head right, up the hill, leaving the riverside lights to twinkle on the dark water as it falls away behind them. The air is chilly; Samantha pulls her hat as low as it will go, muffles her mouth with her scarf.

'So, you said you used to teach in a secondary school?'

'I did. Up in Liverpool. I did my teacher training there and walked into a job teaching history.'

'What kind of school was it?'

'What do you mean, what kind of school?' He laughs. 'A secondary school. Catholic, is that what you mean?'

'No, I just meant private or state or … I don't know really. I guess I was thinking of my school.'

'Ah yes, the school of hard knocks, wasn't it? Pig fights in the yard?'

She bristles. Her rural upbringing amuses him, along with other aspects of her life – the fact that she worked as a waitress, as a Saturday girl in the village shoe shop. She doesn't see what is so funny. Someone like Peter would have been hung out to dry at her school; he wouldn't have lasted five minutes. He hasn't had to constantly adapt to his surroundings as she has – soften his accent, correct his grammar, refrain from verbal tics, originally adopted for survival, in case they make him sound stupid. She doesn't say this, doesn't say much else as they make their way home. In fact, it is only when they get home that she realises that he never really answered her.

Samantha reaches the crèche almost an hour before class. She needs the extra time if she's going to settle Emily and still have a moment to catch Harry Boyd. To her surprise, her student Suzanne is chatting to one of the nursery assistants. The assistant says something out of the corner of her mouth and they both laugh. Samantha hasn't seen Suzanne laugh before, she realises. She looks pretty; her brown hair, which previously looked dull, today is glossy. Samantha thinks perhaps she's straightened it.

'Hi,' she says, cursing the heat creeping up her neck.

They look up and promptly stop laughing. When she sees the baby, however, Suzanne breaks into a warm smile.

'Oh, Samantha,' she says. 'Is this your little girl?'

Samantha feels the blush spread up onto her face. 'I'm trying her in the crèche today. Peter's working, so …'

Suzanne is walking towards her, her smile still wide and warm. 'Oh my God, she's gorgeous.' She bends forward, brushes her forefinger against Emily's cheek. 'Hey there, little one. Aren't you beautiful, eh? You're like your mummy, aren't you?'

The corners of Emily's mouth turn up in a gummy, idiotic grin.

'There's a smile,' Suzanne sing-songs – her accent is northern, well-spoken. 'There's a lovely little smile.'

It is the most Samantha has ever heard Suzanne say. She is blossoming, as if she prefers the company of babies to adults. Samantha understands her. Babies don't care who you are, whether or not you've pronounced the name of a composer correctly, got the wrong century for an artist, asked for sugar for your coffee. All they need is a kind voice.

'She's gorgeous.' Suzanne is looking at Samantha finally. 'What's her name?'

'Emily.'

'Aah, what a lovely name.' Suzanne holds out her arms, raises her eyebrows. 'Can I have a little hold?'

'Of course.' Samantha hands her over, watching with something like delight as the other woman cradles Emily and looks lovingly into her eyes.

'I didn't realise you had a child in the crèche too,' she says.

'I don't yet,' Suzanne replies, her eyes not leaving Emily's face. 'I was thinking of bringing our Jo next week, so I just wanted to have a chat, like, see how I felt about the set-up, but they seem nice here. And it means I don't have to leave her with my mum. I live quite far away, so I don't like leaving her too long, you know?'

'Good idea. How old is she?'

'Only little. Not much older than Emily, to be honest.' She glances up at Samantha. 'Shall I take her over to Gail?'

'No, it's OK. I can't chat actually, though. I have to see my boss about something before class.'

Suzanne nods, her expression flattening before animating once again. 'Listen, do you want me to stay here for a bit, make sure she's settled? That way you can get off and do what you need to do.' She turns towards the nursery nurse and calls over, 'Gail, this is Samantha's little one, Emily. I was just saying I don't mind staying on a bit, make sure she's OK?'

Gail waves and gets up from the floor, where she is playing with bright outsize Lego bricks, the kind Peter has said he will never have in the house.

'Hello,' she says, holding out her hand. 'I'm Gail.'

Samantha shakes her hand. She looks so young – late teens perhaps. Finally, someone younger than her in charge of an infant, although she'd rather leave Emily with someone more experienced. Gail tells her there's a form to fill in, so, leaving the baby clearly very contented with Suzanne, Samantha follows her into the office.

'I'm in RBS27,' she adds, scribbling the number for the classroom on the form. 'But she's been fed and changed so she shouldn't need much. There's some spare nappies in here and a bottle. Can you warm it? She takes a bottle from my partner, so she should be OK. Is there anyone else working with you?'

'Sandra's gone on her break but she'll be back in a mo, don't worry.' Gail is smiling at her with patient benevolence beyond her years. 'She'll be fine,' she says slowly.

'Thank you. I'll be back a little after two.' Samantha remembers her arrangement with Aisha and Jenny. 'Actually, it'll be nearer three, but call me if there's any problem. I'll be in the canteen from two.'

Suzanne is already sitting on a wicker chair with Emily in her arms. Emily has fallen asleep, the pale brown brush of her eyelashes, that pink bow of her top lip, the same as her father's. Samantha sighs, kisses the palm of her hand and presses it to Emily's head.

'Bye then, little one,' she says softly, then, meeting Suzanne's eye, 'See you in class.'

Suzanne hunches her shoulders briefly and smiles once again. 'See you there, hon,' she calls out as Samantha heads out of the crèche.

Harry Boyd is not in his office. He is not in the admin office either. Penny McKay, the woman who, it appears to Samantha, holds the entire college together, tells her she saw him in the cafeteria a moment ago.

'Thanks.'

Samantha half runs across the courtyard, through the canteen, the foyer where the art students' exhibition hangs. Her own wretched little poetry collection comes into her mind. She wishes Peter hadn't sent it to the university press. She wasn't ready. *It* wasn't ready. And if it gets published, she will know it is because of his status, not her own talent. She should have argued more boldly. But she was at the end of her pregnancy and more tired than she had ever been. And Peter's powers of persuasion hit her only afterwards, as is so often the way.

Harry is nowhere to be seen. Time is ticking. She heads for the photocopier to find Sean hovering in the foyer. A stress pain pushes at her sternum. She should ask him what he was doing in her street. But he looks more anxious than she is. He is shifting his weight from foot to foot and fiddling with the zip on his anorak.

'We're in PK23 in the old building.' He zips up his anorak, unzips it a few centimetres, zips it up again, unzips, zips. His brow is furrowed, his eyes round. 'It says it on the classroom door but it's not on the noticeboard. How will people know where to go?'

Samantha can't ask him about his presence outside her house now; he is far too rattled, and besides, any sinister intent just doesn't square up. Now that they are face to face, the idea that Sean would hurt a fly is unimaginable.

'Hold on a sec.' She jogs down the corridor – sure enough, there is a sign Sellotaped to the glass:

Spanish exam. Please be quiet.
Creative Writing for Beginners moved to PK23.

'Oh,' she says, a little perplexed. No one told her. She can sense Sean standing behind her, almost touching her shoulder. When she turns, his nose almost grazes hers. She takes a step back. Oh, but how worried he looks. She could cry for him.

'Actually, Sean,' she says gently, 'could you maybe wait in the foyer and redirect the others? Save them making noise outside the classroom, as there's an exam on? That would completely solve the problem and you'd be doing me an enormous favour.'

He almost beams, nods violently. 'I can do that.'

'Brilliant. I won't start without you, don't worry.'

'I'll stand in the foyer so they won't disturb the exam. I'll tell them to go to PK23.'

'Exactly.' She gives him a thumbs-up and heads back towards the main building to find keys for the classroom, her heart still with him. There will be a moment to ask him what he was doing in her road, but that wasn't it.

In the courtyard, Suzanne is heading towards her.

'Settled in fine,' she says. 'She's fast asleep in her car seat, bless her.'

'Brilliant. Listen, we're in PK23 today.'

Suzanne doesn't appear to register the information. 'I'm sorry I didn't make it last week,' she says. 'I was under the weather.'

'That's OK, don't worry about it. It's not like school – you won't get a detention.'

Suzanne laughs, perhaps more than the joke deserves, and Samantha remembers that she left school at sixteen. At the reception desk, she stops to change the classroom keys and together she and Suzanne take the staircase to the first floor.

'I've booked our Jo in for next week,' Suzanne tells her. 'They can have a play date.'

'Aw, that's lovely.'

They reach the first floor landing. Aisha and Jenny are waiting outside PK23.

'Actually Suzanne,' Samantha says, her pace slowing. 'I've just realised I've given the nursery the wrong classroom number. They won't know where to find me if Emily needs me.'

'Yes they will!' Suzanne's face is pure triumph. 'I saw the sign before and I told Gail.'

'Oh. Oh, OK. That's … that's brilliant, thanks.'

Suzanne beams back at her before disappearing into the Ladies, leaving Samantha to face Aisha and Jenny alone.

'We were just talking about you,' Aisha says. 'Do you have time for a quick coffee after class?'

Samantha nods, eventually produces a strained, 'Er, sure.' She's gone all weird, she knows she has, but she can't help it. She fumbles with the key, which rattles in the eroded fitting of the lock. With a stiff clunk, the door opens suddenly and violently. Samantha almost falls into the classroom.

'Steady as she goes,' Jenny says with a laugh. 'You almost went flying then!'

Without making eye contact, Samantha heads for the computer. Shit, she didn't do the photocopying.

'I won't be a tick.' She dashes out with the day's lesson notes, almost bumping into Suzanne. In the corridor, she stops, curses again. She's left her bag in the classroom, but to go back now will look like she doesn't trust those women. She *doesn't* trust them – well, two of them. But no, she has the folder. The bogus work has always been placed in the folder.

A shadow is moving towards her. Sean.

'I've told all the others like you said, Miss. They're on their way. I told Tommy, Reggie, Daphne—'

'Sean, you've saved the day,' she says. 'Excuse me, I just have to dash and get these copied.' She holds up the folder and smiles.

'I'm a bit earlier today,' he says. 'Tried the bike again because the roadworks have moved north of Kew now so it's not as bad.'

'Right you are, Sean.' Samantha's forehead prickles.

Behind Sean, Lana appears and says a gruff hello. Seeing her chance, Samantha makes a run for it.

By the time she returns, the class is full. Her bag is on the desk and appears to be as she left it. No one will have dared touch it in full view of the others. Focus. Lead the discussion. She pulls a tissue from her bag and wipes her forehead, takes a gulp of her water.

'OK,' she begins. 'Today we're going to look at dialogue …'

She takes them through a couple of scenarios, gets them to split into pairs and write an argument over a parking space in a supermarket car park. After fifteen minutes, she asks Reggie and Daphne to read theirs.

'"Excuse me,"' Daphne reads aloud from her notes. '"I think I may have been here before you."'

'"Were you?"' Reggie peers at the same sheet. '"I'm afraid I didn't notice."'

When they have finished what must be the most polite argument ever recorded, Samantha encourages the class to help her analyse what they have written.

'Good dialogue needs subtext,' she tells them, scribbling a few lines from Reggie and Daphne's script on the whiteboard. 'Can anyone tell me what subtext is?'

Aisha raises her hand. Samantha scans the room, tries to make eye contact with someone, anyone else. No one will look at her directly.

'Aisha?'

Aisha gives one of her sickly smiles. 'It's what lies beneath what we say.'

'Can you expand?'

'It's what you really mean but you don't say it in words. So, like, "I think I may have been here before you" means something stronger.' Aisha's face is so earnest. She simply doesn't look like someone who could spend even one second being mean-spirited. But then, appearances …

Daphne giggles. 'It's really saying "I *was* here before you", isn't it?'

'Good,' says Samantha. She does adore Daphne. 'You could argue that the subtext is even stronger, couldn't you? What would be stronger still?'

Again, Aisha raises a hand. Samantha checks the rest of them, but no one else appears willing to answer.

'Aisha,' she says, through her teeth.

'It means "You're in my space."' Aisha meets her eye. 'It means "Get the hell out of my space."'

The hairs on Samantha's arms stand on end. She holds Aisha's gaze, tries to read it but can't. With a sense of capitulation, she breaks eye contact.

'Exactly,' she says. '"Get the hell out of my space. I was here first."' She looks around at the others, sweat prickling once again on her forehead. 'And there are lots of examples,' she blusters on, trying to lift a mood it's possible only she can feel. 'If your boyfriend puts on a shirt you don't like, for example, and you're going out to a restaurant with some friends, and you say, "Darling, are you wearing that shirt?" what would you actually mean by that? Anyone?'

Boyfriend, shirt, restaurant. Samantha cannot get Peter out of her mind. Peter in their living room, looking her up and down and saying, *Are you wearing those jeans?* Subtext: *Don't wear those jeans – I don't like them.*

No, she had replied, although she had intended on wearing them. And she had gone upstairs and changed. She imagines Aisha in their living room, Peter saying the words to her. Would she have changed, or would she have stood her ground and said, *Yes, what's it to you?*

But a ripple of laughter has run around the class and she forces herself back.

'Anyone?' she manages to say. 'What is the subtext of "Are you wearing that shirt?"' She cannot look at Aisha.

'It means don't wear that bloody awful shirt,' Reggie says. 'You look a right bugger in it.'

Again, the class laugh. Relief runs through her like cool water.

'Exactly,' she says, forcing a smile. 'So try and remember – we hardly ever say what we mean.'

*

The students file out, leaving their dialogue pieces on the desk.

'See you over there.' If Aisha picked up on any subtext in class, she doesn't show it. 'Shall I get you a peppermint tea?'

She remembered. Too nice, too nice by far.

'No, it's OK,' Samantha says. 'Give me five minutes; I have to mark the register.'

Once the room is empty, she dives into the pile of students' work. Eight students. She told each of them to copy out the dialogue and continue it individually for ten minutes so there should be eight pieces. Her chest expands, deflates. Nothing sinister. If it has been Sean all along, perhaps he's now too scared after she caught him hanging around her house. Hopefully it's enough to stop him doing it again. Alternatively, if she meets Aisha and Jenny now and then finds an extra sheet once she gets home, she will know it is Aisha and will tackle her directly. She has her phone number. She will call her and ask her what the hell she's up to. How unpleasant.

The door flies open. Peter is there, looking flushed and a little out of breath.

'Peter?' She stands up, alarmed. 'Are you OK? Is Emily OK?'

'I'm fine.' He smiles, presses the flat of his hand to his chest. 'I've been running all over the college trying to find you. They'd listed the wrong classroom on the noticeboard. I ended up over in the business centre.'

'Oh no, sorry about that. There was an exam. If I'd known you were coming, I'd have texted.' She kisses him on the cheek. 'Anyway, this is a nice surprise.'

'Just thought I'd meet you, give you a lift home, make sure you were OK. Did you speak to Harry?'

'I couldn't find him. But it's OK. There's nothing this week. It's exactly like you said: ignore it and they'll get bored.' She hands the folder to him. 'Listen, can you indulge me and just check there are eight?'

'Sure.' He takes the papers from the folder, licks his thumb and forefinger and counts. 'Eight,' he says after a moment. 'Eight students?'

She nods, her eyes prickling with tears of relief.

He looks genuinely relieved and she loves him in that moment. That he would care so much, that he would run all over college just to find her and offer her some support. He is taking it so seriously.

'It's nice of you to come for me,' she says. 'We can go and get Emily together.'

She could bring Peter with her to meet Aisha and Jenny. That would really put the cat among the pigeons, as her mum would say. But something tells her not to. Aisha might well have Peter in her sights. The way she said 'Get the hell out of my space' in class a moment ago. A shiver passes through her. Aisha is really quite beautiful: large brown eyes and luscious black hair, not the thin, straggly mop that Samantha invariably finds herself pushing into her hat to prevent it flying away altogether. No, let's not flirt with danger, not today.

As they cross the courtyard, she thumbs a quick text to Aisha to tell her she can't make coffee. She doesn't give a reason. There is more to this situation, she knows it, and she wants to keep her powder dry.

See you next week instead, she adds and presses send.

'Can't you catch up with your texts later?' Peter asks, striding slightly ahead.

'Sorry.' Samantha slides the phone into her pocket, though not before reading Aisha's reply.

Next week then! Great class by the way. Jenny and I think you're fab.

Despite her misgivings, she feels a flush of pleasure. Aisha really is so generous and supportive. This would all be lovely and flattering were it not tinged with horrible, poisonous suspicion.

As they approach the crèche, she sees Suzanne heading for the car park.

'Suzanne,' she calls out, but Suzanne is too far away to hear and doesn't turn around.

'Who's that?' Peter peers after her.

'Just Suzanne, one of my students.'

Peter nods. 'Shame I missed them. I would have liked to say hello.'

A knot tightens in her chest. Peter claimed to be here to pick her up, but now she wonders at the real motive behind his romantic impromptu appearance. It is quite out of character. Is it possible that he has read more into the rogue homework than he claims? Did he see in those pieces of writing, just as she did, the ghost of an ex-girlfriend? And did he come here to see not Samantha, but Aisha?

CHAPTER 19

On the way home, Peter is talkative, funny even. If he did come to the college to see if he could catch his old flame in the act, then he doesn't show any disappointment that he didn't, and Samantha begins to feel like a paranoid basket case, incapable of reading innocence into any situation. Even if Aisha has been writing insidious notes, using enough guile to disguise her intelligence, that doesn't mean that Peter has done anything wrong. Ninety-nine per cent of her knows this, of course. It is the one per cent that prevents her from mentioning Aisha's name.

They pull up outside the house, the wisteria that usually covers the front fence little more than a muscular stretching arm waiting for green shoots to disguise its cracked and greyish bark.

Peter leans over and kisses her deeply on the mouth.

'Wow,' she says. 'I wasn't expecting that.'

'A down payment.' He grins. 'I'll settle up later.'

She shakes her head. 'You're really quite cheesy, you do know that, don't you?' She gets out of the car and lifts Emily out of the back. Peter is opening the boot. He pulls out the pram chassis.

'Go inside,' he says. 'It's cold. I'll bring the rest in.'

She goes inside shivering, towards the kitchen, where she pops Emily in her car seat on the table and flicks the switch for the kettle.

'Will you be late?' she asks, returning to the hall as Peter pushes the pram in through the front door.

'Shouldn't be. If I am, I'll text. Sure you don't want me to call Harry, by the way?'

She follows him back out to the car. 'Sure I'm sure. I think the nonsense has stopped now. As you said it would, you wise old man.'

He pulls her into his arms and kisses her again. Playfully she hits him with her gloves.

'Whatever will the neighbours think?'

'They'll think, "There's a lucky bastard." That's what they'll think.'

'Thought you didn't objectify women?'

'I don't. But they might.'

She rolls her eyes and waves. 'Cheese,' she calls after him. 'Pure cheese.'

She waits until he's driven off to return indoors. The pram already set up in the hallway, she decides to stretch her legs and catch the last of the day. She heads back down the hill towards town, and when she sees the specialist cheese shop, she has the idea of going in and buying some for Peter, for a joke. Like most of these deli-style food and wine places, he knows the manager – in this case, Jim. And it is Jim who lets her try a selection of expensive vintage Cheddars. She selects a 'mellow, nutty' piece, thinking that when she gets home, she will write a witty label for it, something to do with Peter being both cheesy and vintage. They can have a few cubes with their wine.

She reaches the house as the last of the sun dies away. It is around half past five and she is thirsty and tired. Emily is awake, however, and needs a feed, so instead of tea, Samantha turns the heating on and pours herself a long glass of water before settling on the sofa, still in her coat. Emily sucks hungrily, her eyes closed in concentration. Samantha closes her own eyes and tries to be still and in the moment. But just as she attunes to the calm and the silence, she hears a door latch click. Her eyes open wide.

'Hello?'

She stands. The strength has gone from her legs. Was it the front door or the back? She waits a moment until she feels able to move, then walks slowly towards the living-room door. It is awkward, with Emily still attached. It takes her a second or two to lean out into the hallway. The black and white diagonal tiles run to the front door. The front door is closed. In the dimness, the coats are a shadowy mass. The shape makes her tremble despite herself. She trains her ears against the silence, hears the soft hum of a car passing on the street. She feels like she did when she was a child, alone in her bed, listening for the knock of the chestnut branch against the kitchen window. It only happened when the wind was strong and the worst of it was that the knocking came intermittently. Just as she felt herself drift to sleep once more, another bang would come, muffled through her bedroom floor.

She hobbles, cradling Emily, to the end of the hall and pushes the front door. Shut, definitely. The Yale lock should be enough. But still. Her keys are in her coat pocket. Christ, this is ridiculous, trying to lock the front door with Emily at her breast. Somehow, she manages the mortice lock. Peter will have a key for it.

She stands in the dark hallway a moment, cursing herself. It has taken little to reduce her to this frightened child. She checks the back door. It is locked. Her satchel is on the kitchen table, so she grabs it and settles on the sofa once again. Emily sucks, at peace. Samantha's heart slows. She needs to calm down. This whole poem business is nonsense and it's taking on way too much importance.

The heating clicks.

Samantha half laughs.

'That was the noise, Emily,' she says to her little girl. 'It was the radiator, not the door. Mummy's a scaredy-cat, isn't she? A silly scaredy-cat.'

She wriggles out of her coat and pulls up her legs to cross them. Once she's comfortable, she calls her mother, who asks if it's her.

'Of course it's me. That's why my name and my picture come up on your phone.'

'All right, sarky. It's just a figure of speech. Everything all right?'

Samantha sighs. 'Everything apart from being a nervous wreck.' She tells her mother about the suspicious poems, plays the whole thing down. 'I mean, I'm not going to let it get under my skin – it's pathetic – and anyway, there was nothing today, so with any luck they've given up. I suppose I'm just stressed because of tiredness. And getting used to Peter.' She stops. She has said too much.

'What d'you mean, getting used to Peter?'

'Oh, nothing. He's a bit night and day, you know? Blows hot and cold. I suppose sometimes it feels like I don't know him, or we don't know each other.'

'That's understandable,' her mother says. 'It takes a long time to really know someone, and after everything with your dad, I wonder whether you ever really do.'

'But for most of it, with Dad, you felt OK, didn't you?'

'I did. And I think for most of it, it *was* OK. It was just the last few years. Midlife crisis, money worries. I wonder sometimes if he had a bit of a breakdown. And even if he didn't, he wasn't the first daft bastard to follow his you-know-what and he won't be the last. It's just a shame we lost the farm.'

It is more than her mother ever usually says. Nothing is solid, Samantha thinks. There is nowhere to feel safe. This house should feel safe, but one click from the radiator and she's a gibbering wreck.

'You've had a lot on,' her mother is saying. 'You've gone from student to mother in such a short time. You're so young, though I know you don't like me saying it. And now you're teaching as well. Maybe you should take a step back. Let Peter look after you and go back to work when Emily's a bit older.'

Samantha nods, even though her mum can't see her. 'I know, but Peter wants another child. He told me the other night when we were … talking.' When they'd been in bed. He'd been inside her and she'd had to manoeuvre herself off him, insist that he used a condom. *But you're still breastfeeding*, he'd said. *You won't be fertile.* She'd reached for the bedside cabinet drawer, told him it was a myth.

They would have another baby next year, but not yet. Strange, she thinks now. It's not as if he is hugely interested in the baby itself, not really; more in the idea of making her pregnant. She wonders sometimes if when they conceived Emily, he did it on purpose.

'Plenty of time for another,' her mother says. 'Maybe get married first, eh? The law won't protect you if Peter … I mean, if anything were to happen to Peter. He's a bit older than you, isn't he?'

'Oh for goodness' sake, Mum. He's hardly at death's door!'

'People have heart attacks at forty.'

'Mum!'

The cackle of her mother's laughter comes down the line. 'I'm not saying he's going to cark it next week, love. Just that if anything *happens*, you'd get nothing. If you get married, what he has goes to you, unless he stipulates otherwise. That's all I'm saying.'

By the time Samantha rings off, Emily has reclined, her eyelids heavy as a heroin addict's. Not a very nice comparison, she thinks, Tommy's red-ringed, heavy-lidded stare coming to mind, but yes, Emily does look drugged. On milk, Samantha thinks. On love. This love is what her mother feels for her, always has. It is a love that cannot be understood unless experienced. From nowhere at all, her eyes prick with tears. There are people who cannot, who will never, experience maternal love, for whatever reason. The only saving grace is that they have not experienced it, so perhaps they are spared the knowing. Although the longing must be so painful. Maddening. Dangerous, even.

Carefully she shifts Emily to her shoulder and carries her upstairs. Lays her in her white cot, pulls the cord for her lullaby mobile. Outside, the garden is a jumble of hulks and shadows, as ever. She shivers, pulls the curtains. These evenings without Peter are long, even if she feels oddly at peace in other ways. She is more carelessly herself, perhaps, though she can't say in what way.

She crosses the landing to close the curtains in her bedroom. On the street, at the edge of the halo of the lamp post, stands a man.

A ball tightens in her chest. She pushes her face to the window. His hood is up, his face obscured. She tries to see if he's holding a bike helmet, but the hedge is in the way.

'No,' she says, to the silent window. 'No, no, no.'

She runs down the stairs. Pops the latch and pulls.

'Shit.' She has double-locked the front door. She rummages in her coat pocket for the keys, unlocks the door, pulls it towards her so fast it flies out of her hand and shudders against the doorstop.

'Sean?' She is running down the front path, hugging her cardigan around her against the sudden cold. She is at the gate. 'Sean?'

There is no one. She looks left and right. Both hands clenched white around the iron gate, she roars at the road like a madwoman. Opens the gate, runs into the middle of the street. Nothing. No one. If the door slams, she will be locked out. Her feet are freezing; the damp cold comes through her thin socks as she runs back into the house.

She stands in the hallway, willing herself to return to the living room. Her satchel is on the sofa. In it is her folder, the corner poking out. She pulls it free, flings it open. This time, she doesn't have to leaf through the work. The anonymous sheet is on the top. It is not dialogue, but another poem. Typed. Blank paper. Someone must have delivered it by hand. Someone has been in this house.

Do not go blindly into that bright light

Do not go blindly into that bright light.
It is but glass with only tricks to play.
A mirror's glare – beware! – you must take flight.

Wise girls they know that silver tongues do lie.
Those men are dogs, they hunt their prey by day.

Do not go blindly into that bright light.

Bad men may bark and they may surely bite,
Their only aim to lead young girls astray.
That mirror's glare – beware! – you must take flight.

Farm beasts live better by a good darn sight
Than men who plant their seed and run away.
Do not go blindly into that bright light.

Oh woman, you must hold your baby tight.
You must take heed, please listen to me say:
The mirror's glare – beware! – you must take flight

Yes, you, my dear, alone on this dark night,
Please heed another who has passed this way:
Do not go blindly into that bright light.
A mirror's glare – beware! – you must take flight

She sinks to her knees. Reads it again, and again, the words
and form at once strange and familiar. It's a pastiche, she's pretty
sure, of the Dylan Thomas villanelle, 'Do not go gentle into that
good night'. Dylan Thomas is Peter's favourite poet. Peter told
her once that he read that poem at his father's funeral. Whoever
wrote this must know that.

Sean was outside a second ago. He *must* have put this here. It's
the only thing that makes sense. And yet it doesn't; it doesn't make
any sense at all. Sean is too helpless. If it weren't for the grubby
anorak, she would want to hug him. If it was him outside just
now, he must have broken in. But there's no sign of that and …
he can't have written this, he just can't. Unless … He's so unsure
of himself; easily startled. Could he have been browbeaten into
delivering it for someone else?

Think, Samantha. The themes are the same as the others: bad men, danger, women, herself. Reggie? No, too kind, too old, too cool. Daphne, no – ditto, plus too twinkly and mischievous, too happy in her skin. Tommy, no, too out of it, too disinterested. Lana, no, she would never have this kind of grasp of English. Suzanne, no, she left school at sixteen, knows nothing of poetry let alone which poet to imitate. Which leaves Aisha and Jenny. Jenny who is intelligent and perhaps a little strident … but no. Aisha, then. It all loops back to Aisha, Peter's jilted ex, Aisha the English graduate who casually dropped T. S. Eliot into her first simple poem.

She reads the poem again. Someone seems to be looking out for her, telling her to get away from Peter. Could this be Aisha's long game? Unsettle with veiled menace, then point to Peter as the danger, causing her to become suspicious of him so that she, Aisha, can exploit that corrosive force in order to rekindle their affair?

Suspicion. The one per cent. One per cent is all you need.

She should call Aisha now. Right now. She should call her and ask her what the hell is going on.

An hour later, she is still on the sofa, reading the poem over and over. Torturing herself. The roar of Peter's car on the drive.

'Peter,' she says aloud. 'Thank God.'

By the time he gets out of the car, she is in on the front path, in tears.

'Peter.' She runs into his arms.

'What's happened?' He holds her tight, kisses her hair. 'Darling, what is it?'

'It's not going away, Peter. It's getting worse.'

'But you said there were no more poems. In the college, we checked.' He follows her into the house, into the kitchen, where the folder lies on the table, the imitation poem on the top.

'I checked,' she says, her voice broken. 'You checked too, didn't you, and there was nothing untoward.'

'Nothing.' He pulls two wine glasses down from the cupboard. 'And you're saying there's been another? Is it possible we missed it, maybe two sheets stuck together?'

She shakes her head, offers him the offending poem. 'This time it's definitely aimed at us. Definitely.'

Peter is uncorking a bottle, his mouth a grim flat line. 'Take it into the living room,' he says. 'I need to sit down and really focus on it. I've been standing up for hours and the drive home was a nightmare. And light the fire, will you? It's cold in here.'

In the living room, she waits, already a little calmer now that Peter is home. Even the clink of the glassware is comforting, the ritual of it, the familiarity. She strikes a match and holds it to the paper that Peter has laid in the grate. She should have done this earlier, got the room cosy for him, but she's been too frazzled. The paper takes, the flames lick around the kindling. As Peter has instructed, she waits for two minutes before laying the first log carefully on top.

'Here.' He is sitting down on the sofa, two glasses on the coffee table, reflected firelight dancing in their ruby-red bellies. He picks up the sheet, in his expression something of the patient schoolmaster. No more than a moment passes before that expression shifts, darkens. Second by second, she watches the deepening lines on his brow, the way he pulls with one finger at his collar, the heavy exhalation, and now the reaching for the wine, the glass drained.

'What do you think?' she asks.

'I think we should call the police.'

It is a Tuesday evening, nine o'clock, in Richmond. The police arrive within the hour, two officers, both men. Samantha had not expected a house call. They refuse offers of tea, coffee. One, the older of the two, somewhere in his late twenties or early thirties, sits in the armchair and takes out a notebook. Peter gives a brief history of the poison notes. Samantha interjects, awakening to the fact that she's been sidelined in her own story. It is as if she doesn't have a voice, or if she does, it is not one they can hear. The only answers she gives are to reassure them that she cannot have been mistaken. When she does tell them something, they look to Peter for confirmation.

'And you recognised this Sean … Sean Worth … did you, this evening?' the older of the two PCs asks her.

She shakes her head. 'I wouldn't put it as strongly as that. It looked like him. And of course he was here last week, on this street. I definitely saw him then.'

He looks to his colleague and back to her. 'But this week you're not sure?'

'Not one hundred per cent, no. And I wouldn't want to accuse someone unless—'

'She did see this guy last week,' Peter interjects. 'And as I said, I checked the folder with her at the college at around ten past two this afternoon. There were eight pieces of homework, all dialogues. This poem definitely wasn't there. If my partner says there was someone outside the house, then there was. And it's most likely to be Sean Worth. Who else could it have been? We're not saying he wrote the poems, but shouldn't we get a restraining order on the guy?'

'But we don't know that Sean put the poem in the house.' Samantha feels like she's interrupting. 'We don't even know it was put into the folder after we got home. We could be mistaken.'

'Come on, Samantha.' Peter looks towards the officers. Samantha only catches his expression from the side, but there's something dismissive in it she doesn't like.

'It's a bit premature for a restraining order at this stage.' The older officer tucks his notepad into his breast pocket. 'I'll file a report. That way we'll have it on record. And like I say, keep us posted on any developments and call us immediately you see anyone near the property acting suspiciously.'

Peter shows them out. The front door bangs shut. Samantha looks towards the living-room door, expecting him to appear, but a moment later she hears him in the kitchen. He is whistling. Stravinsky, she thinks, but is not certain. She is not certain of anything. Peter helped her check the folder. She was with him the whole time. When she thought she heard the click of the door, he was at work. Is it possible she can even think he would do something like that, and if so, why? Why would she think that? Because of the pills behind the sofa cushions? She thinks of his absolute precision just now, talking to the police officers, compared to his vagueness whenever she asks about any part of his life that doesn't, or didn't, involve her. The school he taught at, the ex-girlfriends he never discusses, the unnamed PhD student he meets in the pub …

But his willingness to take her concerns seriously has grown naturally according to the perceived threat. His appearance at the college was the action of a loving partner. His immediate calling of the police just now was completely supportive. The cleverness of this last poem, the way it alludes to a deeply personal favourite of his – there's no way he would use it. Why point the finger at himself? And he is desperate to marry her; why warn her off? He has always wanted to save her, from her father, the spectre of financial ruin, her fear of being left humiliated and penniless. Only the other week, he made it clear to her that he was extremely wealthy, a gesture of faith. The moment he met her, he wanted to take her home. The moment he took her home, he wanted her to stay. Why would he try to frighten her away?

'Sam.'

She almost shrieks. He is at the doorway and he is gazing at her. The firelight casts an unflattering glow and she realises his chin is not as firm now as it was even a year ago. But the way he is looking at her makes it easy to forget that he is almost twenty years her senior. Her raging thoughts are nothing more than paranoia. And when he sits beside her and places his warm hand to her cheek in that way he does, she closes her eyes and leans into it.

'You are my one true love,' he says, 'and I won't let anyone hurt a hair on your head.'

This is the side of him that only she knows. All the academic theories, all the jargon and the published works and the culture and the house and the good looks and the car and the nonsense turn to dust. He is her Gregory Peck. He is her romantic hero. And he is as cheesy as it gets.

'I love you,' she says and kisses him.

CHAPTER 20

'I don't like leaving you.' Peter is standing on the doorstep, his case next to his tan Church's brogues. It is a week later, Tuesday morning.

'The world is full of terrorists and gun-wielding madmen,' Samantha says. 'You can't let terrorists stop you from going on holiday and you can't let a few silly poems stop you going to an academic conference or me going to work.'

He grins at her. 'You're amazing.'

'Only because I have you. And the police know now. I'll speak to Harry today and make sure I lock the house. Honestly, I'm not scared.' It is almost true.

He sighs. 'Are you sure you'll be all right? I could stay a few hours longer; that way I can drive you in.'

'I'm not a child, Peter. If I see Sean today, I'll have a word with him, and then if anything happens later, I'll call the police straight away.'

'And me. You'll call me, won't you?'

'Of course. Now go, go on.' She leans out and kisses him on the mouth. 'Go on, f— buzz off!' She congratulates herself. She caught the swear word just in time.

The house to herself, she goes into every room and checks the locks on all the windows. She checks Peter's bedside table too, and the medicine cabinet, but there's no sign of any pills. Suspicion is exhausting, relentless. Her eyes sting, her shoulders ache. For the last week, countless theories have revolved in her head. Aisha, Jenny, Sean, Lana. Aisha, Sean, Jenny, Aisha. Twice she has lain on her bed in the middle of the day, reading the villanelle over and over for clues; pored over the original Dylan Thomas poem on her phone screen, as if some literary close reading could possibly help. Three or four times she has dreamt of the entire class closing in on her, Peter herding them like sheep, goading them to kill her with sharp flashing knives. She has woken up sweating, only to find Peter beside her, as handsome in sleep as he is awake. She's sick of searching for evidence of his drug-taking, sick of thinking evil thoughts about him, sick of herself.

Harry Boyd is in the foyer of the business unit, talking to Gabby, who teaches English as a foreign language.

'Harry.' Samantha waves to him; this is opportune.

'Samantha.' He claps Gabby on the arm and walks towards her. 'Everything all right? How's the teaching going?'

'Fine – but actually, would you have five minutes?'

He checks his watch. 'I've got fifteen. Any good?'

'Brilliant. I'll drop Emily off and come and find you.'

'Great. I'll be in the manager's office.'

She heads for the crèche. Suzanne is there again, chatting to the nursery nurse, whose name Samantha has forgotten. Suzanne smiles and jumps up.

'Hello again,' she says. 'You look stressed; do you want me to take her?' She holds out her arms, and for a moment Samantha feels a flash of anxiety. Could Suzanne have written that villanelle? No, she doesn't think so. No, impossible.

The nursery assistant is right there, smiling over at her. Samantha knows she is not reacting normally. Everything is getting to her, more than she thinks, even the prospect of her first night without Peter. But if she starts living in fear, then whoever it is has won.

'That'd be great, thanks,' she says simply, letting Suzanne take the pram.

Suzanne wheels Emily into the nursery. Samantha waves before dashing to the old building and up the two flights of stairs. The manager's office is actually a classroom packed with desks, desks piled with paper stacks, the evidence of costs cut, of people finding themselves doing the work of three for the pay of one.

'Harry.'

'Samantha.' He moves a pile of paper from a plastic chair and gestures for her to sit down. He asks after Peter and the baby, but when Samantha answers only briefly and glances at the clock, he appears to realise she doesn't have time for small talk and asks how he can help.

Samantha pulls her folder from her satchel and hands Harry the offending pieces of writing, in chronological order. There are only three.

'The last one's at home, sorry.' A bookmark, folded on page eighty-six of her Rebus, under the bed. It doesn't matter; there's enough here for Harry to get the gist. She waits while his eyes flick over the work.

'The first one came at the end of my first lesson and I didn't think too much of it. I know it's not horrific or openly threatening, but it's a bit, well, dodgy. But when no one claimed it, I did feel a bit uneasy. Peter said to ignore it, said it was probably someone having a misguided joke. But then the next one came the following week, and the last two I found in our house, but that's not to say—'

'Someone put them in your house? Did they break in?'

'That's the thing. It's possible someone might have put them into the folder after class when I wasn't looking, or maybe I didn't see them when I checked.'

His expression shifts – it is almost nothing – eyebrows raised a fraction, his mouth flattening.

'It's not baby brain,' she says quickly, justifying herself, hating herself for doing it even in the moment. 'Emily's an easy baby and I'm not overtired. Last week Peter even checked the folder with me.'

She bites her lip. Now she's adding Peter as a kind of ballast. The weight of a man's word, heavier than her own; she can see it in the clearing of Harry's face. It's 2018, for God's sake; are women not to be believed? 'And then two weeks ago,' she continues, 'I bumped into one of my students on my street. Sean Worth. He suffers from anxiety but he's harmless, or at least I think he is. But then last week I thought I saw him outside again, watching the house.'

'Watching the house?' Harry's eyes widen. 'Are you sure it was him?'

She shakes her head. 'It'd be unfair to Sean to say I was sure. But the week before, yes, it was. Last week it looked like him, but he had his hood up, it was dark and I was in the bedroom. I couldn't see him clearly. And by the time I made it onto the street, he'd gone.'

Harry rubs his chin a moment. He looks so much older than Peter, she thinks, considering they were at school together. He is overweight, his cord jacket is too big for him, his hair almost white. 'And you say no one has claimed the poems?'

'I only asked once. Peter said to ignore it. We were hoping whoever it was would get bored. I thought they had, but then last week ... We actually called the police. They took a statement and told us to be vigilant. They've got it on record now, at least.'

'So you've already called the police,' he mutters. 'And you're pretty sure one or two of the poems ... or pieces or whatever ... were planted in your house, possibly by this student?'

'No, not pretty sure. I'm pretty sure he was outside my house, but that doesn't mean he broke in. I intend to ask him today. I don't want to frighten him, so I'm going to handle it myself when I find the right moment. I guess he could simply have followed me home or something. Or been in the area for a completely different reason. I haven't seen anyone outside the house all week, so I wonder if he saw the police car. He's ... a little odd. Kind of lingers and tells me all sorts of stuff, as if he just wants to talk, you know? But I'd say he's harmless. Lonely, maybe.'

'He might have a bit of a crush. It happens, especially with tutors as ... erm ... well, especially with the more youthful and attractive, shall we say?' He coughs, clearly embarrassed. 'But even so, he can't go following you home.' Again, he rubs his chin, checks his watch. 'Right, tell you what. I'll note it on the system. See how it goes today, and in the meantime, I'll try and free myself up and wander along before – two, is it, your class finishes?'

She nods.

'Right. I'll try and pop down, stand at the back for the last ten minutes, how about that? And we'll take it from there.'

'Thank you. Yeah, thanks. That'd be great.'

There is some relief in having spoken to Harry, and to have him take her seriously, if only to know she is not alone at work. But on her way to class, her stomach clenches. The whole thing is going round on a loop, and loops are a classic sign of stress; she knows that from dealing with her mother after her father left – on and on she went, over and over the same ground, expecting to come out with a different conclusion when the only conclusion was the painful truth: she had lost everything.

As for Peter, she has to stop thinking badly of him. He was at work, and apart from anything else, it doesn't make sense that he wrote the poems. Unless ... but there she goes again, round and round. *Stop it, Sam, just bloody stop it.* What she needs is to get on with her job, focus on other people besides herself.

As she rounds the corner, she sees a figure she recognises standing near reception. Sean. Her chest tightens.

'Sean,' she says. 'How are you?'

'Hello, Miss,' he says. Unusually for him, he adds nothing.

They walk on, through to the cafeteria. Lana is sitting at one of the tables, on her own, drinking hot chocolate and scribbling in a notebook, and at the sight, Samantha feels her insides flip.

Sean is still at her elbow. Sod it, she thinks.

'Sean, what brought you to my road the week before last?' She glances at him, sees his eyes dart towards the canteen exit.

'Nothing,' he says. 'I … I was meeting a friend. But she didn't come.'

'A friend?'

He nods. 'But she didn't come.'

'Sean, can I ask you something?' She stops, faces him.

'Yes, Miss.' He stops too, looks down at his tatty trainers.

'Sean, it's not a problem and I'm not cross or anything, but were you outside my house again last week? In the evening, around seven?'

He breathes through his nose, rapidly. His hand flies to the zip of his anorak. He works it up and down, up and down.

'I was just checking you were OK.' He glances up at her through his upper eyelashes. His eyes are blue and sad and she doesn't know what to think.

'Why wouldn't I be OK?'

He shrugs. Still not looking up.

'Sean? Why wouldn't I be OK?' Nothing. 'Sean, can I ask you, have you been in my house?'

This time he does look up. It is no more than a second, but his eyes are wide and scared.

'I would never go in your house,' he says. 'That's breaking and entering. That's trespassing.'

He is telling the truth; she has no idea why she knows this, but she does.

'So that's what you were doing outside my house last week? Checking on me?' She lays her hand softly on the sleeve of his jacket. 'It's OK. I'm not angry. I just want to clear this up. Can you talk about it?'

'I just wanted to make sure you were all right.' He stares at his shoes. All she can see is his greasy hair, his parting a ruler-straight line. 'You're so kind to me and I just wanted … I just wanted to make sure you were safe.'

'Why wouldn't I be safe, Sean?'

He shakes his head but still doesn't look up.

'Sean?'

'You looked scared. In week two. She was …'

'She was what? Who was? Who was what, Sean?'

'Nothing. No one. You said someone had written something about you. You looked scared, so I was worried. I was only trying to make sure you were OK, Miss.' He is breathing deeply, his eyes darting, his hand working his zip so hard she fears it might burst into flames. Poor guy. She has completely stressed him out.

She lets her hand fall. 'Oh, Sean, it's so kind of you to look out for me like that. Thank you.'

He steals a glance, drops his gaze once again. 'That's OK. I wasn't busy.'

'Well, it's really kind. But I don't want you to do that anymore, all right?' She keeps her voice low and gentle. 'I'm not scared, I'm fine. I'm much better now that I know it was you, but if you're waiting outside my house again, that might make me feel scared, even though I know you're only looking out for me. The thing is, we had to call the police last week, and if they catch you there, you'll be in trouble.'

He twitches, begins to move from one foot to the other and back. 'I'm sorry.'

'You don't need to be sorry, Sean. Nothing to be sorry about, all right? Just … just best not do that again, that's all.'

'OK.'

She is about to continue on towards the classroom but stops.

'Did you write those poems, Sean?'

'What poems, Miss?'

'What I mean is, did you write the poem in week one and leave it anonymous?'

'I only wrote my poems with my name on.' He meets her eye. 'For copyright.'

She holds his sad blue eyes with hers. 'All right, Sean. It's OK.'

'Miss?'

'Yes?'

'I'm sorry. I didn't mean to scare you. I won't come near your house again, sorry.'

Daphne arrives and places a multicoloured knitted flower on Samantha's desk.

'I made you a corsage,' she says and smiles. 'I hope you like it.'

'Oh my goodness, thank you!' Samantha inspects the tiny stitches, impossibly neat, the thin green stem, the bright leaves fanning out. Really, it is a thing of wonder. She pins it to the lapel of her coat. 'I love it!'

'You are kind.' Daphne fixes her with her watery stare. 'And kindness is to be encouraged now more than ever.'

For a moment, Samantha is too choked to speak. She has felt her vulnerability as sharp as a blade this week, but there is so much good in the world; she mustn't forget it.

'Emily settled in fine.' Suzanne is at the door. 'Do you want a hand with the desks?'

It occurs to Samantha that Suzanne must have been checking her own child in earlier, as she said she was going to last week, but there is no time to ask about it there and then. Together they arrange the desks into a horseshoe, and as Samantha positions her own desk in the centre, she resolves to say nothing about the villanelle, about the police coming to her home; simply hand out the dialogue pieces and crack on. Whoever is the frustrated would-be author of those mean little poems will get no satisfaction from her.

'So last week we looked at dialogue,' she begins, scanning her students, noting that Tommy is absent. 'But what happens if you go into the dialogue or the action without setting the scene – the where and the who and the what time of day?'

Aisha half raises her hand.

Fuck off, Aisha, she thinks.

'Aisha?' she says, rictus grin fixed to her face.

'If you don't set the scene, the reader doesn't know where they are?' Aisha's eyebrows are keen and diligent. Does the woman have an expression that isn't earnest, for God's sake? Can eyebrows even *be* diligent?

'The reader doesn't know where *the characters* are,' Samantha corrects, pedantically perhaps. 'Or whether it's night or day, or who is there. And if the reader doesn't know where your characters are, what are they wondering?'

'Um, where they are?' Aisha's voice betrays her fear of stating the obvious.

'And if the reader is wondering where they are, who is with them, whether it's three in the morning or five in the afternoon, what is the reader *not* thinking about?' Samantha looks around. 'Suzanne?'

Suzanne blushes, shake her head.

Too soon, Samantha realises. Still too shy. 'Reggie?'

'The … well, the story?'

'Exactly.'

Together they study a scene from *Brooklyn* by Colm Tóibín, one from *Our Man in Havana* by Graham Greene, both Peter's suggestions, and while the Tóibín has a vulnerable young woman at its heart, now it irks her that both authors are men. It could be her raging stress levels, but Peter's help is beginning to seem more like interference to her now, a desire to tell her how to do things, to control how she does them.

'So, clarity is your biggest challenge,' she says. '*You* know what's in your head, you can see it, but you have to remember to let the reader see it too.'

She sets them an exercise: to write a scene around last week's dialogues, focusing on clarity. The class has almost taken her mind off the poems, her first night alone in the house, but when half past one comes, she checks the door, opens it a fraction and looks out. No sign of Harry. Quarter to, ten to. Five to. She peers out once again into the corridor. He isn't coming. He must have been waylaid, as often happens. Everyone in this place is pulled in five different directions at once.

Two o'clock.

Aisha and Jenny mime coffee and Samantha nods. Too right she'll have coffee. She will have coffee and ask the pair of them what the hell is going on. Now that she knows it isn't Sean, it can only be one or other of these two. Or both.

The classroom empties. Pit in her stomach, she flicks through the scenes one by one. There is no anonymous work. She counts them out again, double-checking, then triple-checking, but still there is nothing that shouldn't be there. She picks up the empty folder and, illogically, turns it upside down and shakes it. Seven students were here. Seven pieces of paper. The only other person in this whole circus who isn't here is Peter.

She shakes her head. Nonsense. That idea is nonsense. But even as her mind strays where it shouldn't, part of her almost hopes that this evening, another nasty note will arrive, if only to prove that it isn't her own partner playing some hateful trick.

A hubbub of different languages reaches her from the corridor. She watches the other class file in, led by Gabby, her blonde hair and black-framed glasses whizzing by. Some of the women wear hijabs, one of the men wears a turban, and she wonders what brought them here, how they live, how they cope with so little English.

She should get a move on, she thinks, see what Aisha and Jenny come up with.

CHAPTER 21

In the cafeteria, Aisha is biting into a huge toasted sandwich. Two ropes of melted cheese escape, sending a blob of tomato swinging down like a trapeze. Both she and Jenny are finding this hilarious.

'Hey,' Samantha says, already feeling on the outside.

'We got you a peppermint tea,' Jenny says, wiping her eyes. 'There's sugar on the side. Don't look at Aisha if you're squeamish, it's revolting.'

Aisha raises a hand, grinning through her mouthful of food. Her wrists are so delicate, her fingers long and thin as a pianist's. She is so pretty, even with food all over her face. She could have any man she wanted. Why try and manipulate her way back to Peter?

Samantha sits down, her spine rigid as a pole. 'How's it going?'

'Good, yeah,' Jenny says. 'I've got an interview with a start-up this week, so if you're lucky, you might not see me again.'

'That's great. I mean, that's great if it's a job, not great that you're leaving.'

'Actually, Samantha,' Aisha interrupts. 'I really need to tell you something. I wanted to tell you the other week, but you had to rush off, and then last week you couldn't make it, so I'm going to say it right now in case you have to go.'

Samantha's face heats. 'OK.'

Aisha puts her sandwich on the paper plate and wipes her mouth with a napkin. She glances at Jenny, then back at Samantha. Samantha's stomach clenches – here it comes.

'The other week,' Aisha begins, 'you mentioned you were with a UCL lecturer. As in living with?'

Samantha nods, all speech for the moment quite impossible.

'Well, it's Peter Bridges, isn't it?'

Samantha feels herself blush. 'How would you know that?'

Again, Aisha glances at Jenny, as if to reassure herself that she has permission to continue. 'Well, the thing is, after the very first class, we, um, once we had your name, we, um, we looked you up on Facebook—'

'Not in a creepy way,' Jenny interrupts. 'Just, you know, normal stalking levels.'

'We were only curious,' Aisha continues. 'You seemed so nice and everything, so we just tapped your name in and looked at, literally, three photos.' She turns to Jenny, who nods.

'Literally three or four,' she adds.

'We didn't scroll down your whole history or anything,' Aisha goes on. 'But there was a photo of you and Peter and the baby. You know, about three months ago?'

'Five,' Samantha says quietly. 'Nearer six, actually. It was the week she was born.'

Aisha looks like she's sitting on spikes. 'Yeah, so, the thing is, I didn't know that when I booked onto the course, obviously. I didn't know you'd gone to UCL or read English or anything at all. Well, the college doesn't put the name of the tutor on the course details, so neither of us even knew who it was going to be, did we, Jenny?'

Jenny shakes her head.

'And Jenny didn't even book onto the course until I made her, did you, Jen?'

'Nope. I wasn't planning on doing a course, but when Aisha suggested it, I was, like, yeah, whatever, something to do, you know? I thought it would make a change from mainlining Kit Kats in front of *Loose Women*.' She laughs, as does Aisha.

In her discomfort, Samantha smiles. She doesn't laugh, couldn't even if she wanted to. The photograph of Peter with his arm around Aisha sharpens in her mind. Peter and Aisha, she thinks. Sitting in a tree. K-I-S-S-I-N-G.

'So is that why you wrote the shitty poems?' The question is out before she is aware of herself asking it, of the power in her voice.

Aisha frowns. 'What shitty poems?'

'The clerihew in week one?' Samantha insists. 'Don't you remember I asked about it? Someone wrote a clerihew with my name in it and wouldn't own up to it. Then there was a limerick, a piece of flash fiction. And the villanelle was really impressive, by the way.'

Aisha glances at Jenny, back to Samantha. She shakes her head. In both their eyes, only confusion. Samantha falters.

'What? That's four. There was only one, wasn't there?' Jenny says. 'Why, was it dodgy? You didn't say it was dodgy. Were they all dodgy?'

Jenny's voice floats overhead, but Samantha is staring into Aisha's deep brown eyes. She is staring so hard she can see her own face, pale and small and pathetic.

'Yes, it was … dodgy.' She looks down at her hands. Her nails are bitten, though she can't remember biting them. 'They all were. I didn't mention the other ones. I didn't want to give it any oxygen. Peter said—'

'You've been getting abusive poetry?' Jenny interrupts. 'That's mental abuse. Can we see?'

'It wasn't us,' Aisha says, her voice plaintive, hurt.

Samantha flops back in her chair. Both women are looking at her, and all she can pick up is concern. Their guilt over looking her up on Facebook was palpable; if they knew anything about the poems, she would sense it, surely. But where does that leave her? Where does that leave her and all this poison?

'I'd rather not show you,' she says after a moment, 'if it's all the same. They made me uncomfortable that's all, and we thought that maybe one of them was left in my house, but to be honest, I'm not even sure about that anymore. I just got the heebie-jeebies; forget I said anything.'

But Jenny is leaning forward and looks uncharacteristically serious. She pushes her long red hair behind both ears, something businesslike in the gesture. Her hair is dyed, Samantha realises in that moment. Punk copper rather than natural auburn. And her freckles, even her freckles appear darker, as if they've come out in support.

'Samantha,' she says, her voice deeper, 'if someone is sending you abusive notes, you need to report it. If it's someone from the class—'

'It's hardly abuse. Just words. There's no proof it's anyone from the class.'

'OK, but words are still abuse. It's intimidation. Anything that makes you uncomfortable or frightened is serious. It's abuse no matter how you look at it.' She reaches out her hand, as if to hold Samantha's, but Samantha picks up her cardboard cup.

Abuse. The term is strong, but it soothes something in her. It explains something about the way she's feeling, makes sense of it, gives her the right to feel it, almost.

'If you don't want to show us, that's fine,' Jenny says. 'And just for the record, I can assure you it's neither of us. We only looked you up once we got home, didn't we, Aish? So why would we write anything malicious? But you do need to tell the police.'

'I have,' she says. She will make no mention of Sean. It isn't that she still distrusts Aisha and Jenny; she's just not ready to trust them completely. Simply because someone seems genuine doesn't mean they are. And even if they are genuine in one respect, it doesn't mean they are in all.

Jenny sits back in her chair. 'I hope they catch him and chop his knob off.'

'We don't know it's a man.'

'It will be,' she says, her expression sour. 'It always is, trust me.'

Trust me. That's what Peter always says. And there's that aggression in Jenny too, as in the poems. Samantha shakes her head, shakes the thought away. For a moment, none of them say a thing.

'I need a pee,' Jenny says and disappears in the direction of the ladies'.

Samantha looks at her watch, pulls her satchel strap onto her shoulder and stands. It's only half past two, but she has no idea what to say or where the three of them go from here. She wants more than anything to be alone to think. Maybe write a list of everything that's making her feel so wired. Marcia would know what to do, or at least she would talk it through until Samantha felt better. But Marcia is a blurry memory of something precious lost.

'Don't go,' Aisha says. 'There's something else.'

I know, Samantha almost says, *but I'm too tired to hear it.*

'I used to see Peter,' Aisha says. 'I mean, more than see. We were together. That's why I needed you to know that I didn't know you were teaching this course. I wouldn't want you to think anything … I mean, I'm not here with any darker purpose or anything. And now you've said about the poems, I can't imagine what you must've been thinking.'

'I know,' Samantha replies, sitting back down. 'About you and Peter, I mean.'

'You know? How?' Aisha gives a slow nod. 'He read the names on the homework.'

'No.'

'You mentioned me?'

'No, actually. I found a photograph of the two of you in a drawer.'

'Listen.' Aisha reaches across the table, but again Samantha withdraws her hand.

'You need to know who you're dealing with.' It's Jenny, back from the loo. She plonks herself in her chair and sighs.

The conspiratorial glance passes once again between the two women. Whatever is coming, Samantha has the feeling she's about to be pulled into it, whether she wants to or not.

'Let me tell you how Aisha and I met.' Jenny rests both elbows on the table; her hands weave together in front of her. 'We were in the pub, as we told you. The Marlborough Arms.'

Samantha's stomach churns. Whatever is coming, she doesn't want it in her head, but she's desperate to hear it. And in all of this she has a feeling that she already knows it, the essence of it at least.

'I don't know how we got talking,' Jenny is saying. 'But we were quite pissed, weren't we, Aish? We liked each other, we made each other laugh. We ended up walking the same way to the Tube at Goodge Street. And I don't know exactly how it came out, but Aisha mentioned that she was going out with this guy. She was going through a rough time with him, beginning to think he was a bit of a shit.'

'I was in the second year of a part-time MA,' Aisha says. 'Peter and I started going out in my final year. I graduated, did some crap jobs, and eventually he suggested I do an MA, so I did. I was twenty-six when I met Jenny. I'd been with Peter for five years.'

'So she's talking about this guy.' Jenny takes up the story again. 'And she says he's a lecturer. She tells me he's a little older than her.' She glances at Aisha. 'Mentions his beautiful house, tells me he teaches art history. And before she even said his name, I knew it was Peter.'

Despite herself, Samantha asks, 'How?'

Jenny shakes her head. 'It was obvious. And it was so horrible. I'd met this amazing woman. You know that feeling when you think you're going to be really good friends with someone? Well, that's what I felt, and I think Aisha did too.'

'I didn't. Jenny just stalked me into submission.'

They both crack up. Samantha smiles with as much indulgence as she can muster.

'Why horrible?' she insists. 'Why couldn't you just be friends?'

'Because I knew he was two-timing her. And she was so beautiful and cool and everything, but I didn't know her and I didn't know whether to tell her or whether to just leave it. It would have been easier to say nothing, but I'd had a lot to drink and she gave me this hug and I was, like, mate ...' She rolls her eyes, reliving the moment.

'And she told me,' Aisha says. 'Which I still think was fucking brave.'

'Why?' Samantha's fists are two tight balls, her chest on fire.

Jenny meets her gaze, her eyes a brown-flecked green. 'Because he was two-timing her with me.'

CHAPTER 22

Samantha feels the throb of a pulse at her temple. 'When was this?'

Jenny looks at Aisha, as if to check. 'It was October. October last year?'

Aisha nods. 'It was near the beginning of term, because we'd been to some drinks thing and ended up in the pub. No, hang on, it was the year before, 2016. October, deffo.'

Jenny rolls her eyes. 'It was, wasn't it? Jeez, where does the time go?'

They laugh. But Samantha is blinking hard now, trying to absorb the information without crying. When Peter took her to his house on the hill, when she became special and original, beautiful and intelligent, because he told her that this was what she was, when his deep brown gaze seemed only to focus, only ever to have really focused, on her, he was in fact making two other women feel special and original, beautiful and intelligent. These two women, specifically. The two women sitting opposite her. Sitting opposite her and laughing like it's some big joke while Samantha presses her teeth into her gums and tries to stop herself from smashing into pieces.

The canteen clock reads quarter to three. She should leave, go and get Emily. She is dimly aware that both her hands are being held. Aisha is holding one, Jenny the other.

'Are you all right?' Aisha asks.

She nods. 'I'm fine. It's just … I mean, I know Peter had girlfriends before me. You expect that. I'm a lot younger than him; I knew he hadn't lived like a monk. I'm just …'

She looks to Jenny, then to Aisha. They should hate one another, she thinks. And they should hate her. And she should hate both of them. But here they are, holding hands.

'Can I ask exactly when in October?' she asks.

'It was …' Jenny pulls out her phone, narrows her eyes. 'It was a Tuesday, so let's see … that would've been the … eighteenth.' She looks up. 'Yes, the eighteenth.'

Samantha inhales. She can't speak. She met Peter on the Thursday. Thursday the twentieth of October. Two days later. Two.

'I don't know what to say,' she manages. 'Jenny, I'm sorry. I didn't know—'

Jenny waves her hand. 'I know you didn't. None of us did. Which is why there's no point us shouting and bitching. It's him, Peter, who's the shit here.'

'Don't call him a shit,' Samantha says, her voice louder than she meant. 'He may not have been completely open with me, but that's his past. He has a right to his privacy. He has a right to a past. And he's changed.'

Jenny snorts.

'Don't, Jenny,' Samantha says. 'Seriously. We have a child together. And he asked me to move in with him before I got pregnant. He asked me the first morning we spent together. It was … different.'

Aisha lets go of her hand. 'I know it's hard, and believe me, I feel like the world's biggest bitch for telling you, but it's not different. Do you think you're different because he told you that you were?'

'No! I mean, he did say that, but he … he meant it.' The words sound hollow. She sounds like a schoolgirl.

'Let me guess,' Jenny says. 'He picked you up at a student drinks party.'

'Well, yes, but …' Samantha checks her watch. It is ten to. She should go. She wants to go, but she cannot stand up.

'He picked you up,' Aisha is saying, 'and took you for a drive in the vintage Porsche Carrera.'

'No spoiler,' Jenny chips in. 'Cream leather seats.'

Samantha closes her eyes. She feels sick.

But Aisha hasn't finished and continues with something like relish. 'He took you to a bar. But shock horror, the bar was rammed. So he suggested his place. And he drove you to his incredible house, with his art and his vinyl and his fireplace. And, let me see, he put a record on. Miles Davis's *Kind of Blue*?'

'You got the Miles Davis,' Jenny drawls. 'I got the Coltrane. *A Love Supreme.* I thought it was the most amazing thing I'd ever heard. I thought he was the most sophisticated man I'd ever met, when actually he's no more than a randy dog.'

Dog. *Those men are dogs, they hunt their prey by day.* Samantha stands so quickly her chair falls back, crashes on the floor of the cafeteria. 'I'm sorry, but why the hell are you both here? Why are you so interested in me and Peter? I mean, it's a bit of a coincidence, isn't it, both of you here in this college when I just happen to be your tutor?'

Aisha stands up too, holds up her hands. 'We told you, we didn't know you were teaching that course when we signed up. I signed up for the last one, but it got cancelled.'

Samantha shakes her head. 'I'm sorry, I don't buy that at all. I think you came here so you could … I don't know. I don't know what you're trying to do, the pair of you. I mean, why do you even live round here? That's just … it's just weird.'

'Samantha,' Aisha says. 'I was with Peter for five years. I know this area, I love it. So does Jenny. For the same reasons. Me and Jenny know Richmond and each other because of Peter. If it weren't for him, we'd just be two women who got pissed together in a pub once. We wouldn't have become friends. And when we decided to rent a place together, we looked round here because we liked it, that's all. I know it might seem like a coincidence, but it isn't.

We live here, this is our local college and it was me who fancied a creative-writing course, not an unusual thing for a postgrad with a passion for English. I dragged Jenny along so I'd have a mate to come with me. That's all, I swear to God. There's no way we thought there'd be any connection to Peter, because he works at UCL; he's got nothing to do with this college.' She bends down to help Samantha right the chair. 'Look, I'm sorry. We got carried away. We're in a different place with it all, but we've been where you are now and we shouldn't have—'

'We shouldn't have made light of it.' Jenny is looking up at Samantha with her round green eyes. 'Sorry, Sam, that was well out of order. But everything Aisha says is true. We didn't come here to mess you up or interfere in your life, honestly we didn't, and if you sit down, we'll tell you properly. We're only trying to help, I promise. We just want to make sure your eyes are open. You don't know what he's capable of. Trust us.'

Trust. Fine word. Samantha pulls her satchel strap over her head. The gesture feels petulant already; her cheeks heat with embarrassment at her own angry display. 'Look, things have changed, all right? He told me they'd changed and I believe him. He didn't ask you two to move in, did he? He didn't ask either of you to marry him. And he didn't have a baby then either. I know it's not particularly edifying, but he's moved on from all that now.' Her heart is hammering. Sweat trickles down her sides. She has to get away. She has to get away from their eyes.

'He didn't seduce you the first night, did he?' Aisha is staring at her, her brown eyes almost black, glowing.

'What?' Samantha takes a step back. 'What has that got to do with anything?'

'He didn't sleep with you, did he? That first night?'

'Let me guess,' Jenny interrupts, her voice too loud for Samantha's comfort. 'He asked you all about yourself, told you that you were beautiful and intelligent and generally fucking amazing. Did he offer you the magic pills? Or was it the sprinkles? And the next day, did he take you to see him perform – oops, I mean lecture? And did you watch him and feel like it was all for you, that he was the most incredible person you'd ever met, and now he'd fallen in love with you, with you above everyone else, and you couldn't quite believe it?'

Samantha glances towards Aisha for support, but Aisha's face is motionless.

Samantha backs away. 'He wants me to marry him. It was his idea to have a baby.'

Jenny laughs. But the sheen on her hardened green eyes gives her away. 'That's because when we found out what he was, we both dumped him. Aisha dumped him that night, legend that she is, and I dumped him the next night, and he couldn't fucking believe it, couldn't believe that he, the almighty Professor Bridges, had been rejected. Twice in twenty-four hours.

'And suddenly he was alone and old and he finally understood what it meant to be dropped, and that if it'd happened once, it could happen again and probably *would* happen again. Just like a normal person. He's intelligent enough to know that he's *not* a normal person – he's a very good-looking, very clever little shit. And he knows he's a shit. He panicked, Sam. That's all this is. He's terrified of being alone, can't stand it even for one week. He'd never end a relationship without first starting another. Can't bear not to be admired, desired, revered … he can't bear it. And he found you, all young and lovely and ripe, and he thought he'd knock you up and put a ring on your finger before you—'

But Samantha doesn't hear the rest. She is running across the courtyard towards the crèche, their words landing like bricks in the water, sinking, sinking, down and down, to the dark riverbed of her subconscious where she knows, already knows, they will lurk, waiting for her to stop, waiting for silence, to begin their poisonous decomposition. Peter found her, all young and lovely and ripe, *before her colour changed*. He picked her up the day after

Jenny ended things with him, two days after Aisha, his long-term girlfriend, left him. My God, it's too much to … How can a person move on so quickly? A machine switching to a new power source, oh God oh God, and now this is part of what she knows about him and it's too late to unhear what Aisha has said, what Jenny has said. She cannot unhear it. Cannot unsee their urgent, laughing faces, the blaze of scorned fury in their eyes. She has seen those eyes before, in the face of her own mother, and in some cruel twist, it appears that it is Jenny, bolshie, man-hating Jenny, who wrote those poems, not to get at her, but to get at Peter – her warped revenge for his crimes against women.

She reaches the nursery half weeping with stress. At the sight of her, the nursery assistant's brow wrinkles with confusion. She gets up from the floor and walks slowly towards her.

'Samantha, hello. Are you all right?'

'Sorry I'm late,' Samantha says breathlessly. 'Lost track of time.'

But the nursery nurse is still scrutinising her. 'Did you forget something?'

The blood drains to her feet. The woman's name badge says Gail. She has a cold sore on her top lip.

'I'm here to pick up Emily,' Samantha says, in those last moments of understanding. 'Emily Bridges? My daughter?'

Gail's face clouds. 'Suzanne said you'd asked her to bring her to you. She said you were busy with a student and wanted to feed her yourself.' Her voice falters. 'She had your number in her phone. She said you were mates. You seemed … We called you from her phone but you didn't pick up, so she left a message … She was like *Hi, hon, it's only me*, like you totally knew her, and she said you were busy with the … Didn't she bring her? Oh my God, she didn't. Oh God, I'm so sorry, this is only my sixth week and I've totally messed up. Oh my God, I'm such an idiot, I can't believe I … but I thought you were mates, you seemed like mates … Oh shit, what've I done? I'm so, so sorry. Samantha … Samantha?'

CHAPTER 23

'Help!' Samantha is running across the college courtyard. 'Help!' She is running through the automatic glass doors, into the cafeteria. 'Somebody help me! Help, help, oh my God.'

Aisha and Jenny are running towards her, their mouths two black Os.

'Oh my God, Sam, what's happened?' Aisha reaches for her, takes her in her arms.

'My baby,' Samantha wails, wriggling out of Aisha's embrace. 'Emily. Suzanne's taken Emily, she's stolen her from the crèche, she's taken her, she's taken my baby, she's taken my little girl.'

White heat. Jenny is running towards reception, phone at her ear. 'Police? Hello, yes, police? This is an emergency. A baby has been kidnapped from …'

Samantha is on her knees. They throb with pain. Aisha still has hold of her hand and she too is kneeling, running her thumb over Samantha's knuckles. 'It's OK,' she's saying. 'The police are on their way. They'll track her down in no time; they have all sorts of stuff for that. It's OK, Samantha, just stay calm – they're on their way. We'll find her. We'll find Emily, don't you worry.'

Jenny's feet – her black leather lace-up boots. Samantha looks up into her face, sees only concentration.

'They'll be here any minute.' Jenny is talking to Aisha. 'Get her onto a chair, I'll fetch tea.'

Samantha lets herself be lowered onto a hard plastic chair. She can hear herself moaning. Her leg jiggles. Her nose is running into her mouth. Aisha hands her a tissue. Jenny holds out a steaming takeaway cup. 'It's got sugar in,' she is saying, but Samantha bats it away. Stands. Runs. She is running, out of the glass double doors, back towards the car park.

'Help,' she cries out, to no one. 'Help.' There is a man in the car park. 'Help, excuse me, hello? Have you seen a woman and a baby? In the car park.'

He looks at her, bewildered. 'No, sorry.'

Over an hour has passed since Suzanne took Emily. Over an hour, over an hour, my God. Samantha is running back through the automatic doors, half blind, half deaf, half crazy.

'Samantha!' It's Aisha. She is crying.

Samantha pushes her aside and runs through to the foyer, up the wide college steps, one flight, two, to the manager's office. The door is shut. She doesn't know the code. She bangs on the door with both fists. 'Help,' she calls at the top of her voice. 'Help me!'

The door opens. It is Harry. She collapses onto him. 'Someone's taken my baby. My student Suzanne, she's taken her. She's gone, Harry. Suzanne's got Emily.'

Harry's shirt smells of detergent and sweat.

The floor is blue and white squares.

They rush at her.

She is holding another takeaway cup. She doesn't know if it's tea or coffee. Her face is sticky and she's crying. She's in a hard chair in the manager's office. Her knees still hurt; there is a pain on her forehead, a balled-up tissue in her hand.

A policewoman is crouching at her feet.

'Miss Frayn,' she's saying. 'I'm WPC Townson and this is my colleague PC Davies. You can call me Christine. Can I call you Samantha?'

Samantha puts her hand up to her forehead. A warm, damp lump.

'You've given yourself a right old egg,' says the policewoman – Townson, was it? Townsend?

'Did I faint?'

'Think so. Don't worry, it'll go down. Samantha, love, we need you to tell us exactly what's happened; can you do that for us?'

There's a policeman there too. She remembers now, she saw them arrive. She was already sitting in this chair, or was she down in the foyer? Aisha and Jenny were with her, she's pretty sure. They led her up here. Which means she must have gone back down. She checks her watch. It is half past three.

'Samantha? Samantha, my darling, can you tell us exactly what happened?'

Townson. Her name is Townson. Christine.

'I …' she begins, her voice hoarse. 'I was having a quick cup of tea with a couple of students. We were talking. I realised the time and I went straight to get Em.'

'To the nursery?' The policewoman is writing in a notepad.

'Yes. I'd booked her in till three. I got there at three. I was about a minute late, two tops. And she said that Suzanne had taken her.'

'And by she, you mean …?'

'The nursery girl. Gaynor or Gail, I think her name is.'

The policewoman looks up at her colleague. 'Do you want to check the nursery?'

Harry leaves with the PC.

The WPC, Christine, is still writing. 'And who's Suzanne, love?' She touches Samantha's arm lightly. 'Who's Suzanne? Samantha, can you tell us who Suzanne is, darling?'

'She's one of my students. She was friendly with the nursery nurse. I thought she was dropping off her own child today.' Samantha stops, hand flying to her mouth. A high-pitched noise comes out of her mouth. 'Oh my God. She doesn't have a child. She doesn't have one, does she?'

'We don't know that.' The WPC has got up from the floor and is looking at Harry. Harry is back. He's right there. She cocks her head, talks into her radio. 'Davies? Yeah, mate, can you find out if this Suzanne left with another child besides Emily? Cheers.' She sits beside Samantha on another orange plastic chair. Her shoes are black and big. Jenny's shoes are there too – black, big. And Aisha's shoes. Aisha's shoes are red ankle boots.

'Can you give us her full name, Samantha?'

Samantha looks up, into the pale brown eyes of the police-woman. She knows this woman gave her name, moments ago, but she cannot now remember what it is.

'Suzanne Lewis,' she says. 'I know it's that because the first week I saw it on the register as C. S. Lewis and I thought that was funny, you know, because of C. S. Lewis the writer, and then when she introduced herself as Suzanne, I thought, ah, she obviously uses her middle name, you know? Like some people do if they prefer it or whatever. I didn't think anything more about it. I don't know her first name. Will you still be able to find her? Will you still be able to find her if you don't know her first name?' She looks up. Harry is standing with his hand on Penny Mackay's shoulder. Penny is sitting at his desk, using his computer. Their faces are set, serious.

'All right, so we have an address,' Penny says. She leans forward, peers at the screen. 'It's twenty-two Rosebush Road. That's just on Richmond Hill. She won't be far.'

Samantha shakes her head, sniffs. 'That's my address. That's where I live.'

The air thins.

'Do you have a registration number for her car?' the police-woman asks Penny, her tone preternaturally calm.

Penny shakes her head. 'We wouldn't have that information, sorry. I have her first name, though. It's Charlotte.'

'Do you have CCTV? We'll need that as soon as possible.'

Samantha bursts into tears.

The policewoman has crouched down again, is looking up at her. 'Samantha? I know it's hard, but I need you to stay calm if you can. Can you tell us anything about this Suzanne Lewis that might help us?'

Samantha tries to think. There is a tissue in her hand. She uses it to dry her eyes, blow her nose. 'She was very quiet. She chatted to me last week at the nursery and persuaded me to hand Emily over to her. I let her have a hold. It was just a hold. Most women want a hold of a baby; I didn't think anything of it. The nursery staff were there – I didn't think there was any harm. She said she'd settle Emily while I did my photocopying. The nursery nurse was right there, there was no risk, I didn't do anything risky, I don't think … then this week I was rushing to see Harry about some … about … Oh my God.' She pushes her face into her hands. Her fingers are slick with tears.

'Samantha?'

'There were some poems. Someone was writing dodgy poems and handing them in. They weren't, like, death threats or anything, but they were quite menacing and they were getting to me a bit … and I think Suzanne … It must be Suzanne … I think she's been writing weird things about me and Peter.'

'Slow down.' The policewoman is beside her. 'She's been writing notes to you?'

'Not notes. Poems. I was teaching creative writing. I got them to write these simple poem forms in class. Then when I looked through them, there was one extra and I didn't know who had written it and no one would own up. But I didn't think it was her. She was so quiet. I never thought it was her. But then someone left one in our house and at that point we called the police. And you're saying she knew our address …'

'You've already had the police out for this?'

Samantha's neck prickles with heat. 'Last week. Last Tuesday evening. They took a statement. Then this morning I saw Harry about it. It was creeping me out but I thought it was …' She glances at Aisha and Jenny. 'I thought it was someone else, an ex-girlfriend having a go. I didn't think … I didn't think it was Suzanne. I thought it was Sean for a bit. Another student. But it wasn't him, it was Suzanne, it's obvious. And now she's got Emily, oh my God.'

'There, there, love.' The WPC offers her another tissue. 'Have you got these poems, love? Do you think you can find them for me?'

Snivelling, wiping her nose and eyes, Samantha digs out the folder from her bag. She takes out the sheets and hands them over. The WPC stands up, consults with her colleague, who has returned. Samantha hears her say, 'Scan these and send them,' but that's all she hears, and then the policewoman is on her haunches, at her feet once again.

'All right, Samantha. What's going to happen now is that we'll have a look at the CCTV, plus we've got her name so we can find her car details that way too and put a trace on it, OK? She'll appear, don't you worry. We'll find her before she gets too far, all right?'

'OK,' Samantha says. 'I need to call Peter, my partner.'

'Is he near?'

'No, he's away. I just need to call him.'

'You do that, darling.' The policewoman stands up, walks away. Samantha hears her radio crackle, hears her talk into it, though not what she says.

She calls Peter. Jenny is sitting next to her. Samantha can't remember her sitting down. 'It's all right,' she's saying. 'We're right here. We're not going anywhere.'

Peter's phone is off.

Samantha finds Jenny's green eyes with hers. 'It's not going through,' she says. 'He's probably at the conference by now.'

'He's away?'

'Yes.'

'Did he say whereabouts he was going?'

She shakes her head. Peter was on the front step only this morning. He said he shouldn't go. She told him he must. A conference, he said. That way he has of seeming to give the whole story. A net to catch the sense, let the truth run through. Samantha doesn't like the look that just passed between Jenny and Aisha. Just because he cheated on them doesn't mean …

'He *is* at a conference,' she says. 'I just forgot where he said, that's all. He's back tomorrow. I didn't think to write it down. I didn't think it mattered.'

Peter didn't say where he was going. She calls him again. This time leaves a message.

'Peter, it's me. Emily is missing. Peter, she's been taken.' What little remains of her voice falters, cracks. 'I'm with the police. You have to call me urgently. Urgently, Peter.'

She rings off.

Jenny and Aisha have stood up. They're talking to the WPC. Seeing Samantha look up at them, they break apart.

'I need you to give me Peter's car reg if you can, love, all right?' the policewoman says. 'Then we're going to take you home. Your friends are coming with us. We'll stay with you until we see where we're up to, all right? Do you think you can stand up for me?'

CHAPTER 24

Outside, bright white cloud. She screws up her eyes against the glare. The others lead her to the police car. She ducks into the back seat, feels a hand warm on the top of her head. She is in the back seat, Jenny and Aisha either side of her. They are holding her hands again, as if she is a child. The car is moving. Richmond flashes by.

They hit the Odeon roundabout, head up the hill. She closes her eyes, feels every lurch and swing. The graunch of the handbrake. They are outside her house.

Someone has her satchel. The policewoman is unlocking her front door. Suzanne Lewis has been here, she thinks. She walked into my house and left her sick work on the table. She pretended to be shy. And now she has Emily, the one true thing, the only true thing, in Samantha's life.

The WPC is beckoning her into her own house.

'What's your name again?' Samantha asks. 'I'm sorry, I'm a bit …'

'That's all right, darling. It's Christine.'

'Christine. Yes, of course. Thanks.'

It's chilly in the hall. Freezing. She bursts into tears.

'I can't be here,' she cries. 'I can't sit here and wait, I can't. I have to find her. I have to do something.'

She tries to run out, but Christine and Jenny are holding her by the arms.

'Let the police do their job,' Jenny says softly. The two women guide her into the living room, ease her down onto the sofa. 'I'll put the heating on.'

'It's OK,' Aisha says from the doorway. 'I'll do it.'

'The timer's in the—' Samantha stops. Aisha and Jenny know where the timer is. They know this house. They have both slept here, eaten here, listened to music here. And the rest. With Peter.

Peter only asked her to live with him because he is afraid of growing old alone. That's what Jenny said. He was dumped by two women just as he was nearing forty. This caused a crisis. Yes. It makes sudden and perfect sense. He met Samantha the next day. Samantha's father had a wife and family and he threw it away for sex. Peter didn't have a wife or a family. She, Samantha, is Peter's family, his future, but she is also his crisis. Just as that silly schoolgirl was her father's. Samantha is a thing. She is one of Peter's *things*: the vintage car, the retro music, the old-fashioned log fire. The young wife.

The career, the status, the credentials. The seduction. The wonder, letting her fall asleep untouched on the couch. It wasn't special – she sees that now. She wasn't, was never, special. It was no more than *technique*. Modus operandi. A cliché. Samantha is a cliché. She is her own grim history repeating itself, no more than a flash in some warped mirror. She is a fool, a child. And now Emily is gone. In her stress and confusion, Samantha thought Peter's ex-girlfriend might have written those poems. She even thought *he* was capable of such a thing. He didn't do it, no. But he is morally capable of it.

Otherwise why did she think it?

Christine's radio crackles. She wanders out of the room, neck pressed to her shoulder. Aisha comes in with some amber liquid in a low crystal goblet.

'Brandy,' she says. 'Peter would want you to use the correct glass.'

It is supposed to be a joke, to ease the tension. Samantha knows that, in some distant part of her brain that doesn't reach her mouth. Wordlessly she takes the glass from Aisha's hands. Sips, feels the fire trace its way down her gullet.

'Have you heard from him?' Aisha perches on the armchair.

Samantha shakes her head. She doesn't want conversation, doesn't want Jenny or Aisha to tell her any more about Professor Bridges.

'That picture's new.' Jenny nods to the ink sketch of the trumpeter on the wall.

'Peter drew it.' Samantha sips her brandy, closes her eyes to its heat. How quiet they all are. She is so tired. She could lie down and sleep, block out the world until someone wakes her up and says, *Hey, we've found her, we've found your little girl.*

'He always fancied himself as a bit of an artist,' Jenny says.

'He's good.' Samantha has the impression of watching herself saying this, though she can't say where she is exactly. 'He knows so much about … about everything.'

'Though perhaps not about how to treat people.'

'Please, Jenny.' Samantha opens her eyes, holds up her hand. 'He's with me now and we have a child. He cheated on you both and I'm sorry, but as I keep telling you, he's changed – honestly he has.'

'And you're one hundred per cent sure about that?'

She scrutinises Jenny. What the hell does she want from this? What could she possible stand to gain? Will she not be satisfied until Samantha has not one shred of dignity left?

She steels herself, meets Jenny's eye. 'I'm ninety-nine per cent sure and that's enough. It's all anyone ever is. Look, my dad cheated on my mum with a younger woman and he dated other women after that fell through. But he's met someone else now, they're having a baby and he's left all that nonsense behind him. He has a second chance. People need a second chance. And I'm Peter's.'

Her father. Well, well. How odd that she should find herself arguing his corner now.

Christine strides back into the living room. 'They've got Ms Lewis's registration number,' she says. 'They'll put a trace on the vehicle now. A local unit's been sent to her home. Hopefully we'll hear something in the next hour or two. She's not local. Lancashire, apparently. Ormskirk. Do you know anyone up that way? Any relatives, anyone who'd have a reason to do this? Any connections to that area at all?'

Samantha shakes her head. 'No. No one. Will they find her?'

Christine gives a cautious smile. 'I can't guarantee anything, darling. But she's got no criminal record. She might have a history of depression or something; we'll have to wait and see. What I'm saying is, she's not a pro. She's not trafficking, by the looks of it, so I'd say they've got a bloody good chance. Honestly, unhappiness does terrible things to people.' She shakes her head. 'We see it a lot. Often, it's not evil or malice or what have you. It's sadness. I tell you, enough sadness in your life'll drive you nuts. Something bad happens to you … Anyway, as I say, there's a bloody good chance.'

Samantha rubs her face with her hands. A bloody good chance is not enough, but there is nothing to do but wait. Aisha is cleaning out the grate with the little iron brush. She screws up rolls of newspaper and lays them out, eight of them, arranges kindling around them. Samantha feels a heaviness in her bones. She knows without any doubt that Peter showed Aisha how to do this, as he has shown her. No other way is permitted. As with so many things, Peter's way is the best way. The only way. Those who do things differently – buy Lego for their babies, eat in chain restaurants, drink coffee from popular American coffee sellers – are morons, nothing but morons. Really, he can be quite obnoxious.

Aisha puts a match to the paper. She waits, as Samantha knows she will, for the requisite two minutes before placing a small log carefully on top. After that, she will replace the fire guard.

And she does.

Christine asks if anyone wants coffee or tea. Samantha tells her she'll make it but is shushed by Jenny, who leaves the living room to join Christine in the kitchen. Perhaps it is better not to be in the kitchen, watching Jenny negotiate the cupboards with practised ease. Everything in its place and a place for everything.

'I'm so sorry we stressed you out about Peter.' Aisha has come to sit beside her on the sofa. 'It was with good intentions, I promise. You're probably right, he's probably turned a corner. We shouldn't have slagged him off like that. We got carried away.'

'That's all right.'

Aisha opens her mouth – an intake of breath. 'It's just, there's—'

'Aisha?' Samantha feels her blood heat. 'You need to stop talking, all right?' Anger has made her voice loud, deep. 'I've lost my kid. You get that, don't you? I've lost my baby, so you and Jenny need to stop fucking talking, all right? I don't give a shit, frankly, about you and your scorned-woman agenda, all right? My baby is missing and I don't know if I'll ever see her again, so if you don't mind, I need you to stop. I really need you to shut the fuck up.'

Visibly chastened, Aisha gets up. 'I'm sorry. I didn't mean—'

'You didn't mean, you didn't mean … Why don't you and Jenny just fuck off, actually? Fuck off and leave me alone.'

Samantha's face burns. She doesn't, cannot look up. Shocked silence rushes at her. She senses Aisha stealing out of the room. Minutes later, in a small, subdued voice, she calls goodbye from the living-room door. Rustling, whispers in the hallway, the latch. At the click of the front door closing, Samantha shuts her eyes a moment in relief. Madwomen, the pair of them.

Christine comes to sit with her on the sofa.

'I told her to fuck off,' Samantha says.

'Apparently.' Christine pats her leg. 'Don't worry about it, she'll understand.'

'I lost my temper.'

'Don't worry about it.'

It is better, now, with this woman she doesn't know, who is here only in a professional capacity, whose motives Samantha doesn't have to guess at. It is almost calm.

'Listen,' Christine says. 'They've spoken to most of your students over the phone. PC Davies, do you remember him from the office? He made a house call to Mr Worth and had a chat.'

'Sean?'

'Sean Worth, yes. He admitted to being outside your house last week and the week before. He was worried about you because he'd been sitting next to Suzanne, he said, and he'd seen her writing mean things on her notepad.'

'What things?'

'Just words, he said, and some doodles. He didn't see her write anything specifically about you, but he said that when you mentioned the poem, he was worried. He followed her to the car park and took a note of her registration and went to check if her car was anywhere near your house. He said he saw it parked in the next street.'

That is so Sean, Samantha thinks. The precision of it.

'Oh, Sean,' she says, tears spilling.

Christine pulls out yet another tissue. 'Second thoughts, have the lot,' she says, handing over the whole packet. 'He's got a bit of a soft spot for you, I think.'

Samantha shakes her head, tries to take it in. 'He tried to tell me. He started to say something but then he got all muddled and stressed.'

Christine nods. 'Could be that he wanted to tell you but couldn't find the words, do you know what I mean? Perhaps he didn't want to cause trouble, you never know. He's quite highly strung, apparently. Anyway, it's looking likely that Suzanne's your dodgy poet, although we can't know until we hear what she's got to say, obviously.'

'Poor Sean. Bless him.'

Christine sighs. 'Like you say, bless him. Might not have gone about it in the right way, but his heart was in the right place, wasn't it?'

'It was.'

For a while, Samantha and Christine sit in companionable silence. A siren out on the street causes Samantha to run over to the window, listen to the atonal whine as it passes. She sees Emily in the ambulance, tiny and helpless on a white stretcher, tubes up her nose, a needle in her arm, paramedics with set faces bent over her fragile form. A strange growl escapes her. She buries her face in her hands.

'Come on, love.' Christine puts an arm around her and leads her away, back to the sofa. 'Try and stay calm if you can.'

Minutes become hours. She calls Peter again, but his phone is still off. She has left three messages. The sky darkens. Christine asks if she could eat something. She shakes her head, tells her to help herself. A moment later, there are sandwiches on a plate on the coffee table. Samantha stares at them. There is tea too. It is sweet, and she drinks in sips while the bread triangles harden and curl. Time is slipping. It has been slipping since the nursery assistant frowned at her and asked if she'd forgotten something.

The police radio crackles. Christine dips her head. Her trousers make swishing sounds as she strides out of the room. The living-room door clicks shut. Silence but for the occasional crackle from the fire.

Samantha presses her face to her knees. Cradles the back of her head. She hears the door handle rattle, the hinge creak. Sees the tips of Christine's black shoes.

'Thank God for CCTV, eh?' she says. 'Samantha, they've found her.'

CHAPTER 25

The ANPR picked up a red Toyota Yaris on the M58, Christine tells her once she has calmed down, once she's stopped crying loud, messy tears of relief. The police tailed the vehicle and pulled the driver over on the A570 after she'd left the motorway at Junction 3 in the direction of Ormskirk. Emily was found safe and well in the back seat. The suspect, Charlotte Suzanne Lewis, was arrested at the scene and has been taken into custody.

'Can I go to her?' Samantha asks.

Christine shakes her head. 'They'll bring her to you, love. They're on their way.'

Samantha can't stop crying. Christine keeps her arm around her, tells her over and over that everything will be all right.

'Do you want to call your partner?' she asks after a moment.

'Yes. Yes, thanks.'

But Peter's phone is still off. Anger explodes in her chest. Where the hell is he and why isn't he picking up? It's been hours. She calls back, leaves a message.

'Peter, it's me again. It's after eight.' Her voice cracks. The flashing thought comes to her – she should leave him to stew, let him suffer, suffer like she has, but she pushes it aside and goes on. 'Emily's safe. The police have found her and they're bringing her home.'

Christine takes updates over the police radio. 'They've taken Suzanne in for questioning. She's cooperating.'

'Why?' Samantha asks. 'Why did she do it?'

Christine shakes her head. 'We won't know until she gives her statement. Sounds like she had some sort of episode. Not sure if there was any logic to it. We just need to be grateful it didn't go any further.'

They leave that there.

'She planned it,' Samantha says after a moment, the thought crystallising as the words leave her. 'Last week she was getting cosy with the nursery staff. And with me. The first time she saw me with Emily, she knew her name, I'm sure she said her name … or maybe she didn't, oh, I don't know! But she made sure the nursery girl saw us together, you know, chatting like friends.' Her face burns with realisation. 'I wondered why she was being so familiar when she'd been so quiet in class. She was getting more confident, maybe preferred being outside the classroom, that's all I thought. Oh my God.'

'We don't know that. Let's see what she has to say, eh?'

Samantha's phone rings. Peter.

'Sam?'

'Where the hell have you been?' She bursts into tears, her voice shrill. 'I've been out of my mind. Peter; it's been hours. Where the hell were you?'

'Calm down, Sam. It's been stressful for you, I understand that.' Peter's voice does not change, not in pitch, not in volume. He sounds exactly as he would if he were ordering a meal or attending to an innocuous yet irritating enquiry. 'I was in a conference,' he continues with dogged calm. 'I never have my phone on if I'm lecturing, you know that.'

'She took Em,' Samantha sobs. 'She took our baby, Peter. I thought I'd never see her again. And you were nowhere …' She is gasping for air, the words a slurred mess. Christine gives her shoulder a squeeze.

'What happened exactly?' Peter asks. 'Where is she now?'

'They're bringing her home.'

'Who? The police?'

'Yes.' She can't stop her nose from running, her eyes from leaking down her face. Fat tears run into her blouse, her bra. Peter's voice is a switch, a valve. One word from him and relief is pouring endlessly from her. Everything she's heard about him today is meaningless. It's in the past. What matters, all that matters, is that their child is safe and Peter will be here soon.

'Where was she?' he asks. 'Who took her?'

'Suzanne, one of my students. Emily was in the crèche. Look, just come home. We can talk about it when you get here.'

'I'm in the car now. I'll be there by ten, latest. Have you got someone with you?'

'Christine. She's the policewoman. Just get here, Peter. I need you.'

Samantha rings off, buries her face in her hands. Christine rubs her shoulders, shushes her, tells her it's all over. But something is knocking at her, the branch against the kitchen window of the farm. Some tenebrous thing: *tap, tap, tap.*

'Excuse me a moment,' she says and leaves Christine on the couch.

Tap, tap, tap. Suzanne's earnest expression – *Do you want me to make sure she's settled?* Something in the set of her eyes, her brow. Her chin, perhaps, when she turned to the side. Something.

In their bedroom, Samantha opens Peter's bedside cabinet drawer and pulls the photo wallet from beneath the rest. *Tap, tap, tap.* The branch knocks louder, quicker against the darkened pane. She knows which picture she's looking for. She knows exactly. And she finds it.

Twenty schoolgirls stand around an adored, good-looking young teacher. Samantha stands up, walks to where the overhead light is brightest, holds the photograph under it. She looks. She looks and looks. Twenty schoolgirls, having the time of their lives. The handsome teacher, arms around them. A school trip to York, a day out – laughs and larks, trying a little cheek because you're not in the classroom now. It's not so long since Samantha herself was that age. *Hey, sir, what's your first name? Hey, sir, how old are you? Sir, have you got a girlfriend?*

One girl is not looking at the camera. One girl is looking at Mr Bridges. She is laughing with shiny-eyed delight. The line of her jaw, the profile of her nose … The handsome teacher has his arm around her around her around her; he has chosen her, oh the bliss.

'Suzanne,' Samantha whispers into the silent room. 'Suzanne Lewis.'

She sinks onto the bed. In the photograph, Suzanne's hair is darker. She is fuller in the face. But her thin shoulders are the same, her white knees protruding from her grey school skirt rather plump. She is pretty. She is attractive. This is not, has never been, about a jilted girlfriend. This is about something else – a teenage crush turned sour? That's not enough, is it? Not nearly enough to sign up for a class halfway across the country, drive hundreds of miles, write poisonous poems, kidnap a living, breathing baby. Suzanne could have written notes and posted them if she'd wanted. She knew their address, used it to enrol. But that wasn't enough for her. She must have wanted to progress from leaving the pages in the folder to delivering her handiwork personally, taking the intimidation up a notch each time. It's so bloody extreme.

Peter said he left secondary teaching when his father died. He gave Samantha to understand that his wealth handed him a new opportunity, that his father dying was the reason for his career change. *Tell them you hope to be published next year.* This is his brand of truth. Tell someone something with enough conviction and they'll either fill in the rest or forget to ask. Opportunities cannot have been rare for Peter Bridges, with his private education and his familial wealth and his beautiful, beautiful face. He would not have had to wait until his father died to change career. So is *this* why he changed? These girls look no older than fifteen. They are children.

What to think, what to think. She is full of boiling water. Frantic thoughts bubble and pop to nothing. She has the same precipitous feeling as when he first asked her to come home with him, except now she is on the edge of an abyss. This dark hole is her partner's past. The past life of her lover, the father of her child, the man who wants to marry her. This is Peter's less artful history come back to haunt not just him but Emily and her too. It's possible she and her daughter are but collateral damage in other harm done long, long ago. Peter is the bullseye, but the dart pierces where the dart lands, and so far he has not felt the slightest prick.

'Bastard,' she mutters. Abuser, she does not say.

She replaces the photographs exactly where they were. Visits the bathroom then makes her way back downstairs. What she really wants to do is turn the house upside down, looking if not for skeletons then at least for bones. She has become suddenly adept at piecing together half-told stories. And it would help her pass the agonising time waiting for Emily to come home.

'Christine,' she begins while still in the hallway. 'There's no need for you to stay if you've got other things to do. I mean, you must have finished your shift by now.' She stops at the doorway, pats the door jamb, leans against it. 'Really, I'll fine now. Peter's on his way.'

'Oh, it's all right,' Christine replies. 'I'll wait until they get here with little Emily. Or Peter, whoever arrives first.'

Later, then. It's a waiting game now.

The police are first. Samantha has been trying to watch television in the snug but has not taken in a single scene. Christine knocks, opens the door.

'Samantha, love,' she says in a low, quiet voice. 'They're here.'

Samantha is out of her seat. She is running barefoot over the black-and-white floor of the hall, out onto the front path, into the cold, surreal night.

'Emily!' Her baby's name is shrill in the chilly air.

A WPC gets out of the passenger side. The street lamp throws its vanilla light onto her cropped blonde hair, her skin pale as porcelain.

'Samantha,' she says, smiling. 'Don't worry, she's fine. Your little girl is fine.' She has a northern accent. Like Suzanne's. She pulls open the back door of the patrol car. 'We gave her some formula and she's slept all the way home.'

Samantha's throat blocks. A whimper escapes her. Her fingertips are cold against her mouth.

The WPC reaches in, pulls out the car seat. In it, Emily, asleep, as if nothing has happened.

Samantha's legs fold beneath her. She collapses against Christine's warm, solid form.

'You see,' Christine says softly, holding on to her. 'Told you she'd be all right.'

'Thank you,' Samantha sobs into her hands. 'Thank you all so much.'

CHAPTER 26

The police have gone. In the firelight, Samantha feeds her little girl, weeping intermittently. On the coffee table is her laptop, which she pulls towards her. It's awkward – her back is stiff from all the trauma – but she manages. On the back of the photograph was written *St Catherine's*. She googles St Catherine's School, Ormskirk. Nothing comes up. She tries the same school, widens the search to Merseyside. Nothing. She googles Ormskirk, discovers it's in Lancashire, not Merseyside, and tries again. Nothing. She tries the school together with Lancashire, gets a school in Edge Hill. It must be that one, though there is no useful information. She tries the school, the town and Peter's name. The turn of the millennium. She herself was only a few years old. Again, nothing. No news reports, no scandal, no information.

Emily rolls away from the breast, sated. Samantha lies cuddled up beside her under a blanket on the sofa, stroking her soft head.

'I'm not letting you out of my sight again,' she whispers, pressing her lips to Emily's button nose. 'Oh my darling. My darling, darling girl.'

The deep roar of a car engine. She opens her eyes, hears the engine cut. Peter. She is still on the sofa, Emily asleep beside her. The rattle of a key in the lock.

'Peter,' she mumbles, blinking, rubbing at her eyes. Her mouth is dry and stale. Her face is sticky. Her shoulders are sore and stiff. When she sits upright, she has the impression of hot fluid draining down through her bones, through her arms and legs, out through her feet.

'Sam.' Peter is at the door of the living room. Another step and he is by her side, holding her hand, kissing her on the head, kissing Emily, who is still asleep. Samantha thought she'd done all her weeping, but she has not.

'Don't cry,' he says. 'Don't cry, my love. It's over. I'm here now. You're safe.'

For several minutes, they cling to one another in silence, until Peter eases himself away.

'Long drive,' he says. 'Need to use the little boys' room.'

She hears the door, his cough, even hears the stream of pee, the flush, the tap, the door again. The sounds comfort her. They are his sounds. His footsteps don't return but go instead into the kitchen. The chink of glasses, the roll of the runners on the cutlery drawer. She checks her watch and sees that it's almost midnight. It is so late to be pouring a drink. She doesn't know if his dependency should worry her. And what has happened is so utterly traumatic, the idea of their evening ritual, performed as if life were normal, almost offends her.

She waits, and then there he is, a glass of red in each hand.

'Here.' He hands one to her and goes over to the fire to stoke it. Throws on a couple more logs before coming to sit beside her and the baby again.

'It's so late,' she says. She wonders if she should lift Emily from the sofa, but for the moment, she cannot bear for her to be out of sight.

'Traffic was hideous.' He drinks, a long slug, sets his glass down. 'So, start from the beginning. Tell me everything.'

She tells him, though not everything. She didn't plan to be sparse with the facts, but in the moment, it is what she does. It is his brand of the truth, she thinks. She has learnt it from him.

She is glad that he is here, she is. But trust will have to be built by degrees.

She tells him that two students came home with her and the policewoman, that they stayed a while. She does not mention their names, nor does she tell him about the photograph of Suzanne. At a certain point, it occurs to her that she is leading up to the revelation of Suzanne's full name, and that when she tells him, she will be watching his face.

And so the moment comes.

'They've taken her in for questioning,' she says. 'They said she'd been cooperative from the outset. Christine said it looked like a rash act of madness. An episode, she said. But I haven't heard anything yet.'

He takes a long, slow slug of wine. 'Her name was Suzanne, you said? And she'd come all the way from Ormskirk?'

'Ormskirk, yes.' Samantha says. 'It's in Lancashire. Not that far from Edge Hill.' She glances at him. Nothing.

'And did you get a surname?'

'Lewis. Suzanne is actually her middle name. Her full name is Charlotte Suzanne Lewis.'

He frowns, appears to chew his cheek. He takes another sip of wine, coughs, as if it has gone down the wrong way.

'Charlotte Lewis,' Samantha says. 'My guess is she used her middle name on the course in case I talked about her at home.'

Peter coughs again into his fist. 'What do you mean?' He is no longer looking at her.

'I mean, I think she intended a kind of slow-drip effect: to unsettle first, then unnerve, then full-on freak us out. Well, you.'

Their eyes meet. In his, something flickers.

'You knew her,' she says. 'Didn't you?'

His mouth presses tight, his forehead creases. 'Knew her? What gives you that impression?'

'Well, let's see. The details in the poems? The fact that the last one was a spoof of your favourite poet. That would suggest she knew you reasonably well. Possibly even knew that it was the poem you read at your father's funeral and chose it for that reason, to really get under your skin. So I'm guessing she knew you around the time of your father's death, when you were teaching in a secondary school. St Catherine's.'

'Sam, what are you talking about? You're being cryptic and it's actually really irritating. If you've got something you want to accuse me of, then come out and say it. I've had a long day and I'm not in the mood for riddles, frankly.'

'Riddles? Have you any idea how pompous you sound? This isn't a riddle, Peter. Not to you. I'm the one trying to figure out riddles here. You know exactly who I'm talking about. I don't believe for one second you don't recognise her name. Charlotte Lewis. Charlotte, Charlie, Lottie, whatever she called herself. Your former pupil. St Catherine's School. Peter, it's almost midnight, I've been to hell and back and I'm very, very tired. So can we just lay our cards on the table for once? All of them.'

'All right.' It is the first time she has heard him raise his voice. His arms fly up; the palms of his hands flash like wings. But no sooner has he done this than he regains that immutable control once again. 'All right,' he repeats, more quietly, picking an imaginary speck from his navy chinos. 'It's not an episode I'm particularly proud of.'

'Well it's an episode that has had some pretty serious repercussions for your partner and your daughter, so I think you owe me an explanation, don't you?'

'All right. It was a long time ago. A very long time ago. I was very young and I behaved … irresponsibly. My father was dying. I was stressed. Lottie was … she was so full of life. She was an antidote to the death I could feel all around me. I'd lost my mother, I don't have any siblings and Lottie was … she was silly and funny and she adored me. I didn't seduce her. If anything, she seduced me.'

'How old was she, Peter?'

He stretches his neck, opens his mouth wide, as if to realign his jaw. 'She was sixteen when I left.'

'Peter.'

'All right. But she was.'

'She was a child. A child does not seduce a man. Even at sixteen, she was still a child, supposedly in your care.'

He pushes his fingers through his hair. It is thinner even than last year, she thinks, but still so brown. 'There was nothing childlike about her, believe me.'

She takes a step towards him, close enough to feel the heat of his breath on her face. 'She was a child,' she repeats, her heart battering. 'You abused her. You abused your position of trust. You do get that, don't you?'

He grabs hold of her arm. His fingers dig in, hurt.

She tries to step back, but he has tight hold of her, shakes her so that she staggers first back then forward. Her face bumps against his chest; she cowers.

'Look at me.' He shakes her again by the wrist.

She looks up; his dark eyes are almost black – red-rimmed, mad.

'I get it,' he spits through clenched teeth.

Another second, two. He lets go.

She reels backwards, rubbing at her arm. Her legs are trembling and already a hint of blue has started to cloud the red marks on the inside of her wrist. Peter has turned away from her. He is leaning against the fireplace as if exhausted, one hand pushing over and over through his hair.

'We didn't …' he says. 'We weren't … we didn't *consummate* our relationship fully until she was sixteen, not that it's anyone's business but mine.' He swings round to face her, his mouth an ugly rectangle, hair sticking up strangely. 'Honestly, you appear to be suggesting that I was a dirty old man, but I wasn't that much older than her. For God's sake, it didn't even last that long.'

'Did you bring her here?' Her own voice sounds chastened, even to her.

His mouth flattens. He glances towards the fire. 'Once. Once, yes. But it was a long time ago. To be honest, I'd pretty much forgotten all about it.'

'She hasn't though, has she?'

'Apparently not.'

For a moment, neither of them speaks.

'So,' Samantha begins – carefully. 'Why would she take our baby?'

'I have no idea.'

'You told me you left secondary teaching because your father died. Is that true? I'm guessing not. I assume *she's* why you left.'

Peter shakes his head. His hands are on his hips. He gives a weary sigh.

'Peter?' she insists. 'You told me it was because your father died.'

'I told you I left teaching *when* my father died. I didn't say it was the reason.' That ugly rectangle again: Peter's mouth, spitting its own particular brand of truth. It's possible he said exactly that; Samantha cannot now remember the exact wording. All she knows is that he gave her to understand that his father's death precipitated his career change. And he knows it.

'So why *did* you leave?' Gingerly she lowers herself onto the sofa, in the hope that he too will sit down. It feels safer to do this, to try to take the heat out of this ... whatever this is. 'Did someone find out? Were you prosecuted?' She gasps. 'Peter, are you on the sex offenders register?'

'For Christ's sake, Sam!' He slams his hand hard on the coffee table.

Emily flinches, gives a soft cry. Samantha pulls her into her arms, unsure who needs the comfort most. Never, never has she seen Peter like this. Though she is less afraid of him now than she was a moment ago.

'Don't raise your voice at me,' she says quietly. 'You're bigger than me and stronger than me. It's intimidatory.'

'Don't be ridiculous. I'd never intimidate you. I'd never shout. But you're determined to drive me to it, baiting me like a bull, sneering from up there on your moral high ground.' He looks at her with something like hate, then appears to compose himself a little. 'Think about what you've just said. I'm not a monster. What you're accusing me of is … it's very serious, Sam.'

'What you've *done* is very serious. You were in a position of power. It's enough that you even touched her before she was sixteen. If you'd been caught, you'd be on the register. Let me put it another way: were you caught?'

'It came out, yes. But I'm not on the … I'm not on any criminal register. It wasn't like that. It wasn't like that at all.'

'So tell me, what was it like?'

'I … As I've said, I was young. I behaved badly – I'm not saying I didn't. But it was a relationship, Sam. Misguided, yes, but I didn't pressurise her in any way. For God's sake, I didn't rape her.' He exhales heavily. 'Her parents found out and I was discreetly dismissed, and that was the end of it. My father died soon after.'

'So you were never prosecuted?'

He shakes his head. 'Neither the school nor her parents wanted a scandal. It would've been too hard on Lottie. I was dismissed on compassionate grounds on account of my father's ill health and I moved on. That's it. Whatever mental-health problems Lottie went on to suffer, they were not my fault. If she has since obsessed over me, that's not my fault either.' He drains his glass, rubs his eyes. 'I need a shower.' He gets up, leaves the room.

The fire crackles, a *schlumpf* as a log falls against the chimney breast. Samantha drinks her wine, at first in sips, then pours the rest down her throat. Emily snuffles against her neck. Above her, Peter's footsteps creak back and forth on the landing. A moment later, the rainy sound of the water in the pipes. What did he just say? No one wanted a scandal because *it would've been too hard on Lottie*. Did he actually say that? What a joke. Avoidance of scandal favours the abuser, leaves the victim with no closure, no validation, no justice. Man moves on, gets new career, invents new way of telling truth. Bullies women, two-times, damages, controls and humiliates them. Knocks up girlfriend, sticks her in the big house, goes to conferences who the hell knows where with who the hell knows whom.

Samantha is exhausted. Her bones feel like tombstones, her head a bowling ball. She is dizzy from her thoughts swinging first one way then the other. But she gets up. She takes Emily up to her cot and tucks her in. Peter is still under the shower, trying to wash off his filthy lies, no doubt. Samantha returns downstairs. Grabs the car keys from the bowl on the phone table. Props open the front door with one of her boots.

No central locking, she thinks, walking around to the passenger side door. *Makes me appear more chivalrous than I am.*

Look at me, I'm a wreck.

Marry me immediately.

I would never objectify you.

You got a ride in the Studmobile.

He's the opposite of a predator, the absolute opposite.

We have a child together … he's changed.

She opens the car door. Inside, a thick smell, floral but stale. She bends to the passenger seat and sniffs. Perfume, she's pretty sure. Not her own. She opens the glove compartment. In it is a silk scarf the colour of the palest blue sky. It is a woman's scarf, unmistakably. She pulls it out, pushes it to her nose. The same floral smell as the car: stale perfume transformed over hours, made specific by the oily odours of someone else's skin. She screws it up in her hand, is about to put it back when she sees the familiar clear plastic bag, the flash of coloured pills.

'Jesus Christ.' She stuffs the scarf into the glove compartment and slams it shut.

Peter is coming down the stairs just as she closes the front door behind her.

'Sam?' He steps heavily onto the last stair, lands in the hallway. 'What are you doing? I've brought everything in from the car.'

'You said there was a lot of traffic coming back,' she says, studying his inscrutable face. 'Was there?'

'Yes, why? What is this? Look, Sam, I've told you the truth. It was bloody difficult for me, but I told you the whole story because I respect you too much to hide things from you. If you're going to bring something I did years ago into every last thing going forward, that's not going to work, is it? We need to put this behind us. Otherwise she's won, hasn't she? Bloody crazy Lottie who should have moved on a long time ago. And by the way, we're not pressing charges, and you say nothing about this to the police, all right? I've trusted you with it, do you hear me? I don't want any more of our life ruined by that madwoman.'

Madwoman. Madwomen. Samantha dismissed Aisha and Jenny as madwomen, only a few hours ago. Madwomen in the attic. That attic must be getting bloody crowded. What was it Christine said? *Unhappiness does terrible things to people.* Yes, Samantha thinks, it does. In the months that followed the revelation of her father's affair, her mother bought a silver miniskirt, had her hair cut and coloured, acquired a brash new friend, Clare, who talked about getting a bit of action, who brought bottles of spirits to the house and kept her mother out all night. There were conversations about minor plastic surgery – tummy tucks, lip fillers, Botox – procedures she could not even begin to afford. Unhappiness does terrible things all right. It can drive a person mad.

'All right,' she replies eventually. They are in agreement about Lottie, though not for the same reasons.

'And I've changed the password on the home computer and on both our emails,' he says. 'It's Samantha1996 on all of them for now, but you can change yours again to whatever. Your name and year of birth, easy to remember.'

Peter is still standing in the hallway, drying his ears with a hand towel. He is attempting to be casual, but the tendons in his throat are thick cables. His hair is wet. His feet are bare. He has washed her off, she thinks, the wearer of the pale blue silk scarf. He has changed into his pyjamas and robe, his cheeks hang a little and he looks about ten years older than he did this morning. If you didn't know him better, you'd say he was just some middle-aged man. You'd say he was a vain old fool who had realised that he was no longer at the height of his powers.

'Let's get to bed.' In one stride, he is in front of her, up close. He smells of citrus; she recognises his Dior shower gel. He pushes her hair behind her ear and kisses her on the temple. 'We could both use a little comfort, don't you think? Relieve some of this stress? And everything will look very different in the morning, I promise.'

'I need a shower too.' She leaves him to lock the doors and rake the fire. By the time he comes upstairs, she is already in bed: exhausted, wide awake.

'Gave Sally a lift home, by the way,' he says, spooning her from behind, kissing the back of her neck, sliding his arms around her waist. 'Professor Bailey, you know? Not sure if I mentioned she was coming to the conference. Did you know she's married to Olivia Ford?' He runs his hand up her belly, takes hold of her breast. 'Didn't she teach your Chaucer module?'

So he knows she's seen the scarf. He is offering up his alibi before she challenges him so that his innocence is beyond doubt. Clever, she thinks. Very clever.

But she is no slouch on the brains front either.

She turns over, kisses him on his lying mouth.

CHAPTER 27

Samantha wakes up naturally for the first time since Emily was born. She was dreaming about Marcia. They were in the late-night Spanish bar off the Tottenham Court Road. They'd had too much to drink and were dancing flamenco. It's the dream of a memory, and for a moment she keeps her eyes closed to prolong it. Before that came nightmares: Emily's lifeless body grey in a ditch; Emily crying and alone in a dark, dripping warehouse; a coffin smaller than any coffin should be. Each time Samantha woke with a shout, covered in sweat, parched, panting. Peter was asleep, the wide bow of his shoulders all she could see in the shadowy room. She left him sleeping, went to lay her hand on Emily's warm body, waiting for the rise and fall. At around four, she must have drifted off, her subconscious finding this last, happier memory to polish and hold up to dream's hazy light.

Light filters now through her eyelids. She gives up, opens her eyes, sees the time. It is almost half past eight. The bed is empty. It is later than usual; the sky is too bright.

Emily.

She throws back the covers, grabs her nightdress from the floor and dashes into her daughter's room. Emily is asleep. Samantha holds her finger under the baby's nose. Feels the warm, sweet breath of life. It is two hours later than she's ever slept. Since last night, Samantha has told herself over and over that Emily will not have felt one moment of fear. If she is still asleep now, it is because she must be exhausted from the chaos of yesterday. She places her hand on Emily's chest. And there it is, just to be sure: the swell and sink. She forces herself to turn away and go downstairs.

Peter is drinking coffee. He is standing up, facing the bank of charcoal-coloured kitchen units, looking at his phone. They don't have coffee in bed anymore, she thinks. Haven't done since Emily was born.

'Hi,' she says.

'Morning.' He barely glances at her, last night's attentions lost in the cold light of the morning. And up she comes, into the clarity of realisation that it has always been like this: nights full of warmth; mornings full of this, whatever this is. He is flushed, she notices. He must have been for his usual early-morning run. She did not hear him get up. It amazes her how unaltered he is. He has slept, has got up at his usual time, has completed his custom-ary route along the river, back through Ham House, Richmond Park, Petersham, and is now drinking his morning coffee. He has ploughed forward.

She, meanwhile, can barely hold her cup. Her nightdress, she notices then, is on inside out. Her baby is safe but her life is a shattered windscreen, held in place only by cracks. One more tap and it will rain down shards on all of them.

'Are you going in?' she asks.

He takes a sip of coffee, swallows. 'Tutorial at eleven.'

That he is going to work the day after their child was kidnapped has not come as a surprise. She has not, she realises, expected him to do anything different, has not expected more. Night's empathy is day's near indifference, even today. Night will come; day will dawn. Life goes on, repeat ad infinitum.

She tells him – tells the back of his head, at least – that she'll see him later. She doesn't ask what time he'll be back, doesn't ask if he could take the afternoon off and be with her *under the circs*, as Marcia would say. Marcia, who would *see* her fragility, who at one glance would *know*. If Peter notices the cracks, he says nothing about it. He will come home exactly when it pleases him. His day will not be conditioned by anything she might say or do, nor by anything she might feel. Even *under the circs.*

Leaving him in the kitchen, she returns upstairs. Checks on Emily. She is so peaceful, fists up, head to one side, lips a pout. Another kind of indifference altogether.

'See you later then,' Peter calls up. A moment later, the door shuts with a bang.

The house is so silent that she can hear a bird calling outside: a waxwing, possibly, or a chiffchaff. It's not a song, she knows that. It's a territorial war cry.

In the bathroom, she undresses, stares for a moment into the full-length mirror. It is not something she does often, at least not with any real intention – she is usually too busy grabbing a shower while trying to sing to Emily through the glass screen – but she looks now. Is she still attractive? Would or could she appeal to someone nearer her own age now that her eyes are ringed in black, the whites bloodshot, now that pregnancy has struck silver lightning onto her abdomen, now that her stomach is not taut as a drum? Her hips are wider than they were yet her ribs protrude in a rack. Her body looks like it's been in a fight. Like it's had a rough time and needs tenderness, a softer light, understanding.

'Poor body,' she whispers, stroking the loose pouch of her belly. 'Poor, poor you.'

No such ravages for Peter. At forty, he's pretty much unchanged from the photographs in his bedside drawer. A flare of resentment hits her. How weird that it is stronger than any emotion she felt last night, in the car, nose pressed to his mistress's scarf. She is angrier about his dumb luck than his infidelity. Unless he was telling the truth and it really is Professor Bailey's scarf. Who cares, frankly? Emily is safe; she, Samantha, is tired.

She wonders if this is how bitterness starts, with this not caring, or no longer caring about things that once meant so much, whether you work through disappointment after disappointment towards weary expectation, until even the most serious transgression barely ripples the surface. She wonders whether in five years she'll have left Peter in this beautiful house on the hill, told him to go to hell, in ten be drooling over younger men in dark bars, drunk, proselytising, telling strangers what's what, jabbing at them with an ash-piled, lipstick-smudged cigarette, or living in a shoe with ten kids by as many different fathers. Or maybe even dead, found only weeks after complete organ failure, empty whisky bottle and a half-eaten tuna sandwich at her feet, dozens of cats clawing at the ratty second-hand sofa upon which she's exhaled her last.

'Madwoman,' she says to her reflection and laughs.

She stays under the hot shower for a long time, much, much longer than three minutes.

She cleans the shower screen with the squeegee and places it carefully back in the correct place in the cupboard. Still no sound from Emily, so she takes her chance: moisturises her legs and arms, combs her wet hair back from her face, brushes her teeth with her electric toothbrush for the full two minutes, even though Peter isn't there to check that the beeper goes off.

She is watching the steam clouds shrink from the mirror when she remembers Peter's pills. She wonders if he has taken them out of the glove compartment and hidden them in the house, or taken them into work along with the scarf.

She pulls his robe from the hook, wraps it around herself.

In the bedroom, she tries to work methodically. She searches his side of the chest of drawers, her own, his bedside cabinet, his wardrobe, his shoes, the small wooden box with the intricate marquetry in which he keeps his monogrammed cufflinks. Nothing, no sign.

She returns to the bathroom, goes through the shelves. Shaving foam, aftershave, razor, deodorant, aspirin, hair fudge, hair wax, hair gel, moisturiser, anti-wrinkle cream.

Anti-wrinkle cream? She doesn't recognise the brand, assumes it's something expensive. She unscrews the lid, smells it, dips her finger in. It is smooth, unctuous. She wipes it on the back of her hand and, as she does so, drops the pot.

'Shit,' she hisses, falls to her knees.

A blob of thick white cream has escaped onto the floorboards. She scoops it as best she can back into the pot, half giggling at how horrified Peter would be if he were to see her doing this. She smooths the cream with her finger, tries to make the pot look like it did before. It looks OK, she thinks. Hopefully he won't notice. If he does, she can say she tried some, just a tiny bit. She stands up, screws the lid back on and replaces the pot in the exact same spot on the shelf. Turns it a half centimetre, back three millimetres. Yep. She's pretty sure it was like that.

She tears off some loo roll and drops again to her knees. A few satellites have flicked out across the floor. And it is when she is cleaning up the streak on the base of the loo that she sees that the floorboard behind doesn't lie flat. She screws up the tissue and throws it into the toilet. Then, on all fours, she worries the corner of the board with the tip of her finger. It lifts easily. She slides her finger underneath and pulls it up and away. Hidden in the space is a brown leather toilet bag. She pulls it onto her lap. It is the size of her father's old analogue radio. Her heart is beating. From the other side of the landing, Emily cries out.

'Shh,' she whispers.

She unzips the case. Inside is …

'"Chestnut Reflections",' she reads aloud. '"A natural way to cover the grey."'

Emily gives a shout, 'Oi!' It is almost funny, as if she is saying, *Oi, wotcha doin'?*

The box is open. Samantha looks inside, thinking, still thinking, that there must be something else to this, that this cannot solely be a box of hair dye. But inside is a kit – two transparent hand shapes, which look like a pattern cut-out for making gloves. They *are* gloves, of course, to keep the dye from getting onto the hands. They have not been used; however, she is filled with the utter certainty that Peter dyes his hair. Not one fleck of grey. And lately she's noticed a slightly wig-like quality, which she now realises is due to a uniformity in the colour.

'Bloody hell,' she whispers, puts the gloves back, places the box on the floor.

Emily is building up now, though not quite crying.

There is something else in the case – a box of … latex gloves. *What?*

On impulse, she removes a pair and puts them on. They are the type that doctors wear for intimately examining patients, a memory all too recent. But that is not their purpose here, obviously. They are probably stronger and better quality than the ones in the kit. That would be so like Peter, to find what is provided wanting. Although surely an exclusive salon would be more his style. Unless his vanity extends beyond not wanting to go grey, all the way to not even wanting to admit that he dyes his hair. In that case, he would definitely not visit a hairdresser and risk being seen. Could it be that he is so paranoid that he has hidden it even from her? Is it even possible to be so vain? It's like that song her mum used to sing, used to love because she'd loved it as a girl; she once gleefully explained the lyrics to Samantha, telling her that they were so clever because they trapped their subject in a maddening paradox, not that her mother would have used that word. But Samantha remembers the song vividly, how the female singer accused her former lover of being so vain, he probably thought the song was about him. Which, of course, it was.

'Ridiculous,' she whispers to herself now, staring at the evidence of her partner's boundless vanity. 'Pathetic.'

It isn't as if she doesn't know he's older than her. She's known that from the start. What the hell is he trying to prove?

She is about to put everything back when she sees something else in the case: a clear plastic vial, a little smaller than a mustard jar – wide neck, screw top. Inside, whitish-grey powder. Her throat closes. A wave of nausea follows. She unscrews the vial, licks her finger and puts the tip to the powder. She has put the powder to her tongue before she reflects on what she's doing. But she's done it now and winces at the acrid taste. Like eating hairspray. But it's not hairspray. It tastes exactly the same as the pill he gave her the first time she came to this house, the pills he gave up offering. Ecstasy, then, is what this is. In powder form. That's her best guess.

She sputters, spits, wipes her tongue on the back of her hand. Emily is crying more loudly now, building up to a full-on wail.

'I'm coming,' she calls. 'Mummy's coming, lovey.'

Quickly, precisely, she puts everything back. She replaces the floorboard and presses it down with her foot, stands back and scrutinises it. It looks the same. She hopes.

'Coming, baby girl,' she calls out, running across the landing. She picks up her daughter, realises she still has on the latex gloves, which makes her giggle. She'll roll them up in Emily's used nappy. No way Peter will find them there. Nappies are something he avoids if he can.

'Shh,' she whispers, jiggling Emily in her arms, laying her on her changing table. Despite her pumping heart, the breath erratic in her chest, when she looks down on her little girl, she smiles. Emily, her precious Emily, is here. She is safe, she is unharmed. She has her father's beautiful bow on her top lip, but Samantha is her mother and she feels the animal fury of it in her blood, in her bones, in every last cell of her. Whatever happens, nothing, nothing will separate her from this child ever again.

Downstairs, while Emily feeds, Samantha calls the English department and asks to be put through to Professor Bailey.

She waits.

'You're through to Sally Bailey,' comes the pre-recorded message. 'I'm afraid I'm not available to take your call at the moment, but if you leave your name and number, I'll call you back as soon as I can. Many thanks.'

She fills her lungs with air, keeps her tone light. 'Um, hi, this is Samantha Frayn, Peter Bridges' partner. I'm just calling to let you know you left your scarf in Peter's car, and if I know Peter, he'll forget to tell you. So just in case you don't see him or he forgets, don't worry, I've got it. I'll make sure he brings it in with him tomorrow. Such a lovely scarf, be a shame to lose it! Take care. Bye.' She hangs up, exhales. She has only met Professor Bailey a handful of times, with Peter, and has always become a little tongue-tied in her impressive academic aura. But it is not this that is making her heart beat faster. What she's just done is hardly the fraud of the century, but at the same time it is, for want of a better word, unnatural. Slyness doesn't suit her, especially after what she and her mother went through. But like an oversize jacket borrowed in an emergency, she will have to wear it as best she can.

She calls Marcia then, her chest buzzing with nerves. She has not seen Marcia in so long, wonders what thin thread is left of their friendship. But when Marcia hears it's her, her voice warms instantly.

'Oh, Sam,' she says. 'I've been thinking about you so much.'

Samantha feels her eyes fill. 'Me too. I even dreamt about you last night. We were in that flamenco bar.'

'Costa Dorada? Was it two in the morning?'

'Of course. We were dancing with the professionals.'

'Lucky them. Did we pull?'

'You did. After you'd fallen off the table.'

They laugh. It reminds her of Aisha and Jenny. That bond that underlies everything, even when things are tough. She thought it had gone, but it has not.

'How're you doing anyway?' Marcia asks. 'I'm sorry I've not been to see you. This PG Cert's a bloody nightmare; I'm practically sleeping standing up.'

'God, that sounds terrible. Why don't we meet for coffee this weekend? I'm around both days.' She realises that she will not tell Marcia about the last twenty-four hours, nor about Peter; that this is not why she has called her and it is too soon to tell Marcia she was right.

'Cool,' Marcia is saying. 'Text me.'

They won't meet at the weekend either, Samantha knows. This is a holding conversation, a wave over a wall until time and circumstances allow them to rekindle their friendship.

'Listen,' Samantha says. 'Party animal. You've taken E, haven't you?'

'Er, yeah, you know I have, loads of times, why?'

'Well, you remember Peter offered it to me the first time I came here?' She pauses. Mentioning that night, Peter, is difficult. It was when life came between her and Marcia in a way so quick, so violent that neither of them noticed until it was too late. Marcia has never said she doesn't like Peter. She's never had to.

'It was only half a pill,' Samantha adds irrelevantly.

'But you didn't take it, did you?'

'No. Well, sort of. I was planning to take it out and hide it but it dissolved too quickly. It tasted horrible.'

Marcia laughs. 'God, I'd forgotten how square you are. A whole half pill and you're anybody's.'

'Thanks, I love you too.' Samantha waits while Marcia gets it out of her system, reminds her of the time they had to call an ambulance after she drank two cans of extra-strong lager, the time she vomited after her first half joint. 'I just wanted to ask,' she goes on once Marcia's sniggers have died down a bit. 'Do other drugs taste like that, or just E? And can you get E in powder form, you know, like cocaine?'

'Christ, Sam, what the hell is going on in that house?'

Samantha gives a fake laugh. 'Nothing, no, not here. It's just something one of the mums said at playgroup.'

In her ignorance, Marcia is still chuckling. 'Bloody hell,' she says. 'What kind of crazy-ass playgroups are you going to, girl?'

Samantha thinks quickly. She should have got her story straight. She's an idiot.

'Oh, it's all going on in Richmond Hill, you know.' She attempts a chuckle. 'We're mainlining heroin in our flat whites up here. No, actually, one of the mums has a much older child, so they were talking drugs awareness, what to do if you suspect your kid is taking something, or addicted to something, whatever.' Or if your fully grown, hair-dyeing, abusive, narcissistic, academic twat of a partner is, she thinks.

'So, what, had this woman found something in her son's room?'

'She found some pills in, like, a plastic bag, and some whitish powder. And she said it tasted like hairspray and wondered what it was.'

'Sounds like MD,' Marcia says. 'I mean, it could be ket, sorry, ketamine. That's pretty rank too, to be honest, but it's usually a drip. Sounds like he's got a baggy and some stuff to dab. MDMA, I reckon.'

'Right. Cheers. That's helpful.'

'Tell her not to worry about it,' Marcia goes on. 'It's just what kids are into. It's unlikely he's an addict. He probably just canes it on a night out, maybe has a few dabs to keep him going. Main thing is to talk to him, make sure he buddies up and doesn't take more than he should. Honestly, some of Jacob's mates take, like, five or six in a night.'

'Five or six?' What an education this is, talking to Marcia.

'Yeah. Listen, hon, I've got to go. Text me about coffee, yeah?'

'OK, babe. Take care. Love you.'

'Love you.'

She is still feeding Emily when her phone rings. She grabs at it, thinking it will be Christine, but it's Aisha, calling to see if she's OK.

'I'm fine,' Samantha tells her, feeling herself bristle. 'It's kind of you to call.'

'Have you found out what happened?'

Why do you care? she doesn't say.

'Not yet.'

'Do you know who this Suzanne is, or why she did it?'

Yes, but I'm not telling you, she doesn't say either.

'Christine said she'd update me,' she says. 'So I'm actually just waiting for a call from her now.' Subtext: *get off the line and out of my face.*

'All right.'

There is a moment of silence. Samantha has the impression Aisha wants to say something. She wanted to say something yesterday. So. They are both holding back.

'Aisha?'

'Sorry, yeah. Er, I'll see you soon hopefully. Let me know if I can do anything. I'm so sorry about yesterday. Really.'

Samantha feels herself soften. 'That's OK. I'm sorry for being so rude.'

'Don't even think about it. You were stressed out. I shouldn't have pushed.'

Another silence. Despite everything, Samantha cannot stop herself from liking this woman. Instinct tells her that without Jenny there, she would have been in less of a rush to list Peter's shortcomings. Her instincts have been way off lately, but still, there's something else in Aisha, some hint of damage or vulnerability that she can't quite put her finger on.

'Aisha,' she says. 'I'm not coming back to college.' And like that, her decision is made.

'What? Why?'

'It was too soon. I let Peter talk me into it, but I wasn't ready. I thought I could manage it, but after everything that's happened,

I think I need to take some time to be with Emily and try again in six months or so, a year maybe.'

'I understand. That's a shame though – you were a good teacher.'
That pause again.

'Aisha, can I ask you a weird question?'

'Sure.'

'Don't be offended and I'm not saying you have, but … have you ever taken E? You know, as in Ecstasy? What I mean is, did Peter ever ask you to take it?'

Another pause, though this one is different. Heavier. Samantha tries not to fill the space with a thousand dark thoughts.

'Shit,' is all that Aisha mutters eventually.

'Aisha?'

'I, um, I think we need to meet.'

CHAPTER 28

As Samantha is leaving the house, a call comes in from an unknown number.

'Samantha?' It is Christine Townson's voice.

'Christine?'

'Hi. How're you feeling today?'

'Ah, not bad,' she lies. 'Not much sleep, but Emily's fine. It's just a question of time now, isn't it?'

'It is, it is.' Christine sighs. 'So, I've just spoken to Ormskirk branch and they released Charlotte – or Lottie, as she likes to be called – this morning. You're not pressing charges, apparently?'

'I, er, no. No, we're not.' Peter must have rung them first thing; how efficient. 'I guess there's nothing to be gained, is there?'

'No. I shouldn't say this, but I think that's the right decision. She's troubled, poor thing, has a history of depression, a couple of delusional episodes, but she's never done anything like this before and she was very upset apparently.'

'Will she get help?'

'She might. But mental-health services are stretched to breaking point, to be honest.'

'That's so sad.'

'Well, it's very kind of you to see it like that. Not many in your position would.'

Not many would have the inside track. 'Did she say why she did it?'

'She reckons the dodgy poems was all she was ever going to do. For her homework, is that right?'

'So she did write them?'

'She did, darling.'

Samantha's shoulders drop. At last. Confirmation. 'That's right. We were quite frightened.'

'Well, it seems it was your husband she had it in for, not you. Partner, sorry.' Another piece falls exactly where Samantha knew it would.

'Why would she want to hurt Peter?' Her face glows with her own disingenuousness.

'She claimed she and Peter had a relationship and she never got over it. She said it was years ago but wouldn't say more, wouldn't say how she met him or when, nothing. They tried to get her to talk about it, but she wouldn't, I'm afraid. She clammed right up apparently.'

'Peter told me,' Samantha blurts, unable to stand the lie. 'Sorry, I should have said – I'm a bit all over the place – but he recognised her name, said she was an ex. He feels sorry for her too, but I suppose he can't be blamed for whatever grievance she carried forward.' Her breath catches. She has just betrayed a vulnerable woman, albeit one who stole her baby.

'Ms Lewis reckoned she was trying to teach him a lesson, but she said once she'd started, it all went a bit out of control. She told you she had a child, is that right?'

'Yes.'

'Well, she doesn't. My guess is that the lies got on top of her and as soon as she put the baby into the car, she panicked. She said as much, said she realised the one who'd be most upset was you. She asked the officers to tell you she's sorry. She asked them to tell you it was never you she wanted to hurt. She just wanted to have a baby.'

'Have a baby?'

'You know, for a bit. Reading between the lines, she's not been lucky in love, so to speak. She couldn't say what her plans were regarding little Emily. I don't think she had any, to be honest. Your guess is as good as mine. As good as hers, if you like.'

Samantha is about to tell Christine about Peter's actions all those years ago. She should, really. But she doesn't. Clearly Lottie hasn't clarified the specifics. So here they are, herself and her child's abductor, keeping Peter's shoddy secrets for him. How utterly messed up.

Christine sighs. 'Well, as I say, there's nothing to be gained going after her, and it's probably for the best for yourselves too. As I say, she clammed right up, even though something was clearly still upsetting her.'

Samantha's stomach heats.

'From what my colleague says,' Christine goes on, 'pressing charges in this instance could well backfire, you know, if she feels cornered.' The subtext is so loud, the sense is distorted; Samantha cannot quite reach it. *Pressing charges could well backfire …*

'I see.'

'I have to go anyway, so I'll leave you to it. Good to hear you're coping well. You've got my number if there's anything you need to talk about, all right? Anything at all.'

'Thank you,' Samantha manages. 'And thanks for yesterday. I couldn't have got through it without you.'

'Well, that's a lovely thing to say. Take care of yourself, Samantha; you're a nice girl.' A hesitation. 'And call me if there's anything – I mean it.'

The phone line goes silent. Emily starts to fret in her pram, desperate to be on the move. *Pressing charges in this instance could well backfire … call me if there's anything – I mean it.* There it is, definitely, the indefinable subtext. Clearly Christine suspects something but is not prepared to say what.

Samantha heads down the hill to meet Aisha and Jenny. The more she thinks about the conversation with Christine, the more she is sure that there was a veiled allusion to an underage relationship, possibly abuse. How else could pressing charges backfire? Yes, it was definitely there, lurking in the words not said, not even attributable to a facial tic or gesture. *Child abuse* is the term that she pushes away, along with *paedophile*, along with *rape*. Suzanne – Lottie – may not have entered into a full sexual relationship with Peter until she was legally of age, but he groomed her while still only fifteen from his position of trust.

As she walks, Samantha remembers a documentary she watched with Marcia when they were living together. The woman in question had been taken to a grubby flat with her friend when they were both fourteen. The two of them had been lured into sleeping with two seedy guys who preyed on schoolgirls, giving them free cigarettes and alcohol. There was a photograph of the girls in their school uniforms, grinning, full of it.

'We thought it was a bit of fun,' the woman said in the interview. 'We thought we were rebels. It was dangerous, you know? And secret.' Twenty years or so later, she could not talk about it without weeping. She had become an alcoholic for a time, had a history of failed relationships. Unhappiness came off her in waves.

'He stole her childhood,' Marcia said, shaking her head at the screen. 'Look at her, a wreck all these years later. He deserves to go to prison. I don't care how long ago it was. Nonce. They'll murder him in there.'

He's the opposite of a predator, the absolute opposite, Samantha told Marcia that first giddy morning, before she found out his not touching her was simply his little trick to bind young, naïve women, women like her, to him. A trick refined over years. Christ, he must have smelled her a mile away, with her social anxiety, her ignorance of recreational drugs and her dislike of the city.

Is Peter, her partner and the father of her child, really the absolute opposite of those seedy men in the documentary? Or is he absolutely the same – the same but richer, better spoken, better educated, separated from those lecherous bastards by class alone? She, Samantha, is not underage. But she is much, much younger than him. *This is not about love at all* is the dark thought that hits her. This is about something much less romantic.

This is about power.

On she walks, to Richmond, her cheeks aflame. She reaches the bottom of the hill, the mini roundabout, where the town centre begins. Tears are pouring down her face, and only now, at risk of someone seeing her, does she become aware of them. She cannot put the tender, loving, safe man that Peter is in the same frame as some grotty predatory beast, no matter what Aisha and Jenny have said. But nor can she unsee the photograph of him with a bunch of schoolgirls, his arm around the one he was blithely violating. She cannot square away what he has told her about his past with what she feels about it, nor can she reconcile the affectionate partner he is in the evenings with the cold, abrupt semi-stranger of the mornings. In that photograph, Lottie Lewis did not look like an innocent teenager. She looked full to the brim with cheek and a healthy thirst for kicks. But she was wearing a school uniform. She was as dangerous to herself as any ignorant young teenager. Samantha knows how out of control she herself was in the confused and dissociated aftermath of her father. Even though it was with boys her own age, the memory of that time haunts her. It's possible that, ultimately, it is what sent her into Peter's arms.

At that sad, sad thought, her anger dissipates. She feels something reach out from her soul or her heart or wherever empathy is stored, feels it search for this woman who has committed such a terrible crime against her, this woman she has just betrayed. She imagines holding Lottie's hand and saying, *I understand. I believe you. I'm sorry.*

Sobbing uncontrollably now, she pushes the pram into the alleyway that runs alongside the cinema. She stops, finds some baby wipes in Emily's changing bag and cleans her face, blows her nose, composes herself. One hand against the damp stone wall for support, she takes purposeful deep breaths, gets herself together. Slowly she feels herself settle. It is another fifteen minutes' walk to the café. She will use every step to calm herself down. Hopefully her face will have returned to normal by the time she meets Aisha and Jenny. Hopefully, like a mask, she will have slapped on a new face: a brave one. Lord knows, she's going to need it while she figures out what the hell to do.

Aisha and Jenny are already in Butterbeans, at the table by the window. The café is small, packed with mismatched wooden chairs and tables. The smell of coffee is nutty, sweet, delicious. A plate of eggs and slick green spinach sails past in the hands of a hip, bearded guy no older than eighteen. He smiles at Samantha, winks at the baby. She blinks back the new threat of tears. He is so beautiful. He is exactly as young as he should be.

'Sam.' Aisha is out of her chair, digging into the back pocket of her jeans, pulling out a cash card. 'Peppermint tea?'

She doesn't argue. The prospect of sitting down is too tempting; pulling her coat from her overheated body and cooling down.

'Thanks,' she says, touching her hand against her breast. 'Bit late for caffeine.'

Jenny has moved a chair to make room for the pram. She budges along the bench and pats the space beside her. Gratefully, Samantha parks Emily, sits down and sighs.

'You sound like you've been through it,' Jenny says.

'Just a long walk. Did you get your job, by the way?'

Jenny sucks her teeth. 'Nah. Sexist bastard asked me if I was married. Men are twats. Did you hear from the police?'

Samantha nods, and when Aisha returns, she fills them in on what Christine told her – on the surface.

'We're not pressing charges,' she says as briskly as she can. 'I think we've all been through enough. We need to move on and recover.'

'That's good.' Aisha sips her coffee. It is only a second, but Samantha catches the look that passes between her and Jenny. Enough.

'So, you two keep glancing at one another,' she says. 'I have to say, it's beginning to piss me right off. You said we should talk, so I presume there's more I should know.'

'Aisha said you were asking about Ecstasy,' Jenny says, meeting Samantha's indignation with a sober expression.

Samantha nods.

'Have you found some in the house? Is that why?'

'I …' She hesitates. This is all so private. She doesn't even know these women, not really. But she needs the information they clearly have.

'Did he offer it to you?' Aisha asks before Samantha has time to speak.

Samantha looks about her, to gauge if anyone is listening in. They're not, it seems. 'That first night at his house. What you said about … about the way he seduces women by not seducing them. And the drugs. That was … it was very familiar.' And oh, she told herself she would keep it together, but now here she is, crying in a café with two women who weeks ago were strangers. Her best friend, meanwhile, the person she should be telling, knows nothing. Everything is upside down. Everything is wrong.

'I'm sorry.' She sniffs. 'I'm just so embarrassed.'

Jenny passes her a tissue. 'Don't be sorry. Or embarrassed. That's how they get us. You've got nothing to be sorry for and nothing to be embarrassed about. And like you say, it could be that he's finally changed. What do we know? He asked you to move in and he didn't freak when you told him you were pregnant.'

'The reverse,' Samantha says. 'It was me who freaked. He was delighted.'

'Well, that's better than I got.' It is Aisha who has spoken, Aisha whose turn it is to well up.

Samantha meets her eye, sees pain. 'You were pregnant?'

She nods. 'We'd been together five years. I was in my mid twenties. I was surprised, but then when I thought about it, I realised I'd had an upset stomach and … whatever, there I was. But I was pleased. I thought we'd move in together. He was older than me, but … no. He wasn't pleased. To say the least.'

There is no child, so far as Samantha knows. She wonders what Aisha will say next.

'He said I was stupid,' is what she says. '*Irresponsible* was the word he used. He was very … matter-of-fact. He did that low, calm talking thing he does, you know, as he told me that he'd booked me an appointment at a private clinic and that he would pay for *the procedure*.'

'An abortion?'

At the next table, a teenage girl looks over. She is wearing headphones, but even so, Samantha leans forward and repeats the question in a whisper.

Aisha gives a grim nod. 'Cleaning up my mess was how he put it. Soon after that, I found out he was sha— sleeping with Jenny and we broke up.'

'It's OK, you can say shagging.' Jenny gives a brief, mirthless laugh.

'I like to think I would've had the strength to end it even without that.' Aisha rolls her eyes, snorts a little, though her amusement is clearly fake.

'I can't laugh,' Samantha almost whispers. 'Sorry.'

'Stop apologising.' Jenny's tone is light, kind. 'I'm guessing that's a habit you've got into in the last couple of years?'

'I …'

'Don't worry. Just tell us, why did you want to know about Ecstasy?'

Their faces are open. But still. It's hard to admit to what an idiot you've been. That you thought yourself sophisticated, maybe a little superior. Chosen. And now you're in too deep to know what to do.

Aisha leans forward, takes Samantha's hand in hers. 'I know you don't know us well, and I know we've been a bit ... you know, pushy. But we're on your side. And at a certain point, women have to trust each other, don't we? We have to believe each other and we have to look after each other. God knows, the world is against us as it is without us being against each other.'

'Aisha's right,' Jenny says. 'We have to believe each other. We have to be on each other's side.'

Samantha thinks of Lottie. Of all that she hasn't told the police, of the reasons for that. She thinks of her own silent conspiracy.

'I knew that Peter took Ecstasy,' she says. 'I didn't know how often.' She glances up; they smile their encouragement. 'When I first moved in, he offered it to me a few times but I said no. He was insistent, but I said I was happier with a glass of wine or a beer.'

'Oh, he loves his red wine.' Jenny's tone is cynical, hard.

Samantha winces but goes on. 'And then he stopped. I guess I thought he'd got the message. And then I fell pregnant and there were other reasons for not wanting to take anything stronger. Emily was born. We were happy. He was happy. I mean, he was a little controlling. I suppose I'm beginning to see that now. He loves Emily, but I guess, if I'm honest, he doesn't like any evidence of her, if that makes sense. He doesn't like to see dirty nappies even by the back door. He doesn't like it if her toys are out when he gets in.

'Sorry, I'm rambling. What I mean is, he has his fixed ideas, you know? But he lived alone for so long, and he's older, and I understand that. I guess I thought he'd forgotten about the drugs. I thought he'd ... I thought *we'd* moved on. And then when I got home from teaching my first class, he was lying on the sofa and Emily was upstairs crying. And later, when he'd gone to work, I found a bag of pills behind the sofa cushions.'

'Did you confront him?' It's Jenny who has spoken.

Samantha shakes her head. 'I left it. I thought maybe they'd been there a while, that he'd not realised. I didn't for one second think he might have taken one during the day, not while he was looking after Emily. Why would I think that? And then, a couple of weeks later, they were gone.'

Jenny sips her coffee, slides the cup back into its saucer. 'Have you thought about why you didn't confront him?'

'Not really.'

'We're not attacking you,' Aisha chips in. 'We're not suggesting there's anything you should or shouldn't have done. It's just, having been there, I can tell you it took me until that termination to realise what I'd become. I was pretty much doing everything he told me by then. Including that last thing. It was Jenny who gave me the strength to kick him into touch. Even afterwards, when I'd ended things, I kept wondering if I was to blame.'

Samantha nods. She is thinking about these two women, that straight after they dumped him, Peter asked her to move in with him, got her pregnant barely two months later. Because that's what happened, she knows that now. He was not too drunk to fetch protection from the bathroom; he simply didn't *want* to protect her, against anything, and certainly not against carrying his child, against being bound to him for ever. She, Samantha, is not unique or special at all, but a reaction. The panic reaction of a man no longer at the height of his powers. There is so much she doesn't know for sure. But there is so much she *feels*.

'Sometimes he's so tender,' she says. 'Like in the evenings. Then other times he's so distant, you know? Usually in the mornings. And sometimes I wonder …'

'It's OK.' Jenny places her hand over Samantha's. 'You're safe. You can say it, and besides, I think I know what you're going to say.'

But what can she say? That she's realised she's not the love of his life after all but some sort of talisman against loneliness? That he chose her only because she was easily overpowered? She can't say that. It is too private. It is too embarrassing.

'Oh, nothing,' she says. 'I'm just really tired after yesterday. The whole thing was so awful.'

'I know, babe,' Aisha says, squeezing her hand. 'I know.'

After a moment Jenny asks, 'And the reason you're asking about the drugs now is because …?'

Samantha sips her peppermint tea. It is hot and sweet. She feels it trickle down. 'I found some pills in the glove compartment of his car last night, that's all. And this morning I found some powder in the bathroom.' She doesn't specify where. She doesn't tell them about the silk scarf or the hair dye or the sodding latex gloves. It already feels like she's beyond naked, like she's opened up her very guts for surgery. But at the same time, there is relief in voicing it, as if she has taken a hazy whiff of anaesthetic.

Jenny fixes her with her green eyes. 'OK, so there's another reason I finished with Peter.' She inhales deeply, blows out, making her cheeks round. 'I think we both found, like you did, that he was more loving at night. And then, like you said, the cold snaps, the indifference. And then I met Aisha and found out he was a cheat, so I thought maybe that was why his moods changed so much. Anyway, the next night, I went up to the house and I told him I'd found out about Aisha. It's over, I said. You're a shit, basically, is what I said.'

Samantha feels her eyes widen. 'Really?'

'Yep.'

'What did he say?'

Jenny scoffs. 'He was all hand-wringing and apologies, told me he loved me, that he'd meant to finish it with Aisha but she was very needy, very anxious, but the good news was he'd found a way to let her down gently. Of course, I knew she'd finished with him the night before. Anyway, he was the soul of compassion, claimed he was worried about her, she'd been through a tough time. All this bullshit. He told me to sit down, that we should talk about it at least, would I let him pour us a glass of wine, said I owed him that much, then if he couldn't make me stay we could at least part as friends.' She sighs, rolls her eyes. 'I didn't want a scene. I thought I'd drink his wine, hear his BS, then make my exit as gracefully as I could. I was in the living room. And for some reason, I don't know why, I decided to spy on him. It sounds ridiculous, but I'd had the blow of finding out he'd had a serious girlfriend the whole time we'd been seeing each other, plus, like you said, Sam, there were all these other things I couldn't put my finger on but that were adding up. I didn't trust him anymore; I suppose that's all it was. So I crept out into the hallway and I watched him from the kitchen door.'

'And?' Samantha cannot take her eyes from Jenny's pale, freckled face.

'I watched him pour two large glasses of red. And I saw him sprinkle his magic powder into both of them. And I knew two things. I knew that one, he was spiking my drink. And two.' She hits her forefingers together, her eyes not leaving Samantha's. 'Two, I knew the bastard had been doing it the whole time.'

CHAPTER 29

'He was basically medicating both of us,' Jenny continues, shaking her head with the weary disbelief of a much older woman. 'My theory is that Peter Bridges is a narcissist who knows he's a narcissist. He takes E because it manufactures empathy, because there's no other way he can feel it. So don't bother trying to work it out or find it, my darling, because it isn't there. The drugs put it there, end of. That's why he likes the way they make him feel, the way they make him behave. He's intelligent enough to know he's nicer when he's on them, that he appeals to women when he's on them. Sick bastard. That's my amateur theory, and I'm sticking to it. And for the women, myself included, the drugs produced feelings of affection and euphoria.' She gives a flick of her hand. 'I thought I was falling for him when in fact I was loved up, as they say.'

Samantha lets Jenny talk. But as she vents her obviously still fresh anger, she leaves the subject of Peter behind and moves on to the entire world and all its ills. Everything is the fault of men, including her lack of career, Brexit and the state of the planet. Jenny hates men. She has put all of them together and has no faith in any of them anymore.

This is what I will become if I don't get out, Samantha thinks, watching Jenny's mouth curl itself around its venomous topic: not yet thirty, a lava of hate bubbling always beneath the surface of me, informing almost everything I do.

'I mean, who does that?' Jenny is saying, and, 'I mean, men just think they have the right … objectifying … bullshit … so much porn they can't even get it up with a normal woman …'

This lava will spill out of every orifice, Samantha thinks. It will cool and calcify into bitter black rock. That's no future. For herself, for Emily. There *are* good men in the world.

'And as for equality.' Jenny throws up her hands. 'What equality? Look at the fucking pay gap …'

I will be bitter, Samantha thinks. *I will be lonely. I will be alone.*

'I don't care if I never meet another man again. I'm done. I'm fucking done.' With a shake of her head and an emphatic swig of her latte, which must by now have gone cold, Jenny finally finishes.

Samantha edges her bag onto her shoulder. 'I'm so sorry you had to go through that.' She turns to Aisha. 'I feel terrible for what you've both been through.'

And Lottie. Lottie too. And, she knows without a doubt, others, many others, at the hands of Peter Bridges and those like him.

'Yeah, well.' Jenny's voice is still a little shaky. 'It's not you who should be sorry. We just thought we should warn you. As I said, women need to stick together. We need to share our stories.'

Samantha stands up. 'I have to get back. Emily needs her tea and I need to think.'

'All right, babe.' Aisha rubs her arm, smiles that wide, warm smile of hers while Jenny calls an Uber, tells Samantha they can settle up next time.

'What will you do?' Aisha asks, hugging Samantha outside the café.

Samantha shrugs. 'I appreciate your honesty, I really do. I think Peter's behaved appallingly, no doubt about that, but I think it was out of fear. He has a family now and I don't think he'd do anything to jeopardise that.' She sounds like a robot. 'I really am sorry he treated you guys so badly, but it looks like you've both found a lovely friendship on the back of it.'

Aisha smiles a little doubtfully. 'Hey, listen, you've got every right to do what you want to do. Jenny and me were just trying to make sure you had the facts.'

Jenny, however, is staring at Samantha, eyes round, jaw slack with incredulity. Samantha averts her gaze.

'I have Emily to think about.' Ignoring Aisha's move to help her, Emily tucked awkwardly under one arm, Samantha folds the buggy with some difficulty and lets the driver throw it into the boot. She ducks into the back seat of the cab, away from the perceptive glare of the two women.

The taxi pulls away. Samantha waves goodbye. Once they turn the corner, she sinks back in her seat and lets out a long, shaky breath. Peter drugs women. She can't believe it. She doesn't believe it. But of course, she can. She does. Just as she believes that he will have done, is probably doing, the same to her. It makes complete sense, down in her gut. And of course, since she moved in, she has never seen him open and pour their wine. *Go and sit down*, he has said. Or, *Hey, go and light the fire. Take the weight off, relax, I'll bring it through …* She doesn't have to spy on him; every word Jenny and Aisha have said is like a dark mirror – she doesn't need to look into it to know she will see herself and all that she knows. She remembers her mother, immediately after things came out, face streaked with black mascara, balled-up tissue clutched in her fingers. *Thing is, Sam, I knew*, she said. *I knew but I didn't know, do you know what I mean?* Samantha nodded, said she understood. But she didn't. Not really.

Now she does.

She is with Peter because he made her feel safe. But as the cab pulls up outside their beautiful home, with its thick walls, its security system and all its locks, safe is the opposite of how she feels.

Once inside, she checks her phone. There is a text message from Peter asking if she's OK and a voicemail. She listens closely.

'Hey, Samantha, it's Sally here. Thanks for your message. Yes, that's my scarf, and yes, you're right, Peter would never have remembered. If you could give it to him, that would be great, as Livvy'll kill me if she finds out I've lost it.' A chuckle. 'Thanks again.'

Samantha gasps, almost laughs. Peter *did* go to the conference with Sally. He *did* give her a lift home and that *was* Sally's scarf.

Oh, but where does that leave her? Where the hell does that leave her?

Emily begins to grumble. Their child. Their flesh and blood. If she's been wrong about the cheating, wrong about the poems, it's possible she's wrong about the drugs. Peter might have changed for real. She, Samantha, might be more than his last port in the storm. His past stinks, yes it does. But she might be his redemption.

She lifts Emily out of the pram and holds her tight.

'Hey there, lovely girl,' she says. 'I think your daddy has changed his ways, yes he has, yes he has. He's been rotten, but we've fixed him, you and me. Shall we give him a second chance, shall we, eh?'

In all the stress of the first raw months of motherhood, the sudden and cataclysmic change in her life, her first professional job, those awful poems, the whole business with Lottie, she has lost her way. Peter is the love of her life. He is flawed, very flawed, but no amount of white noise can alter that love. He might have used all his lines on her, but only because he knew they would work. Yes, he has behaved badly, but like he told her, it was a long time ago, he wasn't that much older than Lottie and she was of legal age by the time things became serious between them. He didn't know, could never have imagined the hurt he caused that young girl.

'If you see the good in people,' her mother always told her, 'they will see it in themselves.'

Everyone deserves a second chance. Samantha takes out her phone, pulls up her father's number and composes a text:

Heard you and Rhianna are expecting. Congratulations. See you next time I'm back. X

The evening is better than any she and Peter have had in a long time. Peter gets home earlier than usual. He has been worried about her, he says, and wanted to make sure she was OK. Samantha puts Emily to bed at seven, keen to re-establish her routine. A little after seven, Peter hands her a glass of dark red wine. On the stove, tomatoes simmer in a deep frying pan. She can smell garlic, chillies, olive oil. He really is a wonderful cook.

'Chianti Classico, 1996,' he says. 'I thought we should open something special to celebrate having our little girl back safe.'

She smiles at him, brings the glass to her nose. Inhales but can't smell anything suspicious. But then, if she's used to it, she wouldn't smell anything unusual. She shouldn't be thinking like this. Hopefully, with time, she'll learn not to. And she won't mention that the wine is the same age as her.

'Look at you,' he teases. 'Nose to the glass. Very good.' He holds his own glass by the stem, takes a large mouthful. 'Actually, we should have a toast.' He really is all smiles this evening, like a man from whom a heavy weight has been lifted.

'Here's to us,' he says. 'A little prosaic but no less profound for that. To you and me, to putting what is past behind us and embracing what the future has in store. Cheers, my darling.'

'Cheers.' She drinks, only a little, tries to discern a bitter note. But he wouldn't do that, not to the mother of his child, not while she's still breastfeeding. She averts her gaze. She was, she realises, staring at his hair.

After dinner, they watch a French film with subtitles, set immediately after the Second World War. She longs to chill out in front of a comedy or a box set, but Peter tells her it's good for her post-baby brain to watch challenging films, to read only the best literary fiction, that she must not let herself fall into bad habits: inane TV, pacy books, women's magazines. She agrees with him about the magazines; they are, as Marcia says, propagandist tosh, but she makes a mental note to buy a Kindle, then she can read what she likes.

In bed, he is his usual mix of tender yet insistent. He hardly ever misses a night, which can be exhausting and a little stressful. It isn't that he forces her, no. Just that she knows that if she doesn't respond, he will continue until she relents. She is so tired by evening and it is better, quicker, easier to comply – that way she can sleep sooner rather than later.

'That was terrific,' he says, lying back.

She is not sure who or what he means, since she has done little more than lie there. He rubs the hair on his chest as if to give himself a congratulatory massage, before rolling over to face her and teasing into his fingers the white-gold necklace he bought for her when Emily was born. He commissioned the piece from a jeweller in Strawberry Hill. On the fine chain is a tiny pair of hand-made white-gold bootees, which is what he is holding now between his thumb and forefinger.

'So, now that this horrible ordeal is over,' he says, 'how about getting married?'

She cannot meet his eye. His past is in the past, yes, but it bothers her like a stain she can't remove. That he is not, as she suspected, unfaithful is a big thing. But as the hours have worn on, her certainty about his new-found moral compass has waned. The question of the hidden drugs and whether he is giving them to her without her consent is still, she realises, live. Trust does not rebuild in one flashing epiphany. But rebuild it she must. Peter is, after all, the father of her child.

She gives him the warmest smile she can. 'Ask me again. I'll say yes eventually.'

To her surprise, he doesn't sulk or pick a fight or accuse her of not loving him as much as he loves her, but instead laughs and kisses her on the nose.

'You play so hard to get,' he says. 'I love it. But I will wear you down.'

And I you, she thinks. *And I you.*

CHAPTER 30

It is Monday morning. Three weeks later. Samantha is standing in the kitchen, the handwritten letter she has collected from the doormat open in her trembling hands.

> Dear Samantha,
>
> You know by now that my name is Charlotte not Suzanne and that it was me that took your beautiful baby girl. By now little Emily is hopefully back safe in your arms and your life has returned to normal. I know I don't have any right to ask you for any of your time but if you can read this letter just once I would really appreciate it.

Samantha gasps, rests one hand on the counter. From upstairs comes the rumble of water flowing through the pipes. Peter has gone for a shower after his morning run. She reads on.

> First off, I am so sorry for what I did and I hope one day you can forgive me. I am not well. I haven't been well for a long time but that's no excuse.
>
> As I say, I am sorry. I didn't mean to cause you pain. I didn't mean to do what I did, but I just did it and no one else did it but me – trust me, I do know that. When I saw you at the nursery with Emily and you let me hold her, I thought you were so nice, but by then I think I was already on a terrible path.

Anyway, I'm sorry I wrote the horrible poems as well. I didn't know you at all then; all I knew was what I saw on Facebook, which is that you were with Pete and you had a baby together. You looked so pretty and happy, and I suppose I let jealousy get the better of me. I've been following Pete for a few years. I did run away to London once a long time ago to find him, but when I got to Euston everything was too big. It was like looking for a needle in a haystack, so I just turned around and came home.

I've done all sorts but I got a job in an estate agent's in town, just doing filing and that at first, but eventually they let me show a house because someone was off sick and I must have been all right at it because in the end I became an estate agent proper – in fact I have won the Nash and Watson Regional Agent award eight years running. Anyway, so I got a desk and then one day in the office I googled him and there he was. He was on LinkedIn and I recognised him straight away. He hasn't changed that much. Then I found him on his university profile and then on Facebook.

Then last year he tagged you in a post and I looked at your page and that's how I found out you had a baby, and that made me feel like killing someone. I didn't, don't worry! Then you posted that you were going to teach the course at Richmond College and you posted a link to it. I pretended I lived in your house so that I could enrol, but you might know that already. That was wrong too. I shouldn't have done that. I don't know what I was planning to do, to be honest. If I'm honest, I'd say I wanted to see what you were like, see what he went for in the end type of thing, but then I wrote that mean poem and then I wrote more. I was trying to mess with your head and get to Pete that way. But I know Pete is too clever for me. I never had a chance against him. I know that. I never had a chance. It was easier to mess with his wife.

The kitchen walls swing away and back.

'Holy shit,' Samantha whispers.

This is surreal; it's all surreal. Above, the rumbling water stops. The squeak of the shower door.

She reads on, lips pressed tight.

But I've got all ahead of myself, sorry. Pete was my history teacher at school. When he first touched me, I was fourteen. It was after school and I was helping him tidy up and he put his hand on my face very gently and said, 'Thanks for collecting the books, Lottie.' My name, like that. He was very handsome and all the girls were in love with him at our school. I was so proud he'd chosen me. After that, I stayed after school regularly and helped him, and we started kissing and a bit more in the stationery cupboard. He took me out to an Italian restaurant in Liverpool for my fifteenth and made me promise to keep it a secret, which I did.

He took me to other restaurants, then to hotels. I went to a girls' school so we didn't know many lads, and the ones that went to the disco weren't anybody I was interested in, not when there was Pete. I'd only ever been to Burger King and a Harvester before I met him, and I'd never been in a hotel. Pete had a Ford Fiesta and he had his own flat. That sounds silly but he did, and all the girls thought he was the business. He had money and he knew where to go and what to do. He knew everything. He was so clever and he was so funny – he was hilarious.

We started having full-on proper sex the night of my fifteenth birthday even though we'd done everything else by then. Sorry to say it like that. I wanted to wait but he said it was all right and he would look after me as long as I didn't tell anyone. He was nice about it. ~~He wouldn't wear~~ He told me he would do the withdrawal method, not to worry, he knew what he was doing. I trusted him because he was older. He told me he loved me and that we would get married once I turned sixteen. He said that on my birthday he would go and see my dad and ask. I believed him, every word.

A sickness has started up in Samantha's belly, a heavy brick of a feeling. Her forehead is damp.

Anyway, this is what I really want to tell you and it's something I've never told a soul. I'm only telling you because I want to try and make you understand why I did that terrible thing, writing the poems and taking your lovely baby. I'm not asking you to forgive me, but I just want you to understand something about me because I feel so terrible.

The thing is that I fell pregnant. I was fifteen and I was scared stiff, but I thought it would be OK because Peter had always said we would get married when I was sixteen. But he told me to have an abortion. He was really angry. He shouted at me and told me I was stupid and a slag, and I thought he was going to punch me. It was horrible. I remember it like it was last week. I could not believe it. It was like all my dreams getting flushed away down the toilet, but I still thought he loved me and that we'd be together once I left school. He organised everything and he took me there and drove me to the corner of our road after, and he told me if I told anyone he would kill me.

I didn't want an abortion. I just really hated the idea of it, and I've always wanted kids. I wanted to have like three or four. I thought he loved me and we would be a family. But he made me get rid of her. He told me if I didn't, he would never marry me and we would never have a family together. So I did it. And I didn't tell anyone, only myself, and to myself I said I'd had a real baby and I called her Joanne. I still call her that – I call her Jo for short – and I talk to her most days, take her to view the houses and that. I know I've taken this fantasy too far but it was all I had. She'd be not too much younger than you now. Funny that, isn't it? Only, then I got really sick. I had a fever and I was rushed to hospital and I had to tell the doctors what I'd done in the end otherwise who knows what would have happened? They told my parents because I was still a child when he got me pregnant, legally. I didn't think I was, but I know now that I was. I really was. I was a stupid child.

My parents were devastated. I nearly died of the shame. My dad was going to kill Pete with his bare hands but I begged him not to. My school was a Catholic school, St Catherine's. My parents had a meeting with the headmaster and they made Pete resign. No one wanted any scandal. It would have reflected badly on the school and my parents, what with gossip and that. We moved to Ormskirk soon after and by then my GCSEs were a waste of time. I left school with a few Cs and that was it, but I'm not stupid. I just couldn't concentrate. Pete went away. No one knew what had happened. I got better slowly and then years later I did get married, but we found out that I was infertile because of the infection.

I suppose that's when my depression really started. My husband couldn't cope and we got divorced.

I'm not trying to make you feel sorry for me, Miss; I'm just trying to explain. I did some mean things, but I think you're really nice and every time I think about what I did, I feel terrible. I'm returning the key to your house. I took it when Pete and me stayed there one time when his dad was on holiday. I'm sorry for sneaking in. That was wrong as well. It's a beautiful house. It's a palace really. I sell houses myself, I think I said that, and once I get better I'm hoping to go back to it. As I say, I don't want you to feel sorry for me; I just want you to understand because maybe then you'll feel better about everything and you'll know it will never happen again.

Pete isn't a bad man. He just wasn't ready to have a family back then. He doesn't know what happened after he left. I wanted him to know but now I don't anymore. What's the point? I'm glad you're happy together now. I know I will never be a mum but I can tell you're a lovely one and that is a nice thing for me to think about.

It would mean the world to me to know you forgive me. I know you're not my daughter, but I like to think she would have been a nice person like you. One day maybe you'll forgive me, but I'm not asking you to or anything. Sorry again. If I could turn back time, I would. Look after yourself, Samantha – I mean that.

Lottie
xx

Samantha folds the letter and slides it back into the envelope. She puts the envelope in her bag and sits at the kitchen table. She is desperate to cry, desperate. Her eyes and throat ache with the pressure. But Peter's footsteps thud on the stairs and she knows that in a few seconds he will appear at the kitchen door. Which he does.

'Coffee?' he says. He is not asking if she would like one; rather if she's made it.

'On the stove,' she says, getting up to pour a mug for him. 'I made a fresh pot.'

CHAPTER 31

She is still sitting in the kitchen when her phone beeps. In front of her on the table lies Lottie's letter. It has been more than an hour since Peter left for work. She has read the letter over and over, must have drifted into some kind of catatonic state. She lifts the letter. Her phone is underneath, a message from Aisha on the screen.

Hey. It's been a while. How are things? X

The house is cold. Christ, it's freezing. Her nose is an icicle, her fingertips red. Shivering, she takes the heating dial from the shelf and sees that the temperature has dropped to 15 degrees. She resets the thermostat to 19, thinking as she does so that 19 is, for her, a little chilly but that Peter has told her it is the correct temperature for the house. She shifts her thumb over the dial, bumps it up to 21.

Her phone beeps again but it is only Aisha's message re-announcing itself. Samantha reads it again before replying:

All fine, thanks. Don't think Peter is up to anything dodgy anymore but am keeping eyes open. You OK? X

That should do it. Her life from this moment and what she does about it is no business of anyone else's. It is Medusa's face; it is not possible to stare into it directly. Ha! Peter would love that analogy, were he not himself the monster. Samantha is alone. Like Lottie. Poor, bewildered, apologetic Lottie. Lottie, who she has hated for stealing her child, whom she betrayed even when that hate turned to sympathy. Lottie is a schoolgirl ruined, a woman ruined, a life ruined. While she alone has carried the shame and the consequences, the man walked away uncaring, unscathed, unaffected. And that man wants her, Samantha, to be his wife. He wants them to step together into their glorious future in this beautiful house with their beautiful child and every possible material need met.

Everyone has the right to leave the past behind.

Do they?

Do they really?

Her phone beeps. Aisha again.

Just wondered if you'd like to see King Lear at the Curzon next week? 21ˢᵗ? It's the live feed direct from the Playhouse Theatre in town? Jen not fussed. Spare ticket yours if you want it.

A peace offering. But her head is mince. Her face is sticky. Her bones are old. She is sitting in her home, but the thought of her home makes her sick. There is no home for her back in Yorkshire, not really – her mother's flat is too small, and she's damned if she's going to live like an old maid, end up bitter and brittle. There's no way she'd knock on her father's door, face bringing up her daughter alongside her own half-sister, co-exist with a stepmother her own age, endure her mother's devastated gaze. No, no, no. She should never have let Peter persuade her to trust him, should never have let herself get pregnant, let him get her pregnant, oh God, but now it is too late too late too late, and anyway she would never wish Emily away, would never …

She groans, throws her head into her hands.

'Idiot,' she shouts at no one. 'Stupid, stupid, stupid.'

A play sounds like the last thing she should do. But she loves *King Lear* and real life is unbearable. It would give her something to look forward to while she figures out what the hell to do with her life. She could ask Peter to babysit. No, not babysit. Emily is his child too. Samantha's not been out in the evening since Emily was born, not once, not without Peter. Peter has been out, been away, worked late, worked weekends. Peter has carried on as if nothing has changed. Even his early-evening red wine has remained unaltered, though Samantha knows now why that is. Jenny had a point. He knows what he is. A narcissist who is clever enough to know he's a narcissist, who won't be caught looking in the pool, who won't be drowned by his own reflection. She thinks of Dorian Gray, the comparison horribly obvious to her now. The man who wears so well on the outside but whose hideous likeness rots away in the attic. In the attic, she thinks, with all the frightened madwomen driven there by men like him.

The letter on the kitchen table is Peter's portrait.

Yes, yes, yes, so much for all the hand-wringing. There is a child, there are practical issues of money, food, shelter. Again, her mother comes to mind. That first time in the new flat. Sparse, cold, so far from the cosy kitchen at the farm.

'Put the kettle on,' her mum had said, sniffing brightly. 'Small steps, that's what's needed. One thing at a time.'

Small steps, Samantha. One thing at a time. A solution will present itself by degrees. She just has to wait until it becomes clear.

She checks the calendar on the kitchen wall. The twenty-first of March is next Wednesday. Peter has written: *Dep meeting 8 p.m.*

'Bugger,' she whispers. Peter's life: ongoing, undisturbed; everything else fitting around it.

She texts Aisha:

Sorry, but Peter has a meeting. I would have loved to! Thanks for asking. Xx

Aisha must have her phone attached to her hand, because her message flies back seemingly moments later:

Jen says she'll look after Emily. You can drop her at ours.

Samantha chews her cheek. Replies:

Would love to. But Peter won't like it.

'Bugger,' she says as the text sails away. She should not have added that last bit. The conversation with Jenny and Aisha returns to her. How it took a termination for Aisha to wake up to who she had become. They will see what *she* has become – subjugated, afraid, cowed. She is about to send another text when Aisha replies:

Peter doesn't have to know.

No, Samantha thinks. He bloody doesn't. He will undoubtedly go for a drink after the meeting, as he always does, and it will take him over an hour to get back from central London. And if he does get home before she does, well, she will have to think of Lottie and Aisha and Jenny and the others she doesn't know about, and Emily for that matter, and stand up to him.

All right, she texts. *Send me your address and the time. Thanks.* Small steps.

And small steps are what she takes. In a kind of post-traumatic fog. Life by minutes, hours, days. Texts not calls. No live interface, apart from Peter. Smiling survival. Quiet subterfuge. Days pass. Until one afternoon, something clears. Something coalesces from that thick fog. Samantha stops at a gift shop and buys a card and a book of stamps. Takes Emily out for a stroll down to the riverside and stops at the café under the arches. March, the sun is out and with her coat, scarf and woolly hat on, it is warm enough to sit outside and watch the water. Lulled by the movement of the pram, Emily is fast asleep. Samantha sips her hot chocolate, takes out the card and opens it.

Dear Lottie, she writes. Stops. This is harder than she thought it would be. But Lottie wasn't trying for elegant prose; she was simply trying to tell her story. The best thing here is to be honest.

> Thank you for your letter. It meant a lot to me that you took the time to explain your circumstances and it has helped me to move on and to feel safe with regard to my baby, Emily. I accept your apology, I do forgive you

and I am reassured that you won't try to hurt us again in any way.

I am so terribly sorry that you went through what you did when you were so young. I understand how easy it is to fall for the charms of someone older, who appears to know and understand the world and who is more accomplished than one's immediate peers.

She reads this back. She sounds pompous. She crosses out *one's immediate peers* and puts *boys your own age.*

'Yep,' she says to herself and takes another sip of hot chocolate.

I am so sorry that you didn't get to see your daughter grow up. That must be a terrible source of sadness for you. And of course, words cannot convey how sorry I am that you are not able to have children as a result of a termination that you never wanted to have. I can only imagine how painful that is, and I think that the fact you wish me well now means that you really are a very special person. It takes a big heart to be so generous when you have suffered so much yourself. Thank you.

I wish you nothing but happiness and peace going forward. I hope you can forget about Peter now, get back to your job and move on properly, as you deserve to. Keep writing, if you can. It is a worthwhile form of self-expression and I certainly find that it can be good therapy in difficult times.

Take good care of yourself, Lottie.

I really do wish you well.

Samantha

xx

CHAPTER 32

The following Wednesday, Peter texts Samantha at five to remind her that he has a meeting. They will probably head on to the pub. He will be late home. Don't wait up.

She replies that all is fine. Everything is under control. She'll see him later. In her belly burns a rebellious little fire. It is not unpleasant.

At six she takes an Uber to Jenny and Aisha's flat on the far side of Richmond. To be honest, the thought of leaving Emily with Jenny makes her chest hurt, but she knows she has to move on and that moving on means learning to trust and to live without fear.

Jenny and Aisha's flat is supremely tidy and clean, modern white gloss kitchen units, the floors a wood-effect linoleum that is warm underfoot. But, my God, it is small.

Aisha gives her the tour.

'This is the bedroom,' she says with a mock-curtsey, and Samantha's mouth drops into an O.

'We're not a couple,' Jenny shouts from the open-plan living space. She has already unclipped Emily and has her comfortably on one hip. She walks up the little hallway, grinning. 'We take turns having the couch on a six-month basis. Clean but compromised rather than spacious but scuzzy. London for you.'

They are both a few years older than her, yet this is all they can afford. They don't even have a bedroom each.

'If one of us gets lucky, we have a warning system in place, in case you're wondering. There's a bit of eye-shielding and ear-muffling but it suits us fine.'

'You wish,' Aisha says, laughing. 'You mean there would be if either of us pulled more than a muscle.' She smiles at Samantha. 'Come on, we should go.'

Samantha realises that Aisha has not gone near Emily. Wonders if she ever has or will. Too painful, most probably. Bloody hell.

They arrive at the Curzon a little early. Aisha won't take any money for the ticket so Samantha insists on buying them both a drink from the cute little popcorn stand. It will appear on her bank statement; Peter will see. So what? She buys two glasses of Cabernet Shiraz, quipping that Aisha shouldn't worry – she won't spike it. She is becoming like them, she thinks, beginning to treat the whole thing as some hideous joke, albeit one she is still stuck in. She buys a packet of roasted peanuts, which they eat at one of the little booth seats in the foyer.

'It's lovely here,' she says.

'I can't believe you've not been. It's an independent. And you can take your wine in, which is très civilised.'

'How come you had a spare ticket?'

'Um, oh.' Aisha stares down at the tickets, as if confused. 'I was supposed to be coming with Sally. You know Sally, don't you? Professor Bailey?'

'You know Professor Bailey?'

'I did English, remember? She taught one of the MA modules. We got on well and kind of stayed in touch. I see her sometimes for a drink and a catch-up, but she couldn't make tonight in the end.'

'She's friends with Peter.'

Aisha is still looking at the table. 'She tried to warn me off him, back when we were … I was defensive, not reading the signs. She tried to tell me, you know, in subtext, that students were his *thing*, but I guess by then I'd withdrawn. Shrunk, actually, that would be more accurate. And Sally backed off. Well, everyone backed off. That's what happens.' She looks towards the film posters, as if to admire them, but she is not admiring them, Samantha knows, simply searching for somewhere to rest her eyes while she gets through what she wants to say. 'Then afterwards she never said I told you so, which I've always appreciated.' She glances at Samantha but immediately away, to a point behind Samantha's head. 'Ah, we can go in.'

They take their seats. The crowd are older, well dressed and most are white. Samantha wonders if she would have noticed this last if not for Aisha, wonders then what it must feel like to always be in the minority, wonders why the hell she doesn't think about this stuff more.

The curtains scroll back.

'Oh, how funny,' Samantha says.

On the screen are rows of seats, as if they are looking into a mirror. But it isn't a mirror.

'That's the Playhouse,' Aisha says. 'Amazing, isn't it? The play is being transmitted live from the West End and we can see it here in Richmond.'

'Amazing.'

It is. From her seat in Richmond, Samantha watches the theatregoers take their seats all the way over in central London. Some are already sitting, chatting, pointing, whatever, quite unaware of being observed from the other side of the lens. And with no sound at all, the effect is disconcerting.

Aisha leans close, keeps her voice low. 'I remember the first time I came here. It makes quite an impression, doesn't it? They have to rig up the camera for the live feed before the play starts obviously. They'll do the sound check in a few minutes; you'll hear the sound come on, and then a broadcaster will introduce the play. Last time it was Emma Freud, I think. Not sure who it will be today. Anyway, it's weird because we can see them, but they can't see us.'

'So it *is* a mirror,' Samantha says into Aisha's ear. 'A one-way mirror.'

'Exactly.'

They settle and watch, benign voyeurs. The camera shots change every minute or so. Now the stage: black and bleak; now the audience: chattering, fussing, oblivious. Now the stage. Now the audience.

And there. Live from the West End of London, taking his seat and talking to an attractive young blonde woman, is Professor Peter Bridges.

Samantha's entire body freezes.

A burst of static, followed by the dull rumbling of inaudible conversation. The audio feed has come on. Now the stage. Now the audience.

Peter has taken his seat. He has a glass of red wine in one hand. With the other, he is offering a packet of something to the girl. She takes a handful, tips back her head and empties whatever it is into her mouth. Peter gazes at her long neck. She glances sideways at him and laughs. He laughs. He cocks his head and continues to laugh before pushing his face to hers and kissing her on the mouth.

Samantha can feel the tension, electric in Aisha's arm as if it is her own. Aisha has seen. She has definitely seen. White heat. The world suspended.

The house lights dim. Silence. A presenter speaks into a microphone, but Samantha doesn't hear a word. Another silence, then blackness. Blackness on both sides of the screen. Blackness everywhere.

And so the play begins, Samantha thinks. *The play begins now.*

CHAPTER 33

Outside, the cobbled lane is slick, though the rain has stopped now. Samantha matches Aisha's silence with her own as together they leave the river at their backs and wander up towards George Street.

'Amazing, wasn't it?' Aisha says finally.

'Amazing.'

They stop at the crossroads. Aisha looks away, down towards the shops. Peter hangs in the air between them.

'I have to go,' Samantha says, bending down to kiss Aisha on the cheek. Aisha, already petite, has worn trainers this evening. In her mule heels, Samantha is much taller.

'Samantha—'

'I'll talk to you soon.' She turns and waves. 'Bye.'

'Samantha! Emily? Emily's at the flat.'

Fuck. Fuck, fuck, fuck.

She pivots on her heel, slaps her forehead comically. But this is one act she cannot keep up.

'Sorry,' Aisha says, spreading her hands.

Samantha wonders what she's sorry for: that she ever told her about Peter, that Peter is a bastard, that he has turned them all into these strained, shadowy creatures, afraid of talking to one another?

'What did Jenny say?' she says, tipping up her chin. 'We have to stop apologising.'

Has Peter ever apologised, she wonders then, for anything? In all their time together, she can't remember him ever saying sorry, whereas she has said that particular word over and over and over again. But no more.

Together they walk towards the station, in silence. Four, five, six paces and already the tension grips at Samantha's shoulders. Another ten and she stops dead on the pavement.

'Look,' she says. 'I saw him. I saw Peter with the girl. But I don't want to talk about it. I just can't deal with the judgement right now, all right?'

'I'm not judging you.' Aisha's brow creases with hurt. 'I would never do that.'

Samantha closes her eyes, opens them again. 'I know. I didn't mean … I just …'

'But I do need to tell you something.' Aisha falters, glances up but almost immediately looks back down to her trainers. 'It's just that I was talking to Sally and I … I don't know how you came up in the conversation. I might have mentioned that you were teaching me or something, but anyway she said you'd been in touch about her scarf and asked me if I thought Peter was up to his old tricks. I said I had no idea – honestly I did – but she said she thought he might be because he had told her he was going to see *King Lear* and when she asked him who with, he was cagey. I guess she put two and two together. She's known him a long time. I think she only puts up with him because she's not into men, but I got the impression that this time she was appalled, with him having a baby now. Anyway, it was her suggestion that I take you to see the live feed, said we probably wouldn't see him, but if we did it might be easier to have the evidence presented in a neutral way rather than having to hear it second-hand.'

'Might be easier to … Hang on, why would she say that? What did you say to make her say that, Aisha?'

Aisha bites her lip. 'I might have said you … you were convinced he'd changed. I might have said something like that.'

'Christ, Aisha.'

'Look, there was no guarantee we'd see anything. It was a bit of a long shot, frankly, and I thought if we did see him, at least you'd have a friend with you for support.'

Samantha is reeling. 'What …' she begins but gets no further.

'I'm sorry,' Aisha says.

'You set this up? You and *Professor Bailey*?'

Aisha looks wretched. 'It was with the best of … Oh God, I'm so, so sorry.'

'What I don't understand,' Samantha says, 'is why anyone cares quite so much about my private arrangements.' There. She has managed to vocalise it. 'I mean, what the hell has it got to do with anyone?'

Aisha's face has fallen.

Samantha hesitates. But the conversation is not over.

'I just keep coming back to the fact that you and Jenny and Lottie all ended up in my class,' she says. 'And now I find out that fucking Sally Bailey knows my private business too, that she's sticking her oar in, giving me a ticket so I'll catch my partner in the act. I mean, I know you've explained why you and Jenny came to the class, but don't you think it's weird that Lottie was there too? It's like some horrible hall of mirrors. I feel like I'm living on CCTV, everyone watching, knowing stuff about me. You'd tell me if you knew Lottie from before, wouldn't you? I'm asking you, Aisha. I'm only going to ask you once, and if I find out you lied, we're done – do you get that?'

'Sam,' Aisha says. 'I'm so sorry. Our intentions were good, I promise. Jenny and I only approached you after we found out you were with Peter. We genuinely didn't want to see another woman's life ruined by that b— that excuse for a man. You can check it with the college. If you look at the records, you'll see that we enrolled for the previous term but the class got cancelled. And I guarantee that Lottie will have enrolled after you put up the link on your Facebook. That's how she knew you'd be the tutor. The college don't give out that information. You know that, Sam. Come on! This is how abusers get us. They turn us into these secretive little animals, and when we try and come out, we don't believe each other because believing is just too terrible. Peter is an abuser, Sam. He is a serial abuser of women.'

'Don't say that! You don't get to call him that to me! He's my partner and the father of my child. It's me who decides what he is, me that gets to call him an abuser, all right?'

Aisha throws up her hands. She is crying now, quite openly.

'Look,' Samantha says after a minute. 'I didn't mean to make you cry. I know you're trying to help. But I don't need some first wives' club wading into my life, OK? I don't need an action squad, no matter how well intentioned. Just let me handle this. If you genuinely want us to be friends then you'll have to try not to interfere or pass comment or – or judge, OK? Because you won't understand – I don't think you'll understand what happens going forward. And that's fine. I don't need you to understand. I just need you to be here on the other side, OK? I know it doesn't make sense now, but it will. One day. All right?'

Aisha looks confused, as well she might. And looking at her crushed expression, her eyes so wet and solemn, Samantha wants to kiss her on the forehead and say, *It's OK, I don't quite know what I mean either, not yet.*

'But I do want us to be friends,' is what she does say. 'OK?'

Aisha nods, glossy tears brimming on her lower lids. Samantha pulls her into her arms and mutters into her hair, 'Just stop trying to help. You're lovely but you're making a real mess of it.'

Aisha laughs. They pull apart. Aisha wipes her face with the back of her hand.

Samantha digs in her bag.

'Here,' she says. 'Mums always carry tissues.'

*

The rain resumes, quickens. It's still a good fifteen-minute walk, so Samantha orders an Uber. Peter is, if nothing else, generous with money. More than generous – flash, in Samantha's eyes, growing up as she did in more modest circumstances, even before the bankruptcy. In the cab, she takes Aisha's hand and holds it. Aisha is still a little fragile. Odd that she should be more upset than Samantha when it is the singed scraps of Samantha's burning humiliation that float now in the air.

But Samantha is filled not with embarrassment, not with shame or tears, but with a kind of preternatural cool, as if she is able to look down upon herself and direct her own speech and action as she used to control her dolls as a child. She wonders with this same detached calm exactly where and how Peter has seduced or will seduce this new woman. This *girl* – that fleeting expression of delight so like her own not so long ago, back when she herself was still a green fruit, caught in Peter's dazzling light. He can't bring whoever she is back to the house, not anymore. He can't play out the firework display of all that he owns and does and is. He wouldn't deign or risk her student accommodation – assuming she's a student. The back seat of the Porsche, forget it.

A hotel, then. How lovely.

She settles back in her seat. Outside, drops of rain fall against the taxi window. Peter appears in her mind's eye. He is walking towards her. He smiles and holds out his hands, but as he does so, he collapses into columns of numbers that stream down against a dark sky. It is code. A kind of computer code.

A soft laugh escapes her.

'What's so funny?' Aisha asks.

'I just had a thought and I was like, oh my God, that is so original, but then I realised it was actually a scene from *The Matrix*. You know, when Keanu Reeves realises that the baddie is just a computer program?'

'I haven't seen it, sorry.'

'Ah. Well, it's an old film, I suppose, but anyway the baddie seems real, but he's just a program. Or something like that. That's not the point. The point is that even though everything is moving super-fast, Keanu Reeves suddenly sees exactly what this guy is, and from that moment he's able not only to fight him but to anticipate what he'll do next. So from that point on, he has the edge.'

'What does that even mean?'

'It means ...' Samantha looks out onto the rain-drenched streets. 'It means it's time to act.'

CHAPTER 34

Peter arrives home after she does. She lies in bed, listening to his bathroom rituals. He doesn't shower, but when he gets into bed, she smells fresh soap and almost smiles to herself. A lovely hotel shower before leaving the poor cow who currently thinks she is his special one and only. She levels her breathing. He lays a hand on her shoulder, apparently thinks twice, lies back. A few minutes later she hears the low nasal inhalations she has come to recognise as Peter's peaceful slumber.

She rolls over, pushes her fingers through his chest hair, wonders vaguely if he dyes this too and if so, how; whether he uses a toothbrush or cotton buds or what.

'Peter,' she whispers. 'Peter, wake up.'

He jolts, grunts. 'What's the matter?'

She kisses his neck, reaches into his boxer shorts.

'That question you're always asking me.' She tightens her grip, feels him harden. 'I want you to ask me again. Ask me now.'

'Huh?' He is still groggy, confused.

'Ask me.' She bites his earlobe, moves over him, sits astride. Slowly she lowers herself onto him, pulls her nightshirt up over her head.

He groans, lays his hands on her hips.

'Ask me.' She moves, feels her own excitement grow. This night is full of contradictions – coolness in the fire of humiliation, helpless laughter in the midst of despair, and now, let's hope, a whopping orgasm brought about by pure, undiluted hate.

'Sam.' He grips her waist, sits up, clings to her. It is over in seconds, for both of them. She rolls off him, rests her head against his shoulder.

'Ask me,' she whispers.

He props himself up on one elbow and draws his forefinger up her belly.

'Samantha Frayn, excellent woman,' he says in his low, calm voice. 'Will you marry me?'

'Peter Bridges, clever chap,' she says. 'Yes, I will.'

They kiss. And it is this she finds hardest. But she steels herself and does it.

The next morning, he is drinking coffee and reading the news on his phone. She is used to the coldness, can anticipate it. Numbers, she thinks, streaming down in a dark, dark sky. Next, he will run upstairs, clean his teeth. He will return, plant a perfunctory kiss on her cheek and leave. It is possible he won't even mention what passed between them last night. Except he won't do any of these things, not this morning, not if she can help it.

'Good morning,' she says, flicking on the kettle, 'future husband.'

He raises his eyebrows, smiles. Hallelujah, a crack in the stone.

'Mrs Bridges.' He puts down his cup and his phone – a miracle – and crosses the room. Takes her in his arms and kisses her deeply on the mouth. He smells of shampoo, tastes of coffee. 'I thought I was dreaming, but if you remember it too …'

She giggles. 'I do.'

'I do,' he jokes. What a witty pair they are.

'How was your morning coffee, dear?'

'It was almost as good as what followed.' He grins. Oh for fuck's sake, he even winks. 'What are you up to today, future Mrs Bridges?'

'Actually,' she says, 'I was thinking of coming into town. I thought maybe I could pay you a visit. One of the mums said she'd have Emily any time. We could grab lunch or something.'

He frowns. 'I'm lecturing until three. Today is tricky.'

She smiles, meets his eye. 'Another day then? I have an idea you might like.'

'Oh yes?'

She trails her fingertips up his arm. 'I've always had this fantasy that I was one of your students.'

'Is that right?'

'Mm-hm. Maybe a PhD student, you know? So I was thinking, if you give me the keys to your office, I could wait for you there and you could maybe give me a little private tutorial before lunch. On your desk, perhaps?'

His eyebrows shoot up; he coughs into his hand. 'It's not a key, it's a … it's a pass card.'

'Key, pass card, whatever. I didn't mean it literally, it was more about the idea …'

'Yes. Yes, of course.' He appears flustered. 'Of course. I have a spare.'

'Great,' she says lightly. 'Shall we put a date in the diary?'

'How about next week? And I keep meaning to book our Easter holiday, but with Emily getting taken and the poems and everything I've been too preoccupied.'

'You're spinning too many plates, hon,' she says, almost licking her lips at the dramatic irony of the line she's just given herself. 'Leave it all to me.'

The first thing she does is book the wedding ceremony. Emily tucked under her arm, she fills in the forms, cursing at the thirty-day notice period. She thought that was something from back in the twentieth century, earlier even, and only for churches – wedding banns and all that jazz. Holy crap, that means she will have to keep this charade up for a whole month.

Both parties have to give notice – not an issue. The password for the home computer is the same as the one for his Gmail account, unless he's changed it again since Emily went missing. Today is Thursday 22 March – she sends notice from her own and Peter's account and books a slot for a simple ceremony, two witnesses, in York House on the morning of Thursday 19 April. That will work well with Peter's Easter holidays – she's pretty sure he goes back the following Tuesday, so they can have a long weekend honeymoon – with Emily. Tempting as it is to ask Aisha and Jenny to be witnesses, if only to see the look on Peter's face, she decides to ask Marcia and Jacob. Marcia can be told only what she needs to know. Samantha will tell her the rest afterwards, once the dust – and there will be a lot of dust – settles.

Is it too much to buy matching rings? No, she must do everything in the most convincing way possible. She must sweep him off his feet.

In Peter's bedside cabinet, in the little wooden box with the marquetry top, she finds the signet ring he sometimes wears when they go out. This she slides onto one of the candles they keep in the cupboard under the kitchen sink. *Everything in its place and a place for everything.* She draws a line around the candle with a sharp knife, there, where the ring has stopped. She will buy a cheap gold band. If all goes to plan, there will be no risk of it tarnishing.

There will be no time.

Next, she returns to the computer and looks into flights. There is only one possible place. Peter promised he would take her there. It was when he took her there through his words that she fell in love with him. She knew even then that this was what had happened; she felt it, had felt it even before, from that first precipitous sensation when he removed the drink from her hands and suggested they leave. His lecture was the penultimate piece of a seduction she thought was all about her, when in fact it was all about him.

But she's not going over this, not again.

There's a Virgin flight from Heathrow to Rome at 21.00 on Thursday 19 April. That will give them plenty of time to get married and make their way to the airport. They will even have time to go for a celebratory lunch, which will make the whole thing more authentic. Sidetracked, she googles the location of the register office and sees that it is over the bridge, towards Twickenham. They could go to The Crown on the roundabout near Marble Hill Park, but, no, Peter won't like that idea. Ah. Luigi's, his favourite Italian, is on that side of the bridge. Perfect. She can book a cab to take them straight there.

She calls the restaurant, speaks to Luigi and explains that they'll be coming directly from their wedding, that it's a private ceremony; would it be possible to book a romantic lunch for two? Luigi is charmed to be asked. Mr Peter is a special customer, he tells her. Leave it with him, don't worry. He will do something special.

'Thank you so much,' she says. 'That's so kind of you. See you then!'

She puts the phone down, realises that her excitement is not, in fact, fake. She really is keyed up, actually. Purpose, maybe that's what it is. She is full to the brim with purpose.

Back to the flights.

She needs their passports. That's a point. She knows Peter organised one for Emily when she was born but she's never seen his. She's not seen her own since she moved in, come to that. There's been much talk of travel, but actually they've barely left Richmond in their short time together. She was pregnant so quickly and Emily is still so little, they haven't yet thought about going anywhere on a plane.

Peter's passport is not in his desk. It is not on any of his shelves either, not even in the box file with the other official documents. She drums her fingertips against her lips.

Think.

There is a safe in the house. Peter has mentioned it. Everything in its place. The passports are bound to be in there. She knows the layout of every room – God knows, she's spent enough time here on her own – but she's never seen a safe. Although there is one room she never goes into. The cellar.

Emily on her hip, she walks out of the study and down the hall. She is about to open the door under the stairs when she stops. Small steps, yes, but be careful.

She runs upstairs and pops Emily in her cot, passes her a new set of toys and pulls the cord for her musical mobile. The one Peter cannot bear to hear when he's in the house. An insult to music, he says.

She takes a pair of latex gloves from the box under the loose floorboard. On reflection, she takes a few more pairs and stashes them in her bag before putting one pair on and heading back to the cellar.

There is a pull cord for the light. It is still flickering as she heads slowly down the stone steps. The basement is cold, sparse and clean. To the right is a wine rack from which around a dozen dusty bottles protrude. She shivers. An idyllic past looked upon through the lens of betrayal is perhaps the most distorted sight there is. All that was beautiful is ugly; all that was meaningful is filled with a kind of empty horror. She looks closer, torturing herself now. Amarone, she reads. Amarone. Amarone. Amarone. She gasps.

I've been waiting to open this one for a long time, he said that night.

All the bottles are the same.

All that was meaningful …

'Well,' she mutters to no one at all. 'It's not meaningful anymore, is it?'

The urge to pull these bottles one by one from the rack is almost overwhelming. To pull them one by one and throw them hard onto the concrete floor.

But no. Careful, Samantha. Be careful. She straightens up and looks around her. The safe is on top of a beautiful old sideboard that on closer inspection turns out to be riddled with woodworm. One of the feet is missing, and inside the central cabinet, the heart-shaped glass window is cracked, the mint-green velvet lining blackened with mould. It looks like something from Dickens, she thinks. Straight from Miss Havisham's sitting room. The safe on the other hand is a modern matt-grey strongbox with a brushed chrome door, combination lock. She was expecting a lock, of course she was, but even so her heart sinks.

'Bugger.'

If she can't get hold of the passports, the plan is dead on departure. Her advantage lies in a fait accompli. Peter won't be able to tell her how to do it if she's already done it, will he?

There must be some record of the combination somewhere in the house. She knows Peter keeps his bank card PINs in his phone under Caravag1 and Caravag2. It's possible the safe combination is also in his phone under a similarly stupid name. Something imaginative like, say, Caravag3.

With heavy tread, she takes the steps back up to the ground floor, the carpeted staircase up to the first, where Emily is whining and holding up her arms.

'Come on, baby,' she says softly. 'Let's get you out for a walk.'

She is wrestling Emily into her padded suit when it occurs to her that Aisha might know the combination, so it is Aisha she calls as she walks down the hill towards the town, Aisha who answers after one ring.

'Sam, are you all right?'

For a moment, Samantha flounders. 'Yes. Why?'

'Nothing. I just thought … after last night …'

'I'm fine. I … It's all fine. Listen, are you free now? Do you fancy meeting up?' She can ask Aisha what she needs to over the phone but it would be nice to see someone, a friend, if only to reassure herself that she still has one.

'I … I suppose.'

They arrange to meet at the riverside in an hour, on the bench in front of the Pitcher and Piano. In town, Samantha calls in at Courlanders, the jeweller's. She chooses two plain gold bands, gives them the candle for Peter's ring size and tells them she'll pick them up the following Wednesday. She will present them to Peter on Thursday when she announces her surprise. Yet again, she feels a surge of excitement. Taking control is a buzz.

She heads back up George Street and takes the right turn down past the Curzon to the riverside. The bench is empty, so she sits and watches the boatbuilders on the quay. The air smells resinous, the faint whiff of varnish and sawdust, the cooler damp notes of the river. A pale shadow falls.

'Hey.' Aisha is standing over her, hands on hips. She is dressed in Lycra sports kit and is even managing to sweat attractively. She cocks her head and pulls out first one earbud then the other, before turning off the iPod clipped to her sports vest.

'Thought I'd multitask,' she says.

'Impressive,' Samantha replies, aware that on the outside she must appear confident, relaxed, whole, when in fact she is afraid, tense, in pieces. In her belly, a hot flare of nerves rises at the thought of what she must now find to say and what it will mean for her and Aisha. But as of last night, when a plan clarified itself in her mind, her life has been no more than a play; that's all it is, all it can be for now. She just has to grit her teeth and take it scene by scene.

Aisha plonks herself down on the bench. 'So you said it was all fine?'

Samantha pauses a moment before rolling her eyes in what she hopes is a self-deprecating way. 'So, I'm such an idiot. I remembered when I got home that Peter's niece is in town. He actually told me she was coming and he, like, even said he was taking her to the theatre. But this was weeks ago and I forgot and I don't think he mentioned which play it was or I would have remembered. I thought he had a meeting but that's next week. I'd read the calendar wrong.' She makes herself laugh. 'I'm so sorry, I don't know what I was thinking.'

Aisha frowns, her brow knits. 'Sorry, I … His niece, did you say?'

Peter has no sisters or brothers. If Samantha knows this, Aisha sure as hell will. Christ, lying is complicated; how do people do it?

'Niece, cousin,' she spits out. 'Something, anyway, I can't remember. Jen, her name is. Jem. Jemima.' Shut up, Samantha. Really.

'Jemima?'

'Something like that. Gosh, I'm hopeless, aren't I? Baby brain! Anyway,' she blusters – horribly, awkwardly, unable to look anywhere near Aisha's face, focusing instead on her neon-pink running shoes, 'I do have some exciting news, although maybe I shouldn't tell you until you've processed—'

'No,' Aisha says, though her voice is small. 'You can tell me anything, Sam – you know you can.'

'You're not going to be pleased.'

'You don't know that.'

'Trust me, I do. But remember I said last night not to judge? Well, the thing is, Peter asked me to marry him again and I … I said yes.'

'You said *yes*?'

'I did.' Samantha closes her eyes a moment against the shocked expression on Aisha's face, opens them to see it still there. Oh God, this is hard, so much harder than she thought. Lying to Peter is one thing, but …

'Are you sure that's what you want?' Aisha is looking out at the river now, her hands clasped in her lap. There is an almost imperceptible film of tears in her eyes. Samantha wishes she could tell her everything, almost does. But it's best that Aisha despairs of her. It will protect her later.

'I know you had a rough time with him,' she says gently. 'And I know he's been a shit, trust me, I do. But I have to believe in second chances.' That's twice she's said *trust me*. It's the phrase Peter always uses. Funny that it should enter her speech habits now, when she is at her most dishonest.

'You think he's changed.' Aisha's voice is flat.

'I think he's got more to lose,' Samantha says. 'I think he's getting older and his power is ebbing away. Like King Lear, if you like.'

'Come on, he's not that old, Sam.' Aisha is still frowning, but her face relaxes a little. 'But yeah, he's vain and foolish, I suppose. Cruel when he wants to be.'

Samantha exhales heavily. If there were a trapdoor to her life before meeting Peter, she would pull the lever and drop through this second. Rewind. Start again. Hold on to her plastic glass of wine and say, *Actually, this wine is fine, thank you. I'm staying right here.* Meet some skinny, awkward boy, have too much to drink, go home for not very good sex but maybe get the hang of it eventually, together, on equal terms. Except for Emily, of course.

'I know this is hard for you,' she says. 'But I want to book a surprise honeymoon and I think the passports are in the safe. Don't suppose you know the combination, do you?'

They are both looking out onto the river now, to where a tugboat chugs merrily along, its blades rotating nineteen to the dozen at the back, the water churning white.

'I don't know it exactly,' Aisha says, her voice dull. 'But I've got a strong feeling it's the year of Caravaggio's birth. Or death. One of those. Fifteen something. Sorry not to be clearer.' And with an air of finality that makes Samantha's guts churn, she stands up and puts one earbud in, then the other.

'I'll see you around,' she says.

They both know that this is it, this is where their friendship ends, but Aisha's smile is kind, her eyes soft. She is sad too, unbearably so. Samantha has to look away.

'Good luck, Sam,' she hears Aisha say, the words a rock in her chest.

She looks up and raises her hand. 'Bye.'

But her friend is already running away.

CHAPTER 35

It's late afternoon by the time she gets home. She's exhausted; her legs ache. By the time she's fed and changed Emily and settled her onto her play mat under her mobile, she wants only to lie down next to her baby and let sleep take her under. But Peter will be back in an hour and, driven by what has become an obsessive desire to get done what she started this morning, she hurries back down into the cellar.

On her phone, there is a screen shot of the Caravaggio Wikipedia page. Two dates: 1571 and 1610. Caravaggio didn't last long, she thinks. But that's what happens to bastards who live their lives with scant concern for laws of common decency. At forty, Peter is doing well, considering. But he should watch his step.

She inputs the first number into the keypad, is so far from expecting it to work that when it clicks and the door opens without a hitch, her mouth too opens, in shock. Bloody hell. Inside is a slim pile of documents, at the top of which are their three passports, and for a moment she panics that it's all too easy. But it hasn't been, not really. Who keeps their passports in a safe, for God's sake? It's not like they work for MI5.

She runs up the cellar steps and boots up the home computer. The flights are still available; she gives an overenthusiastic whoop and punches the air. She's always wondered if anyone actually does that, but there, she just did. Frankly, this whole deception thing is proving so much more fun than almost anything she's ever done before. And if her entire life weren't in tatters, she'd have to admit that anger is just as good a life force as any other.

She begins to fill in the details. She will have to pay from her account. Peter would notice the money leaving his account immediately, but he won't check hers until the end of the month, unless she's really unlucky. Despite her generous allowance, she will have only just enough to cover the flights plus the wedding fee. She will have to pay for the rings in cash, although who can give her a loan, she has no idea. Later. Cross that bridge when you get to it.

The sight of her passport mugshot catches her off guard. Her eyes fill with tears. She renewed her passport the year she came to uni, convinced that she would travel during the holidays. But the student loan was so intimidating, the rental on the flat had to cover the entire summer, not just term time, and her parents couldn't help. Her holidays weren't holidays at all but spent working in bars and cafés, putting every last pound not towards a trip around Europe but towards her degree, her future, which is now ruined. But it is not this that makes her cry. It is the expression of hope on her face; her own youth makes her feel like a bitter old crone in comparison. Two years ago. Not even that. She worked so hard to escape the ugliness of her life in Yorkshire, only to end up here, in a life so beautiful on the surface but beneath, uglier still.

Her fingers curl into fists, nails digging into the palms of her hands, and she lets out a cry of rage.

Use it, she tells herself. Use the rage. Control it. Small steps. Small, careful steps.

She slides Peter's passport across the desk and opens it. His photo is uncanny – he looks exactly the same as he does now. Peter Pan. Like Lottie's piece of flash fiction said. *No, you're not Peter Pan*, she thinks, running her finger beneath the passport number. *Peter Pan was nice. Dorian Gray is what you are, a beautiful, beautiful monster.*

She types the passport number into the booking form, followed by Peter's date of birth, 5 February 1978. Glancing back at the passport, she pauses. His date of birth there is given as 1968.

Her head throbs. There is a mistake on Peter's passport. She will have to call the passport office and find out how to correct it. Peter is forty. They celebrated just last month. He made no secret of it; just didn't want a big fuss. Rustic candlelit dinner for two at the new pizza place, bottle of fizz, bottle of red. *Low-key,* he said, *if there's a zero on the end. Why on earth would anyone want to celebrate being a decade older?*

Reeling, she reads the date again and again, willing it to change, for her eyesight to prove her wrong, for the numbers to melt and re-form. But they won't. They won't ever. Of course. Peter's particular brand of the truth: present a little, let whoever hears it complete it.

There is no mistake.

Peter is not forty.

Peter is fifty.

'No,' she shouts at his unchanged, uncanny, unbelievable passport shot. 'No, no, no.'

But it makes horrible sense. Every event of her recent life lines up with grotesque precision, drops into an ordered row of slots, the click of the correct combination on a safe door, the rush of two-pence pieces in an arcade waterfall. Lottie is a nearly middle-aged woman. Peter must have been around thirty when he left that school; Lottie was just sixteen. He said he was a couple of years older but he was twice her age! For Peter to be forty, Lottie would have to be in her late twenties now, not her late thirties.

'For Christ's sake, Samantha,' she shouts at no one but herself, tears of frustration at her own stupidity running hot down her cheeks. Why didn't she see? Why didn't she think clearly? Too busy, once the seamy details began their oozing leakage, trying to figure out whether he'd changed, if he was a better man now, if there was a way to put his past behind them, if she, Samantha, could be that way, that person, that saviour. Second chances. Redemption. Bullshit.

There is too much past. Too much of it.

'The hair dye,' she wails into her fingers. 'Oh God, the hair dye.'

She is on her knees on the floor of his study. She is banging her fists against the Moroccan rug, the story of the purchase of which was one of his early anecdotal flirtations. He has never told her, not in numbers, how old he is.

'I'm older than you,' he has said. And, 'Trust me, I've been around a little longer.'

A few too many careful owners. Vintage. Mature. Experienced. Trust me. You're safe.

'Fuck.' She is sobbing now. Too much, too much, too much deception masquerading as transparency. There is no point challenging him. 'What?' he will say. 'I never told you I was forty.' Because he didn't. He didn't say the actual words. Peter's words, she thinks, are as slippery as snakes on the Medusa's head.

CHAPTER 36

A week later, Samantha arrives at the university at one thirty. She trips up the stone steps and swipes Peter's card at the black entrance door. An electronic click. The door opens. She makes her way up the stairs to his office, where she swipes his card once again. She has only been to his office once, with him. It is larger than she remembers, lined with books, of course. On the wall are his certificates, photographs of ceremonies, university visits and socials. His leather desk sits adjacent to the window, which looks out over Gordon Square. But she is not here to look at the view.

In her pocket is a bag of pills. A bag once empty, left on the kitchen table. Peter saw it, picked it up as she knew he would and put it in the bin. Latex-gloved as a surgeon, Samantha retrieved it, put four pills inside, part of the stash Marcia got for her at the weekend from a friend who bought them from a guy in a club. She owes Marcia big time, and that's without even mentioning the cash for the rings.

She closes the office door behind her. The latex gloves have come in handy. This morning she used a pair to remove Peter's little stash from its hiding place, tip it into a tiny travel shampoo bottle and replace it with washing powder. The shampoo bottle is in her handbag, where it will stay until she needs it. Now she pulls on a new pair as she slips the plastic bag out of her pocket and winkles it to the back of the top right-hand drawer of his desk. Shuffles various pens, articles and official-looking letters in front and, satisfied that he won't see it, at least not today, closes the drawer. That's all she has to do for now.

She takes off the gloves and wanders over to Peter's bookshelf. As at home, the books are in alphabetical order. At the Gs, she stops, a title catching her eye: *Artemisia Gentileschi: Images of Female Power*. She pulls the book out. The cover shows a painting at once familiar and unfamiliar – she's pretty sure it's Judith beheading Holofernes. It looks very like the image Peter showed in that first lecture. But this is not Caravaggio's painting, she's almost convinced; there is something even more shocking about this one.

She takes the book to Peter's desk and sits down. Flips through, and yes, she was right, here is the Caravaggio picture, for comparison. Beneath, she reads: Judith Beheading Holofernes, *Caravaggio, c.1598–9*. Intrigued, she finds the cover version on the next page with, beneath it: Judith Slaying Holofernes, *Gentileschi, c.1614–20*.

She skim-reads, flipping back and forth between the two images. Gentileschi was younger than Caravaggio – her painting came later. She was ten when she first met him, and Caravaggio's version is believed to be the main influence on her later work. But in the Caravaggio, the murder appears almost effortless. The image is still bloody, of course, but Judith looks unsure, worried perhaps, standing at arm's length from her victim, her servant almost cowering behind her. Gentileschi, by contrast, has both her women bearing down, working as a team, the physical effort much more obvious in their poses, their faces determined, focused. It has taken two women to overpower this guy, whoever he is. And from the expression on his face, he knows they will not stop until his head has been severed. This is the better painting, Samantha thinks. Why has she not heard of this woman?

She reads on, willing Peter to be late while she finds out more. Gentileschi's work was a protest against the abuse she suffered at the hands of men. Rape, repression, injustice. She used her own face in the painting. Just as Caravaggio was his own Medusa, Gentileschi is Judith. Holofernes ... Holofernes is someone called Agostino Tassi. Samantha's eyes scour the page, find the name once again, lower down. Tassi, she reads, was Artemisia's rapist.

'Whoa,' she whispers.

Of course Gentileschi's work is more violent than Caravaggio's. This woman was working from a place of deep visceral fury. She was exacting her revenge.

The door flies open. It's a little after one forty-five. Peter's face is flushed, his hairline damp with sweat. He has clearly run through the campus and, judging by the look on his face, is surprised to see her there. But he soon rearranges his features.

'You're early,' he says and smiles, almost shyly. She wonders why he has felt the need to run. Perhaps he wanted to take something before she got here, get himself in the mood. Who knows? Who knows how much, how often he takes this stuff? He might simply have rushed so as to see her all the sooner. That's the problem with a loss of trust: everything that comes after is loaded with suspicion; the ninety-nine per cent trust becomes one. The one per cent doubt becomes the ninety-nine.

And so here they are.

Peter stands on the other side of the desk, as if he is the student and she the tutor. For a moment neither of them says a word. She wonders if either of them will be able to go through with what they have planned without embarrassment. But then she remembers the play. This might, she thinks, be Act Two.

'I'm here about my thesis,' she says. She lays down the book, picks up one of Peter's biros and taps it against her teeth.

'I ... I read it.' He looks stressed.

She puts her feet on his desk, crosses her ankles. 'Oh yes? And what did you think?'

He blows at his ridiculous acrylic-like hair and comes to sit on the edge of the desk. She lifts her leg, repositions it so that she has a foot either side of him. For the first and, she suspects, last time in her life, she is wearing stockings and suspenders. Peter has told her so often that he doesn't objectify women. But that was bullshit and this is role play.

'Christ,' he whispers, runs his hands up the inside of her leg.

She whips her feet from the desk and leans forward, unzips his fly.

He stays her hand.

'Wait,' he says. He looks about him, seems to be searching for something.

'I hope there aren't too many corrections,' she insists, pushing her hand inside the loose opening of his boxers.

'Not too many.' His voice has thinned. He bends forward and kisses her hard on the mouth. 'Just a few things we need to go over.'

She almost loses it. The whole thing is so cheesy, like an old film, or even porn, not that she's seen more than a few minutes of that stuff. But he's into it, the evidence is hard in her hand, and she knows she can't bottle out now.

But despite the early encouraging signs, Peter struggles to keep up the necessary enthusiasm. She does what she can, but he fades in her grip like a week-old balloon. She wonders at his initial reticence, right at the start. Is it possible that he's so drug-dependent now that he can't enjoy anything unless he's taken something? Or has he felt the power shift already?

'Sorry,' he says, sitting back from her. 'We'll have to try again later.'

'That's OK. Don't worry about it.'

He zips up his fly with an apologetic grimace, opens the deep bottom drawer of his desk. It is a filing section, she can see the steel runners, but inside are not files but bottles, five or so, housed in a cardboard wine carrier. Something about this makes her feel sad, so sad it almost makes her question what she's doing. Peter is not bad, not really, just pathetic. He pulls out a bottle and waves it at her.

'Maybe if we have a drop of this, we can try again?' he says.

She wrinkles her nose. 'Let's just get to the restaurant, shall we? It's booked for two thirty. It's Mexican; we can have margaritas. I'm in charge today, remember. This is your surprise.'

He puts the bottle back without argument. She can't decide if he's disappointed or relieved, but it feels weird to have him do what she says.

They head towards Fitzrovia. In the restaurant, she orders margaritas – virgin for her; she's still breastfeeding, she reminds him, and a cocktail might be too strong. They arrive crusted with glittering salt. Peter excuses himself to go to the bathroom. While he's in there, she takes out the shampoo miniature and pours a little of his magic powder into his drink. It is astonishingly easy, as easy as taking a painkiller, in the bustle of the busy restaurant. And she has practised. The sprinkles hit the cloudy duck-egg-blue drink and just as quickly dissolve. She knew she'd have the opportunity to do this because the thing about Peter is that he needs the loo a *lot*, much more than boys her age. Not surprising, not anymore. Goodbye, grumpy Peter; hello, nice Peter.

'I've been busy,' she announces when he returns from the little boys' room. 'Very busy indeed.'

'Oh yes?' His smile is the same as when they first met, the same smile he was giving that girl at the theatre last week, the one that says: *Go on, you fascinate me.*

'Oh yes,' she quips. 'But have a drink first.'

He doesn't need asking twice. He puts the glass to his lips and takes a large swig.

'Oh, that's good,' he says.

'Are you ready?' She raises her eyebrows and pulls a face, egging him on as you would a child. She pulls out two small jeweller's boxes and pushes one over to him.

'Look at me.' She giggles. 'I'm a wreck.'

But she is not a wreck – far from it.

'What's this?' He is half amused, half ... something – she's not sure what. He takes another slug, almost finishes his drink.

She reaches out and takes both his hands in hers. 'I'm going to count to three. On three, I want you to slide your box over to me, and I'll slide mine over to you, all right?'

His expression is still amused, a touch of paternal indulgence.

'All right,' she says. 'One, two, three.'

The boxes slide, cross over.

'Now,' she says, giggles threatening to ruin the moment. 'Another three and we open them.'

She closes her eyes for a moment.

'One,' she says, blinking. 'Two.' She grins, gratified to feel her eyes filling with open-to-interpretation tears. 'Three.'

She opens her small burgundy jeweller's box. But she's looking at him.

He frowns, that half amusement again playing at the edges of his pink mouth. He takes out the wedding band.

'It's engraved inside,' she says, and while the reasons might be other than Peter will surely deduce, her excitement is real. 'It's a date.'

'Nineteenth of the fourth, two thousand and eighteen,' he reads.

'Yes,' she rushes in. 'That's when we're getting married.'

He meets her gaze. 'What?'

She knows, can feel, her eyes are shining. Oh, it is so good to be in charge! Energy surges through her. She wanted to wait until this moment to tell him! She has done this for spontaneity! For romance! For love!

'I've booked a wedding at Richmond Register Office. Low-key, like you prefer. We get married that day, on the date on the rings. And afterwards, we're going to Luigi's for lunch – he's going to do something really special – and after that ... guess where we're going? Rome! You've arranged so much for me, so this time I thought I'd arrange everything for us. What do you think?' She's out of breath, which is as it would be.

His features fight – he looks like he can't decide whether to be excited or horrified, as if he knows what is expected of him but has no idea how he could have expected this of her, his little malleable princess, so much younger, so much less worldly than him. She can only hope the sprinkles are kicking in.

But his eyes are soft. The chemicals must have hit his bloodstream. He takes hold of her hands and kisses her knuckles. 'I can't believe you've done all that in secret. How did you ... how did you get my passport details?'

'From the safe!'

His brow creases. 'How did you know the number for the safe?'

'Well, I ... I tried your birthday and my birthday, and nothing. I knew your bank card pins were listed under Caravag1 and Caravag2 and I've seen you type a number into the cashpoint a few times and I was pretty sure it started with fifteen. So I looked up Caravaggio on Wiki and I saw his birthdate was fifteen something and I thought maybe you'd used that, the same as your cash cards.' She shrugs. 'I knew I only had one more try but I thought, well, if it all goes wrong, I'll just ask you, you know.' She reaches for his hands again. 'But I so wanted to surprise you. And when it worked, I was so happy.' She laughs: a merry, feminine trill. 'The only thing is, I am so skint now. I might need you to transfer some money, is that all right? But I thought, you know, you were going to book an Easter holiday, and I know you wanted to take me to Rome, so I thought you, me and our beautiful baby girl ... I thought you'd be pleased.' She smiles with all the warmth she has in her, an attempt to return the power to him. He must feel that she is seeking his approval; he must sanction it before it is allowed to happen. 'You are pleased, aren't you, hon? Did I do a good thing?' That last was maybe a bit over the top.

His face breaks, thank God.

'You're amazing,' he says. 'You've organised it perfectly. I thought you'd want a large wedding, but if you prefer a register office, then so do I.'

'I don't want a fuss. I don't want my mum coming down because then I'll have to invite my dad and … no, too stressful, I can't face it.' She kisses the back of his hand. 'I want it to be just us. It's … well, I think it's really romantic, don't you?'

'Where are we staying?'

She holds up her hand. 'Well, actually, I made enquiries. I hope you don't mind, but I asked Sally and she said your favourite hotel is the boutique place in Trastevere. It wasn't too expensive so I … I just went for it.' She cocks her head to one side. 'Did I do OK?'

He drains his drink, signals to the waiter for another. 'Well, we'll probably need self-catering, with Emily.'

'You're right. Of course. I'll change it.' She gives an excited little shrug. 'Told you I'd been busy.'

She has told him everything, though not of the shock of finding out his real age, as he now knows she has. If it hangs in the air between them, he doesn't show it. Neither of them does. That's another little discovery about lying. Once you know you're being lied to, it's up to you whether you walk away, or stay and play along.

CHAPTER 37
ROME, APRIL 2018

The dusty yellow light sweeps up the Via Veneto, glances off the foreign embassies and the five-star hotels, the Lebanon cedars, the stone pines and plane trees of the vast Villa Borghese park. Doubling back, down it comes, over the Centro Storico, floats over the gurgling brown wash of the River Tiber, over the distant footfall of long-dead Roman soldiers in the Castel Sant'Angelo, over the statues wrestling on the Vittorio Emanuele bridge. Onto the white dome of the Vatican this light sprinkles its hazy yellow dust, downriver, down, down to Trastevere, with its students and its buskers, its homeless, its pizzerias and late-night bars. Its artists and its lovers.

And here are two such lovers … although they are no longer in the first throes of passion, the first exquisite moments of mutual discovery. The tourists eye them as they walk hand in hand, form their instant, baseless opinions. His hair is chestnut brown, his stomach doesn't trouble the buttons of his shirt, but those who observe with a keener eye see the telltale grooves in his forehead and the crow's feet at the edges of his eyes, the creases that bracket his mouth, the chin that is losing its definition. Still, he has kept himself in shape. He's really looked after himself. Probably afraid of losing her, yes, look at her – much younger, and pretty too. He lets her carry the baby, they notice – his back's probably packed up, knees giving him gyp. She really is so much younger, now they look closely. Fine blonde hair slung up in a messy ponytail, limbs like string, too young to be with him. Maybe she's the au pair, maybe a third wife, maybe she's after his money. A baby, though, oh, and look, new, shiny wedding rings, how sweet.

He's taking a photograph of his young wife, positioning her against a dilapidated Roman doorway, telling her exactly how to stand. The picture is composed: the perfect juxtaposition of radiant youth and vainglorious, crumbling ruin. He has an artist's eye.

'Rome,' Professor Peter Bridges says when the photo is taken, straightening to his full height. 'Roma,' he qualifies with a sigh, as if he is the first person ever to be struck quite so hard by the impossible magnificence of the Eternal City. He stretches out his hand for hers. Together, laughing like children, they head for the Ponte Palatino, to the Chiesa di Santa Maria in Cosmedin, the only sight she has chosen, has been allowed to choose, for their itinerary.

'Another church,' he says, with the barest lacing of reticence.

'It's a hidden gem.'

'This city is full of hidden gems.' A dismissal, or note of appreciation, it's hard to tell. 'Rome is a city always with a bunch of flowers up its sleeve.'

Samantha Bridges, née Frayn, smiles – not at her husband's words but at the memory of a time when the way he spoke moved her. It wasn't long ago, though it feels like decades.

'Just when you think you've seen all its tricks.' Peter is warming to his theme now. 'Bam! Rome always surprises. That street with the antiques, Sam,' he says. 'Yesterday, what was it called? The one between the Piazza Navona and the Vatican?' He clicks his fingers one, two, three times. She wonders if he is pretending, to test her. She can't imagine he'd want to concede to her in anything.

'Via dei Coronari?' she offers.

'Yes.' He kisses her on the forehead. A test then, the kiss a reward bestowed from professor to student. Although she is not a student, not anymore. And she was never his.

In truth, what she is is exhausted. They have walked all morning. They had a good lunch in a little place they discovered not far from their Airbnb apartment in Via della Paglia, and like all good lunches, it was a soporific one: fried courgette flowers, tortellini and tiramisu made by the restaurant owner's mother. A carafe of house red, which Peter drank, and now he's complaining of thirst. That's because he's drunk too much, as usual. And it's possible he's taken too many recreational drugs.

I'm thirsty, he complains as they make their way to the church, and she thinks about how he never complained when they first met, well, not about anything pertaining to his physical state. No aches and pains, no grey hair, no bad back. *You give me life*, he told her in those first heady weeks and months. *You give me the energy of a teenager*. His fists thumped against his chest in triumph. And then, in bed, between soft bites of her plump resisting flesh, he murmured words of desire that made her want to giggle and call Marcia so that she could giggle too: *I could eat you alive*. His teeth against her thigh. *I could drink you right down*.

Like a vampire sucks blood.

Or like Emily drains the milk from her breasts, leaving her depleted and sleepy.

She *is* depleted. He has drained her dry.

He squints against the low sun. 'So, we're going to see La Bocca della Verità?'

'The Mouth of Truth,' she translates.

He squeezes her hand, swings it as a father might with a young child. She doesn't enjoy the comparison and yet, deeper still, she does. He smiles at her, but his wariness of her is palpable. As if he fell in love with one person and has ended up married to another. How ironic that it is he who should feel like this.

In the queue, he fusses and grumbles like a child. He is a spoilt child. He has not grown up. And when he refuses to put his hand into the gargoyle's stone mouth, she knows she has finally got to him. She knows that he knows that she has seen him clearly, that she saw him clearly a while ago now. How right he is. To her, he is nothing but code raining down in a black sky. She can read the numbers, make her predictions. She knows what he will do next.

What he does next is stagger, cough into his hand. Moments later, he is pushing through the queue, away from her. She follows, calling his name, the baby heavy on her back. On the tiled floor of the church, he falls to his knees, his face set in a grotesque silent scream. Like the Mouth of Truth, she cannot help but think. Or better, Caravaggio's Medusa – a face with fake hair, caught in the full horror of self-recognition. Peter would be proud of her for the comparison. He has taught her so much.

'*Aiuto!*' she cries. '*Ambulanza!* Someone call an ambulance!'

She holds back the worried crowd with her hands.

'*Lasciaci*,' she begs them. Leave us.

She unbuckles her backpack and lifts Emily out. Cradling their baby against her body, she lies beside her husband and strokes his face. On the floor of the church, their family must make for a tragic tableau worthy of Caravaggio himself. Churches always manipulate the light so well. They can make you think you're in the presence of God when actually what you're looking at is paupers' money spent for the glorification of those in power. Ah well, her husband's eyes are closed now, his mouth slack against the shining tiles. The baby grizzles. Samantha opens her blouse and lets Emily suck and be calmed. This infant, so tender and mild, this young wife, her old man. Around them, the soft buzz of those who stand observing this scene of aching poignancy: a bereft new wife lying on the floor so as to whisper tender words of reassurance to her beloved husband while their baby suckles at her breast. She puts her lips to his hot, clammy ear.

'Peter,' she whispers, pulls her head back so she can see him. She wants him to open his eyes. She wants him to look at her.

His eyelids flicker open. A deep, peaty brown.

She holds his gaze. 'I know what you've done,' she whispers. 'And I know what you are.' She leans further in and, at the risk of a tad too much religious symbolism, plants a kiss on his cheek. 'Trust me, my darling. Time's up.'

Peter gasps, reaches out. His eyes are open wide; he is trying to speak. She lowers her ear to his dry, cracking lips, feels his fingers clasp around her arm.

'But you were the one,' he croaks. 'You. You were my—'

Rubber soles, shouts, bustle. A clamour of paramedics.

'I love you,' she cries over the shoulder of a man in a white overall. Someone helps her up and guides her and her baby back a little.

Her husband's legs are all she can see of him, the rest white jackets who bend over him with tubes and plastic lungs. Their briskness contrasts with Peter's utter stillness, and for a moment she thinks things might have gone too far. She holds Emily to her chest. Sweat runs down her back, tears fall from her chin, roll down her neck. Minutes pass. A paramedic stands back, wipes his gloved hand across his face, a gesture of regret and sympathy she recognises from hospital dramas on the television. A wave of nausea rolls inside her. She knows what this man is about to say, and with a sympathetic knitting of his brow and a sad shake of his head, he says it:

'*Mi dispiace.*'

I'm sorry.

'Oh God,' she says. Blasphemes, there in the church.

CHAPTER 38

ONE YEAR LATER

The dinner is rowdy. Samantha can't hear herself think, can't think for laughing, and the food is delicious. A huge pot of veggie chilli, baked potatoes, sour cream and soft, warm tortillas.

'Sam, this chilli is the best.' Aisha raises her glass and takes a swig of the cheap Pinot Noir – on offer in the supermarket: buy six, get twenty-five per cent off. They will get through all six bottles tonight, Samantha is sure.

'Peter never let me make chilli,' she replies above the din. 'Said it was for plebs.'

Aisha rolls her eyes. 'Don't speak ill of the dead.'

'I'm not speaking ill, just saying, that's all.'

They exchange a look, the kind that only close friends can. In moments such as this, Samantha feels she is both here and not here, within herself and without, living her life now and contemplating the life she might still be living had she remained stuck in it. Her life now is as familiar as it is unrecognisable. But the persistent feeling of unease has gone. It began to fade the moment Peter breathed his last.

The decision to ask Jenny and Aisha to move in was easy compared to other, bigger decisions she has had to make. Peter's house is enormous; their flat was tiny. Samantha was lonely, the idea of a new partner not something she could face for the foreseeable future. They insist on paying rent, but she charges them much less than they paid for the tiny one-bedroom flat, and of course they have their own rooms. Samantha gets to share her home with two funny, generous women, women who were always on her side, even if she didn't see it at first. Her judgement of character has been ropy; she gets that now.

Her mother came to stay immediately after the honeymoon, to support Samantha in her grief and through the police investigation. It felt natural that she should stay on, and the rent on her little flat gives her a little income. Right now, Mum is wearing a wig that Jenny bought for a fancy-dress party they went to recently at another ex-UCL student's house – another of Peter's women, as it turned out. The wig is platinum blonde, and with Mum's dark eyebrows she looks like old pictures of Andy Warhol, or a puppet, or a politician. Whatever, she looks hilarious, her eyelids are heavy with wine, and she is telling the rest of them that when Samantha was little, she would sleepwalk into her parents' room and scare them both half to death.

'You'd open your eyes and she'd be standing right there, pale as a ghost, with her dandelion hair flying about. All she'd be wanting was a glass of water, but honest to God, she used to frighten the living daylights out of us.' Her mother pulls off the wig and smiles at her daughter. She looks happier than Samantha has seen her in years. She is studying jewellery design and elementary guitar at Richmond College, where Samantha now teaches English to foreign students and basic literacy to people who, for whatever reason, left school without learning to read and write. The work is emotional and hard and utterly without status, but she loves it. It's poorly paid too, but money is not an issue. On her days off, she writes when she can. Short stories now, not poetry. Recent experience has made her a better writer; it has given her an edge.

They are all really quite drunk. Aisha is regaling the table with her latest attempt at internet dating, or rather, pre-dating: a Tinder exchange with a bloke who, she tells them, fancies himself as a twenty-first-century gigolo.

'"I'm looking for a woman who isn't afraid to be dominant",' she reads from her phone, and already the women are giggling like schoolgirls. Aisha holds up her forefinger and waits for them to settle down before continuing. '"I like the fact that you're in running kit; it shows you're not scared of strength. I can help you with that."' She looks up, her eyes wide. 'Like, what does that even mean? But, wait for it, how ridiculous is this? He says, "I also like BDSM and would be delighted with a threesome if you have any attractive friends."'

An outraged burst of laughter echoes around the table.

'So,' Jenny says, her head cocked at a coy angle. 'When are we meeting him?'

Another laugh.

'Friday,' Aisha bats back. 'Eight o'clock.'

Hysteria.

Samantha stands up, which silences them. A little shy all of a sudden, she eyes the group around the table. Her mother. A woman called Debs, who Jenny has brought along and who seems all right. Aisha and Jenny, and Marcia, who has brought chocolate eclairs from Iceland, where she is doing two shifts a week to help pay off her overdraft. Samantha told her she could come and live in the house, of course, but Marcia has moved in with Jacob and they are, as she puts it, skint but happy as pigs.

'OK,' she begins. 'I'm going to propose a toast.' She raises her glass, then, realising that what she has to say might take some time, places it back on the table. 'As most of you know, a year ago, almost to the day, my husband, Peter, collapsed while we were on honeymoon and died of a heart attack.'

Debs gasps. The others nod gravely.

'Sorry, Debs,' Samantha says. 'But it's fine, don't worry. We're coping well. And I have this lovely lot to keep me cheery. Like any crisis, it wasn't caused by one single thing. And it wasn't as straight-forward as a simple tragedy.' She glances at Aisha, who smiles. What Samantha says next is most of all for Emily, the baby calf she has licked clean and will now raise without help from the bull. Bully. Whatever. The mythology of Peter's death is part of her protection.

'Turns out that Peter, as most of you know, was addicted to Ecstasy. Addicted, well, maybe not, but he was a functioning user as well as a functioning alcoholic. I didn't realise. I just thought he liked red wine.' She pauses. 'A lot.'

Jenny laughs, apologises.

'That's OK, Jen,' Samantha says, not far from laughing herself. 'He never taught a class while inebriated, never drove inebriated, so far as I know, but there was always something in his system, often more than one substance. Funny how you can live with someone and have their child and think you know them.' She meets her mum's sad eyes for a second.

'But you don't – not always. I fell in love with someone whose past, as it turned out, was much more difficult to accept than I thought it would be. In more ways than one. Speaking of which, I got a card from Lottie yesterday. She's doing much better and is hoping to get back to work later this year.'

The women give a collective mutter, the gist of which is that they're all really pleased. In her card, Lottie thanked Samantha yet again for paying for counselling, and for the cheque, which she has used to pay off the mortgage on her flat. Samantha will write back by hand and continue to do so until Lottie feels up to using email again.

'Peter,' she begins again, since they are supposed to be remembering him in as positive a light as they can, 'I found out after his death, was also taking Viagra.'

A gasp.

She holds up her hand. 'I haven't told any of you this before – it seemed disrespectful – but I'm telling you now. I had no idea, but the results of the autopsy showed that it was likely the combination of drugs and alcohol, stress and heat, put too much strain on his heart. I should have noticed. But then I had no idea he was fifty, not forty, so you might argue I'm not very observant.

'So it wasn't just the drugs,' Aisha says.

Samantha permits herself a wry private smile. No. The realisation that his new wife wasn't going to be taking any more shit might have had something to do with it too.

When the police accompanied her back to the hotel, they found a bag of coloured pills and a small vial of blue ones in his case. Samantha didn't have to feign surprise. She really had no idea they were there. It was only later that she put two and two together and realised that the blue pills were the reason he had run back to his office the day she intended to play his sexy PhD student. Finding her already there, he couldn't take one, of course, and things had gone a bit limp from there.

In his office, the police found more drugs, only some of which Samantha had planted, plus the five bottles of red in the filing compartment. Professor Sally Bailey confirmed that, sadly, Peter was a bit of a boozer who liked his women young, joking with a wry smile that he'd been known to dabble in Mandy from time to time, as well as Sheila from records and Anne from accounts. She was sorry to be disrespectful, but really, what was there to say?

The police never found the vial of soap powder under the bathroom floor, but they did find two more baggies of pills in his sock drawer. His fingerprints, his habit, nothing to do with Samantha, the naïve wife, so much younger, broken by shock and grief.

Grief softened by a substantial fortune, she has found.

She picks up her glass. 'I want to make a toast not to Peter, but to friends. To the women around this table. Without you lot, I wouldn't have had the courage to face … a lot of things. So, yes, to friends. Trust each other, support each other, look out for each other.' She smiles. 'It's not rocket science.'

CHAPTER 39

Samantha had not anticipated how she would feel a year on from her husband's death. There has been, after all, a loneliness to it, despite surrounding herself with the people she loves most. And it is this loneliness that wakes her at four in the morning and sends her wandering like a ghost into Peter's study to sit for a moment at the desk where he worked when he was at home. The others are asleep, as far as she knows. This big, beautiful house hums only with the faint sound of the fridge.

She has not felt able to come in here until now, but tonight, she realises, has brought her a kind of closure. She thinks of her father, who she eventually went to see after Peter's funeral, along with his partner and the new baby. They speak once a week on the phone now, and while she will never be close to him like she was as a child, she can live without the need to punish him for all eternity – a decision that has brought her as much peace as it has brought him, she suspects.

People make mistakes.

She switches on Peter's anglepoise lamp, which throws a warm white light over the artfully mottled leather surface. In the left-hand drawer, she discovers a spare computer mouse, some old receipts and some theatre tickets that were never used – for him and his new girlfriend, no doubt; his PhD student, as it turned out (what a surprise), who thought herself that little bit more sophisticated, who lusted for culture and civilised seduction. Poor cow, Samantha thinks, before correcting the thought – that woman has had a lucky escape. She'll be better off with the inexpert advances of someone her own age, someone she can grow with, find sophistication by degrees, if that's what she wants.

In the right-hand drawer are some A4 batteries, a stapler and spare staples. Scintillating. In the middle drawer, printing paper and a lined notepad. She pulls the notepad from under the ream of paper. In the lamplight, she can see the pressure print of scribblings, and somewhere in her gut, a dark one per cent tingles.

'Are you OK?'

She startles, turns. Aisha is standing at the door. She has on her fleece tartan pyjamas and she is as cute and puffed up with sleep as a child. Aisha, whom Samantha loves and trusts ... ninety-nine per cent. And it is this last per cent, this last drop of resistance, that drains away in the dark of the house they have both found themselves in at different times, lost in the labyrinth of Peter's so-called love, only to find themselves living here together now. How good it would be to trust someone one hundred per cent.

'Come into the living room,' she says. 'I have something to tell you.'

In the hearth, the embers have all but died out. Samantha throws a few balls of newspaper onto them, pushes them down with the fire iron, adds some twigs when the flames come. Not the way Peter would want her to light a fire, but Peter is not here, is he? She puts a small log on, then another. When the fire is going again, she sits top to tail on the sofa with Aisha and tells her about her last day with Professor Bridges.

She reiterates what Aisha and the others already know. She tells Aisha that she knew he was in trouble when he complained of terrible thirst on the way to the Mouth of Truth. She tells Aisha that this was because he'd drunk an entire litre of red wine at lunch.

'But it's also because ...' She sits up a little, coughs into her hand. 'It's because when he went to the loo in the restaurant, I emptied a large dose of Ecstasy powder into the carafe.'

Aisha's brown eyes widen. 'What? How?

'In the hustle and bustle,' Samantha tells her. 'I mean, it was so noisy in there. I had the powder in this miniature shampoo bottle, a travel one, you know? And what with the waiters shouting to each other, the door to the restaurant kitchen being open, the chefs swearing and the pans clanging and God knows what … There was some crappy music playing through the speakers, the other diners were looking out onto the Piazza della Verità, or into each other's eyes, or discussing the next sight on their agenda or whatever, so yeah, I just poured it in. I even had time to pick up the decanter and give the wine a good swill.'

'You drugged him?' Aisha's eyes are round with what looks like wonder.

'I'd been drugging him pretty much since I found out he was drugging me. Well, us.'

'What?' The incredulity on Aisha's face is gratifying. It makes up for that awful moment when Samantha watched her run away down the riverbank, believing their friendship over.

'Yes,' she says. 'The day you and Jenny told me, I thought, me too. I knew he was spiking my wine and that he had been all along. I wasn't even surprised, just kind of depressed. And so I thought, if he could drug women to make them more affectionate, compliant, whatever, it was only fair to do the same to him. Marcia scored me some pills; I ground them up. It was easy. And he really was much more pleasant, for much more of the time.' She smiles.

'Oh my God. You never said.'

'Well, no. And don't you say anything either … ever.'

Aisha shakes her head. 'Of course I won't.' She bites her lip, meets Samantha's eye. 'So … so did he really die of a heart attack?'

The subtext is deafening.

'Yes,' Samantha replies.

Aisha presses her mouth tight. When she speaks, it is a reverent whisper. 'No, I know, but, you know, why marry him? Why organise a big secret surprise honeymoon?'

'Did I kill him? Is that what you're saying?' Samantha shrugs. 'Marcia told me some Ecstasy users take four or five pills a night. I wasn't sure about the dosage. I didn't really know what I was doing. I wanted to keep him pleasant, but yes, I admit that when I tipped that powder into his wine, I wanted him to suffer. I saw the damage he'd done to all the women in his life. And I wanted to do him damage right back. I wanted to freak him out. I wanted to look into his eyes and see fear, make him understand how it felt to be powerless. I wanted to take the power back. And when I got home, I was going to file for divorce on the grounds of adultery and mental cruelty. I wasn't about to leave Emily destitute, Aisha. I needed the paperwork. So I needed him to believe in my warped truth for a change. I kept thinking about Lottie and others like her and thinking that men like him do this stuff all the time and that it's the women who go underground, the women who hide away and become lonely and poor, and it's the women who are silenced by shame. And I thought, what the hell, you know? That's why I took him to the Mouth of Truth. I wanted him to know that I was on to him.'

Aisha nods.

'But I didn't know he was taking Viagra,' Samantha adds.

'But did you … want him dead?'

A different question. Samantha shakes her head. 'He was a monster, a beautiful monster. He was ugly on the inside. He raped a child, ruined her physical and mental health and walked away without a care. The burden of shame was all hers, poor girl. He made you have a termination when you thought you were about to start a family. He was cheating on you with Jenny, and when you both dumped him, he panicked and took advantage of my naïvety and weakness to tie me down because, finally, he realised he needed security. He was cheating on me out of nothing more than habit, must have controlled and abused God only knows how many women over the years, all the while proclaiming his feminist credentials, his refusal to objectify, when in fact that was all he did. That was all he ever did, wasn't it?'

Aisha nods but says nothing. She doesn't need to.

'So, to answer your question,' Samantha says, 'I spiked his wine. I threw the little plastic bottle into the Tiber when we walked over the bridge to the church, told him it was a message, a secret wish for our marriage. I knew I'd committed a crime against him. I didn't intend to kill him but yes, maybe I'm glad he's dead. I'm glad that I looked into his eyes and saw fear – that was what I wanted. I like to think he took a good look into my eyes, saw his hideous reflection and it killed him.' She exhales heavily. The words are shaping her thoughts as they fall. 'Look, I've never done anything big in my life. It was about taking back power, not just for me but for you and Jenny and Lottie – for all of us. It wasn't about him, Aish. It was about us.'

'Yes.' Aisha is looking at her intently. Telling her all this tonight could be a mistake, but not telling her means living with this loneliness for ever. And she has been so lonely, in her subterfuge and secrets. They all have. They have been behind a wall. And why should women, why should anyone, live behind walls?

'I tell you what pissed me off more than anything else,' she says as they begin to make a move back to bed. 'What really did it for me in the end.'

Aisha leans in, the firelight flickering in her huge brown eyes. 'What?'

'The bloody hair dye.'

CHAPTER 40

After Aisha has gone back to bed, Samantha returns to Peter's study to turn off the lamp. The notepad is where she left it, the faint marking of words scrawled across the page. The glimmer of unease returns. She checks that Aisha has gone up, then takes a pencil from the pot – everything in its place and a place for everything – and sits down. Her heart is beating with a strange familiar presentiment, a one per cent of feeling she will from now on know better than to ignore. She runs the pencil lightly over the scribbles, the lead flat on its side. There are crossings-out … there are a lot of crossings-out, but what emerges is a draft of a pastiche of a poem she has seen before, in a hand she recognises absolutely. A familiar unfamiliar villanelle. She rubs the blunt edge across the looping indentations, her throat closing.

Do not go blindly into that bright light.

Back and forth she swipes the lead across the page.

Wise girls they know that silver tongues do lie.
~~They are but dogs which sniff bark sniff and spit and drool~~
~~They are but slavering~~
Those men are dogs, they hunt their prey by day.
Do not go blindly into that bright light.

She drops the pencil. Her hand is over her mouth. The whole poem lies before her, white scrawl in a crazy charcoal cloud. She had thought this poem too clever in comparison to the other offerings. Instinct told her it could not be by the same hand. But as she has done so many times, she dismissed instinct once Lottie confessed. Dismissed it and forgot it.

I'm so sorry I wrote the horrible poems, Lottie said in her letter, though of course she didn't list them. Why would she?

Peter wrote this after all. Seeing that it was him she turned to in her fear and vulnerability, he wrote this presumably out of some desire to capitalise. Here was an opportunity to bind her even tighter to him in all his insecurity and ongoing diminishment. Pregnancy was not enough. She wouldn't marry him, no matter all that he was and owned. He needed more. He claimed to be offering her safety, but it was he who needed it, he who feared being alone. He told her she was the one as he drew his last breath. She thinks now that it was, possibly, the truth. He loved her so much, he took a poem written in love for a man's blind dying father, a poem he himself had read aloud at his own father's funeral, and used it as an instrument of mental cruelty designed to keep her where he wanted her: with him, for ever. She thinks of the seduction that was not a seduction, the lingerie that was in no way a suggestion, and this, this desperate warning to flee from him that was in fact the opposite, the absolute opposite. The most audacious of his double bluffs, my God.

'What did you do?' she whispers into the night. 'What did you do, my beautiful, beautiful monster?'

A LETTER FROM
S.E. LYNES

Dear Reader,

Thank you so much for taking the time to read *The Women*; it means a lot to me that you did. I really hope you enjoyed it and that it gave you food for thought. If you'd like to be the first to hear about my new releases, you can sign up using the link below:

www.bookouture.com/se-lynes

The Women is the first book I have written that, after I handed it in, caused me to shed a few tears. Writing a novel is always a long journey, and like most journeys, not all of it goes well – there are problems, hurdles, moments when you want to give up and turn back. With this particular work, I felt the weight of responsibility very keenly because I was trying to tackle an important topic through story and the particular confines of the psychological thriller.

Human beings have always told stories to help make sense of the world. Around the time of the Me Too campaign, I became interested in trying to weave a story around some of the issues surrounding the abuse of power for sexual gain while trying to underline the challenges faced by women who dare to tell their stories and the collaborative power generated by that. The message that women can give each other enormous strength is one that cannot be reinforced enough. The legacy of Me Too must be made to last, and this means that women must be encouraged to have the confidence to talk to one another instead of hiding in the shadows of shame. This confidence, of course, requires trust, loyalty and believing each other without judgement. We must create environments in which we can tell our stories.

Samantha's story is, for me, one of coming up from the fog of youth into active adult consciousness; of developing the edges and the strength she will need to survive and learning to place her trust in the right people. When she meets Peter, she is naïve, while he is a master of seduction who has had years to hone his craft. He has all the power: financial, intellectual, physical. To have any chance against him, Samantha needs to find strength in her friendships but most of all in herself. I enjoyed watching her transform into a woman prepared to fight not only for herself, but for others.

Experience forms us all. I don't know a single woman who has not, to a greater or lesser degree, experienced some form of inappropriate behaviour that has made them at the very least uncomfortable, and I wanted to try and reflect that. Lottie suffers the most serious abuse, but I believe that, had Samantha not acted, she would have become a long-term victim and finished up a ghost of herself, no longer capable of fighting. I didn't want that for her and hopefully you didn't either.

If you'd like to share your thoughts with me or ask me any questions, I'm always happy to chat via my Twitter account and Facebook author page, so do get in touch. Any writer knows that writing can sometimes be a lonely business, so when a reader reaches out and tells me my work has stayed with them or that they loved it, I am truly delighted. If you enjoyed *The Women*, I would be so grateful if you could spare a couple of minutes to write a review. It only needs to be a line or two and I would really appreciate it!

I have loved making new friends online through my novels, *Valentina*, *Mother*, *The Pact* and *The Proposal*, and hope to make more with *The Women*.

My next book is well under way, and I hope you will want to read that one too.

Best wishes,
Susie

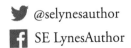 @selynesauthor
SE LynesAuthor

ACKNOWLEDGEMENTS

As ever, first thanks go to my editor, Jenny Geras, who really believed in this project from the start and whose usual light yet laser-like touch means that this story reaches you very much as my original work … only better.

Thanks to Kim Nash, Noelle Holten, Jane 'eagle-eye' Selley and all the team at Bookouture for your incredible hard work and expertise behind the scenes.

Thanks as ever to my writing group, still eating cheese together after over ten years: Hope Caton, Robin Bell, Sam Hanson and Catherine Morris. Our initial thrashing about of the first few chapters of *The Women* was invaluable; thanks for not letting me go off half cocked.

Thanks to my first-draft reader, my mum, Catherine Ball. Our conversation never ends and now you're doing your MFA in fine art; what a role model you are.

Thanks to my dad, Stephen Ball, always on hand for lifts and trout and DIY tips.

Thanks to my agent, Veronique Baxter, for signing me in the first place and for your enthusiasm for my work.

Thanks to the amazing book bloggers, too many to mention individually, who read so tirelessly, write much-appreciated reviews and help to spread the word about my books. I would be nowhere without you and the equally amazing readers … Again, my lovely readers, you are too many to name for fear of missing someone out. Some of you have been with me since the start, and I can't believe you're still reading my books and still get excited when a new one comes out. I owe you all a pint and some chips.

Thanks to my kids, Ali, Maddie and Franci, for not minding when dinner is *Ready Steady Cook* with half a can of sardines and a packet of stale crackers. Thanks for keeping me up to date with the latest young-person words for me to mangle with mumspeak – I am proud of all three of you every single day; you are all sick.

Thanks to Mr Susie. Paul, this year you gave me the best big birthday ever, and as a direct consequence, I love you slightly more than I did before. More than my phone even. And PS, just buy whatever car you think – I don't care as long as it's a nice colour.

Thanks lastly to all my fabulous, funny, feisty female friends. I could not have wished for more support with the whole book malarkey. Some of you have read *all* of my books *and* left reviews and that is astonishing to me; I only ever expected you to pretend to read one and say it was fab to my face. Thank you to those of you who have propped me up against the 'minor wobbles' that happen before publication, on publication, post-publication and between publications. The rest of the time, I'm rock solid, cheers.

22956255R00189

Printed in Great Britain
by Amazon